"You want a love spell."

"Yes," I whispered.

"You are an exceptional young woman, one who experiences the sight."

"You know that?"

"I do, and I am surprised that you are not aware of how binding love spells can be."

"That's what I want! I want to bind him. Won't you help me?"

"There is a price."

I opened the pouch worn around my waist and removed its contents. Two hundred sesterces. "They are all I have, that and this bracelet." I slipped a gold bangle from my wrist.

The mystagogue took the money and the bracelet, sliding them into a drawer in his desk. "There is a far greater price. You will pay that later."

Antoinette May is the author of many books and co-author of the bestselling *Adventures of a Psychic*. She is also a regular contributor to the *San Francisco Chronicle*, *Cosmopolitan*, *Country Living* and many more. *Claudia: Daughter of Rome* is her first novel.

By Antoinette May

Passionate Pilgrim

Witness to War

Adventures of a Psychic

CLAUDIA:
Daughter of Rome

ANTOINETTE MAY

An Orion paperback

First published in Great Britain in 2007 by Orion
This paperback edition published in 2008
by Orion Books Ltd,
Orion House, 5 Upper St Martin's Lane,
London WC2H 9EA

An Hachette Livre UK company

1 3 5 7 9 10 8 6 4 2

Copyright © Antoinette May 2006

The right of Antoinette May to be identified as the author of this work has been asserted by her in accordance with the Copyright, Designs and Patents Act 1988.

First published in the United States under the title *Pilate's Wife*

All rights reserved. No part of this publication may be reproduced, stored in a retrieval system, or transmitted, in any form or by any means, electronic, mechanical, photocopying, recording or otherwise, without the prior permission of the copyright owner and the above publisher of this book.

All the characters in this book are fictitious, and any resemblance to actual persons, living or dead, is purely coincidental.

A CIP catalogue record for this book is available
from the British Library.

ISBN 978-0-7528-9318-1

Printed and bound in Great Britain by Mackays of Chatham plc, Chatham, Kent

The Orion Publishing Group's policy is to use papers that are natural, renewable and recyclable products and made from wood grown in sustainable forests. The logging and manufacturing processes are expected to conform to the environmental regulations of the country of origin.

www.orionbooks.co.uk

For my husband, Charles Herndon

LONDON BOROUGH OF HACKNEY LIBRARIES	
PBK FIC FEB 08	
Bertrams	21.03.08
H	£6.99
DAL	

WHAT IS TRUTH?

—Pontius Pilate

To the Reader

Journalism is a marvelous career. It enables me to be as nosy as I please, delving into old records, newspapers, and letters. My profession enables me to ask anybody anything. Most of the time I get answers that can be corroborated by other interviews and/or checked against recorded facts. Exploring the who, what, why, and how of things has kept me flying since my first newspaper job at fifteen.

Curiosity led from reporting to magazine profiles and biographies. A combination of interviews and archival research resulted in *Passionate Pilgrim,* the 1920s drama of archaeologist Alma Reed; *Witness to War,* the story of Pulitzer-prize-winning war correspondent Maggie Higgins; and *Adventures of a Psychic,* a biography of contemporary clairvoyant Sylvia Browne.

A biographer must be a detective as well as a writer and social historian. I began *Claudia* fourteen years ago as I had my other books—with research. In this case, it involved going back to school. The classics department at Stanford University proved invaluable. For six years I studied with a variety of brilliant professors who opened up the first-century worlds of Rome and Judaea. Steeped in the history, art, philosophy, literature, architecture, and mythology of the time, I then visited the remains of Claudia's world in Rome, Turkey, Egypt, and the Holy Land.

But where was Claudia herself? She was born, she dreamed, she died. Was nothing else known about the visionary wife of Pontius Pilate? For the first time, conventional biography felt constraining. Soon it became apparent that I would have to enter the less familiar realm of the imagination. As I slipped into another world, one by one the questions that were my reporter's stock in trade were answered. Slowly, almost shyly, Claudia revealed herself, allowing me to tell her story.

Prologue

First, let it be said that I did not attend his crucifixion. If you are seeking insight into that tragic affair, you will not hear it from me. Much has been made in recent years of my attempt to stop it, my plea to Pilate telling him of my dream. Knowing nothing of what really happened, some insist on seeing me as a sort of heroine. They are calling Miriam's Jesus a god now or at least the son of a god.

Jerusalem was a tinderbox in those days. Pilate would have forbidden me to attend a public execution. But when have rules mattered? When has risk stopped me from doing anything that I set my mind to do? The fact is, I could not bear to watch the final agony of . . . of . . . who was he really? After all these years I still do not know. Some Jews believed him to be the messiah while their priests cried, "rabble rouser." If his own people could not agree, how could we Romans have been expected to know?

How well I remember Pilate in those days, eyes so blue, mind sharp as the sword hanging from his waist. We were certain that Judaea was only the beginning of an illustrious career.

Isis had other plans. It was a dream of mine that brought us here to Gaul. Yes, of course I still dream. For a change, this one was pleasant. It took me back to Monokos, a village on the Mediterranean coast. I saw myself a girl again, carefree and unafraid, splashing in tide pools, building castles in the sand. Germanicus was there beside me watching as he used to do, the red plume of his helmet fluttering in the breeze. I awakened knowing that Monokos would be good for us.

My solace comes from memories that began here. Sitting alone in the sun, the sea lapping far below, I think often of those days and the momentous years that followed. My granddaughter, Selene, is coming to visit. Yesterday a Roman vessel brought her letter. "You must tell me the whole story," she urged. "Everything."

At first I shrink from the idea. How could I reveal . . . The days pass, the sea mist cool on my skin, the surf sounds at night. Selene will be here tomorrow. I am ready. I know now that the time has come for me to speak of what has happened. It will be good to set the record straight.

All of it at last.

MONOKOS

in the second year of
the reign
of Tiberius (16 C.E.)

CHAPTER 1

My "Gift"

It wasn't easy having two mothers. Selene, who'd given me life, was small, dark, feminine as a fan. The other, her tall, tawny lion of a cousin, Agrippina, was granddaughter of the Divine Augustus.

My father was second in command under Agrippina's husband, Germanicus, commander in chief of the Rhine armies and rightful heir to the Empire. Growing up in one army camp after another, my sister, Marcella, and I were often in Agrippina's home, treated as her own. She favored her sons, but their time was given over to trainers who drilled them daily in the use of sword and spear, shield and ax. We girls remained clay for her to mold.

When I was ten, the ceaseless chatter of the older girls bored me. "Which officer is handsomest?" "What *stola* the most alluring?" Who cared! I was reading Sappho when Agrippina swept the scroll from my hand. Studying my face in the morning light, she admired my profile. "Your nose is pure patrician, but that hair!"

Agrippina grabbed a gold comb from the table, swept my hair this way and that. Then, as I sat rigid under her restraining hand, she began to cut. Slaves scurried to brush away the thick unruly curls fallen to the floor. "Ah, this is much better. Hold the mirror up higher," she instructed Marcella. "Let her see the back, the sides."

Agrippina was always full of ideas, so sure she knew best. I glanced at Marcella, who nodded her approval. The wild hair had been tamed—thinned, pulled back, and bound by a fillet so that my curls cascaded like a waterfall.

Agrippina scrutinized me carefully. "You're really quite pretty—not a beauty like Marcella here, but who knows." She glanced again at my sister. "You're a rose—no doubt about it—but Claudia . . . let me think. Who *is* Claudia?" She reached into drawers, pulling out scarves and ribbons, selecting only to discard. At last, "Of course! Why didn't I see it sooner? You're our little seer, shy, ethereal—pure purple! This is your color; wear it always."

Wear it always! Agrippina was so imperious. Her enthusiasm overwhelmed me. It infuriated Mother. "Those were your baby curls!" she stormed angrily when I came home laden with purple tunics, flowers, scarves, and ribbons. And so it went between them, with me always in the middle.

Still, to this day, I favor purple and take pride in my profile.

People who felt entitled, even obligated, to impose their wills on me were everywhere. *Tata* and Mother, of course, but also Germanicus and Agrippina—I called them aunt and uncle. My sister, Marcella, two years older, expected to dominate me, as did our rich cousins, Julia and Druscilla, and their brothers, Drusus, Nero, and Caligula. Caligula missed no opportunity to tease and embarrass me. He liked to put his tongue in my ear and only laughed when I smacked him. Small wonder I coveted my own company.

Perhaps it was from these quiet times that the sight came. At an early age, I often knew of a visitor's approach before a slave announced the arrival. It happened so naturally that I wondered why others were surprised or even suspicious, imagining that I played a joke. Because the knowledge was trivial and rarely benefited me, I thought little of it.

My dreams were different. They began when we were stationed in Monokos, a small town on the southwest coast of Gaul. For a time it seemed that I could scarcely close my eyes without a vision of some sort overtaking me. They were fragmented dreams. I remembered little and understood less, yet awakened always with a chilling sense of impending danger. The frequency and intensity of these nighttime visions increased; I feared to sleep, forced myself to lie awake late into the night. Then, in my tenth year, I had a dream so vividly terrifying that I have never forgotten it or the events that followed.

I saw myself in a wooded wilderness, a fearful place, thick, dark, almost black. Wet leaves scraped across my face as I breathed the damp smell of decay, shivering miserably in the cold. I struggled to free myself but could not; the dream held me prisoner in its thrall. All about me strange and fearful men chanted words I could not understand. As they crowded forward, surrounding me, I saw that they were dressed as legionnaires, but unlike the soldiers in our garrison, their faces were hardened by anger and bitterness. A huge, fearsome man with pockmarked skin came forward, a young wolf trotting companionably at his heels. This awful person urged the others to violence. Answering cries echoed through the dark forest. He grabbed a sword and lunged toward the wolf who sat trustingly at his feet. With one swift stroke, he impaled the unsuspecting creature. The wolf screamed horribly, or was it I who shrieked? In the last awful seconds of the dream the wolf became my uncle. It was dear Germanicus who lay dying at my feet.

Though *Tata* and Mother rushed in to comfort me, I couldn't banish the ugly picture from my mind. "Someone wants to kill Uncle Germanicus," I gasped. "You have to save him."

"Tomorrow, love, we'll speak of it tomorrow," *Tata* promised, stroking me tenderly, but the morning's talk was brief. My parents agreed: a child's nightmare scarcely warranted bothering the commander in chief. Two days later when a messenger brought word of a threatened mutiny in Germania, I saw them exchange troubled glances.

My retreat in those days was a secluded corner of beach obscured by rocks. I went there alone, waded in tide pools where no one saw me but the tiny sea creatures I called my own. This is where Germanicus found me. Dropping down on a rock, eyes level with my own, he spoke. "I understand we have a seer in our midst."

I looked away. "*Tata* says it isn't important."

"I take your dream as very important and will heed its warning." His rough hand touched my shoulder. Germanicus's hazel eyes lit in a smile. He leaned closer, his tone conspiratorial as though talking to an important adult. "We're going to Germania—all of us. Agrippina is convinced that her presence will restore morale in that wretched corner of the Empire.

Jove only knows, those poor devils have reason for mutiny. Some have grown children they've never seen . . ." His voice trailed off.

What was the matter? I searched the handsome face above me, clouded now, brows furrowed. Timidly, I slipped my hand in his.

Germanicus smiled. "No need for *you* to worry, little one. It will work out, you'll see for yourself. Agrippina needs a woman companion. I've asked Selene to accompany her. And, since my children are going, why not you and your sister?"

MOTHER WAS FURIOUS. IN THE PRIVACY OF OUR HOME, she called Agrippina reckless and absurd. "A woman seven months pregnant making such a journey!" she fumed to *Tata*, unaware that I watched from an alcove. Her face softened as her arms encircled him. "At least I'll be with you—not sitting at home, frantic with fear. It's the girls I worry about. How can we leave them behind when Agrippina makes a show of taking hers?"

I looked about the familiar room as though seeing it for the first time. The walls were a burnished crimson that *Tata* had admired in Pompeii. Mother had painters mix it as a surprise, testing and discarding many times before she was satisfied. Sculpted heads of ancestors watched discreetly from alcoves. Souvenirs from tours of duty added color and nostalgia. There were couches with colorful throws, wall hangings, and cushions in vibrant greens and purples. Mother had created a haven in the midst of an army camp. I didn't want to leave it.

On the first leg of the long journey, I rode in a horse-drawn cart with Mother, Agrippina, and the other girls, my chestnut mare Pegasus tied behind. We played word games to keep our minds busy, but Auntie's voice was louder than usual, reminding us again and again that everything was all right. Mother kept her voice soft, but her eyes flashed angrily at Agrippina. Eventually they abandoned the games, gave us scrolls to read, and whispered among themselves. What I heard was awful: "Mutiny inevitable." What was Germanicus to do?

Gaul's vineyards and pastures gave way to Germania's dense forests. Bushes scratched and scraped like groping fingers. Above us crows and ravens watched. Wild boar scuttled in the undergrowth. I heard wolves howling. Even at noon the light was so dim I felt as though I'd fallen into an abyss. Watching my cousins Drusus and Nero riding with Germanicus, I saw their drawn faces turn often to their father, who nodded encouragement. Caligula rode ahead, brandishing his sword at shadows.

As the days passed, and the leaders guided us through overgrown trails, foot soldiers, two abreast, twisted like a slow sea serpent across an ocean floor. The forced enthusiasm of both Mother and Agrippina frightened me more than the forest. I insisted on riding Pegasus beside Drusus though wretched Caligula jeered at me.

The month's journey across Gaul into the Germanian forests seemed an eternity. At last we reached the outskirts of the mutinous legion's camp. Silently, a few bearded men emerged, eyes guarded. *Not an officer in sight.* Germanicus dismounted, his manner casual, almost jaunty. Motioning his troops back, he approached the men alone. *Tata*'s mouth was grim; his hand rested on the hilt of his sword.

The mutineers crowded forward, their voices an angry babble of complaints. A huge man wrapped in ragged fur grasped Uncle's hand as though to kiss it; instead he thrust Germanicus's fingers into his mouth to feel toothless gums. Others, their scarred bodies covered with rags, hobbled about, eyeing me like a food platter. I urged Pegasus forward as one grabbed for the reins. Then I saw a circle of pikes, atop each a decaying head. *The missing officers.* My stomach lurched. More mutinous soldiers moved in, blocking our exit. I clamped my jaws shut to still chattering teeth.

Germanicus issued an order: "Stand back and divide into units." The men merely pushed closer. I saw *Tata*'s fingers tighten on his sword and wondered if Pegasus felt my legs tremble. Drusus and Nero rode in closer to their father. My heart pounded. It was going to happen. *Tata* and Germanicus would be killed, and with them Drusus and Nero, who'd always seemed like big brothers, and Caligula who never had. Then those fierce, angry men would move on to me. We were all going to die.

Tata glanced questioningly at Germanicus. The commander shook his head, then turned, leaping easily onto a large rock. As he stood calmly surveying the scene, I thought him noble in his cuirass and greaves, the plume on his helmet fluttering in a light breeze. Speaking quietly so that the angry men had to be still, he paid tribute to Emperor Augustus, who had recently died. He praised the victories of Tiberius, the new emperor, and spoke of the army's past glories. "You are Rome's emissaries to the world," he reminded them, "but what has happened to your famous military discipline?"

"I'll show you what happened." A grizzled one-eyed veteran strode forward, pulling off his leather cuirass. "This is what the Germans did to me." He displayed a scar on his belly. "And this is what your officers did." He turned to reveal a back lacerated with scars.

Angry cries echoed as the men railed against Tiberius. "It's Germanicus who should be emperor," the ringleaders shouted. "You're the rightful heir, we'll fight with you all the way to Rome." Many took up the cry, banging their shields and chanting. "Lead us to Rome! Together to Rome!" The angry soldiers pressed forward. I shuddered as I saw them roll their swords back and forth against their shields, the prelude to mutiny.

Germanicus pulled the sword from his belt and pointed it at himself. "Better death than treason to the emperor."

A tall burly man, his body laced with scars, pushed forward and removed his own sword. "Then use mine. It's sharper." As the angry crowd closed in around Germanicus, Agrippina pushed her way toward him. A burly soldier more than a head taller sought to bar her way, but she merely thrust her large belly at him, daring any to lift a hand. The front ranks stepped back. Scarred veterans who'd stood with weapons raised slowly lowered them.

As the soldiers cleared a path for her, Agrippina walked proudly to the rock where her husband stood. Father and I dismounted as the men quieted. Mother and Marcella climbed from the wagon and stood beside us. Her wide brown eyes even wider, Mother slipped her arm in *Tata*'s.

Smiling confidently, she took my hand, calling over her shoulder for Marcella to hold my other hand. We were all trembling.

Every eye turned to Germanicus. He looked so brave, his voice ringing clear and true. "In the name of Emperor Tiberius, I grant immediate retirement for those who have served twenty years or more. Men with sixteen years' service will remain, but with no duties other than to defend against attack. Back pay will be paid twice over."

Soldiers boosted Agrippina up onto the rock. She stood by her husband, the two making a handsome tableau on the great flat stone. "Germanicus, your leader and mine," she said, "is a man of his word. What he promises will come to pass. I know him and I speak the truth." She stood proudly, her face serene despite the silence that greeted her words. At last one man cried out: "Germanicus!" Others joined him, some tossed their helmets high in the air. Their cheers made me want to cry.

"We're lucky," *Tata* said later. "What if they'd demanded their pay now?"

GERMANICUS INSPIRED THE MUTINEERS—AGRIPPINA did too, even Mother admitted that. Hard as it was for me to understand, Caligula, too, was a favorite. He'd been born in an army camp, worn army boots, and drilled with troops when he was still a toddler. Caligula meant "little boots." Now hardly anyone remembered that his real name was Gaius.

Within the week, rumors that German forces were moving

closer rallied the men. It was decided that we women should be sent some forty miles away to the small village of Cologne. Our two families were quartered in what had once been an inn—much too small for so many of us. I hated our cramped, dusty quarters. I hated not knowing what was happening at the front. I missed the sea. Any possible view of the Rhine was obscured by thick pines that surrounded us on all sides, cutting off the sun's weak winter rays. Snow, at first pure magic, inevitably meant slush and clinging frost. I was miserable.

Day by day, I watched Agrippina grow larger. Everyone agreed she was carrying a boy. The prospect cheered her, helping to fight off the bone-chilling cold that no fire could hold at bay. Information about the military operation, now hundreds of miles to the northeast, was sporadic and unreliable. Finally it stopped entirely. Where was the army? What was happening?

Late one night, a shriek like an animal in mortal agony awakened me. When I rose, the stone floor felt like ice. I pulled on my new wolf-skin robe, grateful for its warmth, and followed the awful sounds down the hall to Agrippina's room. As I stood uncertainly, shivering from fear as well as cold, the door flew open and Mother emerged.

"Oh! What a start you gave me!" she gasped, nearly dropping the basin she carried. "Go back to bed, dear one. It's just the baby coming. To listen to her, one would think nobody had ever had a baby before. This *is* her sixth."

Unable to imagine Agrippina ever suffering silently, I said nothing. The midwife, plump like a partridge, moved so fast past us down the hall that her two attendants were hard put to keep up. They trailed breathless, one carrying a basin, the other a tray of ointments. "It won't be long now," Mother assured me. "Go back to sleep."

The door closed. I turned obediently, but couldn't bring myself to leave the dark mystery inside. Agrippina's cries ceased after what seemed an eternity. Had the baby been born? The scent of hot oil and quince mixed with strong, minty pennyroyal assailed me as I quietly opened the door. Mother and the others, faces white and drawn, leaned over the couch where Agrippina lay.

"I don't understand," Mother whispered. "She's full-bodied as Venus herself. Such women are born to bear children."

The midwife shook her head. "She might look like Venus, but best pray to Diana. It's in *her* hands."

My breath caught. Was Agrippina's condition so desperate that only a goddess could save her? The midwife looked up, startled. "Go, child, this is no place for you."

"What's the matter?"

"A breech birth." Her voice softened.

Suddenly Agrippina awakened, arching upward, a mass of tangled, tawny hair, eyes wild in a glistening face. "This boy—this boy—is killing—me!" she panted.

"No!" I heard my own voice as from a distance. "You are *not* going to die." Without realizing it, I'd crossed the room and now stood at Agrippina's side. A picture was forming before my eyes, blurry as though glimpsed through water. I paused as the image sharpened. "I see you with a baby . . . it's a girl."

Mother leaned over Agrippina. "Did you hear that? Take courage from her words." She and the midwife lifted Agrippina, slumped between them. The vision had disappeared. Suddenly, Agrippina's body contorted. She lifted her head, hair matted, eyes like a terrified animal. "Diana!" she shrieked. "My goddess, help me!"

The smell of blood, fetid yet sweet, filled the room, as the midwife held up something dark and shriveled. Slapping the baby's buttocks, she was rewarded by an outraged cry. "Look, *Domina,* look. The child spoke truth. You have a fine daughter."

But Agrippina lay as though dead. Mother was sobbing now, quietly. I touched her hand. "Don't worry, Auntie will be all right. I know it."

"I'll never have a child," I informed Mother the next morning.

Smiling, she smoothed back an unruly lock of my hair. "I hope that's not the sight speaking. I shouldn't want you to miss the happiest moment in a woman's life."

"Happy! You mean horrible. Why would anyone do it?"

She laughed. "You'd not be here if I hadn't."

When she spoke again, her voice was thoughtful. "Childbirth's a test, the measure of a woman's bravery and endurance, as war is a man's. No woman knows when she lies down to bear a child whether she'll survive."

I looked up at Mother's brown velvet eyes; Agrippina's screams still echoed in my head.

"Having children is our duty to the family and to the Empire," she reminded me. "Now, why don't you visit Agrippina? Perhaps she'll allow you to hold her newest princess."

The edge was back in Mother's voice. I guessed that Agrippina was her haughty self again.

Weeks passed without news of the army. Then a messenger finally arrived. A slender boy in his teens, he told us how Germanicus had subdued the savage Germans. I listened, bursting with pride and excitement. Forging on, Germanicus's troops had reached the Teutoburg Forest where six years earlier one tenth of the Roman army had been slaughtered. "When we went to bury our dead, we saw skeletons everywhere." The boy shuddered. "Their heads were pegged to tree trunks. We didn't know if the bones belonged to friend or stranger, but what did it matter? They were all our brothers."

I opened the door a few days later to another breathless courier. Bloodshot eyes fearful, he described a situation grown desperate. Arminius, the general responsible for the carnage, lurked in a treacherous swamp near the battle site. Germanicus was determined to find him.

Soon the rumors began. Wounded men stumbled to our gate. The army had been cut off, surrounded. Fleeing deserters shouted that German forces were on their way to invade Gaul. Soon it would be Rome itself. All around us, panic-stricken villagers insisted that the Rhine Bridge be destroyed. Agrippina, dragging herself from bed, put a stop to that. "In the absence of my husband, *I* am the commander," she announced. "The bridge will stand."

The wounded, returning on foot, using sticks for crutches, would soon have need of it. Agrippina improvised a field hospital, using her own money and soliciting everyone, from noble to peasant, to help. I eagerly fetched bandages and water, washed wounds and held water to the lips of feverish men.

Then the visions started. Though I had no medical knowledge or even aptitude, it seemed that I could tell by looking at the wounded who would survive and who would not.

Late on my second day at the hospital, I sat beside a soldier not much older than myself. His wound seemed slight, a relief after so many gory ones. I smiled as I offered him water. His lips moved in an answering smile as he reached for the cup. Then slowly his round face changed before my eyes into a skull. Horrified, I staggered to my feet.

"What's the matter?" he asked, taking the water, looking at me curiously, normal again. Muttering an excuse, I hurried outside. Forcing myself to believe I'd imagined it, I continued with my rounds. The next day I learned that the boy had died in the night.

It happened again. Then again. Despite the increasing proficiency of Agrippina's hastily assembled staff, the men whose skulls I saw invariably died. When this happened to a merry young soldier of whom I'd grown fond, I fled the hospital sobbing.

Climbing onto a large crag overlooking the river's dark waters, I struggled to compose myself. It was here that Agrippina found me. I looked away, not knowing what to say. Auntie, with her regal self-assurance, would never understand the dread I felt each day, the sense of helplessness at being suddenly possessed by this unwelcome knowledge. I nodded politely and rose.

"Don't go," she said, touching my hand lightly. "I see that you are troubled. It has to do with the sight, doesn't it? You have the gift."

"Yes," I whispered. "This is no 'gift,' it's a curse."

"Poor child." Agrippina shook her head sadly. "From what I hear, the sight chooses *you*. It can never be removed."

"What good is knowing something terrible if I can't change it?"

"Such knowledge could bring you power," she suggested.

"No! I don't want to know bad things," I said, fighting tears that stung my eyes.

"Then pray," she suggested. "Ask that you not be shown more than you can bear. Ask for courage to face your destiny."

"Thank you for understanding. Mother and Marcella don't like to talk about the sight. It makes them nervous."

"*I* am rarely nervous," Agrippina's imperious tone was back. "I think it best we return to the hospital. They need us there."

I sighed, thinking of all those sweet young men, their frightened souls preparing for flight. "There are so many coming now. I'm afraid for the rest, for my father and—Germanicus."

"Your sight tells you nothing?"

I shook my head. "It never does when I ask."

"Then I will." She smiled confidently. "A courier arrived only a short while ago. I was about to post the news when I saw you steal away. The tide of battle has turned. Germanicus lured the Germans from the swamp. He will soon return with his army, victorious. I will welcome them at the bridge."

"My father—my father is safe?"

She smiled broadly, assuring me.

A frisson ran through my body as she spoke of victory, but there was something more . . . "You're certain Uncle Germanicus is safe?"

"Quite certain," she replied, rising to her feet. "You will see him soon."

Agrippina was right. *Tata* returned and Germanicus was hailed a conquering hero, yet the memory of the young wolf remained, his face frozen in surprise and anguish.

CHAPTER

2

A Triumph

One day Marcella was playing with dolls. The next day it was men. Our old slave, Priscilla, laughed about it—when Mother wasn't there to hear her. Priscilla was wrong. Marcella hadn't changed—neither had the men. As long as I could remember, battle-scarred veterans had stared at Marcella, while small boys turned cartwheels in her path.

With time, I could identify the hint of pleasurable fulfillment that clung to her like perfume. At twelve, I knew only that Marcella was special. Mother knew it too. Though warm and loving to us both, Mother's large brown eyes lingered often on my sister. Grateful for the extra freedom granted me by default, I wondered idly what my mother planned.

One spring afternoon Agrippina gave Marcella her first grown-up gown—a scarlet tunica of the softest Egyptian linen, clasped at the shoulders, and a filmy violet *stola*. "Few can wear such colors together," Agrippina said. Clearly they hadn't worked for her own daughters, Druscilla or Julia, or my sister wouldn't have been the lucky recipient.

Delighted by her good fortune, Marcella hurried outside. From the balcony off Mother's room I watched her dance along the orderly rows of barracks. Out of every building she passed came at least one young officer, smiling, waving, hurrying to her side.

"Marcella has so many friends," I commented to Mother.

Mother's eyes strayed absently from the loom before her. As her gaze followed mine, her glossy brows came together. "Friends! Find Priscilla. Order her to bring Marcella in *this minute*!"

THAT EVENING, PLAYING UNNOTICED BEHIND A COUCH, I watched Mother pour *Tata*'s wine. He scattered a few drops on the hearth for the gods, then lifted the glass to his lips. "My favorite," he smiled, "and you didn't cut it with water."

Mother smiled back at him. "Marcella grows more lovely every day, don't you think?" she asked, her voice light and casual.

"Half the camp's besotted with her."

Mother's smile faded. "Such attention goes to a girl's head. In a rude garrison like this, anything can happen."

Father's cup thumped the table, splashing wine on the carefully mended cloth. "No soldier with a brain in his head would risk—"

"Come now, darling. What moved you at that age—surely not your brain."

"Selene! This is not a barracks."

"No, it is not, or I might use any number of words with which you are more familiar."

"Not from my wife . . . not in a while. Do you remember that furlough—"

"In Capri?" Mother's voice softened. "Of course. We conceived Claudia there."

Holding my breath, I moved closer.

"You were lovely. You are still lovely—when you don't frown."

"Who would not frown? Gaul's better than those wretched German forests, but still provincial, so far from Rome. I never thought we would be here this long. And then there's Agrippina. You have no idea—"

"Come now, she means well. The girls often show me pretty things she has given them. Only today Marcella showed me a very pretty tunica."

"Cast-offs! You're a man, a soldier, how could *you* understand? Sometimes I wonder if men and women really suit one another. Perhaps we should just live next door and visit now and then."

Tata chuckled. "That would never work. Your house would be in Rome."

"And yours an army tent." Mother laughed too. "I suppose we'll just have to muddle through." She moved to his couch and made a place for herself close to him. "But you see," she touched his cheek, "I want something more for the girls. Marcella's manner *is* provocative. You can hardly blame the young men for responding . . . and now that she's a woman—"

"A woman!" *Tata* looked startled.

"A woman," Mother repeated firmly. "It is time we took steps to secure her future. You men see only the surface. That girl charms people—women as well as men. She leaves them pleased with themselves. Such a wife would be an asset to anyone . . . why not Caligula?"

"I don't like that lad. Never mind those damn boots, there's something not quite right about him. He's not at all like his older brothers, and nothing like his father."

"All the better," Mother argued. "Let his brothers risk everything on war, dragging their wives from camp to camp. Marcella could have a marvelous life at court."

"Tiberius's court?"

"Why not? It's the center of the world. Why shouldn't she enjoy all it has to offer?"

"Perhaps . . . if she has the stomach for intrigue." Father's face cleared. "Why are we even talking about it? Agrippina will want someone rich for her brat."

"I'm well aware of that," Mother admitted, "but she *is* fond of Marcella. The boy is so spoiled. When the time comes, he'll marry whomever he chooses—dowry or no. After all, it's not as if he will ever be emperor."

My hands clenched as Caligula's image appeared in my mind's eye. *Oh, but he will.* I saw him commanding the emperor's dais, Marcella nowhere in sight. Where was she? And Drusus, Nero? If Caligula was emperor . . . where were they? I shook my head, not wanting to see more.

Father shrugged his shoulders. "Time enough to talk of this after the spring campaign. Germanicus has vowed to cross the Rhine again." His face brightened at the prospect.

BUT *TATA* WAS NOT TO HAVE HIS BATTLE. TIBERIUS forbade it. Suddenly, unexpectedly, the emperor called Germanicus back to Rome. "You have sacrificed enough for your country," he wrote. "It's time the people honored you. A triumph is scheduled to commemorate your victories."

Rome was charmed by Tiberius's generosity. In Gaul we knew better. The emperor was jealous of his relative's military success and the immense popularity that it had brought him. The only way to curb the hero worship was to bring the hero home, toss a triumph at him as a bone to a dog, then assign some new, more obscure posting.

Germanicus sent letter after letter, each a plea for time: "Give us one more year to complete Germania's subjugation."

Tiberius was adamant. "Your triumph will be held on the Ides of August."

Germanicus, *Tata,* the officers, and most of the men were despondent. The women made no effort to conceal their delight. Rome was all that anyone could think or talk about. I'd left the city as an infant and was full of questions that no one had time to answer.

Soon we were on the road, a cavalcade of chariots, wagons, carts, and horses. By day there appeared no end to the line of marching legionnaires. At night the light from many campfires created a field of stars. Once, just before dawn, *Tata* and I climbed a hill to survey the landscape together. Looking down at the flickering lights illuminating the darkness, I felt transported to Mount Olympus. Surely this was earth as only the gods saw it.

Cultivated lands and small towns, laid out in the Roman manner with a public bath, a forum, gymnasium, and theater, gave way to angry, ruptured earth as our ascent through harsh, mountainous country began. Even in late July, long fingers of snow streaked the towering peaks. Often enveloped in the thick mist of clouds, we could only inch our way along the rim of savage gorges. Once a cart skidded on an ice patch and careened off the narrow road, dragging its braying, terrified mules into the abyss. The cries of the plummeting passengers, German prisoners, echoed for hours in my ears.

That night we made camp beside a temple to Jove. "How can you bear it here?" I asked the priest who stood at the entrance. "This is the end of the world."

"But near our god," he replied solemnly. "Listen, you can hear his thunderbolts." A jagged flash rent the sky as the earth trembled. I hastily slipped a coin into his coffer and hurried inside. Kneeling before the altar, I heard the clink of many coins and never doubted that everyone in our party gave something. I prayed that Jove was watching, keeping track of our pious prayers and homage.

As we began our careful descent from the Alps I noticed changes, subtle at first but soon pronounced. The ice and snow were finally gone. Shades of red and amber carpeted the valley below. The sun was bolder, shadows sharper. Marcella and I exchanged glances, sensing laughter and gaiety in the golden light. Mother flung her arms about us. "Yes, darlings. This is Italy. We are almost home!"

ROME WAS A CHALLENGE, A PROVOCATION, DARING everything, promising more. Narrow streets reeked with a smell all their own, a heady mix of perfume and garlic, spices, sweat, and incense. They teemed with ballad singers and beggars, scribes and storytellers. I saw vendors everywhere, heard them cry their wares in singsong. Porters, bearing staggering loads on their backs, swore profusely at whoever impeded their progress. Almost all traffic was on foot, for chariots were rarely allowed inside the city gates. Those who could afford it were carried in curtained litters with slaves running ahead to clear the way.

Even at twelve I saw these people, arrogant with power, as a different breed. How could they be otherwise? Stinking, dirty, brawling, brilliant Rome was—as Mother had said—the center of the world, and any man or woman less for living outside it. Now I understood her dissatisfaction with Gaul—with any place else—for I, too, was hopelessly besotted.

Tears of pride stung my eyes, for we entered this glorious capital as heroes, its haughty residents paying tribute to us. It was my uncle, my beloved father, and all the men who had served under them who were being honored. Beginning some twenty miles from the city, Romans lined the roads, often five deep, cheering and flinging flowers. I felt as though the entire population had come to greet us. A gigantic arch erected near the Temple of Saturn proclaimed the glory of Germanicus. The throngs went wild as our triumphal procession passed beneath it.

Germanicus and Father had planned our entry well. First came runners bearing laurel branches, a reminder of many victories. Floats followed, more than a hundred, heaped with spoils from German temples, some piled high with enemy shields and weapons. Others carried flamboyant tableaux of battles or depicted the spirit of Rome subduing German river gods. One bore a captured princess and her child, collars about their necks. Behind them an endless train of manacled prisoners plodded.

My family rode in a lavish chariot flanked by outriders. Father's parade armor glittered in the sun. Mother eyed him proudly. Her personal triumph was that neither Marcella nor I wore Agrippina's cast-offs. This was my first grown-up gown. The sleeveless tunica, a *chiton* of pale lavender, fell in silken folds from shoulder to ankles. A silver ribbon drew the bodice of a violet *stola* together just under my breasts; I held my breath as much as possible to make them appear larger. Still a child then, despite my new dignity, I shared the triumph with Hecate, holding the kitten up from time to time so that she too might enjoy the spectacle.

Germanicus rode last in the largest and most elaborate float. He was splendid in a golden cuirass embossed with the likeness of Hercules vanquishing a lion, his crimson cloak bright as blood in the morning light. Agrippina stood at his side, her long tawny hair rippling in the sun.

Beside them were the children, Drusus, Nero, Caligula, Druscilla, Julia, and the toddler, Agripilla.

"I'll wager there hasn't been such cheering since Augustus returned from defeating Antonius at Actium," *Tata* exclaimed, his face flushed with pride in his commander.

My heart thumped with excitement as I turned to wave at Druscilla and the others. Just at that moment a man ran up alongside their chariot and climbed on. I watched curiously as he held a gold crown over Germanicus's head. The man's lips moved continuously, but with all the noise it was impossible to catch his words.

"Who is he?" I asked *Tata*. "What's he saying?"

"A palace slave sent by Tiberius. It is a custom."

"But one rarely practiced," Mother observed. "He is advising Germanicus to look back."

"Look back! Why should he look back?" Marcella wanted to know. "*I* never look back."

"It is a reminder," Mother explained. "Sometimes the future creeps up from behind, catching us unaware. The slave warns Germanicus not to be too arrogant or too confident of the future. No mortal knows his fate. One day he may be triumphant, the next day disgraced or even dead."

I WILL NEVER FORGET MY FIRST VISIT TO THE CIRCUS Maximus. The events set in motion that day changed my life, but at the time I thought only of how awfully *big* the arena was.

Following the triumph, my family was invited to share the imperial box with Germanicus's uncle and adopted father, Emperor Tiberius, and Agrippina's step-grandmother, Dowager Empress Livia. We'd approached the arena together through the imperial tunnel leading from the palace. Once we were inside, the immensity of it all made me dizzy. Everywhere I looked I saw faces, thousands of faces. People on all sides of me, tier after tier of them, stomping, yelling, jostling one another.

Trumpets heralded our arrival and, for an instant, the stadium stilled, voices dimmed. Then the crowd roared like some huge, untamed animal. Thunderous cheers welcomed Tiberius and Livia as they entered the box, but they were nothing compared to the greeting received by Germanicus and Agrippina. The cry *"Ave! Ave! Ave!"* rose from every tier in the amphitheater. Germanicus smiled, a boyish grin of surprise and pleasure, raising his arm in acknowledgment. The shouts grew louder, came faster. Agrippina, beside him, her eyes shining, lifted both arms like an actress accepting applause.

The tremendous roar subsided as the last of the imperial party took its place. Pomanders and bags of sweet-smelling herbs were passed about in an attempt to block the stench of some two hundred and fifty thousand Romans crammed into the stands above us. The highest seats were occupied by the poorest of the poor—I could scarcely see that far—but those immediately above us were reserved for war casualties. Catching sight of one of the men I'd nursed in Cologne, I smiled and waved just as another trumpet fanfare announced the arrival of the Vestal Virgins. The crowd cheered again, briefly, as the white-clad figures stepped into their elaborate box.

Another wave of dizziness swept over me as I looked out at the vast sea of faces. Power and restlessness hung like sweat in the air. No one gladiator had yet clawed his way into the glare of popularity since Vitellius had been slain a few weeks earlier. I could feel the crowd's impatience, the tension beneath an undercurrent of laughter and conversation. Trumpets sounded again, announcing a parade of combatants and performers. "Oh, look!" Marcella cried, pointing to the charioteers who entered, rank after rank, four chariots to a rank. Behind them the gladiators. How could they smile so confidently? Today's combat had been designated a *sine missione.* The life of each would depend on killing his comrades before the sun set.

The first part of the show was given over to animal-baiting. Never having seen an elephant, I was thrilled by their size, power, and cunning. Surely that lordly trumpeting could be heard beyond the city gates. My excitement dissolved as I watched trainers pierce the beasts with fire darts until, driven mad by pain and anger, they turned on one another, goring and stamping. The butchery was like nothing I had seen anywhere or could ever have imagined. The dust was impossible to block even in our place of honor and the smell . . . Blood, entrails, excrement steamed in the August heat. I held my ears, hoping to block the angry bellows, the agonized squeals. I couldn't; they were deafening. At last one animal remained, standing alone amid the carnage. A herd of possibly fifty elephants had been massacred. While enormous oxcarts carried off the slain beasts, the victorious elephant knelt before the imperial box as he had been trained to do.

The slaughter of jungle cats was to me even more terrible. I had to bite my lips to keep from crying out as torch-bearing beaters forced the creatures into the arena. Scorched by flames, goaded by sharp swords, the exotic felines snarled furiously, swiping at one another with their fearful claws. Despite their agility and defiant courage, in the end it was hopeless. The black panthers reminded me of Hecate. I couldn't bear it and turned away to wipe away the tears that streamed from my eyes. I am a soldier's daughter, I must be strong, I reminded myself and turned back.

*

From time to time I stole glances at Tiberius, sprawled back in his seat under a purple canopy. The emperor's body was well formed, his shoulders particularly impressive. I thought his features attractive. What would it be like to know one's face was recognized on coins and monuments throughout the world? Yet, despite the power and privilege that clung to Tiberius, I saw sadness. *He's never been happy. His life is a tragedy.* Why I should know this, I couldn't imagine any more than I could fathom why one so powerful should not have everything he desired.

Tiberius looked up, our eyes locking as he coolly returned my gaze. I felt as though I had glimpsed him naked and been caught staring. Blushing to the roots of my hair, I looked away only to catch a glimpse of Caligula's hands, following the folds of my sister's *chiton.* Startled, I wondered why Marcella didn't box his ears.

A fanfare of trumpets announced the gladiators. Fleetingly regal, they marched forward to stand before the imperial box. Eyes on Tiberius, they spoke as one: "We who are about to die, salute you." Father and Germanicus exchanged glances. "One rarely hears that," *Tata* said. "It's to be a fight to the finish," Uncle reminded him. The emperor nodded indifferently, sunlight flashing from his ringed fingers as he idly drummed the arms of his chair. The gladiators broke into pairs and positioned themselves to fight.

Wax tablets were passed from hand to hand as spectators scribbled the names of their favorites and the sums they staked. Everyone was taking part—not only the common people but also senators and knights, even Vestal Virgins.

"Did you know we have a prophet among us?" Germanicus

asked Tiberius. "When we hold our regimental games, Claudia invariably picks winners."

"Indeed! That little mouse?" The empress looked up from her tablet. Until now she had managed to ignore my entire family. *Why does she dislike us so?* Livia's green eyes were disdainful. "Isn't this your first circus?"

"I venture she will know a winner when she sees one," Germanicus assured her.

"And who will win this time, Madam Oracle?" Tiberius leaned forward, a spark of interest lighting a face that had remained impassive throughout the preliminary events.

"I—I—can't do it that way," I struggled to explain. "I don't know something because I want to."

"Then how *do* you know it?" Tiberius persisted.

"Sometimes I dream the winners, or else they just jump into my head."

The empress laughed contemptuously as she tapped her son lightly with an ivory fan.

Tiberius ignored her. "Then look them over and see who 'jumps,'" he challenged me, gesturing toward the gladiators standing below.

Half sick with self-consciousness, I closed my eyes in prayer to Diana: *May the earth open this instant and swallow me.*

"Claudia's choices are often fortunate, but we don't encourage the child's fantasies," Mother hastily explained.

"Some of us do," Germanicus chuckled. "The boys and I have done quite well with them."

Caligula baited me as I sat, sick with anxiety. "I knew all the time that you were making it up."

"I don't make it up!"

"I'm sure you don't." The emperor, his hands surprisingly gentle, reached out, pulling me from my seat into an empty space he created next to himself. "Why don't you just take a good long look at those men down there? If you see a winner, tell us."

"She won't see anything. What does Claudia know anyway?" Caligula, diverted from Marcella, beat his booted foot against the seat.

"That's enough, Caligula!" Germanicus snapped. "If you can't be polite to Claudia, remove yourself and sit with the rabble."

Tata patted my shoulder reassuringly. "We all know it's just a game you like to play. Why not try it now?"

"It's not a game, it's a lie," Caligula insisted, ignoring his father's admonition.

I glared at him. Angrily pushing back the curls loose over my forehead, I turned to the men assembled on the field, studying each face carefully. The pressure was terrible. I tried breathing deeply. Pictures come to me involuntarily, but at that moment, looking at the men waiting for the starting signal, I saw nothing. Desperate, I closed my eyes. Then . . . yes, one face appeared. An unusual face, high cheekbones, blond, very blond. I thought him handsome as Apollo. More important, he was smiling triumphantly. I opened my eyes, eagerly scanning the gladiators below. Helmets covered their hair, but I recognized the striking face, the fair skin. "It's that man," I said, pointing. "Third from the end. He'll be the winner."

"Not likely," Livia scoffed. "Look how young he is. Hardly more than twenty. A thrust or two and it will be over."

"Are you sure, Claudia?" Father asked. "Ariston is the favorite, the one on the end."

My eyes followed his pointing finger. Ariston looked formidable. He was slightly taller than my choice and much broader through the shoulders. Now, as I studied the gladiators, I realized that the man I'd chosen was more slender than any. Though a large man, tall and broad-shouldered, he looked almost frail beside the massive veterans of many combats. All I could do was shrug. "He's the one I saw."

"You're just showing off," Caligula accused me.

"Do you have any pocket change, boy?" Tiberius asked him.

"Sir, I'm fourteen."

"Very well, then. I'll wager one hundred sesterces against whatever you have that Claudia's choice wins."

"Tiberius, you're not only a poor judge of gladiators but a spendthrift," Livia chided him.

"If you're so certain, suppose we have a little wager of our own?" Germanicus suggested.

"Taken," the empress responded. "What about two hundred sesterces against my fifty?"

"Agreed." Germanicus nodded.

Mother and Father looked at each other in consternation. Even Agrippina was subdued. Marcella leaned over and squeezed my hand. "I hope you are right. That gladiator is just too handsome to lose."

"Marcella!" Mother reproved, but everyone laughed and some of the tension eased.

What followed has become legend. It began routinely. The men were evenly matched—*retiarii* brandishing nets and tridents and *secutori* countering with swords and shields. Each man moved slowly, warily, as he sought to gain an advantage over his opponent. The pair would fight until one man was killed, the winner then going on to challenge another until only two remained—one final dance of death.

As the struggle began, Tiberius sent a slave for information about my choice. The young *secutor*'s name was Holtan, we were told. He was a Dacian captive only recently brought to Rome. Nothing was known of him. It was unlikely that he had ever attended a *ludi*.

Holtan's unfamiliarity with the arena was apparent from the beginning. "He won't last a round," Livia scoffed. I feared the empress was right. Without gladiatorial school training, what chance did he have? After a few tentative swings, the young gladiator, who'd taken his eyes off his opponent for an instant to look up at the stands, was knocked to the ground. The other man moved in for the kill. Tiberius shook his head in disgust and turned to order wine. In that instant Holtan was back on his feet, sword in hand. He swung this way and that, confusing his adversary, then moved in for the kill, blade slashing cleanly into his opponent's chest. From then on the man was Hercules himself.

An excited buzz ran through the stands, echoing around us: "*Who is that man*?" Tiberius patted my shoulder approvingly. The orchestra played, a frenetic accompaniment to the drama below. Horns and trumpets blared wildly. A woman hunched over the water organ, face changing from pink to purple as she furiously pumped the bellows. Attendants dressed as Charon rushed here and there striking the fallen gladiators on the head with hammers. Pluto, king of the underworld, had claimed them for his own. Body after body was dragged away through the Porta Libitinensis while the slaughter continued. At first I hid my eyes from the brutal melee, but soon the exhilaration of the howling mob infected me with its madness.

Across the amphitheater an improvised banner was lowered. My whole body tingled with excitement as I read the hastily scrawled words: HOLTAN OF DACIA. I screamed myself hoarse with excitement. We all did. Often Tiberius was on his feet beside me, cheering with the others: "HOLTAN! HOLTAN! HOLTAN!" Incredibly, this young unknown fought man after man until only he and one other, Ariston, remained. Warily, they circled one another. Ariston lunged forward, tripping Holtan with his net, throwing him to the ground. Trident raised, Ariston moved in for the kill. I closed my eyes. Beside me, Marcella shrieked; cries echoed everywhere. Cautiously opening my eyes, I saw Holtan roll sideways, eluding Ariston's blade by an inch. He was on his feet, swinging, slashing. A slicing, sideways plunge, and it was over. Holtan stood above the prostrate form of his opponent, awaiting Tiberius's verdict.

The emperor turned to me. "Well, young lady, he's your champion. What is your pleasure? What will you have him do?"

The excitement of the crowd was palpable. Many indicated their own verdicts: thumbs down. "Go ahead, give the people what they want—another corpse," Livia urged.

"You may be doing him a favor. He looks more dead than alive," Father agreed.

Just then the fallen gladiator's eyes opened. Though his

blood-splattered face was impassive, I felt his plea. The man wanted to live. My heart beat wildly as I felt the eyes of the entire stadium on me. Smiling shyly, I raised my arm—thumb up. *Mitte*. Tiberius nodded, then raised his thumb beside mine.

CHAPTER

3

Aftermath of a Triumph

I was a heroine at the imperial banquet that followed the circus—at least within our family circle. Agrippina and Germanicus saw to it that I met many of their friends. Clearly, Rome's most prominent families liked and respected them, anticipating the couple's eventual ascent to the throne. Though their reflected glory was heady, I turned away when the conversation shifted to people and places I didn't know, jokes I didn't understand.

For a time I wandered through the palace, drinking in the magnificence around me. Hundreds of lamps flickered on walls and tables, illuminating the elegant women, some in Roman dress, others in exotic Eastern gowns, their hair piled and pinned into pyramids and towers or wreathed in flowers. The men, too, were grand—many in wide-bordered togas, others wearing brightly colored tunics with gold half-moons gleaming on their knee-high sandals.

Tiberius had invited Holtan on a whim. Hoping to meet him, I searched out the gladiator only to find him surrounded by new admirers. He shared his couch with a woman whose legs, entwined with his, were nearly as long. Her hair fell like a golden skein across his chest. Did I imagine for an instant . . . his eyes on me?

Nearby, Drusus and Nero watched a pair of Nubian dancers. The boys' hands rested nonchalantly on the gold hilts of their ceremonial swords, but their eyes widened as each filmy veil slipped to the floor. Again I passed unnoticed. Marcella, face flushed with excitement, enjoyed a silly game of slap and tickle with Caligula. Druscilla and Julia, hiding and chasing among the couches, waved for me to join them.

No one paid the slightest attention to us, but we caught glimpses of things we couldn't have imagined. Why did grown-ups make such fools of themselves? I wondered more than once. I was shocked sometimes, but also amused. I'd never seen an adult naked before—a real adult, not merely a dancing slave. Often we held our sides from giggling. All too soon an attendant arrived to collect us.

She was short and plump, not sleek like the usual court slaves, nor as confident. "Where are Marcella and Caligula?" she asked. Her small eyes narrowed anxiously as they roved the crowded room.

"What difference does it make?" I replied, annoyed by her intrusion.

The slave looked uncertain. "Your mother ordered me to find all of you and see you to your beds. She will be angry."

Why was Mother doing this? It was still so early. Standing tall, I tried to sound like an adult: "Don't trouble yourself. Marcella and Caligula are old enough to find their beds without a nurse."

"Why don't you go look for them and come back for us?" Druscilla suggested hopefully.

Clearly the slave was taking no chances.

Her gait a brisk waddle, she led us down a wide corridor inlaid with agate and lazuli. Julia and Druscilla were taken to nearby rooms where their own attendants waited to serve them. I bade them good night and followed the house slave further down the corridor. It was no longer as well lighted. Our sandals echoed against the marble floors, and the woman's lamp cast eerie shadows on frescoed walls. It seemed to take forever to reach the small, ill-appointed room that had been assigned to Marcella and myself. At least there were two sleeping couches. I dismissed the slave and settled into one. Recalling the excited sparkle in Marcella's eyes, I wondered uneasily: Where was she?

Sleep, when it finally came, brought a bizarre, troubling dream. Down, down, down I slipped into an unfathomable world of dark, sobbing figures. Who were they? For whom did they cry so piteously? It was for me, it had to be for me, but what had I done? Why had these phantom shapes turned their backs on me? The air was heavy, weighing me down. I gasped, barely able to breathe. The mourners slowly faded. I was alone. All was blackness but for a small candle. It cast eerie shadows on the rough wall, ugly shadows. The candle flickered, such a tiny flame. Now it too was gone. The darkness was heart-stopping. I was trapped, enveloped. I struggled frantically to free myself, screamed and scratched at the damp, clammy walls. No one answered, no one came. I knew then that it was not me who thrashed and flailed in that fearful crypt. It was

Marcella—Marcella imprisoned in darkness, Marcella abandoned and alone.

My own frightened cry awakened me. Sunlight streamed through a small window. I looked over at Marcella's couch. It was empty, not a cover mussed. A sense of dread swept over me. Just as I was getting out of bed, the door burst open. My sister rushed into the room, hair undone, face red from crying. My careless words of the night before echoed in my ears, as, throat choked with tears, she tried to explain what had happened.

"It was awful," Marcella gulped between sobs. "Caligula's *grandmother* came in! She—she caught us. There she was, standing over the couch, the *empress*, with those two huge guards that follow her everywhere. Now the whole palace will know. Mother says I'll be ruined. The empress called me a slut. She hates me—I think she hates our whole family. She says it was my fault—but it really was not. Caligula has been after me for months—"

"Caligula!" I stared at her, astonished. "Why did you go with that slimy boy? But what's the fuss about? We used to take naps with our cousins all the time. Surely sleeping with Caligula won't harm you."

"We weren't sleeping."

It took a moment before I understood; perhaps I didn't want to understand. "You actually did *that*? You let Caligula—oh, Marcella, how disgusting!"

"It is *not* disgusting." Marcella giggled through her tears. "It's even . . ."

I shuddered. "No one's ever going to do that to me. I'd like to see anyone try!"

Marcella sighed. Her face wore that superior look I hated. "Oh, what do you know! You are a child."

"We're only two years apart," I reminded her.

She sighed. "Those are the two that matter." Marcella poured water from a pitcher near the couch and bathed her eyes. "Oh, little sister, what will they do to me?"

It didn't take long to find out. Within minutes Livia entered with her guards. There was barely enough space left in the tiny room for Mother, who followed, her face white and drawn. Agrippina stood behind them, for once in the background. She looked guilty. I didn't need the sight to tell me that Marcella's punishment would be awful.

In fact, Livia's plan was unthinkable. "I will send her to the Virgins," she announced gleefully.

"The Virgins!" Marcella's lips parted in a gasp. Her eyes went wide, her skin deathly pale. I moved closer, fearing my sister might faint, but Marcella stood firm, her eyes unwavering as she faced the empress.

A cruel smile lit Livia's face. "They have ways of dealing with unruly little bitches." Mother's arms encircled Marcella, holding her wordlessly. "Come, Agrippina." The empress crooked her finger. An emerald sparkled in a shaft of sunlight. She turned abruptly and swept from the room followed by her two guards, huge men, black as ebony. Agrippina trailed behind, her eyes down, not looking at any of us. What was the matter with her? Agrippina was our aunt, our friend. Why wasn't she standing up to Livia? Mother and Marcella clung together, sobbing quietly, scarcely aware of me as I hurried into my clothes and slipped out the door.

I'd always believed that my father could do anything. Now, as I approached the garden bench where he sat, I began to have doubts. His shoulders were hunched, his face buried in his hands.

"*Tata,* isn't there something—"

Looking up, he took my hand and drew me down beside him. "Livia is the empress. Her word is law. To go against her is to go against Rome itself."

"But Tiberius is the emperor."

"And Livia's son. Do you think he'd cross her for anything so trivial?" Father touched his finger gently to my lips, forestalling an outburst. "Trivial in *his* eyes."

I sat mutely for a time, casting about for ideas, discarding them one by one. The garden, ablaze with summer blooms, mocked me, forcing my gaze to the far end of the planting where an immense marble statue of the Divine Augustus stared down. The whole world was displayed across the emperor's chest, a constellation of conquests—Parthia, Spain, Gaul, Dalmatia. Father, who loved to tell war stories, had made certain that I was well acquainted with each victory. A cupid at Augustus's feet also reminded viewers of his descent from Venus. Mother had taken care to explain that myth. As family members, we claimed the same divine ancestor.

"If Augustus were alive this wouldn't happen," I ventured. "He'd stop Livia."

Tata shook his head sadly. "Who knows? When the last Vestal died and everyone scrambled to save his daughters from the lottery, Augustus swore that if either of his granddaughters were eligible, he'd propose her name."

I heard a sharp, bitter laugh and turned. Mother had come

down the path and now stood behind us. "He only said that because Agrippina and Julia were safely married. The emperor was forever holding up ideals of morality, though everyone knew he'd left his own wife and baby daughter to steal Livia—a mother with a young son—from her husband."

"Hush, Selene," Father warned, glancing in my direction.

I hadn't missed a word, each a precious piece to the puzzle. The ancient scandal explained the dowager empress's hostility toward Agrippina, Augustus's granddaughter from that first marriage. Apparently it even extended to our remote branch of the family. Hadn't she anything better to do than persecute poor relations?

"The empress thinks she's so clever, but her plan won't work. Marcella's too old," I reminded them. "The order will refuse her."

Mother sat down beside me. "The Chief Vestal won't quibble once she feels the weight of Livia's purse."

I hesitated, searching for words. Marcella had been my window into the adult world. Talking to a parent was much harder. "The whole idea is wrong. Marcella is not a—a virgin."

Mother's white face flushed. "You are so young, it's difficult to speak of such things, but you've learned so much already . . ." She sighed. "It's true, initiates are young children. One would scarcely question their virginity. All that's required is that they not be deformed, deaf, or dumb. Both parents must be alive and neither one a slave. So you see, in all respects but one, Marcella is qualified."

"But," I argued, "that one is *the* one. Livia is cheating the goddess."

Mother shrugged helplessly. "A fine point that doesn't trouble the empress."

"What about Agrippina? How can she just stand by and watch this awful thing happen?"

Mother shook her head. "I believe Agrippina is genuinely sorry about the wretched Vestal business, but Livia has played cleverly upon her ambitions. She promises a brilliant marriage for Caligula while threatening a terrible scandal if the affair is not settled to her satisfaction. None of us wants a scandal, but poor, dear, foolish Marcella. Her life is over—*over*."

I put my arms around Mother who had quietly begun to sob. "Must she remain a Vestal forever?"

"It might as well be forever. The term of office is thirty years. At the end of that time a Vestal may return to the world, but few do. Most remain in service to the goddess until they die."

"Thirty years!" I exclaimed. "Marcella will be an old woman."

"Indeed."

I cast frantically about. There was no way, no one . . . and then it came to me . . . *Caligula*! If anyone could help, it was he. It hadn't taken me a day in Rome to realize that Caligula was the only grandchild the empress gave a fig about. The mere thought of him made me ill. But what choice did I have? A decision had been made. He alone might change it.

WHEN I FOUND MY WAY TO THE SUMPTUOUS APARTMENTS assigned to Caligula, I waved away the attendant slave in the foyer, and, taking a deep breath, pushed open the door to the *cubiculae*. Caligula lay sprawled across a massive sleeping couch, his shoulders propped against a bank of pillows covered in leopard skins. A wave of revulsion swept over me as I looked at the crumpled sheets. They were black silk.

Caligula grinned at me. "Well, hello, Claudia! Do you like my room? Your sister did."

"What you did to her was horrible."

"Marcella didn't think so." Caligula folded his arms behind his head, that awful mocking smile broader still. "So why did you come?"

"Because of you, the empress wants to punish Marcella. She's forcing her to become a Vestal."

"Really! How amusing." Caligula smirked delightedly as his fingers absently played with the fringed pillow behind his head. "My first deflowering and now the maid is to be turned into the ultimate virgin. That makes me a sort of god."

"This isn't a joke! We're talking about Marcella's life. Surely you must have known someone would find out."

He laughed heartily. "I *wanted* Livia to find out. I sent a slave to tell her. Why not? It is never too early to build a reputation."

I stared at him incredulously. I wanted to fling myself at him, scratching, biting, kicking. I wanted to kill him for his ugly insolence, his thoughtless cruelty. My hands clenched tightly into fists. "But you like Marcella," I reminded him when I could speak at last. "You've always chased after her. I thought when you knew the trouble she was in you would want to help."

"Oh, I like her well enough," he said, watching me thoughtfully.

My heart quickened. "Then it will be easy. All you have to do is marry her."

"Marry her!" Caligula laughed mirthlessly. "Not likely. She's a lively girl all right, very lively, but a bit too full of herself for my taste. None of you Proculas know your place. You, Claudia, are the worst with your uppity ways. I don't know why my parents are so fond of you. Who do you think you are, walking in here and presuming to tell me what to do?"

I looked down, feeling that I had only made matters worse. It was hopeless.

"So where is your famous sight now?" Caligula goaded. With a flourish, he threw back the covers. "Has it ever shown you anything like this?"

"Oh!" I gasped, my cheeks flaming as I stared at his naked body.

Caligula gloated, his eyes gleaming with pride. "Come now, Claudia, you always have something to say. Aren't you impressed?"

A wave of violent nausea swept over me. I gritted my teeth. "Is that all?" I somehow managed to ask. "I'd heard they were bigger."

THE TEMPLE OF VESTA IS A MASSIVE GOLD-DOMED building, round, signifying the hearth, its circular *cella* enclosed by handsome Corinthian columns. On the day of Marcella's initiation, two priestesses, white gowned and veiled, met us at the entrance. Marcella, standing straight and noble, walked with them to their adjoining palace. We were very proud of her courage. No one would have guessed that the girl had lain awake the whole night long, sobbing until there were no tears left.

An hour later we joined her in the grand chamber. Marcella was clad like the others in flowing white. Father took my trembling sister's hand and led her to a dais where Tiberius waited before the sacred flame. Marcella had never looked more beautiful, her blue eyes almost the shade of violets as she met his solemn gaze.

Father moved back as the Chief Vestal motioned for Marcella to kneel. Acting as Pontifex Maximus, Tiberius stepped forward. Placing his hands lightly on her shining black hair, he spoke the ritual words: "*Te amata, capio!* My beloved, I take possession of you." Slowly, lock by lock, Marcella's curls were shorn. Since her hair was long and very thick, Tiberius seemed to take forever.

Sitting between my parents, hands in theirs, I tried to control my sobs. Occasionally I stole glances at Mother, tears coursing down her pale cheeks. My father's face was set in grim lines, but from time to time I saw his eyes glisten. Agrippina had the grace to look away, but Livia and Caligula made no effort to conceal their pleasure. Both appeared to delight in every minute. Sometimes they nudged each other. Once they even laughed. My sister seemed impervious to everything. As I watched the last curl fall and the wimple go over her head, the Marcella I'd known all my life faded before my eyes.

CHAPTER 4

The Voice of Isis

The day after Marcella's initiation Tiberius startled us all with a proclamation: Germanicus was to tour the empire. *Tata* would accompany him.

Within an hour Mother was packing for all of us. I could scarcely believe my eyes as I watched her move from one trunk to another, folding this, discarding that. "Surely we aren't going with them?"

Looking up from a stack of tunicas, she brushed a tendril of hair from her forehead. "Have you taken leave of your senses? Can you imagine your father refusing Germanicus?"

I couldn't, any more than I could imagine Mother refusing to accompany Father, yet the long journey, the close shipboard confinement with its unavoidable proximity to Agrippina, felt intolerable. Her defection was harder to bear than Livia's and Caligula's evil. As long as I could remember, Auntie had been there: bossy, generous, irritating, and lovable. How could I ever forgive her betrayal?

Arrangements for the tour fell smoothly into place. Too

smoothly. I overheard *Tata* comment to Mother: "Tiberius must have planned it months ago."

So little time remained to spend with Marcella. Bittersweet hours, my sister's sparkle fading before my eyes. All Marcella's impetuous charm must, as a Vestal, be submerged. Though Vesta's priestesses are honored above all others, they are set apart and expected to exist chastely as the goddess herself. Sitting with my sister in the great temple's marble anteroom, it dawned on me that, though Vesta and her sacred flame provide the focus for the home, for the family, for Rome itself, there's no statue of her anywhere. *Vesta is invisible.*

"There's so much to memorize," Marcella complained. "Vesta's divine lore can't be entrusted to writing; we learn it word by word. Rituals are hardest. One mistake and the whole ceremony must be repeated from the beginning. It will take ten years to learn it all."

How brave she was to joke. I forced myself to laugh. "What are you really doing?"

"I just told you," she said, a bit of the old flash in her eyes. "It is nothing to laugh about, I assure you."

My heart ached for her. I'd struggled to put the best possible face on Marcella's new life. Vestals were highly respected, their box at circuses or theaters second only to the imperial ones. They were allowed visitors and could come and go as they pleased, never answering to men. I liked that. I'd admired her white gown, too—beautifully fashioned from the finest silk. Now I realized that the ethereal look was romantic only because it emphasized her remoteness. The enormity of it hit me once again: Marcella—mischievous, high-spirited Marcella—lost to us, lost to the world, imprisoned for a lifetime.

"What follows?" I forced myself to ask.

"Ten years of practicing those rituals."

"And then?"

"I get to teach the rituals to novices." Marcella smiled tremulously at my incredulity. "Yes, it's truly so. Thirty years of ritual." Her eyes brimmed with tears. "That isn't the worst."

"What is?"

"The Vestals are very kind . . ." Marcella began to sob. "But it's all such a . . . woman's world."

ONCE SHIPBOARD, MY PARENTS AND AGRIPPINA SETTLED into accustomed routines that shocked me. Father was polite and deferential as always, Mother appeared to resent her no more nor less than she ever had. Though overt disrespect was unthinkable, I politely ignored Agrippina's attempts to slip back into the old familiarity and avoided her as much as possible.

The rhythmic pounding of the ship's drums awed me at first. Soon I scarcely noticed. Only at night in my bunk was I aware of the steady cadence that kept the slaves rowing. Reflecting on the eight hundred men who manned the ship's oars in continuous shifts, I saw similarities between their lot and my own. No overseer lashed my shoulders, but was I any less a slave? Rome was master of all our fates.

Germanicus's command ship, a massive quinquereme, sailed at the center of an honor guard, six triremes, purple sails stretched across four masts of Lebanese cedar. Galley slaves praised Neptune for the stiff breeze that eased their labors.

I continued my studies, sharing the same pedagogue with Julia and Druscilla. We all missed Marcella. Bright, though not a scholar, she had livened many tedious hours with her quips. Nero and Drusus, too, were absent, junior officers serving their first tours of duty, Nero in Carthage, Drusus in Spain. My consolation was that Caligula no longer studied with us. At Germanicus's suggestion, the ship's resident expert—*Tata*—drilled Caligula in the use of shield and javelin. I hated the thought of my father working to improve the martial skills of Marcella's seducer. The disgusting ironywas worsened by *Tata*'s unquestioned acceptance of his commander's order. For order it was, no matter how casually voiced.

In the past it had been Marcella and me paired against our cousins at whatever game we played. Now, when Julia and Druscilla sought my company for our favorite dice match, I felt Marcella's loss all the more acutely. Better to escape into a scroll, allowing a story to just happen to me. Not even Rome could interfere with that.

As I reclined on the top deck, sea rhythms subtly tempering my resentments, the days blended seamlessly. Lost in the mirrored blues of sea and sky, I filled scrolls of my own with attempts at poetry, odes to the foamy miracle of Venus's birth. Daughter of Jupiter and a sea nymph, Venus had emerged full-grown from the tumult of their union. Below me, five banks of oarsmen rowed in tiers using giant sweeps requiring all the might and muscle of their bodies. From time to time, I left my couch to look down at them. Staggered, some sitting, others standing, they bent over the shafts of their oars, gripping tightly and grunting in unison as they flung themselves forward, then back, responding with all their strength to the insistent beat. Sometimes my pulses throbbed.

Without warning, the weather changed. A series of battering storms pounded our ship, driving all passengers belowdecks. Although nearly everyone was ill, the turmoil exhilarated me. Despite Father's orders, I climbed the ladder to watch the great waves crash over the sides.

The skies cleared when we reached Nicopolis, but our ship limped into port with severe storm damage. Our steering system, on the verge of collapse, would require extensive repairs. Germanicus wanted to make use of the time to visit the gulf of Actium. His grandfather, Marcus Antonius, had fought the great sea battle there—a losing one against Augustus. Father dutifully organized an expedition and many of the officers set off to locate the remains of Antonius's camp. I was delighted when Caligula insisted on going too. Though under strict orders from Germanicus to treat me with respect, he taunted me mercilessly. I tried to ignore him and succeeded most of the time, but only the night before I'd discovered a dead rat under the wrappings of my bunk. When I flung it in Caligula's face, he grabbed my wrists tightly, pulling me toward him, glowering down. "Have a care, Madam Sybil. Next time it will be a live rat."

"You wouldn't dare," I said, pulling free. I'd hated sharing a cramped cabin with my parents. Now I was glad. Even Caligula wouldn't risk *Tata*'s wrath.

The morning the party departed, I awakened to unaccustomed cramping pains. Pulling myself from the narrow bunk, I caught my breath at the crimson streaks. Just then Mother entered the cabin. She smiled, noticing immediately, and put her arms around me. "Ah, it has begun. How do you feel?" she asked, rubbing my back.

"It hurts, like something pressing hard."

Mother nodded. "It's that way for some of us. Once you have your first child, you will scarcely notice."

I grimaced, one big pain replacing a lesser one. At Mother's bidding, I climbed back onto the bunk. She left the cabin but quickly returned with a female slave who bore fresh linen and cloths. While the slave remade the bunk, Mother carefully explained what must be done each month. Such a nuisance! My carefree life was gone forever.

"Roman women must be strong," Mother reminded me. "We never submit to pain. We go about our duties." She hesitated, then added, "Since this is your first bleeding—" She turned abruptly and left the cabin with the slave. Moments later Mother returned alone, carrying a pitcher with two cups. Sipping from the one offered me, I tasted undiluted wine, slightly heated. The full-bodied flavor warmed my body. It was good. I lay back on the freshly made bunk, feeling loved and cosseted.

Mother pulled up a campstool and sat down. "I was sixteen," she confided. "So late—I thought I would *never* become a woman. Then finally it happened—on the Feast of Matronalia. Imagine! As the Fates would have it, I was wearing a white tunic. A female slave whispered in my ear. I still shudder at how many may have seen. Your grandmother called it a good omen. She said that becoming a woman on the day most sacred to Juno would bring me good fortune in marriage. It has."

We talked on, sharing jokes and fancies. Even as I laughed

with Mother, I thought of Marcella. If only she were with us, but after a time a sense of drowsiness crept over me. Mother quietly removed the pitcher and cups from the sea chest and tiptoed from the cabin.

The next thing I knew, Agrippina stood at my side. "Good morning, *Domina*," she said, winking like a serving girl. In one hand she held an exquisitely cut glass vase containing a single red rose, in the other a slender strand of blood red garnets.

I moved away.

Agrippina placed two ringed fingers gently over my tightened lips. "It's no use, Claudia. You can't run from me any longer, any more than you can run from the facts of life. You are a woman now; it is time you acted like one. You have much to learn about being an adult, just as I continue to learn."

Her words surprised me. Agrippina acted as though she knew everything. Silently, I watched her place the vase in a wall niche.

"I have brought these gifts as symbols of your passage into womanhood. It is my pleasure," she explained, fastening the necklace about my throat. "Good bye, little girl, welcome, my sister."

I held myself stiffly, refusing to meet her eyes.

"Yes, I know." Agrippina sighed. "You blame me for what happened but I was not the cause. Marcella knew the risk. The woman always pays. That's a lesson you must learn, but hopefully, *not* from personal experience."

"You could have tried," I protested. "You thought only of Caligula."

"What mother doesn't want the best for her son? No one could have saved Marcella. My own mother has spent much of her life exiled on a tiny island, the price for a handful of indiscretions. Imagine, the only child of Augustus existing on bread and cheese, not even permitted cosmetics."

I nodded. "Mother told me. I doubt she has need of cosmetics with no visitors allowed. Mother said that Livia exaggerated the Lady Julia's . . . ah, indiscretions, that she poisoned the emperor's mind against his own daughter."

"That's quite true." Agrippina nodded. "It's another valuable lesson for you to keep in mind. One doesn't cross the empress. Livia hates me and doesn't appear overly fond of you. Avoid her at all costs."

I wavered. How could I withstand the force of Agrippina's charm or her logic? Nothing could change what had happened. The bitterness hurt only me. When Agrippina's arms enfolded me, I hugged back.

MONTHS PASSED INTO YEARS AS THE IMPERIAL TOUR continued. There were state visits to Colophon, to Athens, to Rhodes, to Samos, and to Lesbos. Eavesdropping more and more frequently on conversations around me, I realized that it would be a long time before I saw Marcella again. Tiberius was not about to allow his charismatic step-nephew to return to Rome. Agrippina and Germanicus were a golden couple. Everywhere we went, the client subjects, as we called those puppet kingdoms, rallied adoringly around them. These exotic potentates offered a potential power base. Even I saw that.

"Why doesn't Germanicus rebel?" I asked my father one night as we stood at the ship's rail looking out at the twinkling lights of one more receding shoreline.

Tata looked quickly over his shoulder. "Careful, little one. We never know who may be listening. Don't think for a moment that youth will protect you." He put his cloak about my shoulders, shielded me from the rising breeze feathering the sea with whitecaps. "Remember Germania? The mutineers wanted nothing more than to overthrow Tiberius. Germanicus wouldn't do it then to save his life. He won't do it now. Caesar—whoever he may be—*is* Rome. Germanicus's duty is clear and so is ours."

Well, not so clear to me, but I was young and found much to divert me. As part of the imperial entourage, I met each client king. Some treated me almost as a woman; I loved it. The world itself was a kind of playground in those days. I still remember the performers: the brightest, most talented each country had to offer—acrobats and magicians, animals and mimes. Every capital brought out its best for us.

Marcella and I wrote often, our letters entrusted to ships that plied the waters between Rome and its dominions. My sister's were little more than notes: "The Chief Vestal fell asleep during the dedication of a new palace hearth. No one dared wake her. She snores like an elephant." I, on the other hand, loved to write and filled scroll after scroll with the sights, sounds, and even smells of the countries we visited. Then an event occurred that I could find no words to describe, not even to Marcella. It happened in Egypt after a day of sightseeing.

My parents took me on a small skiff out to Pharos where the white cylinder of Alexandria's famous lighthouse shimmered in the early morning sun, its sparkle almost blinding. Even Father breathed heavily after climbing the four hundred steps to stand beside the watch fire. Although the flames, kept blazing from sunset to sunrise, were ebbing now, the rays from the great polished reflecting mirror dazzled my eyes. "Nothing that man has ever built or ever will build can equal this," Father told me.

From there we'd made our way to the equally celebrated museum. Exploring the gardens where every known flower blossomed and the library filled with more scrolls than anyone could read in a lifetime, I thought the learning center truly a temple to the muses. I wanted to stay there forever, but Father insisted we move on to the tour's highlight.

No one visited the city without a pilgrimage to the tomb of its founder, Alexander the Great. The remains of a legend lay encased in an etched glass chamber reflecting every hue of the rainbow. Revolted but curious, I moved forward. The corpse's embalmers had been masters. Though some flesh receded from the strong young bones, the broad brow, high, arched nose, and firm chin had settled into a bizarre kind of beauty.

Offerings were banked about the sarcophagus, images of the god-king, amulets of metal, bone, and stone, wine, sweets, and flowers, fresh and withered. So much homage to a ruler dead three hundred years. Studying the corpse, I marveled at the vision of a man who had created a capital rivaling Rome. "Is the city really just as Alexander planned it?" I asked.

Father pushed back the heavy folds of his woolen toga. "The story goes that he walked the site, pointing out locations for temples and city buildings to architects hurrying after him. At one point, he ran out of powdered chalk and used grain. When birds swooped down to feed, seers predicted that Alexandria would prosper and nourish many strangers."

"That's a wonderful story," I said, enjoying the idea of a prophecy that turned out well. My own were generally so awful. I didn't add the doubts that had plagued me throughout the day. What was the point? What good was Alexander's power in the end? Only a shell remained. The lighthouse, the museum, the city itself had been built by men, long gone. Might these stupendous monuments also someday disappear? Was there nothing more? With a last speculative glance over my shoulder at the sarcophagus, I followed my parents from the shrine.

Night was falling as we reached the street. At my urging, *Tata* waved aside the litter bearers and agreed to walk back to our rented villa. I smiled up at him appreciatively. "We have so little time in Alexandria. I want to see everything." Until we'd reached Alexandria, I thought I *had* seen everything. I was fourteen, remember. There was little I didn't know.

Nothing could have prepared me for Alexandria. As many as a hundred ships docked there in a single day bringing people from far-off worlds of which I'd never dreamed. I saw camels, not one or two in someone's private menagerie, but endless caravans passing in and out of the city led by men who looked like princes in their flowing robes and silken turbans. All about me every shade of human mingled freely. I sensed, without understanding, a seductive tolerance and felt myself on the edge of adventure. I loved it.

On this night I saw a pair of cheetahs strolling freely with a woman black as ebony. We stopped to watch an amber-skinned snake charmer and then a fire breather with hair to match his flaming breath. The rhythms of many languages assailed my ears at once. My cheeks flushed as somewhere a high-pitched male voice, speaking in Greek, praised the luscious ripeness of a boy's buttocks. What a contrast to the rapid gutturals of a trader's Persian and rough soldiers' Latin.

Then one voice cut through them all, brasslike and imperious. "Way! Make way for the Voice of Isis!" Almost magically, the dense crowds parted for a procession. First comically dressed comedians leaped into view, creating lighthearted confusion as they passed among us. An old man sat astride "Pegasus"—a donkey with wings attached to its shoulders. A bear dressed as a Roman matron rode a sedan chair. An elegantly clad monkey appeared as Ganymede clasping a gold cup. Women, white-gowned and garlanded, showered us with roses. Musicians with pipes, flutes, cymbals, and drums followed, and then a choir of sweet-voiced children singing the praises of one they called "Daughter of the Stars."

Lamps, torches, and candles gleamed in the twilight as the priestess was carried forward. My breath caught at her beauty, wrapped like some rare confection in transparent white linen. Her jewelry too was marvelous, a golden belt and anklets, snakelike bracelets with emerald eyes that matched her own brilliant orbs drawn long with kohl and malachite. Adorning her throat was a necklace of gold, ivory, lapis, and carnelian, and in her hands were the crook and flail of the Great House of Egypt.

The priestess surveyed the crowd from her lofty vantage on a great golden chair, a gentle smile playing about her full lips. With a serene expression, she surveyed the crowd. As her eyes moved over the throng, she caught sight of me standing spellbound. Our glances locked. My heart was choking me; I felt the stones beneath my feet move. The priestess's smile deepened as though in recognition.

I started forward, drawn as to a magnet, but was held firmly in place by Father. The procession moved on, the sound of gongs and flutes fading as the crowd drifted forward until the priestess was obscured from view.

I sighed longingly. "Who was that?"

"An abomination!"

I looked up, shocked by an angry tone I rarely heard.

Mother's small hands flew up in a protective gesture to avert the omen. "Marcus! She *is* the high priestess of Isis."

"The goddess of that bitch queen, Cleopatra."

"You don't still think it was *all* Cleopatra's fault!" Mother exclaimed.

"I do! If she hadn't bewitched him from his duty to his family, to Rome—forced him to play Osiris to her Isis—"

"Can a woman force a man to do anything he does not desire?"

"Who are you talking about?" I wanted to know.

Mother and Father exchanged glances. Mother sighed. "Why not tell her?"

"It happened long ago. Such things are better forgotten."

"Not *that* long ago," she reminded him. "Tiberius has not forgotten. I notice he wasn't at all pleased that Germanicus chose to come here for a holiday."

"No, he was not," Father admitted, his gray eyes thoughtful. "Another message arrived yesterday. Tiberius is angry."

"I'm not surprised. I thought it risky of Germanicus. No potential heir has dared come here since—"

"Since what? Who are you talking about? I'm not a child," I reminded them.

"No, but you are a daughter of Rome who should know

better than to press her father." *Tata*'s voice was stern, but his expression melted as he looked at me. "Whoever controls Egypt controls Rome's grain supply. The emperor is always suspicious of Germanicus."

I had sat, an attentive mouse, through many policy debates. Now I waited expectantly. When no one spoke, I prompted, softening my voice. "There's more to it than that. I know there is. Who are you talking about?"

It was Mother who answered. "Antonius. Marcus Antonius, Germanicus's grandfather."

I nodded. "He shared the empire with Augustus, didn't he?"

"For a time, before he was lured away by his Egyptian—consort." The anger was back in Father's voice.

"Here, I'm told they thought of him as *her* consort," Mother reminded him.

"It's Antonius's disgrace that he allowed himself to forsake the gods of our fathers, that he walked at Cleopatra's side while she was carried above him on that wretched throne."

"It *is* incredible," Mother agreed. "Imagine a man forgetting Rome so completely, sacrificing everything."

I said nothing, remembering the invitation in the priestess's eyes. I'd glimpsed a new freedom there. A chance, perhaps, to escape the imperial restrictions I resented. At the very least I'd seen the promise of an adventure unlike anything I'd ever known.

CHAPTER 5

Isis's Quest

Mother had never taken me to the slave market. Now I saw why. The stench alone was dreadful. Many of the terrified slaves had fouled themselves, staining their garments and the filthy straw where they stood.

"Disgusting!" Mother muttered, holding her *stola* tightly about her. "No Roman would behave in such a manner."She handed me a small crystal vial of perfume. "Hold this to your nose and stay close beside me."

Clutching the vial, I followed Mother from one small crowd to another. The smell was only part of it. I heard horrible screams, curses, and shouts. The slaves wore metal collars fastened to chains secured by heavy wooden posts. Some of the men swore at passersby, straining as far as their chains would allow. So fierce, but I felt their fear, clinging like sweat. Older ones stood straight, but looked frail. Who would want them? Mother pulled me past a slave woman, her arms shielding three young children who clung to her skirts. All of them were crying.

"It's awful, Mother. I had no idea."

Mother nodded. "I can't pretend that it isn't, but someday you'll have a home of your own to run. It's time to see how things are done. Look around, we must find a replacement for old Priscilla. The banquet's next week."

I scanned the possibilities. They might as well be a herd of dumb oxen. And then one piqued my interest. She stood tall and still among the trembling, often whimpering men and women. "What about that girl?"

Mother gestured to the slave master standing nearby. He quickly handed her the girl's bill of sale. "A fine choice, *Domina.* Rachel is today's best."

Mother turned her back to him, frowning over the scroll. "Rachel, is it? The stories those masters tell! This claims she's fluent in both Greek and Latin with a father who was adviser to Herod the Great." Regarding the slave closely, Mother speculated, "I wonder what's wrong with her, only four years older than you and sold three times."

I searched Rachel's lively, intelligent face, liked her bright, hazel eyes, longish nose, and broad, humorous mouth. "Perhaps she was just unlucky."

"She looks delicate to me." Mother turned away.

Disappointment flickered in the slave's eyes. "Hungry is more like it," I ventured. "I think she'd be the very one to help with the banquet."

The only other prospective buyer was a large man whose belly bulged over an Egyptian kilt. Round face flushed, he leaned forward to lift the girl's wiry arms, managing to cup a breast in the process. His large hand moved to the slave's jaw, forcing her mouth open. She ended the examination abruptly, catching two of his short, fat fingers in her sharp teeth.

"Seth's shit!" he swore, cuffing her hard with one hand while trying to extract the other.

The slave master rushed forward. "Take care! You don't own her yet."

"How much is she?" I asked.

"One thousand sesterces," replied the master. "A woman with such spirit"—he looked at the examiner, who swore again and sucked his bleeding hand—"such fire, is worth far more."

"One thousand be damned," the man growled. "She isn't worth ten."

"No, she isn't," Mother agreed. "Claudia, what *are* you thinking!" My cheeks flamed. Two men laughed openly; old women in black watched us with little fox eyes, missing nothing.

The slave master's eyes shifted to Mother as one hand, weighted with rings, adjusted the folds of his embroidered tunic. "Surely a *domina* of your obvious discernment sees that a bright young woman with a cultured background would be a bargain at one thousand. It's only because I'm forced to close my establishment to attend family business in Etruria that I'm willing to part with her so cheaply."

Mother shook her head firmly. Taking my arm, she led me away from a knot of curious onlookers. "You're so anxious to be treated as an adult, it's time you acted like one. I've five hundred to spend, not a denarius more. That one"—she glanced discreetly at a matronly figure standing docilely at the far end of the line—"looks right. I've been watching her since we came in. The young slave is anyone's guess. With such a temper, it's no wonder she's had so many masters."

"What would you do if some man touched you like he did her? I'd bite him even harder than she did."

"I'm sure you would," Mother allowed, "but it's hardly the same, now is it? The girl brought her troubles on herself. The slave master's gambling that man will pay more than she's worth and now he thinks you're a potential buyer as well."

"The man's already angry," I pointed out. "If he buys the slave, he may hurt her."

"That's life, my dear."

"Oh, Mother, the poor slave . . ." I felt my eyes fill with tears.

"Don't 'Oh, Mother' me. I *am* your mother, not your father. Save your drama for him."

I dried my eyes. "How much were you planning to pay for a slave?"

"I told you, five hundred is my limit. I am expected to entertain the governor this week. You attended his reception. You saw how lavish it was. Those gold dishes, the sword swallowers—well, why not? He's got the whole treasury of Egypt to steal from!" She paused, watching me speculatively. "Do you have any pocket money?"

"Fifty sesterces," I admitted reluctantly. I'd been saving for a gold ring fashioned into a coiled snake with bright green eyes. The shopkeeper told me it had magic properties.

We looked back at the prospective buyer, still haggling with the slave master. The latter had come down to nine hundred, the former up to seven. So close. I looked at the slave, who stood still as stone, her face impassive but for the eyes—fixed on me.

I sighed. "I do have one hundred more hidden at home in Hecate's basket . . ."

"Oh, very well"—Mother sighed—"if it means that much to you. We'll pay seven hundred and fifty," she called out in a clear voice. The buyer considered the girl for a long minute, muttered a curse, and stalked from the market.

RACHEL, OUR FAMILY SOON AGREED, KNEW EVERYTHING worth knowing about Alexandria. The girl fit effortlessly into our household, behaving as though she'd served us for years. Skilled at hairdressing, clever with a needle, she made herself indispensable to Mother while managing to work with Hebe and Festus, our cook and house manager, an ill-tempered but gifted pair. For that alone Mother blessed Fortuna, but soon she came to suspect that Rachel knew every bargain in a city renowned the world over for its variety.

The governor dined on the finest cuts of sterile sow womb. He delighted in boiled ostrich served on a bed of Jericho dates and rhapsodized over minced sea crayfish spiced with *garum* sauce. Orchids from the far reaches of the Upper Nile transformed our modest atrium. Athenian lute players entertained while an Ethiopian Venus performed with panthers that cavorted like kittens. Everyone marveled at the feats of Mithradites, a magician said to be the cleverest in a city of wizards; but Mother and I privately decided that Rachel was the true wizard. She'd accomplished the event for a fraction of the amount originally budgeted.

*

For days banquet preparations had absorbed Rachel's life. All the while I'd thought of little but the great goddess Isis and her handmaiden, Cleopatra—exotic, intriguing, and forbidden. Returning to my room after the festivities, I sighed in anticipation. Let my parents keep their secrets, I knew exactly where to turn.

The lamps had been dimmed. A pink shift lay draped across the couch. Rachel rose to greet me. "Would you like a massage?" she asked, unfastening my tunic.

"Yes," I answered, stepping out of my garments. "A massage and some information. Tell me about Cleopatra. *Tata* called her a bitch. Was she evil?"

Rachel carefully removed a vial of sandalwood oil from the small collection near the couch. "She was worshiped as a goddess. Alexandrians still mourn her. Cleopatra was the last of the Ptolemies, Alexander's dynasty."

"I know that!" I exclaimed impatiently. "When we conquered Egypt, Augustus installed a governor. One has ruled ever since. But what about Cleopatra? Was she very beautiful?"

Rachel's hands kneaded my back. "Her statues show a shapely body dressed splendidly in the Egyptian manner."

"Egyptian styles leave little to the imagination. What about her face?"

Rachel's experienced fingers moved impersonally over my buttocks. "Her nose was large and her jaw pronounced."

"But Antonius and, I'm told, Julius Caesar before him—"

"It couldn't have been her face," Rachel remarked with certainty. "The old ones say she had a beautiful voice and everyone thought she was awfully smart." Rachel paused. "Then there's the other thing."

"Other thing?"

"You're very young."

"I'm fourteen! Another year and my parents will be searching for a husband. Tell me!"

"Cleopatra was heady wine. She thought that marriage, first to Caesar and then to Antonius, would unite the world in one bed—"

"Her own," I finished. "But that was all so long ago. *Tata* never saw Cleopatra, yet he hates her. There must be something else . . ." I sat up, raising my arms as Rachel slipped the shift over my shoulders. Yawning, I lay back on the couch. My eyes felt heavy. "I don't suppose even *Tata* knows why he hates Cleopatra," I murmured sleepily, "but it's that power he fears—the power of Isis."

I DREAMED THAT NIGHT OF ISIS. A PLEASANT DREAM, FOR, once, but not surprising. I'd been thinking of her, after all. What did surprise me was Rachel's reaction."It's an omen," the slave insisted excitedly. "The true beloved of Isis are always dreamers."

"How do you know so much about Isis?" I asked, looking up from my breakfast figs.

"I go to her temple whenever I can."

"*You* go there? A slave?"

Rachel smiled at my surprise. "Isis welcomes everyone."

"How remarkable." I reached absently for a pot of honey. "Your bill of sale said you are Judaean. I've heard that your people have only one god. He must be strong. Why have you left him?"

Rachel hesitated. "Yahweh punishes people. He turned one woman into a pillar of salt—just for looking back. A goddess would be more forgiving."

"Some of them," I conceded. "Diana turns men into stags if they take liberties, like spying on women bathing. She loves animals, though. When a chariot hit Hecate, no one thought she would live. *Tata* wanted to get another cat, but Diana heard my prayers. Hecate's leg mended. She doesn't even limp."

"A miracle, I'm sure, but tell me please, what of your dream?"

"There's little to tell," I answered, surprised again by Rachel's intensity. "It was mostly her face, so beautiful, full of love and . . . compassion. Isis wouldn't turn anyone into anything. She called me to a lovely blue sea. We flew there together, she holding me in her arms. Sometimes we rested on the wave, rocking as in a cradle. I felt so . . . so safe."

Rachel nodded knowingly. "The sea is sacred to her. She's chosen you, I'm sure of it."

LATER WHEN I JOINED MOTHER IN THE SUNLIT CORNER where her loom rested, she did not agree.

"Don't let your father hear you talking about Isis," she warned.

I nodded obediently, then after a pause, asked, "Are you happy worshiping Juno?"

"Happy?" Mother looked surprised. "I seek reassurance from Juno, nothing else." She smiled at me. "When I was your age I worshiped Diana. She is a virgin, which is all very well when one is young—*very* well. But then I met your father . . . My offerings to Venus were well received. In recent years, Juno has grown very dear. She protects our home, I feel it."

"But Juno . . ." I hesitated.

"Juno is the goddess of marriage," Mother reminded me. She picked up a skein of mauve wool. "What more could any woman want?"

"I don't know." I paused again. "Her husband seems a strange god, always chasing one tunica after another, but Juno . . . isn't very forgiving. She does such cruel things to her rivals—changing them into cows and things."

Mother picked up her shuttle. "When you are a wife you will understand."

RACHEL TOLD ME ISIS'S STORY EARLY THE NEXT MORNING while we walked to the fish market. At first Father had forbidden me to go; then, at Mother's suggestion, he agreed to a litter. I didn't want a litter. I wanted to *see* things, so I pleaded: "I need the exercise." *Tata* sighed, finally agreed, but later I noticed two house slaves trailing discreetly behind us.

"If ever there were a pair of soulmates, it was Isis and Osiris," Rachel said, lightly swinging the basket she carried. "They met and loved each other in their mother's womb before their birth as twins."

I had heard that Egyptian kings and queens sometimes married siblings. It seemed strange, but still, who would you know better than your own brother? "Their happiness must have been eternal," I ventured.

"Anything but," Rachel explained. "A jealous brother tricked Osiris into trying a casket on for size, then locked it and flung him into the Nile. Isis set off to find her husband. It was a long, hard journey. She even pretended to be a temple love priestess."

"A love priestess!" I was shocked and thrilled.

"She had to," Rachel quickly explained. "It was the only way she could get Osiris's corpse back to bury. Even that wasn't the end. The same awful brother unearthed the body, dismembered it, and scattered the pieces all over the world. So what could Isis do but set off once again, this time to find and join his missing parts?"

"Did she find them?"

"All but the most important."

I tried not to giggle.

"It's the means by which a woman brings life to her husband," Rachel reminded me. "The goddess used her powers not only to reconstruct the missing member, but to bring immortality to her husband through their child."

We'd reached the seaside market. Brightly colored boats bobbed in the water as men hauled in tubs of flailing fish. Rachel darted from one makeshift stall to another searching for the rare bream, Mother's favorite. Sniffing from a perfume vial, I leaned against the sea wall, staring absently out at the harbor. Pharos, the great lighthouse I'd visited the week before, was emerging from early morning mist when Rachel touched my elbow. "We should return home," she urged. "Look what I have here. Your father will want these sardines for breakfast." In no time, she'd purchased not only sardines and bream but mussels and crabs.

All around us slaves and sellers bargained and cursed, crying out to be heard above the market din, but my thoughts were of a female deity who roamed the world surviving by her wits. "That was the most beautiful story I've ever heard," I said at last. It was also the most exciting.

Turning to Rachel, I announced: "You will take me to the temple of Isis."

She jumped, nearly dislodging the basket from her shoulder. "Your parents would kill me!"

I laughed at the idea. "Mother fusses a lot, but wouldn't hurt a bug." I paused, considering. "*Tata*'s a soldier. What he does, he does for Rome—not himself. Besides, he'd think it poor business to injure his own slave."

"I know that," Rachel said. "Your mother reminds me of my own. Had life been different, had they met at Herod's court, they might easily have been friends. Your father's a fair man. More than fair, he's kind; but if either of them thought I'd wrongly influenced you, they would sell me. I couldn't bear that, not again. I want to stay with your family forever."

"I want you to," I assured her. "Often I forget that you're a slave. I was so lonely after Marcella was taken—" I paused, overcome by sudden emotion, then continued. "We'll go tonight when they're asleep. No one will ever know."

CHAPTER

6

In the House of Isis

Even in the dim lamplight, I saw that Rachel's skin was pale, her jaw tense. I pretended not to notice as we stole out into the night. We were dressed simply. I wore Rachel's threadbare *palla,* not the new one that Mother had given her after the banquet. It was as though I wore a costume. Having never been out at night without my parents, I found the prospect thrilling.

Walking briskly, we passed unnoticed and soon reached the market square where many stalls remained open. Crowds still jostled. The air was heavy with the scent of roasted lamb, temple incense, and human bodies at work. Rachel rushed me forward, her eyes constantly watching, wary as a cat.

After much bargaining, she hired a litter. I wondered if the rickety frame would hold together, then fretted over the slow, clumsy bearers. Behind the soiled curtain, confused by the many twists and turns, I lost all sense of direction until I smelled the sea. I pulled the curtains aside to look out, but Rachel yanked them back. "No, no, you must not," she admonished me, her voice anxious. "What if someone were to recognize you?"

At last the litter was roughly deposited on the ground; Rachel and I climbed out unassisted. I paid the bearers, then looked up expectantly. Before us a broad flight of stairs led to a garden illuminated by at least a hundred torches. I caught my breath at the sight. Ibises and peacocks strutted along walkways of green serpentine bordered by multitudes of many-hued roses, their scent hovering seductively on the balmy air. I pushed back the hood of my *palla* as an unexpected sense of familiarity swept over me. The faint sound of chanting grew louder as we passed row upon row of fluted columns, then entered the temple's anteroom, where Isis's many trials were depicted in mosaics on the floor. I shivered in anticipation as I read the words inscribed in gold beside them.

I am the first and the last
I am the honored one and the scorned one,
I am the whore and the holy one

Beyond, gauzy draperies stirred gently in the soft breeze. The splendor of lights, great circles and squares, arcs and clusters of lamps hanging from the vaulted ceiling, dazzled me with their luminosity.

People stood talking softly in small groups or sat on marble benches. Men as well as women. Some were dressed fashionably, but not all, yet even the most simply garbed appeared immaculately clean. Many recognized Rachel. I was surprised by the smiles and friendly nods she exchanged. How could it be that a mere slave could be accepted, even welcomed, into such a grand place?

As I looked about the large marble room studying the people gathered there, I became aware that I, too, was being watched. Beneath a broad column a young man sat alone. The scroll that he'd been holding slipped unheeded to the floor as his eyes studied me. Intense eyes, great, dark, filled with . . . what? I shivered. Straightening my shoulders, I turned away. Who was that man, how dared he look at me as though . . . as though he could see into my very soul?

I looked back, couldn't help myself. He'd gotten up, retrieved the scroll, and was smiling at Rachel. She nodded a friendly greeting, and he moved toward us with an easy grace. He was taller than most, long-limbed and slender. "Do I know you?" I asked, raising my chin as Mother sometimes did.

"For a moment I thought I knew *you,*" he said and bowed low. Then, his eyes again on mine, laughing eyes. "I was mistaken. How could I, a simple wanderer, know such a grand lady?"

Was he mocking me? The young man's manner was humble, his Greek thickly accented, yet I wondered at his assurance.

Rachel muttered a few impatient words in a language I'd not heard before. He nodded in agreement.

"What are you saying?" I demanded to know. "What tongue are you speaking?"

"It is Aramaic, the language of our country, Judaea," he said. "Rachel says that your high station should not be known in this place."

"Yet you knew it. How?"

He shrugged. "You are who you are. Simple clothing cannot change that."

I looked at the man curiously. His own garments were simple enough—a brown homespun tunic, partially covered by a dark blue mantle. There was nothing to attract notice and yet . . . something set him apart.

"Why are you here?" he surprised me by asking.

"Why are *you* here?"

I studied the clear, unlined face and guessed him to be about twenty. For a moment I thought that he'd been mistaken, that perhaps we had known each other. I'd traveled so much in the past years, but no, that was impossible. I'd never seen that calm, confident face before. He was young, but sure of himself. A natural leader, *Tata* would say. He'd want him to be an officer. Shrugging at my foolishness, I answered. "The priestess called me. I want to know what she knows. What about you?"

"I will teach, but my time has not yet come."

"Now he asks endless questions, challenging everything. The way of the goddess is new to him," Rachel said. For a moment I'd forgotten she was there.

"I came to Egypt when I was a baby," the young man explained. "I remember this temple. My mother brought me here—against Father's wishes. When I was four, the politics changed at home and we went back. Mother never spoke again of Isis, no longer sang her hymns as lullabies, but one day Father found a small clay statue that she had kept—Isis holding her baby Horus. He ground it to dust. Our ways in Galilee are different."

"I should say they are!" Rachel agreed. "That difference is why we are here, is it not?"

"I don't know . . ." The man's serene, open face clouded unexpectedly. "I have studied with other teachers as well—great rabbis. Soon I must return to my home. My father has need of me. His health is failing. I am the eldest." He sighed, looking about the marble anteroom. "There is great strength here . . . strength and compassion. My Father in heaven is also compassionate, but that has been forgotten."

A great gong sounded. The massive golden doors before us were thrown open. People pressed forward. I was eager to go inside, but hesitated uncertainly. "I am Claudia Procula," I introduced myself, "and you?"

"I am Yeshua—Jesus, you Romans would say."

Impulsively, I took his hand, looked into his eyes, solemn now and a little sad as he returned my gaze. "I hope—I hope you find that for which you are searching."

"I wish the same for you."

Turning, I moved forward, following the crowd. "What an intriguing young man," I commented to Rachel as we passed into the inner sanctum.

"You cannot imagine," she answered cryptically. "He is like no one I have ever met."

My questions were forgotten as I looked about me. Despite the hour, worshipers filled the white alabaster chamber that shone in the reflected glow of hundreds of lamps. Advancing slowly, I saw a slender figure seated on a golden throne. It was the high priestess that I had seen in the parade. Once again the woman's eyes held me, glittering green and bright. Though painted in the Egyptian fashion, they needed no artifice. She raised her brows in a private greeting that sent pleasant chills down my spine.

While the priestess kept time with a golden sistrum, white-gowned women played lutes, their voices rising in a hauntingly sweet hymn. Finally as the music faded, the priestess rose from her golden chair. I gasped at her gossamer blue gown. Golden stars and crescent moons glittered from its silken folds. Her radiance filled the room.

"I am the mother of nature," the priestess said, addressing the group as Isis's earthly embodiment. "Only through me can fields flourish and animals multiply. It is I who makes the barren wife fertile." Her soft voice filling with tenderness and compassion, she continued:

"Come to me if you seek truth,

"Come to me if you have lost your way,

"Come to me if you are sick and desire to be healed.

"Come to me if you have sinned and seek forgiveness,

"There are no divisions in my house. I bring peace to all. Woman and man, slave and master, rich and poor—all are welcome. Come to me for I am Isis, loving mother to you all."

My knees felt weak with wonder. I knew then that Isis was more powerful than Fortuna, for she could conquer fate. She was every goddess, every god, evoked in every name. *She is the one.* My soul cried out. The group surged forward, seeking to be closer, to touch the hem of the high priestess's robe. I was swept along with them, wondering if I dreamed.

I dropped to the marble floor, kneeling before the priestess. Slowly, deliberately, she raised me to my feet, gazing for a long moment into my eyes. Then, without a word, she handed me the golden sistrum that rested in the crook of her arm.

I stared wordlessly at the instrument, a graceful oval, surprised at the way it fit my hand so naturally. As the priestess turned me about to face the group, I began to shake the rattle to an instinctive rhythm as if I'd done it many times. I knew then that all I had ever sought was waiting here in the House of Isis.

CHAPTER 7

The Initiation

The morning after my visit to the temple, Tiberius issued a four-word order that could not be ignored: *Proceed immediately to Antioch.* The household plunged into a whirlwind of activity. Most of our furnishings had been rented with the villa, but personal belongings remained to be packed. Throughout the frantic activity, my thoughts whirled.

"How can I leave Alexandria?" I whispered to Rachel as we stood together sorting clothes. "How can I leave Isis now that I've found her?"

"She is everywhere," Rachel assured me.

Exasperated, I threw down the tunic I'd just folded. "Isis's power is here in Egypt."

"Her power is everywhere," the slave repeated, picking up the tunic and folding it again. "If she has a plan for you, you will know it."

My cousins, Druscilla and Julia, kicked their slaves when they were annoying. For the first time I felt tempted.

That evening at dinner Mother chattered on and on about

Antioch. The highly political and very social capital of Syria was second only to Rome. She was already plotting alliances. It was Selene's kind of place, but *Tata,* too, was pleased. Antioch was a military stronghold, strategically located, a window on the east. He and Mother, so full of plans, were finishing each other's sentences.

Hebe, our cook, had spent the afternoon shopping for Egyptian herbs and spices to take with us on the voyage. As a result, the evening meal was a light supper of roasted lamb, peppers, onions, and rice. Mother, signaling for more, observed my plate, barely touched. "Are you ill?" she asked, patting my forehead. "No fever, but you do look tired."

"I am tired, Mother. It's been a busy day," I answered, my eyes cast down.

"Then you had better be off to bed," *Tata* advised. "Remember, we sail at dawn. Everyone must be ready."

Nodding to my parents, I rose from the dining couch. Their enthusiasm merely added to my depression. On lead feet I walked to my bedroom, but inside, my pulse quickened. Rachel was there. The room felt charged. "What is it?" I asked, puzzled by her flushed face.

She placed a finger to her lips. "Follow me, come quickly." Silently, Rachel led the way down to the kitchen. "Don't let Hebe see you. Wait here." Opening the door cautiously, she looked in. Satisfied, she turned and beckoned. We crossed the room on tiptoe, hurrying to the rear entrance.

A curtained litter rested on the ground outside, two burly bearers beside it. A third, larger man approached, his clean-shaven head gleaming in the light of the torch he carried. "I am Thoth," he introduced himself. "The high priestess bids you come to the temple—but only if you desire it."

I looked inquiringly at Rachel. She nodded, encouraging me. "I know Thoth well. Besides, I will be with you."

I shook my head. "Not this time. There's no need for you to risk more than you already have."

"You're certain?" she asked, searching my face.

"Certain," I replied, trying to sound like I meant it.

I felt Rachel's relief as she wrapped a *palla* about my shoulders. Thoth helped me into the litter. I wondered if he could hear my heart thumping. I forced a smile and settled back. At least the litter was comfortable. The cushions were soft. A porcelain jar filled with almond oil and citron lightened the curtained stuffiness. Nevertheless, the ride seemed interminable as I tried to imagine what lay ahead. Often my thoughts strayed to Marcella. She had been forced to dedicate her life to a goddess who never went anywhere, while my goddess roamed the world. Vesta just tended a fire. Isis did everything. Would Marcella envy me for what I was doing or would she think me disloyal—even demented? Whatever she might think, I missed her at that moment as I never had before.

Suddenly, it seemed we had arrived; Thoth was helping me to alight. The great temple loomed large before me. It was as exquisite as I'd remembered, but so vast, so very mysterious. My legs trembled as I climbed the marble steps. The high priestess rose from her golden throne as I entered the sanctuary. How lovely she was, but otherworldly, untouchable. Silently acknowledging me as I knelt before her, she lit incense in a white alabaster censer, sending sweet smoke into the lofty reaches of the great marble chamber. Somewhere, perhaps in the next room, I heard chanting. At the priestess's nod, I rose. Just when the suspense seemed unbearable, she spoke. "Surely you are not afraid?"

"No," I answered, surprised that I spoke the truth.

The priestess's dazzling smile enveloped me. "Of course you are not. The goddess has called you. She invites you now to become an initiate."

"Oh! I would love that!" I exclaimed, almost overcome with emotion. Sadly I shook my head, explaining, "It is impossible. My parents are sailing to Antioch . . . I love my parents," I added almost apologetically. "I must go with them."

"Of course you must. Isis knows that. She would never ask you to give up your family. She asks nothing that you do not give willingly. She is never capricious." The priestess paused, searching my face, then continued. "If you choose, your preparation can begin tomorrow. The process will take ten days."

"But we're leaving tomorrow."

"Perhaps." A gentle smile played about the priestess's lips. "We shall see what the goddess decides. For your part, do you truly want to become an initiate?"

"Oh yes!"

"You do realize that you can always worship Isis in your mind and heart? There is no need to even go to a temple, though there is an Iseneum in Antioch. You can worship there any time without subjecting yourself to the risks of initiation."

Risks? I paused briefly. What did it matter? "I would gladly brave any risks to become an initiate, if only that were possible."

"Then you must prepare," counseled the priestess. "I admonish you to refrain from sexual intercourse, though I doubt that will be an issue."

I fought an impulse to giggle.

"Tomorrow," the priestess continued briskly, "you will begin your fast. Consume nothing but water and juices for the next ten days. Most important, set aside a part of every day, at the same time each day, to be alone with Isis."

"Alone with Isis?"

"This is how it will happen," the high priestess explained. "You will sit with your spine straight and both feet flat on the floor. Place your hands together with your palms and fingertips touching—no, not like that, like *this*."

I nodded politely, copying her hand positions, listening obediently as she instructed: "Focus upon the goddess, holding her image firmly in mind. Whenever your thoughts wander, gently draw them back. After ten minutes of concentration, turn your hands over palms up and rest them on your lap."

Ten minutes sounded like an awfully long time to sit still, but I nodded dutifully.

"Perhaps," the priestess continued, "you will see pictures or images, experience strange sensations or hear voices. Whatever happens, do not be afraid. Accept what occurs as a gift from Isis. Allow it to progress without attempting to hold on to one particular idea. Do this every day. Then, on the tenth night, Thoth will call for you."

I looked at her in surprise. All these instructions . . . it was as though she had never heard me. "But I told you, I am leaving. I won't be in Alexandria ten nights from now. Neptune willing, I shall be in Antioch."

"We shall see."

I left the temple with Thoth, quickly descending the marble stairs to the waiting litter. Earlier the night had been clear and star-filled, but now I was surprised to feel light drops of rain. Before long the bearers were trotting. A strong wind had come up and heavy rain pelted the roof. By the time I reached home the curtains were soaked through and my *palla* was damp.

Rachel waited anxiously. "Be very quiet," she whispered. "Your father is awake. A servant from the lord Germanicus arrived minutes ago. They are in the library."

I slipped off the *palla* and handed it to her. "Most probably last-minute arrangements for the journey." Tiptoeing quietly, we made our way up the stairs to my room. All but a few essentials had been taken to the ship.

I shook my head in bewilderment as I unclipped the fillet that bound my hair. "It was wonderful," I told Rachel who was putting away my clothes. "The priestess invited me to begin my initiation tomorrow; but, of course, that's impossible."

"It is indeed." Rachel stifled a yawn. "You'd best sleep now. Your father wants you up at dawn."

Dawn when it came was barely discernible. Rain poured in torrents and savage winds battered the house from all sides. The departure had been delayed until the storm subsided. At mid-morning Rachel appeared to pull back the draperies. Sleepily, I looked out. The sky was dark as twilight.

"There is little for breakfast because it was expected that you would eat on the ship," she apologized. "Your father had the last egg. He is in the library going over maps. *Domina* is there too, writing letters. She will finish the lamb unless you want it."

"I'll have a little. I was too upset last night. Now I'm starved." I stretched, sat up, then started at a sudden thought. "Never mind the lamb. The priestess said, 'nothing but liquids for ten days.' It's ridiculous—this storm will soon blow over. Perhaps we'll sail this afternoon, surely by tomorrow. Still, I'll follow her wishes."

"There are oranges," Rachel recalled. "I will make juice for you."

Later that morning I went to the reception room and sat beside the water clock, an elaborate structure with a large wheel and floats, rented with the villa. Sitting as the priestess had instructed, I tried to focus my mind on Isis. Too many thoughts vied for my attention. The clock made an irritating trickling sound that I'd never noticed before. Outside, the wind howled, rain lashing down with no sign of stopping.

Rachel and Festus braved the storm for dinner provisions, returning with oranges as well as grapes to be squeezed into juice.

The rain continued.

The next day brought no sign of clearing, nor the one after that. At first I'd been excited by the idea of fasting but soon wearied of it. As my parents resumed normal meals, the seductive cooking smells wafting from Hebe's kitchen made my ordeal all the more difficult.

It seems in retrospect that the fifth day was the hardest. The rain, the close confinement, frayed on the nerves of everyone. Tempers grew short, very short. Once Mother had established that I wasn't ill, she grew angry with me for not eating. Unable to explain my reasons, I said nothing. This only made it worse. "Stop sulking and *eat*!" she snapped. "How many times do I have to say it? I'm not hungry!" I screamed back. *Tata* was furious. "Jove's balls, what's the matter with you two?" he roared. I ran off to my room, slamming the door. I thought I heard Mother's slam too.

My daily meditations were no consolation. To the contrary, they merely added to my frustrations, focusing attention on the angry emptiness in my belly. "Surely this rain can't last much longer," I complained to Rachel that night as I lay down on my couch.

"Who knows," the slave replied. "My people tell of a man named Noah. In his time the rain lasted forty days and forty nights."

"Enough! Extinguish the lamp," I ordered, turning my face to the wall.

THOUGH NO VISION APPEARED AT THE NEXT MORNING'S meditations, I took comfort in the knowledge that my fast was half over. The rain had lasted five days. If by some miraculous chance it was to last five more, I could become an initiate of Isis.

Everything seemed to change after that, not only for me but for the entire household. No longer was the rain deplored as an exasperating personal inconvenience. Overnight it became an amazing phenomenon viewed with awe. The servants came home with disaster stories. "Oh, master! The whole east wall of the market has collapsed." "*Domina,* a great ship from Athens crashed into the rocks below Pharos!"

Rachel rushed back one afternoon with news that the governor's palace was flooded. Yet despite the chaos around us, our home and its inhabitants remained snug and safe. Each family member settled into a routine, finding new activities to occupy his or her time. For me, it was writing poems and letters to Marcella. *Tata* sent to the museum for scrolls. By the end of day six, he was well into a rare history of Alexander's conquest of Persia, a tome written, for once, by a Persian. Mother had her loom brought back from the ship and began a new tapestry, using Egyptian themes. Rachel experimented with vegetables, pounding and grinding them into juices. Some were quite tasty.

As the days passed and the rain continued, I became aware of a growing sense of peace and purpose. The storm was, I felt certain, the will of Isis. I knew it would continue until the goddess's desires were met.

On the afternoon of the tenth day, the heavy buffeting winds calmed. By four, the skies cleared, the cloudburst ceased. People were venturing outside, some of them dancing and splashing in the great puddles. *Tata* set off immediately to confer with Germanicus. Jubilant, he returned to announce that we would sail the next day. "Everyone get ready!" Once again possessions were assembled and packed. I was certain that within twenty-four hours we would be on the sea, but in the meantime . . . the priestess had said that on the tenth night, Thoth would come for me.

AS MY CLOTHING WAS STRIPPED AWAY BY TEMPLE WOMEN, I thought of Diana. Might she strike me dead for my defection?

And what would *Tata* say? The thought of his reaction frightened me more than Diana's. Standing naked and trembling before the priestess, I searched the room as a trapped animal might, yearning to escape, but buried the impulse by force of will.

Myriad lamps cast flickering shadows on a large burnished golden bowl resting on the altar. I watched the priestess ladle the contents into a chalice. She extended it to me. My hand shook as I raised the vessel to my lips. The liquid's tangy sweetness was unexpectedly pleasant. I drank again and again, at last draining the chalice. A comforting warmth stole over me. It no longer mattered that I was naked. After a time I ceased even to be aware of it. The chanting of those around me grew louder, the sounds of drums and sistrums more insistent.

The priestess motioned for me to follow her. We exited the grand chamber from the back, walking down a long torch-lit hallway that seemed to stretch forever. My head felt light, the will that moved my feet no longer mine. The priestess stepped to one side, revealing a flight of stairs that descended into a black abyss. She signaled that I was to go on alone. Her glance seemed somehow appraising. Was I being tested?

The marble steps were worn. How many had walked there before? I wondered. Step by step, I made my way down. The stairs were wet. I was descending into water. The steps were slippery. I walked gingerly, downward, deeper and deeper. The water was up to my knees, then my hips. I looked back over my shoulder. I couldn't see the priestess.

The next step was steeper and threw me off balance. I slipped into the abyss. Once I thought I felt the pool's bottom, but was buoyed up by water. I struggled not to breathe, not to swallow, but the water began to pour in, burning my throat, filling my lungs. Black water covered my head now, blotting out everything. Three summers before, a broken ankle had kept me from learning to swim with the other children. Now I cursed Fortuna.

Frantically flailing, sometimes floating up to the surface, only to slip back again, I scrambled wildly for the stairs but couldn't find them. Terror gripped me as I struggled to hold my breath. Once more I reached the surface but only to gulp more water. My lungs felt as though they would explode as I fought the desire to open my mouth. I could no longer hold my breath. I was going to die. Why, Isis? Why have you done this? Did you cause the winds to blow, the rain to fall for ten days and nights merely to drown me? Recalling the sense of purpose that I had come to feel during my meditations, I would not, could not, believe it. Surely the goddess of the sea could lead me out of a pool! Help me, Mother Isis, help me! You who can do anything, guide me now.

Trying desperately to remain calm, I slid one foot forward across the pool's bottom, then the other. Struggling to ignore the suffocating pain in my chest, I lifted one arm above my head as though to grasp Isis's hand. It cleared the water.

Surely there was a wall somewhere that would lead me to the stairs. The floor was slippery, my progress slow, the pain in my chest crushing, unbearable. I gasped and inhaled more water. Just then my toes touched a hard surface. The wall? No, a step! Coughing and gagging, I struggled upward. Twice I slipped and lost my footing. At last the unforgettable moment when I lifted my face out of the water. Each breath pure ecstasy.

Sputtering, belly aching, body bent like an old woman's, I reached the top step and fell sprawling across the marble floor. The sound of my own labored breathing echoed in my ears until I became conscious of a faint, rhythmic pounding. Eyes streaming, I looked about. Where was the priestess? I'd expected welcoming arms, congratulations. She wasn't even there—no one was. In the distance I saw a broad veranda supported by seven marble columns. Beyond that the sea. Slowly, painfully, I pulled myself up.

Seven shallow steps led to sand fine as face powder against my bare feet. The clear night was filled with stars, the full moon a dazzling disk of light. As I reveled in the miracle of fresh air filling my aching lungs, the moon waxed brighter still. Slowly a radiant form rose from the sea. First the face appeared framed by luxuriant locks the color of flames; then the shapely body emerged from cresting waves. She wore a crown in which was woven every flower that I had ever loved and over her long white gown was a blue mantle covered with glittering stars.

This time Isis was no dream.

CHAPTER

8

Aftermath of Isis

Isis stood before me, great waves crashing about her. Rising from the sea even taller than Pharos, she was awesome in her grandeur, glorious in her radiance. Overwhelmed by emotion, I dropped trembling to the sand and yet, curiously, felt no fear.

A soft hand touched my shoulder, then another. The high priestess and her acolytes had appeared seemingly out of nowhere. Now they clustered around me. "You saw her?" one young priestess asked excitedly.

"Yes, yes!" I gasped, looking up. I turned back to the sea, but Isis was gone. I sighed in disappointment.

The high priestess smiled gently. "If she remained, you would no longer be of this world."

"Oh, but how can I go on without her, now that I have *seen* . . ."

"You will go on, I assure you. You have many years of life before you."

Tenderly, but with a kind of wonder, the acolytes helped me

to my feet. Taking my hands, they led me down a labyrinth of halls to an inner sanctum deep within the temple. The floors, the walls, the vaulted ceilings were of gold laced with lapis lazuli. Everywhere I looked, jeweled lamps reflected their brilliance.

There, in that magnificent room, I was anointed seven times with sacred Nile water poured from a golden ewer encrusted with emeralds. Temple priestesses patted me dry with soft linen towels and rubbed my body with fragrant oils. I was dressed in a flowing white robe and garlanded with red roses, their scent sweeter than anything I had ever smelled.

It was then that the high priestess pressed a miniature gold sistrum into my hand. "It is sacred," she explained. "Isis, the eternal woman and goddess of life, has many symbols but only one weapon. The sistrum is an instrument she plays upon when she wants to create change or to see the true meaning of circumstances others merely accept. You, Claudia, have earned one of your own. Take it back with you into the world."

"Back?" I looked at her uncertainly.

The high priestess smiled again. She put her arms around me, led me through the twisting passageways from which I had come until I stood forlornly in the temple's immense atrium. How could I leave this place? How could I leave the acolytes who now seemed as close to me as Marcella?

The high priestess embraced me once more, then stood back. "Before your enlightenment you were the daughter of your parents. You are still the daughter of your parents. Nothing has changed."

"Everything has changed!" I exclaimed.

"Everything and nothing." She nodded her head toward

Thoth, who must have ascended the stairs silently, for he stood now at my side. "Your litter is waiting to take you home," the high priestess said. She wrapped a soft blue mantle about me, then turned and reentered the temple.

There was an awful finality about it; somehow I knew that I would never see her again.

What could I do then but allow Thoth to help me into the litter? Everything and nothing. What was the meaning of it all? I wondered as the slaves carried me homeward through the streets. Surely I would never be the same and yet I was exactly the same. A part of me knew every secret of the universe. For an instant Isis and I had been one, and yet here I was as I had always been, Claudia Procula, going home to her ordinary life as though nothing had ever happened.

I was also a fourteen-year-old girl with a big decision to make.

My fingers closed about the tiny gold sistrum that the high priestess had given me. For an instant I felt again the rush of joyous zeal that had followed the initiation, the moment when Isis had risen before my eyes. I sighed. Despite the miracle that had happened to me, I felt even younger than fourteen as I approached the villa. There was still my father to confront.

It was nearly dawn when I stepped from the litter. The villa was dark but for a single light coming from the library. I tiptoed into the atrium and stood for what seemed a very long time arguing with myself. It would be so easy to just slip up to my room, remove the gown and garland—hide them somewhere. With all the excitement of leaving for the ship, no one would find them. No one need ever know what had occurred. *Tata need never know.* And yet if I wasn't honest, if I didn't tell him of this wonderful thing that had happened to me, what meaning did the experience have?

"Who's out there?" *Tata* called out. "Claudia, is that you?"

My hand tightened once again around the sistrum. Taking a deep breath, I pushed open the door to confront him.

A large map slipped unheeded from his fingers as he surveyed my garments. He rose from his chair, staggering slightly, and shouted, "By Jove, what have you done!"

I thought of all the prisoners he must have questioned and felt sorry for them. My voice shook as I answered: "Isis called me."

"Have you lost your senses?"

I took a deep breath. "I had to go to her."

"What nonsense is this!"

"Isis is queen mother of us all," I began. The tip of his nose was turning white, a bad sign. It only happened when he was very angry. "She protects us here on earth, and when we die, we don't go to some awful place like Hades. Isis promises peace and joy for everyone and only asks that we keep faith with her and be the best that we can be."

"Aren't the gods of Rome good enough for you?" Father demanded, his voice a roar.

"No, sir, they're not." I took a deep breath and plunged on. "The old gods are like naughty children, but are the new ones any better? Can we really be expected to worship Tiberius . . . in our hearts?"

He looked as flabbergasted as if the cat had spoken.

Sensing an advantage, I ventured: "Perhaps you feel the

same. Perhaps, sir, that is why you so often visit the Temple of Mithras."

"What do you know of Mithras?" he asked, leaning closer, his eyes studying me. I knew I'd caught him by surprise.

I thought of Mithras, such a manly god, all about courage and brotherhood. It was easy to see why that would appeal to *Tata*'s sense of dedication. "Mithras is a warrior's religion, his worship is forbidden to me," I reminded him. "Isis is for everyone." I reached for his hand as the words tumbled out. "Oh, *Tata,* after my initiation the moon was so bright and close that I felt possessed. My veins coursed not with blood but with Isis's light. For the tiniest instant I knew all that had ever been or ever would be. I was a tiny part of her immense power."

His gray eyes widened. He looked shocked as though seeing me for the first time. "And then what happened?"

"Most of it just seeped away. If I try to tell you more . . . I'll lose everything." I shook my head helplessly, fighting the sudden tears. "What happened isn't something you can talk about, you only feel it. All I can say is that I saw the goddess as clearly as I am seeing you. I understand now why the poor, the lame, and the ill are welcomed by Isis. Don't you see, *Tata,* we are all part of each other like leaves in some giant tree."

He sat mutely for what seemed a very long time, his face impassive. Finally *Tata* shook his head, almost sadly. "Why did it have to be the goddess of that whore, Cleopatra?"

"You hate Cleopatra, but what would you have done if you were an Egyptian with all her power?" Seeing his face redden, I lowered my voice. "Cleopatra thought she was mistress of the world. Wasn't it only natural that she would appear on a golden throne at Antonius's triumph?"

"Natural?" *Tata* raised a bushy eyebrow. "Natural to whom? She rode, he walked at her feet." His voice rising again, he asked, "Is that the kind of woman you want to be?"

"No, *Tata,*" I bowed my head contritely, then looked up at him. "But Antonius loved Cleopatra. It was his choice."

"Enough of this," he said, rising to his feet. "Take off that—that costume and get to bed. Do you hear me? In a few hours we will be on the sea headed away from this accursed country. Perhaps one day you and I will talk again of Isis, but never of Cleopatra." He put his arms about me. "There, there, dear," he said, patting me on the shoulder. "Get a good night's sleep and you'll forget all about this nonsense."

"Yes, *Tata,*" I agreed, but even then I knew it could never be so.

ANTIOCH

in the eighth year of
the reign
of Tiberius (22 C.E.)

CHAPTER

9

Casting the Spell

I worried about the upcoming party, dreaded it—my first as an adult. So much expected of me, so much for which I was unready. Oh, I knew well enough what to say and how to say it, had been drilled in how to walk and sit and stand. That was the trouble. Now the training was expected to pay off. Soon, very soon, I must find a husband. The auction block waited for me as surely as for any slave.

As for the party . . . I'd never possess Marcella's careless confidence, but a noble dress might help. Not for me the pale pastels selected for my friends by their mothers or the bright maroons and oranges flaunted by my cousins, Julia and Druscilla.I wanted to look like me. Now, turning this way and that before the mirror, I wasn't sure who me was. My gown was the subtle white of an eggshell shot with threads of gold, but the way it clung . . .

"That material came all the way from India," Mother reminded me. "Marcus paid a fortune for it."

Dear *Tata,* how good he was . . . my fingers played absently with the small gold sistrum I wore about my throat, recalling my initiation and our talk that followed it. Egypt seemed far away now. Had it been only two years? Though neither of us had referred to the exchange, it had brought us closer. *Tata* had, I suspected, dismissed the whole thing as a youthful indiscretion. Perhaps he was right. I meditated daily before a small shrine to Isis, but had yet to visit Antioch's Iseneum.

Once we reached the powerful city-state, Mother had kept me busy. There was a new metropolis to learn. Then a home to furnish and maintain, for Tiberius had decreed early on that we were to remain indefinitely in Antioch. Mother saw to it that I learned every detail of running a house. It was time-consuming when combined with lessons: dancing, singing, lyre. The end result stood reflected in the mirror, a young woman admirably trained for marriage yet so unready.

Rome must be served, but that duty was nothing compared to the obligation I felt to my parents. If only it were Marcella preparing for the party. My sister would have adored every minute. She had looked forward to marriage, would have made a dazzling match, too, even without a dowry.

Marcella had loved to flirt, had done it instinctively, impulsively with any male of any age. I wasn't good at it, didn't care to be. Such a waste of time, encouraging people into my life who didn't belong there. So I didn't flirt, I talked. Would-be suitors seemed satisfied with that—anyway they came back often to see me. I liked them all well enough, yet the thought of spending a life with any—worse yet, sharing a couch . . .

"Who is coming tonight?" I asked Mother, barely suppressing a sigh.

She smiled, obviously pleased by the question. "I imagine

that means what young men will be present at the party." Not waiting, she began to list them. "Horacius will be there, of course, and Flavius. Hardly a day goes by that they don't drop by to see you. Tell me, which do you favor?"

I thought of Horacius, an *aedile,* so young he had pimples; and *Tata*'s aid, Flavius, a bit older but still callow. My pleasure at the new gown ebbed. "They are both quite nice, Mother," I said, trying to sound polite. "I could not possibly choose between them . . . Is there no one else?"

"I've asked Drusus and Nero to bring their friends. Perhaps one of them will suit you." She smoothed the folds of my gown. *"Somebody had better, Claudia, and soon."*

Slightly ill with apprehension, I hesitated outside the atrium where guests gathered. Glints of gold sparkled in my gown . . . all the way from India. Chin up, I entered the room smiling and was rewarded by a muted gasp of appreciation. From then on, it was easy to move from group to group, couch to couch. I felt tiny tingles of envy and admiration radiate around me and loved it. Drusus and Nero were home at last—and Caligula away hunting. The party was already wonderful. Why had I worried?

As I hugged Drusus, my glance wandered over his shoulder to an alcove where my parents talked with a man I'd not seen before. He was possibly twenty-seven, a good ten years older than I. Slim, yet broad-shouldered, he carried himself with an easy grace. Sleek and handsome like a young leopard. He was looking at me now, smiling, so confident.

"Who's that?" I asked Drusus.

"Don't even think about it."

I drew back, looking up at my cousin in surprise.

"He is said to be a fortune-hunter and much too fond of women."

"Really?" I turned away from Drusus and approached the newcomer slowly, pulling in my breath, arching my back. Julia and Druscilla walked that way all the time, I'd only begun to practice.

"Pontius Pilate, a centurion just returned from Parthia," my father introduced him.

The centurion nodded, smiling at me. "I came with a message. Your father was kind enough to invite me to stay for your party."

His words floated by. Lost in his eyes, I thought of a blue pool, deep and dangerous. Pilate stepped closer. "Some women are not meant to be Vestals."

What was he talking about? Oh! Not me at all. He was looking at a bust of Marcella that rested on a nearby pedestal. But now Pilate's eyes shifted, an appraising glance that wandered the length of me. "It would not suit you either."

"It would not?" My voice quavered. I took a deep breath, paused a moment and raised my head. It was my turn to study him.

Pilate had even features, a finely defined jaw, a well-chiseled nose; he had full lips bracketed by barely perceptible lines. Was there a touch of weakness? Surely not. A shade of cynicism, perhaps. Was that not to be expected in a soldier?

"No, it would not," he repeated, a slow smile lighting his face.

Pilate turned to *Tata*. "You are a fortunate man to have two such beautiful daughters, but then," he nodded toward Selene, "to have daughters like that, you must look to their mother. Fortuna has been good to you."

"Fortuna, yes," my father agreed, signaling Rachel to refill Pilate's glass, "but I believe we should lighten the goddess's task whenever possible and make our own luck. Don't you agree?"

"I do indeed, sir."

"I thought you would," Father commented dryly.

Mother smiled brightly. "It was a great honor for our eldest daughter to be made a Vestal—the empress herself intervened for Marcella—but we still miss her dearly. It has been nearly five years since her induction."

My heart ached for Mother. "We saved a number of sketches that street artists made of Marcella," I explained to Pilate. "Mother took them to Marius here in Antioch. The bust he made is a composite of those impressions. We think it a fine likeness."

"You made an excellent choice," Pilate assured me. "Marius is the best. Last year my father had a full form of himself sculpted as Apollo."

Having met the elder Pilate, I tried to imagine his heavy jowls, broad nose, and protruding eyes above the god's slender form. I couldn't. "I am sure it's quite—quite arresting," I said.

"Oh, it is," he agreed. That smile again. I wondered what it would be like to be alone with him. New guests had arrived; Mother drew me away to greet them.

The comic actors she had engaged were a great success, but my eyes strayed often from the improvised stage to the couch where Pilate reclined. Once I caught him watching me. I smiled slowly, then turned my attention back to the actors.

The comedians' repertoire seemed endless. Then at last, the final applause. As it faded, Germanicus and Agrippina rose to make their farewells. The other guests took their cue from the royal couple. Standing beside my parents, bidding each good night, I was surprised by the weariness in Germanicus's face. When Pilate's turn came his manners were impeccable—deference to *Tata,* gallantry to Mother. He said nothing of consequence to me, yet paused, I thought, possibly a moment longer than necessary, lingering in the archway, his knight's toga falling in beautifully ordered folds from left shoulder to ankles.

I could scarcely sleep for thoughts of him and was ready with questions the following morning. "Forget Pilate," Father advised. "Only a bride with a handsome dowry will do for him."

"But, *Tata*—" I began.

He silenced me with a headshake. "Pilate's star is rising. I have seen his kind before. Those eyes miss nothing."

"Eyes like ice, clear, so very blue, and that charming smile! No wonder you are drawn to him," Mother sympathized. "Pilate is considered the most eligible of all the young knights. Everyone talks of him."

"The mothers as well as the daughters." *Tata* smiled at her. "Pilate's adopted father only recently attained equestrian rank. He is said to have made his money peddling chariots, a fortune; but mark my word, that young man will more than double it. Only the most lucrative alliance will satisfy him."

I cursed the Fates. At last, here was a man I could imagine sharing a couch with . . . imagine it very well. I turned away to conceal my blush.

In the ensuing weeks my path crossed Pilate's many times. Often I felt him watching me, yet his manner when we spoke was merely polite. He divided his time among many women, all of them wealthy.

One afternoon, seated two rows behind Pilate at a chariot race, I watched him with Sabina Maximus, arguably the richest of the city's young, unmarried women. The narrow seating spaces compelled them to sit quite close. I saw Pilate solicitously pick up the hem of Sabina's gown from where it dragged on the rough stone floor. It afforded him an excellent view of her ankles—thick ones, I noted with satisfaction. Oblivious to the thunderous crowd around me, I speculated. Perhaps a man with many women friends isn't too fond of any one. A wooden chariot had overturned, spilling the driver. The four horses continued to gallop. People all around me were shouting advice and imprecations. The unguided horses crashed their chariot into two others, smashing both. Beside me, my father, who backed an underdog, was on his feet cheering.

My fingers played absently with the small gold sistrum at my throat. "The sistrum is sacred," the priestess had said. "Isis, the eternal woman, has but one weapon." Whether my father liked it or not, Cleopatra *had* captured Antonius and Caesar, subduing them as completely as any army. Cleopatra's only weapon had been her femininity.

I pulled a mirror from the small leather pouch I carried. It was an exquisite piece, the ivory handle carved in the likeness of a sea nymph. Agrippina had given it to me the previous Saturnalia, predicting that I'd soon spend much of my time looking in mirrors.

Now I turned the polished surface this way and that. The reflection for which I longed eluded me. My eyes weren't blue like Agrippina's, but smoky gray, large and tilted slightly at the corners. My face wasn't oval like Mother's but heart-shaped. My nose, short for a Roman, was at least well formed. My lips, not as lush as Marcella's, were full enough. I wished I was allowed to color them as Julia and Druscilla did. I wished too that my hair was burnished gold like Agrippina's instead of black, but at least it was thick and curly, an impressive mane when released from the fillet that usually bound it.

My fingers rested again on the sistrum, *an instrument to play upon when one wants to challenge the status quo.* I sighed; it was hopeless. Everyone knew the laws of destiny were written in the stars . . . To attempt to override their cosmic imperatives was unheard of . . . yet Isis had helped Cleopatra . . . *If I must have a husband, why not the one I want?*

Just then Pilate glanced over his shoulder and saw me sitting behind him. A long look passed between us, warming my body, filling me with excitement and strengthening my resolve.

ANTIOCH IS A CITY OF LUXURY AND DECADENCE. constructed of marble and lighted by thousands of torches, its streets and shopping arcades shine throughout the night with the luster of day. Each arcade is lined with elegant shops packed with treasures brought by caravan from the East: silk, amber, amethysts, ivory, ebony, sandalwood, carpets, spices, and herbs. Mother and I often frequented these pavilions accompanied by Rachel, who had rapidly developed a network of shopping informants that my father claimed was more accurate than his political ones. He was only half joking.

One day Mother chose to enjoy an afternoon at home with *Tata*. It was the opportunity for which I had been waiting. Rachel and I set forth to shop for a birthday gift for Agrippina, selected a strand of large amber beads, then quickly embarked on a different mission.

Antioch's Iseneum, though smaller than the one in Alexandria, reminded me of a delicate jewel. I hurried past the exquisite mosaics, promising myself to examine them in detail another time. Pausing to kneel before a statue of Isis, I whispered a few words of entreaty, then rose to face the elderly priestess who greeted me in the atrium.

"I must speak with your mystagogue," I explained.

The priestess shook her head, smiling apologetically. "This is his time for meditation. Come back later, perhaps this evening."

"I can't come later. It must be now. This is a very important matter."

"Everyone always thinks theirs is a 'very important matter.' I don't believe I have seen you here before."

"This is my first visit," I admitted, adding, "I was initiated in Alexandria."

"Ah, an initiate," the priestess regarded me with more interest. "I see you wear the sistrum."

"The high priestess of Alexandria gave it to me. Do you have a crypt here?"

"Indeed we do, and it is filled with sacred Nile water. Would you care to see it?"

"No, once was enough, but I would like to see the mystagogue. Would you ask him for me?" My eyes pleaded with the older woman.

She paused for a moment, then beckoned for me to follow. "The decision will be his."

My heart raced as I left Rachel in the foyer and followed the priestess down a marble corridor. If only the mystagogue had been a woman. Could I possibly explain my problem to a man? As much as I wanted help, it would almost be a relief if he refused to see me.

He did not.

Slightly built, the mystagogue wore stylishly cut robes of white linen. His skin was light olive, his curly, neatly trimmed hair lightly threaded with gray. I searched the limpid eyes and thought I detected sadness behind the sophistication.

"There is a man," I began haltingly. "I think I love him."

"Think?" The mystagogue raised a glossy dark brow.

"I *do* love him," I amended. What else could it be? My cousins, Drusus and Nero, dear as they were, had never kept me awake at night, thinking, speculating, longing to touch. What I felt for Pilate was unlike anything I had ever experienced. It had to be love.

"And does he love you?"

"He could. I know he could—I feel it—but money and position are important to him. Everyone speaks of his ambition."

The mystagogue studied me for what seemed a very long time. "Yes," he said at last. "You are right. He could care for you, care for you very much. Someday he will come to depend upon you in ways you cannot imagine, but that does not make him right for you. There's someone else. You would be wise to wait for him."

"I don't want to wait. I want *this* man."

A wry smile played briefly about the mystagogue's lips. "Then pray to Isis."

"I need more than prayers. My parents have little money for a dowry. They say it is hopeless."

"You want a love spell."

"Yes," I whispered.

"You are an exceptional young woman, one who experiences the sight."

"You know that?"

"I do, and I am surprised that you are not aware of how binding love spells can be."

"That's what I want! I want to bind him. Won't you help me?"

"There is a price."

I opened the pouch worn around my waist and removed its contents. Two hundred sesterces. "They are all I have, that and this bracelet." I slipped a gold bangle from my wrist.

The mystagogue took the money and the bracelet, sliding them into a drawer in his desk. "There is a far greater price. You will pay that later."

Turning from me, he wrote briskly on a piece of parchment. "Read this and say it aloud three times each day. Visualize the man you love. Hear the words you want him to speak. Feel your reaction to those words as though they were being said. And," he emphasized, "pray to Isis for guidance. You will surely need it." He handed me the parchment.

I placed it unread in my pouch. "Thank you, thank you so much. You've been very kind."

"I have not been kind at all, but that you must learn for yourself."

I nodded and hurried from the temple. It wasn't until night when I was finally alone that I removed the parchment and read the words inscribed there:

> *When he drinks, when he eats, when he has intercourse with someone else, I will bewitch his heart, I will bewitch his breath, I will bewitch his members, I will bewitch his innermost part. Wherever and whenever I desire, until he comes to me and I know what is in his heart, what he does and what he thinks, until he is mine.*

"Yes! Mother Isis! Yes!" I whispered, folding the parchment carefully.

CHAPTER

10

Hymen Hymenaeus

It was a quiet party—only a few guests—not Agrippina's style at all. Why? I wondered, but not for long. Pilate was there. He was all that mattered.

Julia, Druscilla, and I shared a couch, nibbling absently at grapes passed to us on golden plates. My cousins laughed a lot, showing their teeth and profiles. I pretended to listen, savoring my own thoughts. Drusus winked at me from across the room. Ever the protector, he had managed earlier in the evening to block Caligula's attempt to spill wine on my new silver gown.

Yes, Caligula still clouded my life. Recently he had begun staring at me. He called often at our house, leaving flowers and trinkets; but when I ignored them, he turned ugly once again, seeking ways to hurt or embarrass me.

Looking about the room, so opulent in tones of burnished gold and bronze, deep blue and vibrant purple—Agrippina's colors—I noted how carefully the bachelor guests had been selected. There were army officers, of course, but also a promising young augur and the son of the puppet prince of Antioch. Julia favored the latter. I knew she had stolen out at least once to meet him. I should have liked to do the same with Pilate but something warned against it.

My glance shifted to his. He was watching me. I shivered with pleasure. When Pilate smiled that slow smile I felt as though melted honey oozed down my back. He nodded to the centurion with whom he had been talking and crossed the large room in a few strides. Settling on a tufted stool beside my couch, he murmured into my ear, "Some say that sooner or later every woman gets the face she deserves."

Puzzled, I followed his glance to an alcove where Mother held court, the center of a small circle of friends.

"She is still very beautiful," he said.

"Beautiful on the inside too," I added, "but you have to know her to discover that."

He nodded to a passing slave, took two wineglasses and handed one to me. "You have her beauty and something more . . . a touch of mystery. No one knows what you are really thinking. You have that and . . ." He leaned forward, whispering again, ". . . perhaps some mischief. I think sometimes you like to raise Hades just for the fun of it."

"Perhaps," I conceded. Studying him over the goblet's rim, I reflected on how well the spell was working.

Behind him, I saw Germanicus approaching. He carried a lyre under his arm. How annoying! I didn't want anyone to interrupt us.

"I dismissed the jugglers," Germanicus explained. "The heavy one dropped his torch twice. Besides, the noise they make—all the shouting. I would like you to sing, Claudia—

the way you used to in Gaul. It has been a long time since I've heard your lovely voice, too long."

I nodded toward Druscilla and Julia. "You mean the three of us?" My thoughts shifted longingly to Marcella. Trained by the same tutor, we four had sung often at family parties, even occasionally at military gatherings.

"Your voice was the sweetest. Never mind the others." Perhaps sensing my reluctance, he added the imperative. "Sing for me."

I studied the kindly, surprisingly unassuming man I had known all my life, aware that his natural charm overlay a quiet authority. Why now did he look so tired? Lately, it seemed, Germanicus was always rubbing his forehead; his walk, too, seemed slower. *Was something wrong?*

The hum of conversation ceased as all eyes focused on me. I felt slightly ill. In recent years I had rarely sung outside my home and never alone. I didn't want to now, but Germanicus was handing me the lyre. "Sing!"

How could I refuse?

Strumming a few chords tentatively, I breathed a prayer to Isis and began. First a mild military parody that had always amused Germanicus. Then, my confidence growing, a street ballad burlesquing the fable of Leda and her swan lover. Pilate moved closer, smiling. Pulling my eyes from his, I saw expressions of polite boredom change to surprise. I enjoyed the moment until another face came into focus. Druscilla watched with angry intensity.

Druscilla loves Pilate. That knowledge would once have plunged me into despair. What man wouldn't aspire to marry the great-granddaughter of the Divine Augustus? But now, with the spell working so well, I merely pitied her the hopeless longing I myself had felt only days before.

GERMANICUS'S WAN FACE VISITED MY MORNING meditations with increasing frequency. What is troubling him? I asked. Almost immediately another face—sallow, pockmarked—appeared before my mind's eye. *Governor Piso.* I scarcely needed the sight for that. The man had been a thorn in Uncle's side from the beginning. Tiberius had appointed him governor while we were still in Egypt. By the time our party arrived in Antioch, Piso and his wife were already settled into the palace. Germanicus let it pass. So like him to be generous, but now we saw daily reminders of how the governor mistook kindness for weakness. Piso's army was contrary to everything Germanicus stood for. Bullies promoted, good officers with honest records demoted and replaced by scoundrels . . . There was more, I felt it. *Something terrible was going to happen. Perhaps it had already begun.*

I wanted to talk to *Tata* about it, but between his political duties and my new social ones, I rarely saw him. Finally the sudden cancellation of a banquet at Germanicus's villa gave our family an evening at home. My parents' animated conversation stopped abruptly as I entered the *triclinium.* Mother's dark eyes sparkled. *Tata* looked concerned. Each watched me with an anticipation I was at a loss to understand.

Determined not to be diverted, I sat down on the couch opposite them and asked point-blank: "Is Germanicus ill?"

"Why ever would you say that?" Mother exclaimed. "He

has always been healthy as a horse. The banquet was postponed because of a fire in their kitchen."

"You are sure? He seems thinner."

"He is concerned about Piso." *Tata*'s eyes were thoughtful. "City guilds and farmers are appealing to him. They say the governor's men force them to pay for protection."

Piso again. The lean, hungry-looking governor and his wife, Plancina, a proud, vain woman with a boundless taste for luxury. I recalled her in Rome, never far from Livia. The conversation shifted as Hebe and Festus entered, poured wine, passed plates of stuffed grape leaves and dates.

"Why hasn't Germanicus complained to Tiberius?" I wanted to know when we were alone again.

Tata shrugged. "He has. The emperor claims to be surprised that Germanicus would be swayed by malicious rumors. By no means is Piso to be removed from office."

I hesitated. Hebe and Festus were back with a platter of wild boar, a gift from Drusus, who had speared it himself. It took a while to carve and serve. Then, at last, they bowed and left—for a while anyway. Now a chance to say what I'd been thinking. "The business with Piso is threatening to us all, but I feel there is something more—something evil—hanging over Germanicus."

We sat quietly for a moment or two. Despite the warm spring evening, a chill raised little bumps on my bare arms. Then Mother shook her head impatiently, "Why are we so gloomy when your father has wonderful, exciting news for you?"

I moved over to the edge of their couch. "What is it, *Tata*?" My heart raced. Suddenly I knew the answer.

He was silent for what seemed a very long time, all the while watching me thoughtfully. "Pilate came to me this morning," he said at last. "He has asked to marry you."

My hand moved to the sistrum at my throat. *Pilate was mine.* "Oh, *Tata,* it has happened," I gasped, flinging my arms around him.

Tata disengaged my arms, but held both my hands in his. "He knows your dowry is small, but says he would marry you if you had none at all." *Tata*'s eyes were puzzled as he studied me. "It must be your Claudian lineage. A patrician connection could be useful to an ambitious young knight . . ."

"Of course it could," Mother agreed. "Besides, our little girl has blossomed into a true beauty. Really, my dear"—she turned to me, smiling—"you grow lovelier every day, almost, it seems, before our very eyes. I'm not surprised at all by Pilate's proposal—not anymore. I saw him at the games yesterday. Even when the lion was at the throat of the gladiator he looked only at you. The man is positively enchanted."

I glanced down, embarrassed. Of course Pilate was enchanted, that was the whole idea. For the first time, I felt a tiny twinge of guilt, then quickly dismissed it, assuring myself that I would be the perfect wife for Pilate. I would find every way to please him. He would be the happiest man in the world. Once again I sent a silent prayer of thanksgiving to Isis, who had delivered to me the man of my dreams.

THE NEXT TIME I ATTENDED THE CHARIOT RACES IT WAS with Pilate. We sat with Germanicus and Agrippina in the Sponsor's Box, for it was Germanicus who had subsidized the event. Beside them were my parents and Pilate's adoptive father.

The elder Pilate was a portly man. Beneath the peacock blue of his silk tunic, I saw rolls of flesh that quivered as he moved. Still, I noted, he moved quickly and his eyes were sharp. Here was a man who missed nothing. Though he was cordial and complimentary, I knew his true opinions were guarded. From time to time, his eyes rested on Druscilla, who sat nearby. I felt certain he questioned his son's choice. Had they quarreled about me? I moved toward him, casting about for something to say, something that would both flatter and reassure him. "Pilate tells me that you have raised champions," I ventured. "You must be a fine judge of horses . . . I know so little. Which team would you suggest I bet on?"

He smiled, leaned closer, whispered in my ear. "Go with the blue team."

Just then Plancina, sitting below, turned and looked up—scrutinizing me. She seemed to be taking in every detail of my attire. Then with a sweeping, contemptuous glance, the governor's wife looked over at Druscilla. My hand strayed to the amethyst brooch Pilate had given me that afternoon. I knew it was exquisite and matched my pretty lilac gown perfectly; still, the older woman's disdain frightened me. What if the rich, established families didn't accept me? Pilate was ambitious . . . *What if I were to fail him?*

I stared at Plancina, focusing all my attention upon the buxom matron, willing her to turn again. Slowly, her head began to move until she faced me once more. This time Plancina's round pie-face wore a puzzled expression. I watched her intently, all the while smiling sweetly as I raised one hand casually and parted two fingers in a horn shape.

Plancina gasped at the hex sign, her painted cheeks like full moons against a face grown pale. My smile deepened as I raised my other hand to arrange a small curl loosened from its fillet. Suddenly I was aware of Pilate sitting next to me. Isis! What if he had seen me? I turned slowly. He was engrossed in conversation with *Tata.* What a relief. Pilate would not have been amused. What had I been thinking of? Plancina was the governor's wife.

The trumpets sounded. Germanicus rose to address the throng. "It is my great pleasure to announce the betrothal of Claudia Procula, daughter of my closest friend and aide-de-camp General Marcus Procula, to Centurion Pontius Pilate, commander of the First Cohort. This race is dedicated to them. May it be a grand beginning."

A roar of applause greeted the announcement. I trembled with happy excitement. What difference did Pilate's father or Plancina make? We were a golden couple. What could ever change that? Turning to acknowledge the cheers, I saw Druscilla watching and looked away.

As the betting tablets were being passed, Pilate's father watched me expectantly. I wanted to flatter him. He had given me advice. Should I trust it? I could not rid my mind of the thought that the race was somehow symbolic of my future with Pilate. Where was the sight now when I wanted it? Forcing a smile, I took the tablet and stylus. "It's the blue team for me."

The trumpets sounded again. All eyes moved to the field. I clutched Pilate's hand as we watched the four teams approach.

The chariots were splendidly draped in their brilliant colors—red, white, blue, and green. Curried and preened to perfection, the horses pranced for us. The crowd roared with anticipation as drivers whipped and hailed their two-horse teams to charge the starting line. Wheels spun and bounced, dust flew. The red team, a splendid pair of matched blacks, burst into the lead leaving the green and white teams neck and neck. A dull roar hung over the crowd as the blue team driven by Diocles, the favorite, drifted to the rear. My heart sank.

For the first three laps I watched tensely as the blur of movement remained unchanged. Reins whipped, ribbons flew as the white team nosed to the inside and made its move. The red driver, perhaps sensing the challenge, looked over his left shoulder. I gasped as his ebony stallions swerved wide to the outside. The stadium vibrated as all around us people chanted and cheered, urging their favorites forward. Perhaps, perhaps there was a chance for the blue team.

By the fifth lap, the red, white, and green teams were three abreast, with Diocles pulling his steeds up behind the red chariot in the middle. I was on my feet cheering him on. Turning into the sixth lap the red team wavered. Diocles's tunic was a blue blur as he reined his horses into the outside lane to avoid the slowing chariot. The green and white chariots charged into the turn, seeking their opportunity for leadership. Both demanding the center lane, they crashed into each other. The white chariot bounced into the air and capsized in the path of the blue pair. Diocles pulled his horses to the inside, the flailing legs of the downed pair kicking at his chariot as he inched by. The red team driver was not so skillful. His pair thundered into the fallen chariot, causing him to be thrown.

I could hardly stand the excitement as the two remaining teams prepared for the final assault to the finish. "Blue! Blue! Blue!" I shrieked. Diocles, feet planted squarely on the floorboard, leaned over the chariot, urging his horses forward. The green team charioteer, diverted by spectators' cries, turned his galloping horses too far in the direction of the stands. Driving straight and fast, Diocles passed the green driver, who recklessly pursued him, whipping his chestnut pair frantically. I jumped and screamed for joy and then, in an instant, everything changed. The green driver, in a last effort to overtake Diocles, cut too sharply across the track. His horses stumbled and fell. Legs, tangled in spinning wheels, snapped. The driver slipped off the chariot. It collapsed on him in a heap of twisted wreckage. His body lay still.

I remained quiet despite the pandemonium. Danger was what racing was all about. Still, *this* time, for my betrothal race, I wished it had been different.

I turned to Pilate. "One person is certainly dead, maybe two. Why did it have to be this way?"

"A good driver has to be ruthless," he reminded me. "It's about winning. Everything is always about winning. You should know that."

Germanicus patted my shoulder. "Your race, my girl. It is you who must present the driver with his award." He handed me the victory palm branch brought forward by a slave. I looked up at Pilate and saw his eyes, usually so cool, light with sudden pride. I felt the protective pressure of his hand at my elbow as we descended the stairs and walked onto the track. All the while I knew that thousands of eyes were following us.

Diocles was young, fair, and a slave. It was his owner, a wealthy merchant backing the blue team, who would benefit from the victory. I hoped he would be generous. Looking into the charioteer's smiling face, I thought fleetingly of the young gladiator whose win I'd predicted four years before. What was his name . . . Holtan? Where was he now? I wondered, recalling the handsome face, virile and vital, looking eagerly ahead to a lifetime of victories. What were the odds on that? Not good.

I handed the victor his palm branch and turned to Pilate. Nothing mattered now but the image of myself reflected in his eyes.

THE FOLLOWING AFTERNOON AGRIPPINA DROPPED BY TO see me. IN her hands was a gorgeous package wrapped in apricot gauze. "It is an engagement gift," she explained. "Germanicus and I wanted you to have it right away."

Carefully I removed the wrapping. It was so lovely I wanted to save it. Inside was a carved ivory box, and inside that twin star sapphires glittered up at me. "Earrings! They are exquisite!" I exclaimed.

Agrippina smiled. "We thought you would like them. Gray to match your beautiful eyes. They come from far away—India, I'm told."

I hugged her happily. Then backed off, taking her hands in mine. "I have decided on a June wedding."

"Marvelous! I could not be happier. The month sacred to Juno is always lucky."

"I am sorry about Druscilla," I ventured. "I know so well how she feels."

Agrippina shook her tawny head. "I doubt that. You have always taken things far more seriously than Druscilla. I know my daughter. She fancies Pilate today, tomorrow it will be another. This is *your* time, don't spoil it worrying about anyone else. Just be happy."

I was more than happy, I was delirious, but there were still things that worried me. Mother, absorbed in preparations, looked up from her many lists to answer housekeeping questions, but found excuses to avoid anything more intimate.

"She won't talk about the most important thing," I complained to Rachel.

Rachel looked up from mending one of my undertunics and smiled. "You mean the man and woman thing? Surely *Domina* knows where babies come from."

"Of course, I know that!" After a pause I added softly. "But what's it *like*? Mother just says I should not worry, that it will be the most beautiful night of my life—as though I planned to spend it stargazing in the atrium."

Rachel's teasing smile faded. "'The most beautiful night of her life' . . . Not every woman is so fortunate."

I considered her a moment. "How do *you* know that?"

Rachel's laugh was raw. "Slaves are rarely virgins. My first master had four sons who took turns with me. One of them, Isis only knows which, was my child's father."

"You have a child! I can't believe you never said anything."

She shrugged. "What is there to say? David would be six, if he is alive."

"You don't know where he is?"

"He was weaned and then sold." Rachel's voice was flat.

I put my arms around her, but she disengaged herself. "David was never mine and surely I had no love for any of his possible fathers. Let us talk of pleasant things." She picked up her sewing. "Your mother is a happy woman who adores her husband. I am sure her wedding night was beautiful. Why should yours not be?"

I hesitated, looking at my hands. "Pilate is so handsome, so confident. He has been everywhere, done everything. All sorts of women are drawn to him, everyone from grand ladies to field slaves. He knows so much; I know nothing."

"That is good," Rachel assured me. "His experience will make things all the more pleasant for you. Your husband will guide you, be certain of it."

"But what . . ." My voice trembled. "What if I don't please him?"

"Isis has seen fit to help you thus far," Rachel reminded me. "Why should she desert you now?"

It is bad luck for a bride to be seen by members of her household, yet I knew exactly what was going on downstairs as though I were there. We had been over it all so many times. On the day of my wedding, Hebe whispered a prayer to Juno as she set the wedding cake of wine-steeped meal on its bed of bay leaves. The smell of roasting peacocks, pheasants, and suckling pigs wafted up the stairs. I knew the kitchen staff were hard at work. Slaves had already washed down the walls, twined garlands about pillars, and strewn green boughs over marble floors polished to gleaming. In the *triclinium,* Mother still fussed over the proper order of banquet couches.

Upstairs, Agrippina, assisted by five of Antioch's most noble matrons, officiated. I had little acquaintance with any of them, but knew that each had been chosen with an eye to Fortuna—all well married, no widows. As Agrippina approached with the ceremonial spear, my scalp tingled. Lowering my head, I stood still while the cold blade slowly parted my hair, dividing it into six plaits to dispel the evil spirits. Then each of the women took a turn at applying a subtle tinge of makeup to my face.

At last the filmy cloud of white was slipped over my head and tied at the waist with the knot of Hercules. According to custom, only Pilate could untie it. I had thought a lot about that, both dreading and longing for the moment. Would he be pleased or disappointed by what he saw?

Now I forgot that I had ever been nervous. Everything and everyone was revolving around me, bathing me in love and reassurance. Even Druscilla seemed happy. As Agrippina had anticipated, my cousin's fancy had already been captured by a Parthian prince. She gave me a gentle pat and stood back as Julia adjusted my crown of marjoram, securing the scarlet wedding veil.

"You look like a bride is supposed to look—absolutely beautiful," Agrippina said, hugging me.

The lyre players were at the door; it was time for the procession to begin. I knew so well what to expect, the roles we were to play. I was relieved to see a slave handing Druscilla and Julia white thorn torches. Diana must be propitiated. Everyone knew the goddess opposed marriage, preferring women to remain virgins. Slowly I followed my two attendants down the stairs to the great hall where guests sat facing Pilate, his father, and *Tata*. Every head turned.

Tata allowed himself a proud smile before solemnly pouring a few drops of wine onto the household altar. Lares, the ancient guardian spirit of our family, must have his portion first. As if in a dream, I listened to my father invoke Hymen Hymenaeus, god of weddings, and watched as he filled glass after glass with wine. Incense wafting up from the altar made me dizzy. When all had been served, *Tata* signaled the augur to bring in the lamb. The flutes and harps went silent. My heart quickened as the creature's throat was slit with a silver knife and its belly deftly opened. My breath caught as the augur examined the entrails. Would it be the bad luck of a heart distended with disease? Or the good luck of a liver folded at the bottom like a pocket? "Many happy years to you both!" he cried, nodding approvingly at the healthy pink liver. Instantly the music of flutes, harps, and lyres welled up around us.

Shivering slightly, I turned to Pilate. Smiling, he threw back my diaphanous veil. We joined hands and I heard my voice, soft but clearly audible intoning the ancient vow, "While you are Gaius, I am Gaia." The eternal couple. He took my right hand in his. We were truly married.

After we had shared a small piece of cake, the wedding tablets were brought for our signatures. Our guests applauded, then rushed forward to embrace us. Pilate and I led them into the *triclinium* for the feast, where we reclined together on a dining couch for the first time. I wanted those moments to last forever.

So soon Mother's hand rested lightly on my shoulder. It was time to withdraw. I looked back at *Tata*. I belonged to Pilate and his family now. Standing with Mother in the deserted atrium, I began to sob. "I don't know why I'm crying . . . this is what I wanted . . ."

"Of course it's what you want," Mother assured me, dabbing at her own eyes. She blew her nose daintily. "It is time to go, darling, your husband has come to claim you."

Pilate was there, pulling me from Mother's arms. It was an ancient ritual that I had always considered foolish, but now there was no need to feign reluctance. If Pilate noticed, he gave no indication. Grabbing me firmly, he hurried us from the house. Following close behind were *Tata,* Germanicus, and a number of their officers. All shouted for Pilate to stop and made a show of brandishing their swords. Outside, a groom waited with a chariot. Pilate leaped on and swept me up beside him.

The wedding procession was forming. Some followed in chariots, others on horseback, more than one hundred on foot, all laughing and singing. My thumping heart calmed somewhat as I looked with wonder at the cityscape around us. It was as though I saw it for the first time. Antioch is a brilliant city at any hour, but then, late at night, the glow of moon and torchlight rivaled the sun. Nowhere else in the world could one ride for two miles beneath a marble portico, and this wonderful, amazing place was the city of my wedding procession.

It wasn't all magic and moonlight. Having attended other weddings, I was prepared for the bawdy epithets that were an inevitable part of the procession. Many well-wishers were carrying statues of Priapus, the lusty god of fertility. Some just carried replicas of Priapus's enormous penis. It was embarrassing, yet how else could friends ward off the evil spirits who might be jealous of our good fortune? I stole a look at Pilate. He was smiling broadly.

Then, at last, we reached the villa that he had recently purchased. Reining in his chariot, Pilate jumped down and helped me to dismount. By now the others were catching up. The songs and jokes had gotten worse. People—mostly the men—were waving huge leather penises at us. I felt my cheeks flame.

The heavy door of the villa was thrown open by the steward. Quickly, Pilate swept me into his arms and carried me over the threshold, slamming the door behind us with his heel. There was a loud pounding. I could hear *Tata*'s voice angrily demanding entrance, still playing the role of the irate father.

So quickly it faded.

CHAPTER

11

Two Trials

At first we merely reclined together, sipping wine and talking quietly of the ceremony and our guests. Then gently he untied each of my plaits until the unruly curls tumbled down my shoulders. I forced myself to meet his eyes and was surprised by their intensity. The Pilate I had known was cool, in control, his manner toward me lightly teasing. This man was altogether different. I shivered when he undid the knot of Hercules.

Pilate gently put his hands on my face, brushed his fingers through my hair, tipping my head up as his lips came toward me—my nose, my forehead, my cheeks—gentle kisses. Then my mouth, my mouth that now wanted his. I slid my arms around Pilate, pulling myself toward him, eagerly returning his kisses.

It was several minutes before he released me, but when he did, it seemed too soon. Opening my eyes I saw him looking at me with faint surprise, though whether at himself or me, I did not know. He slipped the strap of my tunica down and kissed my shoulder, my neck. When he reached my breasts, a rush of warmth flowed through me. I breathed into his hair, kissed his ears, and sought his mouth again.

Pilate caressed my skin as his warm hands slowly undressed me. Though he asked nothing of me, I clung to him as he gently pushed inside, whispering, "*Claudia, Claudia.*" How strong and sweet and vulnerable he sounded whispering my name. I clung to him, intent on what I had feared most, the pain a small price to pay for being this close to the man I loved so much.

"Well?" Pilate asked at last, gently turning my face to his.

"I fear I did it all wrong," I whispered. *What if the woman wasn't supposed to move?*

"No, my dear. You did it all right. Very right, surprisingly right. And, if you did not feel everything there is to feel this time, I shall remedy that."

LATER, ALONE, I TURNED A SMALL HAND MIRROR THIS way and that, studying my reflection. The worldliness I had anticipated was nowhere to be seen. I looked the same as always, not one whit more mature. But inside, well . . . I smiled, setting the mirror down. Inside was a different story. I recalled the disgust I had expressed to Marcella. How naive I'd been! Small wonder she had called me childish. If only Marcella were in Antioch. There was so much I longed to ask and tell. I wished, too, that I could show her my new home. I was so proud of it.

A few weeks before our marriage Pilate had purchased a house for us on the Daphne road. Lush, green, and lined with elegant villas, the road followed the course of the Orantes River. The earth there, fed by underground springs, was rich and the gardens reputed to be the most beautiful in the world. Each year the residents held a competition to judge whose grounds were the most pleasing.

Our own villa, though smaller than some, was a jewel. I had fallen in love with it at first sight; but my home, like my husband, posed a challenge. I determined to be the perfect matron, worthy of both. Just as Pilate was expected to devote himself to his career, I was supposed to focus my attention entirely on his well-being.

Surprisingly, the requirement that had worried me most was the easiest to fulfill. I was an eager pupil, Pilate a delighted teacher. Quickly, we discovered the joy of coaxing, teasing games rewarded by kisses, of a private language and silly jokes. Sometimes we took a small barge out on the river that adjoined our property. The gardens that reached down to the banks were thick with blossoms and flowering shrubs. Lilies spread over the water and tangled masses of sea grass, like green hair, floated on the current beside us. We spent hours twined in each other's arms or lying stretched out on deck cushions, soaking in the warmth. Pilate often lay naked, his body turning a rich, dark brown, while I stayed under the scarlet awning. He had admired my skin, comparing it to pale amber; I would take no chances. Often I would sing to him, each note an intimate caress, but there were other days when we never got out of bed.

Two weeks after the wedding the morning came when Pilate rose early, announcing that he would meet with clients.

"Must you? So soon?" I sighed.

"I would like you to accompany me."

When I looked up in surprise, he explained. "I want to present you to them. You may leave afterward, our business would hold little interest for you."

I felt my face flush with pleasure. The patron-client relationship excluded women. My husband's desire that I be there, however briefly, was a great compliment.

From Rome's earliest beginnings ambitious men had sought out patrons better educated or more powerful than they for advice and influence, becoming, in return, retainers providing services for their protectors. Just as Pilate had sought out Germanicus to be his patron, he himself had many clients looking to him for favors.

I had grown up with the system, taking it for granted, but an hour or so later, standing beside Pilate in our atrium, watching the twenty or so men who attended him, I saw it all in a new light. I could almost smell the soap, feel the barber's blade. How fine they looked in their best. The tall and the short, the young and the not so young stood before us, their eagerness palpable. I watched the eyes focused on Pilate, admiring, deferent eyes. Each man so earnest, so . . . I felt a tiny shiver. The man at the far end. Thickset, not much taller than I, with a wide, protruding jaw and narrow blue eyes. He caught my glance, flashed a disarming grin. Clearly, the patron-client alliance emphasized deference, even obsequiousness on the part of many toward a few. That precarious balance could change overnight. Still, for that moment it was delicious to be introduced as Pilate's wife, the lady of the villa.

"What do you think of my clients?" Pilate asked that evening at dinner.

Snuggled beside him on the dining couch, I reflected on how fortunate I was. My heart surged with pride as I raised my head to look at him. "They like you."

"They like what I can do for them," he corrected me.

"That surely, but I think more."

"Hardly," he said, reaching for the wineglass his slave had filled.

"No," I insisted. "They believe in your future and hope to benefit from it, of course; but there is more to it than that."

Pilate studied me curiously over his glass. "What are you talking about?"

I paused a moment searching for the right words. "They want more than a nod on their behalf to a magistrate, a moneylender, or an officer. They don't just want something *from* you, they want to *be* you. They think that if they are around you enough, some of you—your vitality, your purpose, maybe even your youth—will rub off on them."

Pilate shook his head, regarding me almost warily. "That's a strange thing to say. How could you possibly have known what they were thinking?"

I hesitated again, sensing his discomfort. "It is more what they were *feeling*. This morning I knew a little of that."

Pilate set his glass down on the table. Eyes still on me, he asked, "Did you like them all?"

I considered, savoring the wine on my tongue, the seeming importance of my words to him. "They were all well turned out, trying to make something of themselves," I said at last. "Most know where they are going. They don't expect you to do it all for them. I like them . . . except for one. Plutonius. I should watch him."

"Why?" That guarded look again as his eyes met mine.

"I don't know." I felt suddenly reluctant. What was it about Plutonius? I recalled the broad smile . . . His flinty eyes had not smiled. "There is something . . . the others were open enough. You know what they are about. Plutonius . . . is cloudy. Has he been your client long?"

"No, not long at all. I wondered today what caused him to leave Governor Piso and come to me."

PILATE'S FATHER'S WEDDING GIFT WAS THE LAST TO arrive. My breath caught as I unpacked the first plate. It was gold. There were twelve, each exquisitely inscribed with a different astrological sign.

"Let's put these to use right away," Pilate suggested. "Is it not time we had a party?"

I thanked Isis for my favorite wedding gift. My parents had given us Rachel.

Germanicus and Agrippina would head the guest list. I knew Pilate was impressed by my connection to Rome's ruling family. He would be pleased by their presence and I less nervous with my family there. If only, I thought wistfully, this first party could be left a foursome. So much would ride on it. People would expect a hostess like Mother or even Agrippina. Our social and perhaps political future could ride on the dinner. What if I failed Pilate? The challenge was formidable. I was glad there were only twelve plates; Pilate might have insisted on a banquet.

Later, scratching my head absently with a stylus, I pondered the menu with Mother. "Pilate has given you a generous household allowance," she reminded me. "He will expect something ambitious."

"I know. That's why I am worried." I gestured to a slave who was crossing the room with an armload of flowers. "Bring us two glasses of Falerian."

"Yes, *Domina*," she replied, impatience apparent in her face.

"Who is *that*?" Mother asked, nodding in the departing slave's direction.

"Psyche. Pilate brought her home the other day with two new garden slaves. He was so pleased—she used to cook for the former governor. Very full of herself, you would think *I* was the slave. At least she likes our kitchen. I saw her admiring the new brick oven."

Psyche returned after a time with two goblets. She placed them on the serpentine table before us and started to leave.

Mother took a sip and then set the glass down. "This will not do! It will not do at all. Psyche! Come back here."

Psyche retraced her steps and bowed before Mother. "Is something wrong, *Domina*?"

"Something is very wrong. Not only has this wine not been cut properly with water but it is not even Falerian."

"Oh, oh . . . Forgive me, *Domina*. I am very sorry."

"I should think so. My daughter expects better and will receive it. Do you understand?"

"Yes, *Domina*."

"Now bring us what she requested and serve it correctly."

"I think she is used to an older *domina*," I explained once Psyche was out of earshot.

"Claudia, *you* are her *domina.* Remember that always."

"Yes, Mother." I picked up my tablet and began to take notes. "Last night Psyche fixed raisin-stuffed flamingo. It was good. And what about Germanicus's favorite—suckling pig with plum sauce?"

"Perfect," Mother agreed, "but you'll need something more . . ."

"The other night I cooked a dish for Pilate myself. He acted amused, treated me like a little girl playing house. I know he was dubious, but it turned out wonderfully. I surprised him."

"I am sure you did. What did you fix?"

"Numidian chicken. Remember the asafetida we found in the market? I added a little of that. It was quite tangy."

Mother looked impressed. "Why not give the recipe to Psyche," she suggested. "This time, the slave will do the honors."

For three days Rachel and I auditioned entertainers: jugglers, actors, singers, dancers and musicians. I would have preferred a poet, but settled on a Thracian dance troupe. The women guests would be impressed by their superb skill, the men by the scanty costumes.

Again and again, I reviewed the placement of the guest couches. Naturally, Germanicus and Agrippina would be at our right. From there it grew more complicated. I had originally omitted Piso and Plancina from the list. Pilate noticed immediately. "Are you out of your mind!"

"Just this once . . . for our first party?"

"Our first party is the most important. Piso is Tiberius's man. You know that! We can't afford to offend him."

I wheedled, I sulked. Pilate's jaw set. The couch to our left would be occupied by Piso and Plancina. High-ranking officers and their wives, my parents among them, would sit on either side with two of Pilate's most promising clients and their wives at the lowest couches, those farthest from us.

Up early the day of the party, I was in and out of the kitchen, watching carefully as each dish was prepared. The Numidian chicken was to be a surprise. I watched approvingly as a chastened Psyche deftly ground the asafetida root and then combined it with powdered nuts and dates, which had arrived that morning by caravan from Alexandria. Inside the brick oven, tender young chickens poached slowly in white wine. Savoring the tantalizing aroma, I dipped a finger into the sauce, and nodded approvingly, confident that my dinner would be a minor sensation. Psyche was a born cook and loved it—no doubt about that. I was glad she liked our oven; she would be spending a lot of time before it.

Leaving the final preparations in her hands, I retired to my living quarters. I had overseen every detail of the party just as I'd observed Mother do it many times. Rachel had gone to the flower market at dawn. The fragrance of roses filled every room. Reviewing my list in the bath, I thought with pride of the polished floor, the gleaming silver. Everything had been done. The party's outcome rested with Isis.

THE FEEL OF DAMASK MADE MY BARE SKIN TINGLE AS Rachel slowly lowered the filmy lace overgown past my shoulders. Revolving slowly before the mirror, I studied my reflection critically. Lace, fashioned like an airy cobweb, subtly accented the silver damask that clung to my body like a glove.

Settling down at the rosewood dressing table, I tried to sit quietly while Rachel adjusted the silver fillet which held my elaborately casual curls.

"You look like a nymph of the mists."

Pilate stood in the archway watching me, so noble in his white wool tunic. A necklace of star rubies dangled from his hand.

"It was my mother's," he explained, fastening the strand around my neck. I jumped up and flung my arms around him. Pilate laughed softly, holding me back at arm's length. His fingers deftly caressed my throat and shoulders. "Perhaps you should remove this," he said, lifting the small sistrum with one finger.

I backed away. Surely not on a night when I needed all the help that Isis could give. The goddess had treated me well in the past months but never once had I imagined that I could get along without her. I smiled up at my husband, gently removing the charm from his hand and tucking it inside my gown. I would wear his necklace on the outside.

Just then Rachel announced that the first of our guests had arrived. From then on I was kept busy moving from one to the other. At first conversation was an effort for me. I knew that I was being judged and more than a generation divided me from many. The first to arrive were old, really old, Lucius Raecius, bald as an egg, and his wife, Lucretia, leaning heavily on an ebony cane. Fortunately, listening had always come easily to me and none of our friends, young or old, were the least reluctant to speak of themselves. Once I caught Mother watching, a proud smile on her face. My heart surged with pleasure, but even more precious were Pilate's words, whispered in passing. "I am a lucky man. You are a woman for every room in the house."

After that I floated. The guests mingled, talk flowed freely. I even found myself chatting easily with Plancina, wondering if I had misjudged the governor's wife. She was more than pleasant, complimenting me first on my gown, then on the couches, the frescoes, the mosaic floor. Apparently she admired everything. "I am surprised that Germanicus and Agrippina aren't here," Plancina said at last. "Surely you invited them?"

I glanced apprehensively at the elaborate water clock. The golden bowl was nearly filled. What could be keeping them? With a murmured excuse, I slipped away. Placing my hand lightly on Pilate's shoulder, I drew him away from a small group. "What shall we do?" I whispered. "The dinner will be ruined if we delay longer."

"If our guests drink much more wine, they won't know the difference."

"I will send a slave to inquire—" Even as I spoke, Rachel appeared and whispered softly, "A messenger has just arrived. The lord Germanicus has been taken ill. The lady Agrippina bids you begin without them. I have taken the liberty—"

I was swept by an ugly sense of certainty—a confirmation of the growing fear I had chosen in my happiness to ignore. Something was very, very wrong.

CHAPTER

12

The Curse

Though it was almost dawn when the last of our guests left, I slept fitfully, plagued by dreams, confusing fragments, frightful pictures of my beloved uncle. Awakening only a few hours later, I gently disengaged myself from Pilate's arms. He was still sleeping as I dressed hurriedly and slipped from the room.

Our groom took me by chariot from the villa to the edge of town, where a city ordinance had recently banned all horse traffic. The dust, the congestion of carts and chariots—not to mention the smell—had gotten out of hand. Now the streets were forbidden to all but foot traffic. As we approached the city gates, the area was jammed with waiting litters, bearers competing raucously for early-bird customers.

I chose the team that appeared most aggressive, but their initial eagerness and brawny muscles proved deceiving. The ride seemed an eternity. "Faster," I urged as we jogged through the early morning streets. "You must go faster!"

At last I reached my destination and ran up the wide marble

stairs leading to the villa of Germanicus and Agrippina. The heavy, brass-fitted door opened, but only a crack. A familiar slave peered out, his grim face lighting at the sight of me.

"Good morning, Achilles. I've come to see—"

"Yes, yes, *Domina,* come in." He swung the door open to admit me. "They will be happy that you have come." He led me through the leafy atrium, down the frescoed hall. I'd been there many times, knew the villa well. Nothing had changed, nothing that I could see or touch anyway. "I shall tell them you are here," he said, indicating that I wait in Agrippina's *tablinum.* At one end was a shelf filled with scrolls neatly tucked into their stylish sleeves—bold, bright colors. All the popular writers, my favorite Ovid among them. Augustus would be spinning in his grave if he could see that. The old emperor had banished the poet for work deemed salacious. Now here was his granddaughter displaying Ovid prominently. Idly, I speculated—had any of the scrolls ever been out of their coverings? Vibrant and sociable, Agrippina rarely sat still long enough to read.

Scarcely a moment passed before Caligula appeared in the archway rubbing his eyes sleepily. "Up so early?" he inquired with a smirk. "I am surprised your husband would allow you out of bed. I wouldn't."

How arrogant of him to greet me in his sleeping tunic. "I came about your father," I replied evenly. "What is the matter with Germanicus?"

Caligula shrugged. "I have only just returned from a hunting trip in the north." He settled himself onto a couch. "Sorry to have missed your little party."

"You were not invited, but your parents were. It worries me

that they didn't come," I said, sitting down on the couch across from him.

"How sweet you are. Very sweet, like your sister. Tell me, how is Marcella?"

How dare he mention her name? Through clenched teeth, I repeated, "I came about your father."

"That was good of you," Agrippina said. I looked up, startled. She had appeared silently, like an apparition in her stained and wrinkled party gown. Auntie's pale face, gaunt in the early morning light, frightened me as I stood to greet her.

"I know I look awful," she apologized, tucking up a strand of hair that straggled over her forehead. "I was up all night with Germanicus. Every day he grows weaker. His surgeons can tell us nothing."

Caligula, still sprawled on the couch, looked up at her. "Mother, I had no idea—"

Agrippina lowered herself wearily onto the couch beside me. "It is worse since you left."

I looked from one to the other. "When did it start?"

"Three months ago, perhaps more. The symptoms began gradually."

I took Agrippina's hands in mine. "Why didn't you tell me?"

"At first we could not believe it, later we did not want to."

"But when you did?" I persisted.

"You were so happy with your marriage plans. We did not want to mar your pleasure. Germanicus would not even tell your parents, though I am certain your father suspects. By now everyone must know."

"Has it grown that bad?" Caligula asked. His questions struck me as strange, not so much what he said but how he said it. He seemed merely polite, almost detached. I have never understood Caligula.

"The progress has been slow," Agrippina explained. "One day he is very ill, the next almost normal. Germanicus looked forward to attending your party, Claudia. He wanted to see you happy in your new home. We planned to come right up until the last minute. Then, as he started to dress, the nausea came over him again. It was terrible . . . terrible."

A cold certainty closed about my heart. "You suspect poison, don't you?"

Agrippina nodded. "The soldiers would give their lives for Germanicus. He treats the slaves well—they love him. Still I prepare all his meals myself."

Caligula drummed idly on the arm of his couch, a roaring lion's head. "So much wasted effort, the poisoner is not in this house."

"Who then?" The awful coldness persisted as I faced him.

"You cannot guess?"

"If I could, would I ask you?"

"Think about it." Caligula raised a cynical brow. "Who stands to gain most by my father's untimely demise?"

"The governor! It is Piso."

"The governor or his wife," Agrippina answered.

"Plancina?" I frowned, thinking of the dumpy little woman with her permanently rosy cheeks.

"Do you imagine that women are less ruthless than men?" Leaning over, Caligula chucked me under the chin as though I were a child. "How naive you are."

I backed away, ignoring him. "Do you have any proof?" I asked Agrippina.

"Do you know Martina?"

I thought a moment. "Once at the baths she had tried to strike up a friendship. Mother did not encourage her." I recalled Martina's short, stubby fingers, each encircled by a flashy ring. "A rather vulgar-looking woman—all that jewelry."

"Thank-you gifts, no doubt." Caligula's lip curled.

"In exchange for what?" I wanted to know.

"Martina has an evil reputation," Agrippina explained. "She's known to be an abortionist. Some accuse her of witchcraft."

I paused, remembering an afternoon at the central shopping arcade. Plancina's petulant face animated pleasantly for once as her caramel curls bobbed in conversation. Beside her, a dark woman with large emeralds dangling from her ears. "Yes . . . they're friends, aren't they? Plancina and Martina are friends." Puzzled, I looked up at Agrippina. "Surely you didn't let her into your house. If Martina is the poisoner, how . . . ?"

"If I knew that, would I allow it to happen?" Agrippina's eyes flashed. "I boil every plate and cup, prepare each dish myself. I have chopped grasshoppers and mixed them with egg, I have mashed eels and boiled them in milk. Anything that any doctor or apothecary suggested, I have done myself. I try everything, I do everything, but nothing helps. I'm so afraid . . ."

Agrippina, who never cried, suddenly seemed to explode into tears, great wracking sobs that shook her body. I put my arms about her, gently stroking her back. "I know you have done everything," I said after the awful crying had ceased. "Now, please let me help. Let me do whatever I can."

Drying her eyes at last, Agrippina rose wearily. She took my hand, leading me to Germanicus's personal quarters. The air felt close, drapes were drawn, torches flickered eerily on the walls. My eyes traveled to a large couch where he lay propped up by pillows. A chill passed through me. Though scarcely a month had passed since the wedding, Germanicus must have lost fifty pounds. His face resembled a death's-head. Impulsively, I dropped to my knees, burying my head in the fur robe he wore despite the heat.

"Don't hide your pretty face," Germanicus said in a tired, reedy voice I would not have recognized. "Sit opposite me where I can see you."

"Uncle, I am going to help care for you," I promised, choking back my tears. "I am going to bring food every day, things I fix myself. Pilate says I am a very good cook. We will have you better in no time."

"My dear girl, there is nothing that you or anyone can do for me. The stench of death is in this house. It grows stronger every day."

"That is nonsense," Agrippina said, grabbing his hand and holding it in hers. "How many times must I tell you, *there is no smell.*"

EARLY THE NEXT MORNING RACHEL AND I SET OFF WITH five litters filled with flowers and fruit, Numidian chicken and roast young kid that I had prepared with my own hands. En route, I stopped at the temple of Isis. This time I had no difficulty getting to see the mystagogue. In fact, he came himself to the atrium where I waited, greeting me with a quizzical smile. "So you have returned to us."

"Yes." I nodded, taking his outstretched hands. "And once again I have come to ask a favor. It is something highly confidential."

"Indeed? And I thought you had come to take religious instruction."

I darted a look at him; was he laughing at me? "Not now, at least not this time," I said, following him into his consultation room. "I need special incense, something to cleanse the air immediately, something that will remove evil."

"Not for *your* house, surely?" he asked, his silky brows raised.

"No, for a dear friend. He has not been well lately and he . . ."

"Believes himself to be cursed," the mystagogue finished for me.

I hesitated, picking my words carefully. "Something like that. Of course," I assured him and perhaps myself, "it is merely his illness that creates such fancies."

"They are not fancies. The *Dominus* Germanicus *has* been cursed."

I drew back, shocked. "You know!"

"For weeks there have been whispers. Now people speak openly."

"Supposing what you say is true, can you help us?" I looked at the walls behind him, shelves from floor to ceiling filled with bottles and jars.

"I can give you something to make him more comfortable, perhaps poppy seeds ground in honey."

"Surely you can do more than that. Please," I urged, "anything."

"His fate is in the hands of the goddess."

"There must be something . . ." I searched the mystagogue's face for a sign of encouragement, however faint.

He paused, considering. "The goddess appears to favor you, despite your neglect."

I flushed. "I should have come back weeks ago, but your love charm—"

The mystagogue watched me, I felt him totaling up the cost of my gown, my jewelry. "Obviously succeeded," he finished for me.

"Oh yes! Very well indeed. I cannot thank you enough. Your charm—the goddess's grace—has changed my life, changed it completely. I have been so busy. Learning to be a wife has taken all my time."

"But there is more . . ."

I looked down, feeling guilty. "My husband does not understand about Isis. The idea that I should seek something more, something outside our home bothers him. I love my husband, I want to please him in every way." I forced myself to meet the mystagogue's eyes. "Love is everything—is it not?"

"There are many who think so, for a time."

"It will always be that way for us," I assured him.

"But now there is the *Dominus* Germanicus. You wish a remedy for him? It occurs to me that you might demonstrate your sincerity to the goddess with a gift."

"A gift? Of course, anything. What shall I give?"

"Celibacy is customary for a woman requesting a boon."

I felt myself coloring. "We have only been married a few weeks . . . Celibacy for how long?"

The mystagogue smiled. "Merely for the duration of the *Dominus* Germanicus's illness."

"Merely! Who knows how long that will take?"

"You say your uncle is very ill . . . perhaps dying?"

"Yes," I whispered. "You are right, it is a small price to pay." But what about Pilate?

Agrippina and I saw to it that each room was scrubbed down, then filled with fragrant blossoms. The strong but pleasing incense prepared by the mystagogue wafted through the entire house, yet Germanicus insisted that the smell of death pervaded everything.

I dismissed his complaint, but as days passed and I arrived each morning with fresh flowers and more incense, a strange, indefinable odor became apparent. The smell was vaguely sweet yet increasingly unpleasant. I hesitated to mention it to Agrippina, who looked more frightened with each passing day. Then the morning came when Auntie brought it up herself.

"I have noticed a bad smell for days, but did not want to admit it."

"Surely there is a natural cause," I insisted.

"Surely," Agrippina echoed faintly.

But was there?

"I feel so hopeless," I admitted to Mother later that afternoon as we sat drinking snow-chilled grape juice on her balcony. "Nothing we do helps. I am frightened and I cannot talk to Pilate. He has grown so distant . . ."

"Distant?" She looked up, frowning. "Why should he be distant? Surely he is concerned about Germanicus?"

"Very concerned. Germanicus is a friend as well as his patron. It is just that . . ." My voiced trailed off. I knew better than to discuss my bargain with Isis. Mother would never understand, but perhaps . . . I took a deep breath. "I know how you feel about Agrippina, but if you saw her . . . She adores Germanicus and now he . . . he is dying before her eyes."

Mother's lips tightened. "Do not involve me, Claudia. Agrippina likes to do things her own way."

"She is different now. You would scarcely know her. Suppose it was *Tata.* Does this terrible tragedy not go beyond past differences?"

Mother looked down as though considering the depth of her goblet. "Yes, I suppose it does," she said at last, putting the glass aside. "Of course it does."

WE MARSHALED THE SLAVES. THE SCRUBBING BEGAN anew. This time, Mother noticed a loose tile in the floor of Germanicus's bedroom. Lifting it, she discovered the decaying corpse of a baby. "Ugh!" she shrieked. The slaves backed off in disgust. Recovering herself, Mother picked up the dead baby and handed it to the nearest slave. "Burn this poor creature, burn it immediately—outside the building. Then search every room in the villa."

Almost immediately other macabre objects turned up under floor tiles or in niches gouged out of the walls behind hangings. I myself found the corpse of a black cat with rudimentary wings growing from its back. Beside it was a twisted cord holding a lead tablet inscribed with Germanicus's name. I screamed, overwhelmed by so much horror. Then slowly the realization came to me. No matter how hideous these grisly objects were, they were nonetheless *real.*

Rushing to Germanicus's couch, I took his hand in mine. "The search is over," I assured him. "You were right all along. We have covered every inch of the house. None of those awful things remain. They have all been removed and burned. The smell will leave now."

"I believe so too." He nodded. "At least now I know the smell is real and not merely some wretched figment of my imagination. It is Piso. I don't know how he did it, but he is responsible."

Agrippina agreed. "It is about time you admitted it! I always suspected him and now his slaves are coming three times a day to inquire about your health. Ha! Of course he is to blame, he and Plancina and that witch friend of hers, Martina."

Germanicus smiled up at us. "It will take more than a witch to get the better of you two."

I left him propped up on his couch surrounded by scrolls, reports, and petitions that he had been too weak to address before.

"GERMANICUS IS BETTER, HE IS REALLY BETTER," I TOLD Pilate that night as we settled down on our dining couch. "Agrippina and I both noticed an improvement in his color, and just before I left he said he was tired of broth and wanted meat."

"I am heartily glad to hear that." Pilate shifted to face me. "Glad for my sake as well as for his. It would seem that Isis has heard your prayers and recognized your sacrifice—not to mention mine. Surely tonight . . ." He caressed my cheek lightly.

I shook my head, smiling ruefully. "Dear one, Germanicus is still very ill, dangerously so. It would be premature to assume that he is out of danger."

Pilate rose abruptly. "You realize that it has been ten nights."

"Of course I realize it. I have been counting too." I got up and stood before him, my eyes pleading.

Pilate placed his hands lightly but firmly upon my shoulders. "My dear Claudia, you must know that what we do or don't do has nothing to do with Germanicus's recovery."

"How can we be certain of that? If he dies and I have not done all the goddess asks of me, I could not live with myself. Besides, Germanicus is your patron, does he not deserve your loyalty?"

Pilate stiffened, his arms dropped to his sides. "Are you accusing me of disloyalty? I would do anything the man desires, but your obsession with Isis is something else entirely. It is unseemly, un-Roman. Who worships Isis but a bunch of demented foreigners?"

"Foreigners, yes, but hardly demented," I corrected him, struggling to keep my voice down.

He was not appeased. "My mother—and every other Roman woman I have ever known—was content to worship Juno. Homage to *that* goddess would never involve anything contrary to a husband's wishes."

"No, I do not suppose it would," I agreed, "but I owe Isis a greater debt than you could ever imagine. Please be patient with me just a little longer."

"Not much longer, Claudia." He turned from me and picked up the cloak he'd flung casually over a chair.

"What about the wild boar—it is your favorite." I placed my hand softly on his arm. "You have hardly touched a thing."

"Offer it up to Isis. I'll dine tonight with livelier companions."

GERMANICUS DID NOT GET BETTER. THOUGH WE ALL pretended otherwise, the smell was back. The slaves discovered cocks' feathers, then human bones. I noticed when I arrived one morning that, despite the warm summer weather, the house was unaccountably cold. Germanicus, weary of the darkened room, the row of basins and medicines beside him, forced himself to rise from bed and walk unassisted to the atrium. Following behind him, I gasped in horror. There above us was his name scrawled high on the wall, each letter upside down. I called the household together. No one had any idea how the words, Germanicus Claudius Nero, got there. With much scrubbing, the slaves removed them only to have the inscription reappear the following morning. This time the last letter, the *o* in Nero, was missing.

Agrippina had insisted that Germanicus send a message to Piso ordering him out of the province. The governor reluctantly left. Now he was reportedly anchored off the nearby island of Chios. "He's waiting for news of my death," Germanicus told me when I arrived one morning. "He means to return then, like a vulture."

"Then he will wait forever," I assured him, sitting down beside the bed. A slave removed a wet towel from Germanicus's forehead, gently wiped the dried saliva from around his white lips. I pressed my face against the bouquet of red roses I had brought from my garden and took a deep breath. I had been slightly ill upon waking; now the smell, which no amount of scrubbing or incense could eradicate, was all the more pervasive. Hoping that a drink of water would help, I rose to my feet. For a moment I stood staring unsteadily at the floor. Dizziness swept over me in waves, bringing with it the sensation of standing in the midst of a swirling sphere where floor and walls no longer existed.

"Is something the matter, Claudia?" Germanicus asked. "You look pale."

I tried to orient myself. "Nothing is wrong."

Very carefully, for my arms no longer felt a part of me, I set the bouquet down beside him. Germanicus extended one thin, bony hand from under the tasseled coverlet and grasped my wrist. Only a few days before, I had found the skeleton of a hand buried under a couch cushion in his sitting room. Now, with dazed detachment, I noticed the similarity.

"Claudia." He stared at me, his hazel eyes narrow, searching. "You're not—sick too?" The words came out with a slow, forced reluctance.

I attempted a reassuring smile, but at that moment the nausea started to rise. Then before I could reach the door, I began to vomit.

CHAPTER

13

And a Blessing . . .

Snakes undulated above my head. I closed my heavy eyes, then opened them. Slowly the swirling motion ceased. The serpents remained. An elegant stylized pattern, gold and green, rippled across a marble ceiling. I lay on a couch, red satin cushions beneath me. Where was I?

Somewhere people talked in hushed, frightened voices. As the words became clearer, I realized they were speaking of me. Germanicus, weak and tormented: "It's my fault. I will never forgive myself . . ." Agrippina: "Dearest, you are not to blame. Claudia wanted to come." Mother sobbing: "Yes . . . she . . . she did. My poor child wanted to help. Now she's caught the—the curse."

Caught the curse! The room spun, my head ached from where I'd struck it when I fell. What was happening to me? Terrified, I sat up.

Mother, at my side in an instant, murmured, "Claudia, darling, are you all right?"

I grasped her hand. "I want to see Pilate."

"If I may be allowed—" Petronius, Germanicus's personal physician, entered the room with Rachel. I breathed a sigh of relief as the tall, gray-haired man approached the couch where I lay. "Your slave tells me you fainted. Has this happened before?"

"No, never." I was embarrassed by the quaver in my voice. With the doctor's help and Rachel's, I walked to an adjoining room, where they settled me on another couch. Petronius pulled up a small chair and sat down beside me. "Do you feel the nausea only in this house?"

I paused, considering. "Sometimes in other places . . . Last night's wine was harsh. No matter how much water I added, it tasted bad." I forced myself to ask, "Could it have been poisoned?"

The doctor's heavy-lidded eyes regarded me intently. "Did your husband drink it?"

I laughed nervously. "As a matter of fact he did, quite a little. He had a headache this morning, but was fine otherwise." The laughter faded as I searched Petronius's face. "Do you believe as they do that I have been cursed?"

The doctor sighed wearily. "I will be honest. In this house anything is possible." Taking my hand, he rearranged his tired face into a smile. "How long has it been since your last bleeding?"

WHEN I RETURNED TO GERMANICUS'S ROOM I WALKED unassisted, feeling the silly grin on my face. "It is not a curse, but a blessing! I am going to have a baby!"

Mother and Agrippina looked at each other. Mother

shook her head. "What is the matter with us! The nausea, the fainting . . ."

Turning from the midst of a three-way embrace with Mother and Agrippina, I saw Pilate framed in the archway watching. Disengaging myself, I rushed into his arms.

"What's going on here?" he asked. "Good news apparently. I hope it means you are better, sir." Pilate looked questioningly at his patron.

Germanicus smiled broadly. "May I offer my congratulations?"

Pilate, one arm tight about me, set his plumed helmet on the table. His blue eyes were thoughtful as they regarded the proconsul. "Congratulations? Have I been promoted?"

"Something better, I trust. But I must say that dear girl of yours gave us a scare, fainting the way she did."

"Fainting! Claudia fainted?" Pilate looked down at me. "Are you all right?"

"More than all right," I assured him. "But can you imagine—I actually thought myself cursed."

Pilate's eyes narrowed as he took in the banks of flowers, the incense wafting from every available niche. His nostrils pinched slightly as he inhaled. "Why did you think that?" he asked quietly.

"I was ill—frightened—but Petronius has just examined me and it seems that I—we—are going to have a baby."

Pilate smiled happily, but then, so quickly, his expression hardened. A chill swept over me. What was the matter? "You *are* happy, aren't you?" I asked, looking up at him.

"Very happy," he assured me, stroking my back lightly, "but also concerned." He turned to Germanicus. "You know my loyalties are always to you, but I cannot allow my wife to remain in this house. She must not return until you are fully recovered. I trust that will be soon."

"Pilate, no!" I exclaimed in shocked surprise. "I am fine now, and Petronius says my symptoms are quite common."

"Hush! You heard your husband," Germanicus admonished. "I understand perfectly." He turned to Pilate. "Take Claudia home immediately. I insist on it, but promise to keep me informed of her progress. It will ease my—I shall be eager to hear how she is doing."

"Gladly, sir." Pilate reached for his helmet, half dragging me toward the door. At the threshold I turned and looked back. Agrippina sat at Germanicus's side, holding his hand, but her eyes followed us, a wistful smile about her full lips.

THE NEXT MORNING THE CAPTAIN OF A LARGE MERCHANT ship arrived with a scroll from Marcella. Clearly, such an important man would not have brought the message himself if he wasn't seeking personal news of Germanicus's progress. He wanted to gossip. It was difficult to go through the motions of civility, sitting with him over wine and date cakes, while my fingers itched to unroll the scroll. Happily, Pilate joined us and I was able to slip away.

"From Marcella of the House of Vesta," the note began in the formal way, as though I wouldn't recognize her scrawl anywhere. Smoothing back the parchment, I noted fewer of the familiar dashes and exclamation marks. The reason for her restraint was soon apparent. News of Germanicus's illness had spread to Rome, where public life had ground to a standstill as people awaited further bulletins.

Recently a rumor had mysteriously surfaced. "Is it true that Germanicus has recovered?" Marcella asked. She described how hundreds of celebrants had rushed to the palace carrying torches, awakening Tiberius with the joyful chant: "All is well again in Rome. All is well again at home. Here's an end to pain, Germanicus is well again."

Marcella's hastily written letter ended there. It worried me. How had Tiberius reacted to such an extravagant public display of affection for Germanicus? The contrast between the two men was cruelly obvious. Tiberius was an indifferent orator, Germanicus a brilliant one. The emperor's military achievements were negligible, Germanicus's world-famous. More devastating, Tiberius had been disliked and distrusted from the beginning, while everyone adored Germanicus. Agrippina, the granddaughter of Augustus, and Germanicus, his grand-nephew, were blood heirs to the throne. Tiberius, Augustus's stepson, had assumed the imperial reins when Germanicus was still a boy. Most of the world believed that Rome was merely being held in trust for the rightful heir.

For the first time I thought beyond the personal loss of my beloved uncle. *Tata*'s future and, to a lesser degree, Pilate's had been aligned to the proconsul. What would happen to them if Germanicus was to die?

I SENT RACHEL TO UNCLE'S HOME EVERY MORNING. SHE took flowers from our garden and meals that I had prepared myself. Julia and Druscilla returned from summering with cousins in Ephesus. They were tender, solicitous nurses, but nothing that anyone did helped. Despite the slaves' vigorous scrubbing, Germanicus awakened each morning to find that his name had been rewritten on the wall, always with one additional letter lopped off.

With every passing day, Germanicus grew weaker. When the morning came when only one letter remained, family and friends were summoned. As Pilate prepared to leave, I begged to go to him. He forbade it. "Jupiter's balls! What are you thinking? Your own mother found a dead baby in that accursed house."

"I am in no danger, none of it has to do with me," I reasoned. "I should have realized I was pregnant, but my mind was on Uncle Germanicus. I didn't think."

"No, you didn't think."

I looked up, startled.

Pilate's voice softened. "You are not thinking now. How would you feel if our child were marked in some way by this evil?"

I looked at him stricken, my hand involuntarily straying to the sistrum at my throat. I nodded in agreement, turning away.

THAT EVENING AS I WATCHED THE LAST RAYS OF SUN ON the river, a grim-faced Pilate sat down beside me in the garden. "He's dead, isn't he?" I whispered.

Pilate took my hand, holding it in both of his. "Germanicus was brave to the end. Even seasoned officers wept." My husband's voice was hoarse. "He had a kind word for each of us and a message for you."

I waited silently.

"He sent his love and wished you much joy in this life. He said he hoped you would be as fine a wife as your mother is to Marcus, and Agrippina has been to him." Pilate frowned. "There was something else, words I didn't understand. He was very weak."

I struggled to keep back the tears. "Tell me."

"It was confused, something about a dream. He remembered your dream from long ago—something about a wolf. He regretted not taking it more seriously. 'The prophecy is clear now,' he said." Pilate shook his head. "Surely the delirium of a dying man."

"Surely," I agreed, eyes down. "Did he say anything else?"

"He charged us to avenge his death. 'Tell Tiberius that Piso and Plancina are responsible,' he said. 'Tell the people of Rome that I entrust my wife and children to them.' Then he reached out and took Agrippina's hand." Pilate's voice caught. After a time, he continued, "It was over."

"I should have been there," I gasped, no longer able to contain my sobs.

Silently, Pilate pulled me toward him, but I held myself stiffly.

THE ENTIRE CIVILIZED WORLD HAD VIEWED GERMANICUS as a just and tolerant man, a harbinger of peace and prosperity. Recalling our two-year-long inspection tour of client kingdoms, I saw again the eager throngs, thousands of men, women, and children, cheering their hearts out. I remembered marigolds fluttering like golden snow from the rooftops, women who had broken past guards wanting only to touch the hem of

Germanicus's toga. The proconsul's charisma had imbued everyone with confidence, for surely what was good for Rome was good for the world.

Now the world was plunged into mourning. People stoned temples and threw their household gods into the street; even barbarians stopped fighting one another and sued for peace as though afflicted by a grievous domestic tragedy.

Germanicus's embalmed body lay in state for nearly a month. It did not surprise me that ministers from as far away as Spain, Gaul, and North Africa came to pay tribute. The funeral itself was splendid. Thousands of mourners flowed through the gates of Antioch carrying bouquets of brilliant blossoms. Bright sun shimmered off the marble buildings of the massive forum. The armor and jewels of the mourners who passed by the bier one by one blazed in the glow. As our family joined Agrippina and her children beneath a purple canopy, an officer suddenly appeared and whispered in *Tata*'s ear. I caught a look of concern on my father's face before he excused himself and hurried away. What now? I wondered.

Musicians played. They were, I hoped, helping to prepare Germanicus's spirit for its journey to the afterlife. One potentate after another knelt before the pyre, then rose to eulogize the fallen leader. Julia and Druscilla sobbed; Agrippina bit her lips; Drusus and Nero were dead white, their hands clenched into fists at their sides; Caligula sat quietly, engrossed in thoughts of his own.

Finally the orations came to an end. Flanked by an honor guard, Agrippina rose and slowly walked to the bier. Gently her hands passed over her husband's face for the last time. Her fingers parted his lips. I watched as she placed a small golden coin beneath his tongue. Germanicus would need it to pay the ferryman who would row him across the River Styx.

Agrippina stood back as Sentius, the newly appointed governor, ignited the bier. I reeled back in spite of myself as flames shot twenty feet into the air. Drums rolled and trumpets blared as Germanicus's children advanced to the burning pyre. Each threw lavish gifts of food and clothing into the fire. The departed spirit might have need of them in his new life. Who knew? When the fire died down, wine would be poured onto it. Eventually the ashes would be gathered and put into an urn. I could bear to watch no longer.

"Germanicus was like Alexander," Pilate said to me. "Both were great leaders with even greater promise, both died too young, victims of treachery in foreign lands."

I looked out over the assembled throng, many crying openly. "If only he had acted against Piso in the beginning. A friend of Mother's has written from Chios saying that Piso offered up thanksgiving sacrifices when he heard of Germanicus's death. And Plancina!—she threw off the mourning she was wearing for her sister and put on a red gown. Can you imagine?"

"It's worse than that."

Startled, I looked up and saw *Tata.* He had shouldered his way through the crowd and now stood beside us. "Piso has written Tiberius claiming that Germanicus was the real traitor." Tapping Pilate on the shoulder, he continued, "There's more bad news. Piso is mounting an offensive. He intends to invade Syria. Get ready for a fight."

CHAPTER

14

All Roads to Rome

As the weeks passed Mother and Agrippina changed before my eyes. Who were these strange women who bore almost no resemblance to their former selves? Agrippina, a pale shadow, sat silent, lost in thought. Mother darted here and there with pillows, compresses, and tinctures, trying always to anticipate the widow's slightest need or whim. Clearly the enormity of Agrippina's loss had eradicated past slights, real and imagined.

Mother took a seldom-used alcove in Agrippina's apartments and turned it into a *textrinum,* or weaving room. A loom was brought in—I doubt that Agrippina had ever spent much time at one. Now she seemed to welcome the idea. Weaving would occupy her hands, if not her mind. With Pilate and *Tata* at war with Piso, we all needed a project to keep us busy. It was decided that we would work together on a classic scene from the Aeneid. Slaves busily set to work carding the wool for us. All that fuzz made everyone sneeze, but soon they had the room swept out and ready for us. The sun shone cheerily through large windows as we sat down to spin the wool.

As Mother began a preliminary sketch, I suggested, "Why not Aeneas's reunion with his father in the Underworld?"

Druscilla thought it a splendid idea. She and Julia came every day for almost a week.

We spun much of the wool into silvery threads that would provide the weaving's misty background and fastened this warp to the loom, weighting it at the bottom. As we spun the weft, knotting it into skeins, Druscilla and Julia's enthusiasm waned. Even for girls in mourning, the fall season held many attractions.

Mother showed Agrippina how to knot the first top cord of the weaving, deftly doubling the weft yarn to form a loop, then drawing a pair of warp threads through that loop. Agrippina was surprisingly good at it. She worked quietly for a time, silent, face impassive, while Mother and I set to work on other sections of the project.

"I know it is unlikely," Agrippina spoke at last, addressing no one in particular. "You will think I am grasping at straws."

"My dear, what is it?" Mother asked gently, resting her shuttle.

Agrippina's wide eyes fastened on her with unaccustomed intensity. "Is it possible—could it be that we truly *are* reunited with our loved ones somewhere beyond this world?"

Mother paused, her own eyes grown thoughtful. "Through all the years, through all Marcus's many battles, I have prayed that it is so."

"I *know* it is so," I broke in. "Isis has promised."

"Not Isis again," Mother chided me.

"Isis promises eternal life?" Agrippina watched me curiously.

"She does, and I believe her."

"You are very sure of yourself for one so young—perhaps because you *are* so young."

Mother smiled wryly. "That is what I thought years ago when Claudia began asking questions. 'What do you believe?' 'Why do you worship Juno?' " She shook her head. "Such thoughts never occurred to me when I was a girl, but then"—she glanced at me affectionately—"Claudia has always been different. I paid scant attention to what I thought were her idle fancies. The next thing I knew she had gone off in the dead of night to some strange temple—"

"No!" Agrippina, busy knotting the weft, looked up in amazement.

"That was only the beginning, my dear. The impetuous girl risked her life to join an Egyptian cult."

"An Egyptian cult! Ugh! I had no idea! You never told me."

Mother was knotting from left to right, pushing her work upward so it advanced to cover the warp, tightening the threads at each turn to maintain an even weave. "It is not the kind of thing one talks about even to family. Marcus was furious. Of all the foreign gods, it would have to be Isis." She looked up from her work. "You know—that whole Cleopatra tragedy."

Agrippina nodded. "Germanicus resented her terribly. He adored his grandmother and spoke often of the pain Antonius caused her—not to mention the disgrace." She picked up the threads again, fingering them absently. Her eyes shifted back to me. "What does your husband think of your devotion to Isis?"

"He used to say that nothing under the sun surprised him, that life was full of inexplicable matters that defied logic." I paused uncertainly. "What I said amused him then. I doubt that he took it very seriously. I don't think he took *me* very seriously."

"Every young couple goes through adjustments," Agrippina reassured me.

"Did you?" I asked, doubting it.

Agrippina sat for a time, her eyes thoughtful. "Not many," she admitted at last. "Our families were so closely aligned. I was Augustus's granddaughter, Germanicus the grandson of his sister. I think we loved each other even as children. Besides, we were raised with the future of Rome in mind. It was taken for granted that Germanicus and I would marry"—her voice trailed off to almost a whisper—"and eventually rule."

Such grand hopes dashed forever. I thought for a moment she would cry. Mother hastily changed the subject. "Your father and I have had our share of problems. He might have married any number of army daughters better suited to military life than I, but then . . ." She held up a new ball of yarn, tying it to the old and then twisting the knot to the inside. "I had my share of well-placed suitors. Father favored one young senator—surely you remember him, Agrippina—but I would not hear of it. It was Marcus or no one. He needs me," she reflected, "if only to smooth his rough edges." She picked up a skein of scarlet yarn earmarked for Aeneas's cloak and studied it absently. "You and Pilate are also quite different. Perhaps it is your 'strangeness' that most appeals to him. You are lovely—Agrippina will agree, it is more than a mother's pride—but we all know that Pilate had his choice of beauties.

He wanted something more, and got it. I am certain that he finds you both fascinating and frustrating. It will work out." She hesitated a moment watching me. "You do miss him, don't you?"

"Oh yes! Yes, of course!" I looked up from my knotting, surprised by the question. "I miss him terribly. This war against Piso goes on forever."

"Scarcely a month," Mother reminded me gently. "You have no idea what a real separation is. I pray you never will."

"It is amazing that Piso has held on this long at Celicia," Agrippina said. "He can thank his mercenaries for that—the best that money can buy."

"I had a message from Marcus yesterday," Mother said. "He does not expect the blockade to last much longer."

"I light candles to Isis every night and stare into the flame," I told them. "Sometimes she seems very close. I know then that Pilate and *Tata* are safe."

"I never gave much thought to gods and goddesses," Agrippina said. "Whether they were 'real' did not matter. It was enough that they were beautiful. Now I wonder . . . life is so empty without Germanicus. I am frightened for our children."

"Isis knows what it means to lose a husband," I assured her. "When Osiris was murdered, she traveled the world searching for pieces of his body. When she recovered them, she brought him back to life and bore his child."

Agrippina smiled at me. "That is a very sweet story."

Mother shook her head. "But little consolation under the circumstances."

There was an uncomfortable silence. I felt that I had been

dismissed as a child. Agrippina was quiet for what seemed a very long time, her eyes resting on the shuttle in her hands.

"Perhaps it is," she said at last.

"What are you thinking, Auntie?" I asked.

Agrippina put down the shuttle and looked up at me, the old fire shining through the fog of her grief. "I cannot return my husband to life, but I can avenge his death in Rome. I can make certain that his name lives on. We cannot conceive another child, but I can protect the legacy of the ones we have." She stood up, tossing back her tawny mane in a gesture that I had not seen in months.

A sense of relief swept over me. We had our Agrippina back again—ready to play the heroine once more.

MOTHER AND I DISCUSSED THE DAILY WAR COMMUNIQUÉS each night at dinner. We were so proud of *Tata,* who figured prominently in most of them. Sentius, the newly appointed governor, a senator with little military experience, relied heavily on my father. As the siege continued, Piso stood on the ramparts of a seaside fortress offering extravagant rewards to individual soldiers whose skill he coveted. When the color sergeant of the sixth brigade defected, *Tata* ordered barricades thrown up, ladders braced and mounted by crack troops. A rain of spears, stones, and firebrands from his battle engines provided cover while blaring trumpets drowned out Piso's blandishments. His defiance crumbled. Soon Piso pleaded to remain in the fortress in exchange for surrendering his arms. He would wait there, he promised, until Tiberius himself decided who would govern Syria. When Sentius denied the terms, Father stormed the fort, captured Piso, and sent him back to Rome under armed guard. Now, we were certain, Tiberius would see to it that the vile murderer got the punishment he deserved.

Agrippina was taking no chances. Despite winter's menacing approach, she, too, would go to Rome, would lay the true facts, with Germanicus's ashes, at the feet of Tiberius and the Senate. I had expected the announcement while dreading it. It was taken for granted that Father would command her military escort; and, of course, Mother would go with him. Pilate volunteered to accompany them but Father forbade it. "Sentius needs you here to help maintain order," he explained. I breathed a grateful sigh that I hoped went unnoticed. The mourning ship was already carrying not only my parents and Agrippina but my closest friends, Julia and Druscilla.

"I NEVER THOUGHT THE DAY WOULD COME WHEN I WOULD not be overjoyed at the prospect of Rome," Mother admitted to me as we stood on the wharf.

I struggled with a smile. "You will be happy enough once you are there. Besides, there will be Marcella. You will be able to visit her often."

Mother nodded. "It *will* be wonderful to see her again after all these years, but dear one—if only I could be in two places. I want so much to be with you when the baby is born—only another six months. I remember how frightened you were as a child . . ."

My back straightened. "I am a woman now. Bearing children is my duty. Besides, I want this baby very much. I pray to

Isis for a boy. That will please Pilate. All men want sons, don't they?"

"Probably, but most are quickly reconciled to daughters. Witness your father."

I thought of *Tata*. His love had always been there, I had never doubted it. "Pilate is different, he expects a son. I know it. I must not fail him."

"Fail him! My dear, Pilate adores you. If this child is not a boy, there will be others. Surely there's no trouble between you two? This past month since his return from Celicia, he has appeared most happy."

"No, no trouble." I hesitated. "It is only that I hope the baby will bring us even closer. Children do that, don't they?"

"Of course they do, but there is more to marriage than children, no matter how truly they are loved. You know that."

I nodded, at a loss for words. Since my marriage, I had come to see Selene as a woman as well as my mother, a very fortunate woman. She and Father were like two interlocking pieces of a puzzle.

When the final moment of their departure came, we all strove to be stoic. Not even Father, who had lingered out of earshot while I said goodbye to Mother, was very good at it. He held me a long time before admonishing Pilate, his voice grown gruff: "Take care of this girl."

I stood on the wharf, waving long after the black sails receded from view.

Pilate wandered off to speak animatedly with Sentius. That is as it should be, they have important matters to discuss, I reminded myself, trying to ignore a faint cramping in my belly.

THE WINTER WAS FIERCE. FEW SHIPS PLIED THE STORMY waters. Weeks passed without any messages; some when they came were merely duplicates of others. No one could know which ships would make it through the troubled winter waters, so correspondents took no chances. Pilate dispatched a slave to wait daily at the port. Finally, to my great relief, the man returned breathlessly with a letter from Mother. The voyage was over, they were alive. She had written from Brundisium, their port of disembarkation:

> *Our arrival was moving—none of the usual brisk rowing, slaves chanting, overseers marching back and forth cracking their whips. Our ship was guided silently with slow, measured strokes. Agrippina, dressed all in black, a veil covering her hair, was first to disembark—alone, eyes lowered, carrying the urn with Germanicus's ashes in her arms. Close friends and officers who had served under him were among the waiting throngs crowding the wharf, the walls, and the housetops. Men, women, and children waiting at the dock cried out, their voices blending into a single eerie moan.*

A few days later I was confined to bed. "Minor complications," Petronius said. "Nothing to worry about," I heard him assure Pilate. Turning this way and that, struggling to escape the pain, I thought of Mother so far away.

Like Petronius, Rachel was reassuring, her manner always cheerful, yet sometimes I saw concern in her eyes. Once I heard her angrily chiding Psyche for gossiping with another slave about a neighbor who had died in childbirth. They thought I hadn't heard.

Mother's next letter, so vivid, was a fresh reminder of how much I missed her. Tracing her handwriting on the papyrus, I could almost see the royal progression to Calabria, Apulia, and finally Companía, where thousands waited to pay their respects.

Two black-robed battalions provided an escort, their axes and rods carried reversed, their standards undecorated. Company commanders took turns bearing the ashes while poor Agrippina walked all the way, dry-eyed, white-faced, without a word to anyone. Oh, Claudia, if only you could have seen it. At each successive settlement mourners, some villagers from hundreds of miles away, joined the procession. Shoulder to shoulder with knights in purple striped tunics, they erected funeral altars and offered sacrifices for their dead hero's soul. I thought my heart would break.

A few days later a quick note arrived from Terracina, where Nero and Drusus, who had been serving with their units, joined their mother, along with Germanicus's brother, Claudius. The emperor and Livia were conspicuously absent. "What is going on here?" Mother asked. "Do they consider mourning beneath their dignity, or do they fear that the public gaze would detect insincerity in their faces? I am frightened for Agrippina, frightened for us all."

Anxious to discuss this new development with Pilate, I pulled myself from the couch. Turning, I saw a red blotch where I had been lying and was suddenly, sickly aware of a sticky dampness between my legs. I screamed for Rachel, who in turn dispatched another slave to flee in search of Petronius.

Lying on the couch with my feet elevated, the wait seemed an eternity. Where was that doctor? Why didn't he come? Petronius's manner, when he finally arrived was hearty, falsely so, I thought. "The bleeding has stopped. There is nothing to worry about," he insisted.

Petronius handed Rachel a pouch of crushed poppy seeds. "This will calm the *domina.* Mix it with milk and honey," he directed her. "Most important, the lady Claudia must remain in bed."

His smiling manner did nothing to allay my fears. I dispatched Rachel immediately to the Iseneum with a note begging the mystagogue for a potion. "Dear Isis, please do not desert me now," I prayed again and again and again.

DURING THE FOLLOWING TWO WEEKS I NEVER LEFT MY bed. Sometimes Pilate ate his meals with me but more often business took him elsewhere. The sense of loneliness and loss was scarcely bearable. Finally one rainy morning our chief house slave returned panting from the wharf. He had run all the way. Arms trembling with weakness, I pulled myself up, hands trembling as I unrolled a scroll bearing the royal seal. The handwriting brought a lump to my throat. "We are in Rome at last, surrounded by friends. Each has a story to tell, all so sad." I struggled to make out the rest. Tears had washed out portions of Agrippina's bold script. My own eyes stung as I pieced together the account of what followed the eventual confirmation of Germanicus's death: "Altars destroyed . . . newly born children unacknowledged . . . December upon us . . . Saturnalia . . . no heart to celebrate." At the end she wrote, "It is as though each family mourns a beloved patriarch."

A letter from Father described the final desolate dawn when Germanicus's ashes were taken to the Mausoleum of Augustus. Streets were full, Mars Field ablaze with torches. Despite the closely packed bodies, silence hung like a pall over the throng. "It was a mockery," he wrote. "Not only was the emperor absent, but he had made no state preparations. No family masks were carried, no effigy of Germanicus. No one spoke from the Oration Platform, no state funeral hymns were sung. People from all walks of life, soldiers in uniform, patricians, freedmen, officials, and slaves drew together in common sorrow and outrage.

"Nothing and no one can restore Germanicus to his friends and country," *Tata* concluded. "Just last evening I overheard an old shopkeeper muttering as he fastened down his door, 'It is as though one heard that the sun would never shine again.' "

My eyes closed wearily as I lay back against the satin cushions of my couch. The scroll slipped from my grasp; I was too tired to retrieve it. The unknown merchant's sentiments were easy to understand. The agonizing cramping that had wracked my body was over, the bleeding that had nearly cost my life had ceased, but the son longed for with such hope and expectation was lost forever. I had miscarried.

CHAPTER

15

The Secret Potion

No one, least of all Pilate, understood. "You were only five months along," he reminded me.

Even Rachel suggested, "You can have another child."

Pilate was eager to get on with that, but Petronius advised against it. "There is no reason you cannot have a fine family, but give Claudia some time. You would be wise to wait six months."

Unready to conceive another baby while my arms still ached for the lost one, I felt grateful. Pilate might say it was not yet a person, but to me the lost infant was the product of our early passion. No other child could be *that* child. Why had Isis forsaken me? Days and nights passed like black oxen. Locked within myself, I sat silent and alone. What was there to say? Who would I say it to? Even Hecate, my cat, deserted me. I roused myself to wander the house, calling her name. There was no answer.

Matters of state claimed Pilate with increasing frequency. I spent my evenings in the moon-watching pavilion, a marble *nymphaneum* that I had commissioned as a diversion shortly after my parents' departure. The small circular building with its partially open ceiling was supported by six fluted columns, a small, gently splashing fountain at the base of each. Chandeliers suspended from the colonnade ceiling illuminated the garden; and beyond, the delicate amber glow of small bronze lamps lit winding pathways that descended to the river. The previous autumn I had conferred closely with the best gardener in Antioch, taking into account both the color of the blossoms and the perfume combinations I wanted to achieve. Now, with the coming of spring, I saw those plans taking shape.

One balmy night as I lay musing on my cushioned couch, Hecate appeared beside me. In her mouth was a tiny striped kitten. She deposited the mewling ball of fur at my feet. Within minutes a family of three was presented for inspection. Rebirth, renewal . . . Wasn't spring the time for it? I gently stroked a fluffy yellow kitten that resembled its ebony mother not at all. "Is your new love a lion?" I asked Hecate. She glanced at me sideways, green eyes glinting proudly.

The following day I ordered immediate construction of an outdoor pool. At its center would be a marble statue by Pilate's favorite sculptor, Marius. It was he who had captured Marcella's essence so perfectly and had also, rather amazingly, combined my father-in-law's face with the body of Apollo. This time his subject was Venus rising from her oyster shell, a reminder to the world, and most particularly to Pilate, that my ancestral line was said to descend from the love goddess herself. I planned a special dinner for him, a surprise and celebration. I would ignore Petronius's warnings. More than three months had passed since the stillbirth; surely that was long enough.

I made certain that all Pilate's favorite dishes were served. A trio of lute players performed as we dined, then followed us out to the garden. The new pool and statue had been covered during construction. Now at last the unveiling. I looked up at Pilate expectantly as slaves pulled back the white sheets. The marble statue shone in the moonlight.

"Very beautiful, Claudia. You must plan a party here."

"I have planned one . . . for tonight." I nodded toward Psyche, who approached us with a silver tray, bearing two brimming wineglasses. The lute players, joined now by a flutist, broke into a new selection, soft but lilting.

"Sorry, Claudia, very sorry. I have an engagement with Sentius."

"Must you go?"

"I'm afraid so. Possible trouble brewing on the Parthian border. We have much to discuss. I am sorry." He kissed me lightly on the forehead. "We will celebrate another night."

My eyes stung with sudden tears. How foolish of me. "Of course," I agreed, looking away.

"Perhaps it's time you ordered new gowns," Rachel suggested on the fourth night that she and I played board games together in my sleeping room.

"Perhaps so . . ."

We set out by litter the following day. "What a city!" I exclaimed, pulling back the curtains to admire flowering trees dappled with sunlight. Antioch, with its wide streets and perfumed crowds, was extraordinarily well favored by both climate and location. Small wonder its citizens were said to be the most luxury-loving in the world, living for little but self-indulgence. For the first time in months I felt lighthearted, aware suddenly of my good fortune to be who and where I was. Isis was with me again—I felt her.

I easily found the fabrics I wanted: violet linen for a gown, silken gauze the shade of smoke for a *palla,* rich satin the color of garnets for new couch cushions. I selected a scroll of exquisitely illustrated erotic poetry and savored the thought of unrolling it with Pilate. The cover was rich maroon, his favorite. I bought pretty new tunics for Rachel and a moonstone collar for Hecate. I found peacocks for the garden and exotic fish and lilies for the new pool. I could scarcely wait until evening when slaves would deliver them.

"How long has it been since you visited the baths?" Rachel asked.

"Far too long," I admitted. "It has been ages since I've seen anyone. I don't even know who they're talking about these days."

Though all the women I knew had baths in their homes, most regarded the public ones, particularly the fashionable Daphaneum, as a kind of social club. Here they gathered to see and be seen while bathing and being massaged. If the latest gossip was not entertainment enough, singers, dancers, and poets enlivened the afternoons.

In the Daphaneum's frescoed anteroom, Rachel and I separated, she going off to join other slaves in a small pool of their own. An attendant led me to a private cubicle where another woman stood waiting to undress me. How many bodies had she seen? I wondered as the slave deftly removed my *chiton* and *palla*. Face impassive, she raised a silver ewer and poured water over my shoulders, then seated me beside a large marble basin. Another slave joined us and the two of them lathered me with fragrant soap, then briskly pumiced my body. The thought of being prepared for Pilate made a pleasant sensation even more so. The misunderstandings and sadness that had somehow divided us were being washed away. Pilate would find me pleasing to the touch.

My mind drifted languorously, recalling his smooth, hard body. I thought with longing of the early days of our marriage and assured myself it could be like that again. It *would* be like that again. The sound of laughter coming from the cubicle next to mine intruded on my reverie. I thought one voice familiar, but couldn't identify it.

"I NEVER DID UNDERSTAND WHAT HE SAW IN HER," THE woman was saying. "It's not as though she is beautiful."

"Be fair, she has good bones and those big eyes," the other woman argued.

"Cheekbones aren't everything. As for her eyes, I don't find them at all attractive. She looks lost most of the time, or off in another world."

"Some men like that. He must have once—enough to marry her."

"Did. He *did* like that," the first speaker emphasized. "I wonder if she knows yet?"

"Not likely. I am sure they are discreet. Can you imagine if anyone found out! Marcia's the new governor's wife."

The voices tantalized me. Who were they? And who was the unfortunate wife? I pitied anyone with the glamorous Marcia Sentius for a rival. I was tempted to get up and look out. Only a voluptuous lethargy stayed me. The voices faded as the women moved on to the *frigidarium* for a cool plunge.

A few minutes later, a slave wrapped me in a sheet of cool Egyptian linen. Stepping into the thick-soled sandals she had brought to protect my feet from the heated floor, I followed her to the *tepidarium.* Light streamed through the mist from perforations in the central dome supported by large Corinthian columns and green marble arches that shone like jade. Some twenty women splashed and played in the great green pool. More lounged about the sides, sipping wine while slaves dressed their hair or rubbed their bodies with perfumed oils. Across the pool, two women lay on their backs while slaves applied gold paint to their toenails. The effect was stunning, even if it did last only a day.

Now I realized why one voice had sounded familiar. The woman was Sabina Maximus. I had heard that simpering giggle often enough when I watched her with Pilate at the races. How long ago that seemed, yet scarcely a year had passed.

Just then Sabina and her confidante looked up, startled by the sight of me. I caught the amused smile that passed between them and wanted to die.

But of course I did not. Somehow I found myself smiling, waving in response to their effusive greetings. I signaled to a poetess waiting nearby to read to me, then sank down on a marble slab, eyes closed, pretending to listen. A masseuse's hands moved expertly over my body. "*Domina* is very tense," she murmured. "Relax . . . relax." Relax? My heart was pounding like a wild creature in a trap. "Is *Domina* all right?" the masseuse asked. "I am fine," I assured her, "just fine." I might make it through the next hour if only Sabina and her friend didn't come over to my side of the pool, if only I didn't have to talk to them.

It was not to be. In minutes the two had sauntered around the large pool and settled themselves at my side. Sabina, full of kisses and compliments, hugged me profusely, then introduced me to her eager friend. "I have heard so much about you!" the woman enthused. *I knew she had.*

The poetess stood silently waiting for instructions. I tossed her a gold coin. "Thank you. Perhaps later." I smiled apologetically. In an instant she was gone. How I longed to follow. The next two hours seemed interminable. A virtual prisoner under the masseuse's practiced fingers, I tried to remain calm. When Sabina and her friend asked pointed questions about Pilate, I chatted brightly, describing his generosity and devotion. I was determined to give them no further cause to pity me, yet even as I laughed and sparkled, another part of my mind, at first numbed by shock, slowly came alive.

Pilate was the core of my existence. How could I mean so little to him? I forced myself to consider: Absorbed in my own pain, had I carelessly opened the door to a rival? Marcia Sentius would be the sort to take advantage of such a situation. A chill settled over me as I thought of the worldly, sophisticated Marcia, a woman as beautiful as she was rapacious. How could I possibly compete with her? I couldn't. *I must.*

"So, you have returned to the Iseneum at last." the mystagogue's olive eyes, luminous and almond-shaped, regarded me reflectively. Shafts of late afternoon sun sparkled on the anteroom's brilliant frescoes and exquisitely wrought mosaic floors. Everywhere I looked I saw the trials of Isis recreated by the finest artisans in the land. Their masterworks displayed the adventures of a divine being who had experienced every tragedy a wife might imagine, yet Isis had not only survived but triumphed. Surely I had come to the right place.

"I've been ill," I explained to the holy man. "Actually, this is my first day out of the house."

"And to think you came directly to us! Your devotion to the goddess is touching."

I felt myself flushing. "Not only that."

"Then tell me what you are seeking."

I looked directly into the mystagogue's eyes. "My baby died, despite your potions, despite my prayers to Isis."

"I was saddened to hear of it, but one should never question the goddess's wisdom . . ."

"Must I lose Pilate as well? I won him with your spell. Now give me something stronger. He must be mine forever."

The mystagogue shook his head silently.

"I don't believe you!" I exclaimed. "The spell you gave me before worked perfectly. The match was against all odds, my own mother said as much. Pilate might have had the wealthiest woman in Antioch, but chose me. For a time he loved me. I *know* he loved me. Now I need something stronger than words. Rachel says that you have other things—charms . . ."

"Such things are not for you," the holy man told me. "They bind the one who uses them far more than the recipient."

"What difference does that make? I am already bound. I love my husband, but being his wife means nothing if his interests are with someone else."

"His interests now, perhaps. But he will return, I assure you. He will always return."

"That's not enough! I want him to love me as I love him."

The mystagogue raised a silky eyebrow. " 'Love' him? Is that what you call it?"

"Of course that's what I call it. I adore him and want his love in return. Is that too much to ask?"

The mystagogue inclined his small, well-chiseled head, regarding me speculatively. "Love means many things. Your definition and that of your husband may be quite different. Tell me, instead, of your meditation. Once you were faithful. Do you no longer seek to attune yourself to the goddess?"

"For a time I did, but after I lost my child, the sadness was so intense—Why should I? Isis has forsaken me!"

He said nothing, merely watched me with his strange dark eyes.

With an effort, I lowered my voice. "Lately I've taken to going to a shrine I built in my garden. I hoped to regain what I once had. I will try, I *want* to try," I assured him, "but for now—please—surely you can help me." I looked up, pleading.

The mystagogue shook his head wearily. "What you ask is not only foolish but dangerous. You must learn that for yourself."

I relaxed, realizing that I had won the first battle.

"It will cost you," he warned me.

"Anything." I gestured to Rachel to open the soft leather pouch she wore fastened to her belt.

"Yes, money, of course, a lot of money; but you will forfeit much more than sesterces. That you must learn for yourself."

I nodded to Rachel, who opened the pouch and shook out some thirty or more gold pieces. "No, give it all to him," I instructed her impatiently.

She handed the pouch to the mystagogue.

"Is that enough?" I asked as he emptied the contents onto the table. "I can send for more."

"Enough for now." The mystagogue swept the gold sesterces into a drawer. "Remain here," he instructed me and left the room.

Finally he returned with a temple woman bearing two glass vials. "You," he said to Rachel, "will pour some of this"—he gestured to one container—"into your mistress's bath and later massage her body with the contents of the other."

"You"—he turned to me—"will resume the incantation that I gave you before. Recite it seven times a day."

"Oh, thank you," I exclaimed. "I can't thank you enough."

"Nor should you try." He shook his head, waving me away. "Go now and may the goddess protect you from yourself."

When I returned home, Psyche had a message for me. Pilate was dining out. *He's with Marcia, I know it!* The vision of them together tortured me but then I reminded myself: With Governor Sentius at home, it would be impossible for Pilate to spend the night with her. He would return eventually and I would be waiting.

I ate lightly, then slipped out to the moon-watching pavilion where I repeated the incantation.

When he drinks, when he eats, when he has intercourse with someone else, I will bewitch his heart, I will bewitch his breath, I will bewitch his member, I will bewitch his innermost part. Wherever and whenever I desire until he comes to me, until I know what is in his heart, what he does and what he thinks, until he is mine. Quickly, quickly! Now! Now!

For the first time, I savored the spell's full power. Before my marriage, I realized, I'd scarcely known what I was saying. Now that I had learned the ways of love, the spell took on a new intensity that I couldn't have imagined the previous year. Thinking of Pilate's body entwined with Marcia's, I felt the power of my jealousy was a potent force adding impetus to my words. Again and again I repeated the incantation.

Returning to my quarters, I found Rachel waiting expectantly. "It is time," I said, my voice almost a whisper. We entered the bath, where she poured a few drops from the vial into the steamy water. I savored the heady fragrance, drawing it in with deep breaths. Never in my life had I encountered such a perfume. It was neither sweet nor heavy, yet it subtly piqued my mind and body. Like a delicate wine, insidiously intoxicating, the effect worked slowly on my senses. I imagined how the scent would affect Pilate, arousing him slowly, surely, persistently.

When I stepped into the bath the steam drifted around me in a misty cloud. Sinking into the water, I relaxed while the beguiling aroma wafted over me. At last I rose and Rachel wrapped me in a soft linen towel, drying me carefully.

Indolently, I moved into my *cubiculum*. Lying on the couch, I stretched languorously and closed my eyes as Rachel's hands moved over me. The oil on her fingers had the same scent as the perfume. Working from head to heel, over my entire body, Rachel rubbed me gently until the fragrant liquid had disappeared into the pores of my skin. Then she massaged the flesh, kneading it firmly until I glowed all over and my breasts were proud and pointing.

There was a soft knock; Rachel left me to answer it. In a moment she was back. "*Dominus* has returned."

"Leave me now," I instructed. My voice sounded soft to me and husky.

I lay quiet, eyes closed, listening absently to the sound of the slave's retreating footsteps. Like a sleepwalker, I got up and crossed to the mirror. The flickering lamplight cast amber shadows across my naked body as I unpinned my hair. Masses of thick curls spilled down over my shoulders. *Leave it like this, he likes it loose, he likes . . .*

I picked up the silken gauze I had bought earlier that day for a *palla* and draped it about my body, fastening it loosely at one shoulder. I was pleased with my image, a slim column of smoke reflected in the polished metal. A sudden warmth stole along the hidden surface of my flesh. Slowly, I turned and walked from the room.

Pausing at Pilate's door, I summoned the full power of the spell, then pushed firmly. He stood at the window, looking out onto the garden. As he turned, his eyes widened at the sight of me. "You are very lovely, Claudia," he spoke softly.

I said nothing but stood just inside the door. He raised a brow questioningly. "What is it?" In a few quick strides he had crossed the room. He lifted my chin, looked into my eyes. My arms swept up around his neck, my body arching against his. Blindly, eyes closed, I sought his lips. After a time Pilate gently broke my grip and stood back to look at me. His blue eyes glittered.

"I love you, my husband," I whispered as he undid the clasp of my *palla,* "so much I love you—so very, very much."

CHAPTER 16

Two Trials

Pilate and I lay together on the couch, legs entwined, opening a scroll. Once again we lived a life of companionable domesticity. The potion had worked beyond my wildest dreams. I recited the incantation faithfully while Rachel made twice weekly trips to the Iseneum for magic balms. I was certain my marriage depended upon Isis's grace. Once the goddess allowed me to conceive a son and carry it to term, Pilate would surely be mine.

The spring and early summer had been marked by unseasonable storms. Ships had been lost at sea. Now, at last, one had reached Antioch bearing a scroll written several weeks before. My heart gave a happy tug as I recognized the loops and flourishes of Mother's hand.

> ***What can Tiberius be thinking! Instead of imprisonment, Piso and Plancina are at home, casual and carefree as though charges of murder and treason had never been***

leveled against them. Now they plan a dinner party. That ostentatious house of theirs overlooks the forum where all can watch . . . thousands of sesterces being spent on gold paint. It is an outrage, an absolute outrage!

"Look here." Pilate pointed further down the scroll. "What's that about Martina?"

I folded back the papyrus and read aloud: "We have just received word from Brundisium that the witch Martina died shortly after disembarking. A tiny vial of poison was found clenched in her hand."

"That's bad." Pilate frowned. "She was the chief witness against Piso."

"What do you think happened to her—suicide or murder?"

He shrugged lightly. "It hardly matters. Plancina's involvement is lost forever. The mystery of Germanicus's death may never be resolved now."

I put down the scroll. "The nerve of those people!"

Pilate retrieved it. "Your mother tends to be outspoken."

"Outspoken!" I drew back. "You know—everyone knows—that Piso was responsible. Tiberius is linked to it too. I know he is."

"My dear"—Pilate stroked my shoulder lightly—"*knowing* a thing and committing it to papyrus are quite different. Your mother has not only placed herself in jeopardy but now her words could be used against us."

"Don't you want to know what's happening? My father swore to avenge—"

"Yes, yes, I know. Your father was Germanicus's man.

Everyone's well aware of that, too aware. Marcus would be wise to forge new alliances and we as well."

I tried to keep my voice steady. "You mean alliances with Tiberius?"

"One must be practical." Pilate's finger traced a lazy circle around my breast. "Vengeance won't restore Germanicus to life."

A WEEK LATER, IN THE MIDST OF A DRIVING RAINSTORM, a sailor appeared at the door with a scroll under his cloak. Soon he was inside the kitchen drinking a cup of undiluted wine while Pilate and I poured over a letter from *Tata.* Tiberius had begun the trial with instructions to the Senate: "Did Piso cause Germanicus's death or merely rejoice in it? If there is proof of murder, so be it, but if Piso merely failed to respect his senior, that is not a crime, though I—in my deep sorrow—will renounce his friendship, closing my door to him forever."

"Tiberius is so sanctimonious! Just listen to this: 'He asked the Senate, "Did Piso incite his troops to mutiny? Did he make war to recover the province for himself or are these lies spread by his accusers?"' His *accusers*—that means *Tata* and Agrippina. How can Tiberius say such things?"

"Very easily, my dear. The emperor can say anything."

I hated Pilate's condescending tone, as though speaking to a child, but I didn't give up. "What about this—Tiberius's summation—it's disgusting: 'I grieve for my nephew and always will. But I offer the accused every opportunity to produce evidence to establish his innocence or Germanicus's wrong.'" Germanicus's wrong! "Who is he trying to fool? Everyone knows what happened."

"Let's just hope none of it reflects on our position." Pilate kissed me lightly on the forehead and went off to meet with Governor Sentius.

My heart felt empty as I rolled up the scroll. My husband's cynicism frightened me almost as much as Tiberius's culpability. Germanicus had been his friend as well as a generous patron. Did that count for nothing?

The winter storms continued, big thunderheads rolled up over the sea. Confined to the house by rain, I thought of little but the trial. How would its outcome affect my parents? Pilate's words sprang often to mind. Roman alliances were treacherous, a false move often fatal.

Another scroll arrived, this one from Agrippina, her bold, obliquely slanted script praising my father, a chief witness against Piso in the Senate hearings. *Tata* had described the proconsul's mysterious death in detail, not forgetting the outspoken pleasure both Piso and Plancina had shown. Finally, he had reminded the Senate of the war the former governor had launched after the success of his murderous plot. The evidence was undeniable, only the poisoning charge remained to be refuted.

Piso is so insolent, so sure of himself. "Are you calling me a magician?" he asked, all the while shuffling a small bundle of scrolls, flashing the royal seals so that anyone sitting nearby could see them. Your father asked that they be opened, but Tiberius hastily ruled against the motion. The Senate watched in amazement as the defendant passed the scrolls to the emperor. If anyone doubted there was a connection between the two, they knew it then. Surely we were seeing the very orders that cost Germanicus his life.

"What a fool!" Pilate laughed, looking over my shoulder. "Piso has just signed his own death warrant."

"Wait, there's more—"

At the very moment the Senate was on its feet, backing your father, demanding that the scrolls be opened, a messenger announced that Piso's statues had been torn down and dumped beside bodies of executed criminals. Tiberius hastily adjourned the session. You should have seen him, Claudia, the man was purple with anger. Much as Tiberius may want to protect his accomplice, this is a mandate from the people. Plancina has upheld her husband's innocence—swearing to share his fate whatever that may be—but this afternoon, instead of going home with him, she went off with Livia.

The trial was all I thought about as a series of violent storms closed the port. The suspense was unbearable. Finally, Pilate came home with a scroll that had been carried aboard a newly arrived military ship. "It's from Selene," he said.

I saw the seal was broken. Pilate hadn't waited. I looked at him with surprise and then alarm as a frown creased his forehead. Mother's letter picked up the thread of the trial, which, I realized from the date, was already history. The message had taken six weeks to reach us. Seals can be broken, then repaired. Who else might have read it? I was beginning to think like Pilate. My eyes anxiously scanned the scroll. An angry mob waiting Piso's arrival . . . Tiberius suddenly hostile, aggressive, conducting the interrogation himself . . . Question after question . . . Piso a broken man carried out of the courtroom . . . his next day's defense written in a trembling hand . . . Piso discovered at dawn, throat cut, sword at his side . . . a sham investigation of Plancina . . . Two days and then dismissal . . . Livia's triumphant smile.

I looked up at my husband. "How could Livia, Germanicus's own grandmother, consort with his murderess?"

Pilate shook his head impatiently. "Claudia, Claudia, she's a tyrant. Don't you know that by now?" After a pause he added, "I wouldn't care to be in Agrippina's sandals."

And what about my sandals? Once so proud of my connections, did Pilate now consider me a liability?

SITTING BEFORE THE COSMETIC JARS THAT MULTIPLIED daily upon my dressing table, I gave a surprised shriek as the first eyebrow was plucked. After that I sat patiently. A new slave worked with the quick, polished delicacy of an artist, dusting my face lightly with powdered white lead, plucking and darkening the newly arched brows with antimony, shading my cheeks with rouge and smoothly applying accents of kohl to my eyelids.

With Rachel's assistance, she gathered my hair and bound it loosely back, securing it with jeweled combs and plaiting the remaining locks into one thick braid. This was deftly woven with seed pearls, then placed in a serpent's coil on top of my head and sprinkled with gold dust. Sipping snow-chilled wine, I regarded the stranger who looked back at me from the mirror's polished metal surface. In half an hour I'd been transformed into a creature of sparkle and artifice, a worldly woman, at least in appearance.

Inwardly, I was torn with doubts. My stomach fluttered with nervousness. With each new garment I bought, each new alteration to my appearance, however subtle, I worried—what if Pilate didn't like me that way? And now the governor's banquet . . . Marcia would be there, of course, flirting with Pilate, all the while watching me with those cold, mocking eyes. My hands felt moist as I reached for an almond-stuffed fig on the silver tray beside me.

"You look beautiful, *Domina,*" Rachel assured me.

"Yes? Really? Unfortunately, there are so many beautiful women, *stunning* women. You saw them at our party last night. Pilate was surrounded." I sighed, remembering the long bare arms, the dark-lined eyes, the laughing, reddened mouths.

"He was their host," Rachel reminded me. "What would you have him do?"

I heard approaching footsteps. It was Pilate, I knew his brisk step. As he entered the room, I rose quickly to greet him. "Do you like my hair?" I asked eagerly. He took the finger of one of my hands and turned me slowly about, while I looked back over my shoulder, unwilling to miss the slightest expression on his face.

Pilate seemed surprised. "Yes, my dear, you're lovely. You're always lovely, but you do look different . . ."

"Isn't that good?" I asked, my face stiff under its armor of paint. "Surely you don't want to see the same old Claudia night after night."

"You are never the same old Claudia, you constantly surprise me." Pilate picked up my new *palla* made from a fabric that looked like molten gold. "That's the thing I love most about you," he said, placing it about my shoulders.

THE GOVERNOR'S HILLTOP HOME WAS SUMPTUOUS. Crossing the mosaic floor, a swirl of rose and lime, lavender and gold, I felt dizzy. There was Marcia, her lips wine-coated, dark and startling against porcelain skin. I saw the malice in her amber eyes and realized that the liaison must be over and Pilate the one who ended it. Suddenly the evening became a personal triumph. With a hand resting lightly on my husband's arm, I moved easily from one group to the next.

In this luxurious enclave far removed from the noise and smells of the city, talk centered around recent events in Rome. Sentius shocked us all by announcing that Tiberius had condemned the venerable Titus Maximus, one of Agrippina's staunchest champions. The patrician had been executed without a trial, his body hurled down the Stairs of Mourning, a ritual punishment for traitors, then cast into the Tiber.

"What reason did he give?" I asked, pretending that I hadn't felt Pilate's warning nudge.

"The emperor's will is reason enough," the governor reminded me.

"My, it would appear that friendship with Agrippina could be injurious to one's health." Marcia stood at her husband's side watching me, her words almost a purr.

A sense of foreboding for my parents and Agrippina overcame my earlier pleasure.

While I was chatting with Governor Sentius, my gaze wandered beyond him to a far corner where Pilate talked animatedly with Aurelia Perreius, pure and perfect, flawless as a cut gem, and married to the wealthiest knight in Antioch—some said in all of Syria. Her tranquil poise was broken suddenly by a bubbling laugh. Oh, what was so terribly amusing? I longed to interrupt them, to claim him, but forced myself to continue a conversation with Sentius. Finally, I succeeded in bringing it to a courteous close, but by then Pilate was out of sight. The room felt stuffy, the sound of so many voices oppressive. I wanted to get away, if only for a moment.

My jewel-encrusted sandals made soft crunching sounds on the walkway as I moved rapidly between close-trimmed box hedges, laurel trees, pomegranates and ancient pines. I sat down on a secluded bench overlooking a pool. Opposite me, a marble Venus looked down upon a bed of pale pink roses. I thought of Mother, who loved the color pink above all others and revered Venus for the gifts the goddess had bestowed upon her. If guilt by association was Tiberius's game, then surely my parents were a prime target. I wished Mother was with me, safe and wise. There was so much that I longed to talk to her about. I had never felt more alone.

Glancing up, I saw a man standing in the shadow of the archway. How long had he been there watching? "Who—who's there?" I demanded, rising to my feet.

He moved forward into the light of a flaming torch. "Don't you remember me?"

"No." I hesitated uncertainly, wrapping my *palla* closer about my shoulders. "Are you a guest in this house?"

"Yes, certainly."

"I didn't see you."

"But I saw you." His voice was deep with a slight accent I couldn't identify.

He was handsome in a rough-hewn way and quite tall, possibly a head taller than Pilate. There was something . . . familiar? Creases bracketed the stranger's mouth as he smiled. "It was a long time ago. Rome. The games. You lifted your thumb for me."

Memories flooded back, engulfing me. Livia and Caligula's scorn, my panic. The young gladiator's face, smiling, confident, so, so . . . *masculine.* Then the sudden certainty that he would win. The excitement, the bloody conflict. Two triumphs, his and mine. "Oh, my goddess! It cannot be. You are not *that* gladiator!"

He drew closer, bowed slightly. "I am Holtan. Did you never know my name?"

I brushed back a tendril of hair that had escaped from my elaborate headdress. "Of course, I've never forgotten it, but the Holtan I remember was hardly more than a boy. He was, I recall, a slave."

"Boys grow up. This one is no longer a slave."

I looked into his eyes. "What are you doing here?"

"I came to meet you."

I stared at him in shocked silence.

"Why should that surprise you? I have always wondered about the little girl who predicted my victory."

"I remember that day too—you've no idea—so much happened afterward. Everything changed for me, for my family, almost overnight." I tilted my head to look at him. "What about you? Why have you come to Antioch?"

"I was lucky. You were lucky for me. The last time you saw me was the first of many victories. Eventually I bought my freedom and a few other things." He smiled again briefly. "I came to Antioch for the games. I fought yesterday."

"And won, obviously. I wish I'd known."

"You don't attend the games?"

"Not often." I fell silent, studying him. He was dressed in white, his tunic and toga of the finest Egyptian linen judging from how they draped. The toga was held in place by a ruby brooch, the largest ruby I had ever seen. "You must have everything you desire now."

"And so must you."

I shook my head, smiling at the irony of his words.

"You still have your beautiful smile."

I fought a foolish desire to run my fingers over the cleft in Holtan's chin, to touch the indentations in his cheeks. "Women must find you irresistible."

He shrugged. "Some enjoy flirting with danger."

"What about you? Why continue to risk your life now that you are free?"

"Why not? It is one way—the only way for most of us—to make a lot of sesterces in a hurry. You wouldn't know about that, you have always had wealth."

"Not always, I assure you."

"But now."

"Now I don't find sesterces very important. They buy nothing that really matters."

"Like your husband's loyalty?"

I felt suddenly ill. Was my life such public knowledge that even a wandering gladiator knew of it?

"No one told me," he said as though reading my thoughts.

"Then how did you know?"

"I saw you as I came in. Your eyes so intent, watching him with that blond woman."

"You saw too much."

"In the arena you learn to read signs. A shifting glance means life or death."

I paused a moment. "Will you be in Antioch long?"

"I should leave tomorrow for Alexandria . . . unless . . ."

"Impossible!"

"*You* are impossible."

Our eyes caught and held. "It would never have been possible," I said, wondering if that were true.

"Your husband is a fool."

"I beg your pardon!"

"A fool to take you lightly—to cause you pain. A fool," Holtan repeated, his voice thick with anger.

I brushed his arm lightly, looked away, fearful of tears.

He placed his hands on my shoulders. "Pilate merely plays. I know his kind. He likes rich women, likes their power. Perhaps he uses that to his advantage. It is only a game. You are the one he loves. How could he otherwise?"

My eyes met his. For a second I swayed forward, then caught myself and broke free.

Not daring to look back, I ran across the garden, back to the lighted room and the sound of Pilate's voice.

CHAPTER

17

The Dream Cure

I loved Pilate, I hated Pilate—hated my dependence on him. I was scarcely aware of myself except as reflected in his cobalt eyes. Again and again, pulling him tightly against me, drawing him into me, I thought of the child I wanted desperately, the child that would hold him forever.

One morning, rising from breakfast, he kissed me lightly, gathered his stylus and tablet and set off. Pausing in the doorway, he looked back. "Plutonius and I are going boar hunting this afternoon. We may not return until tomorrow."

"You never mentioned it." *Was the potion wearing off?*

"Come, come!" A hint of impatience flickered in his eyes. "You look like an orphan, not my Claudia. Surely you can find a means of occupying yourself." He frowned, still watching me. "Think about that trip to Pergamum. Plutonius and Sempronia are leaving next week."

Plutonius, Piso's former client. Not to be trusted, his fawning wife no better.

"I don't like them."

"Plutonius is devoted. He will watch over you. You can't go alone."

"I don't want to go at all."

"But you will go—for me and the dynasty we will found." Pilate took my shoulders lightly in his hands, kissed my nose, released me as suddenly, and was off.

That afternoon, acting on an impulse, I visited the Iseneum. To my surprise, a priestess took me directly to the mystagogue's library. Three walls were lined with cedarwood cabinets, packed with rolls of papyri stacked end on end from floor to ceiling, the other taken up by an altar to Isis.

"I've been expecting you," he said, glancing up from a scroll.

"How can that be?" I exclaimed. "It was only an hour ago that I decided—"

"I knew," he said simply, setting the scroll down on a polished rosewood table.

My heart ached with longing for such attunement to the goddess.

"Once you too were close to Isis," he said as though reading my mind.

"I thought I was, but now I am bound to him."

"As you seek to bind *him*?" The mystagogue's voice was silken.

"Are you mocking me?"

He rose from his desk. "It is a lovely afternoon, let's take a stroll."

Curious, I followed him down a broad passage set with mosaic tiles into a sunny garden. Three priestesses, reclining beside a large pool, smiled at us over the tops of their scrolls.

Nearby a fountain splashed. The mystagogue led me past an extensive herb garden tended by two more priestesses to a secluded cypress grove. We seated ourselves before a small pond. A half smile played about his lips as he turned to me. "You were speaking of your husband . . ."

"Your potion worked well. I'm grateful." I paused, looking down. "Pilate is very attractive to women. Every minute that he is away I wonder—" The familiar desperation swept over me. I looked up at him pleadingly. "If there was a child . . . then I could be sure of him. My doctor believes that I will heal in time. All he ever says is, 'Let nature take her course.' "

The mystagogue nodded. "I cannot quarrel with that advice, but apparently you do or you would not be here."

I watched him intently. "You must have a potion or incantation, something that will help. Nature will never take her course if Pilate divorces me for not giving him a son. Such things happen. Pilate can do anything he pleases. With Father so far away there would be no one to intercede for me."

"Has he spoken of divorce?"

"No," I acknowledged, "but there's no doubt he wants sons."

"There is something else, I think," the mystagogue prompted.

"Yes, there is," I admitted. "Pilate wants me to visit the Asklepion in Pergamum."

"Why not? It is the most renowned healing center in the world. One hears every day of miracles performed there. Asklepios cures many through dreams. Of all people, you should be a candidate."

"I would be gone at least two months; what if Pilate fell in love while I was away?"

The mystagogue shrugged his slim shoulders. "So? By your return he might as easily have fallen out."

"I couldn't bear that! I love my husband very much." I felt my cheeks flame. "I came here because I thought you would understand my feelings. Instead you laugh at them."

"Your feelings are anything but amusing. I find them a tragic waste."

My voice dropped. "Once you helped . . ."

"Twice I helped and now you ask me again. If you recall, I warned against both the incantation and the potion."

"But you gave them to me," I reminded him. "Help me again—this one last time. I'll do anything, pay anything. Several times since I lost my baby I've thought I was pregnant and then wasn't. There must be something you can do."

"There is nothing that I *will* do." The mystagogue rose.

"Then there *is* nothing . . ."

"I did not say that." He touched my shoulder lightly. I looked up, my heart filling with hope. He shook his head once again. "What has eluded you will be found at Pergamum."

"Are you saying that Asklepios will enable me to have a child?"

"I'm saying that Asklepios is a mighty god, perhaps he can cure even you."

ONCE BOUND FOR PERGAMUM, I PRAYED OFTEN TO Asklepios. The god's mortal mother, while pregnant with Apollo's child, took another mortal for a lover. Wild with jealousy, Apollo killed her, snatching the unborn child from her body. Their son, Asklepios, was raised by centaurs who taught the boy healing skills he later far exceeded. With such a human background, wouldn't the god understand my problem? I prayed that he would.

The voyage seemed to take forever. One, two, three days passed . . . The farther we were from Antioch the more authoritarian Plutonius grew. His increasing arrogance was unsettling. Sempronia was merely boring. Boring and nosy. Fortunately, both were gamblers who gathered eagerly with others at a far end of the deck. Sometimes the cries "Jupiter!" or "Dogs!" for high or low dice throws floated back in the wind. The weather was clear and bright with a light breeze, the rocky Lycian coast breathtaking. Pine trees stretched to the water's edge. Mountain peaks, some snowcapped even in summer, shadowed sheltered bays, but again and again, my thoughts turned to Pilate. Did he blame me for the loss of our child? Was my stillbirth somehow related to Germanicus's death?

When the *Persephone* stopped to take on provisions at Halicarnassus my heart sank. We would be in port a whole day—one more away from Pilate.

"There is a famous shrine," Rachel reminded me. "You could pray there."

We eluded Plutonius and Sempronia and set off like errant schoolgirls. Our destination was the tomb of King Mausoleus, an elaborate resting place known the world over as the Mausoleum. I wanted to explore it on my own, free from Sempronia's prattle. The multi-tiered ziggurat was not only the largest building I had ever seen but also the most elaborate. Brilliantly white, the tomb towered more than a hundred feet above us.

"Very splendid—and none the worse for almost four hundred years," Rachel panted when we had climbed the lofty brick podium. "Artemesia must have loved her husband very much."

Pausing to catch my breath, I stared up at the colonnaded temple topping the edifice. Its opulence was staggering—every square inch crowded with friezes and statues. At its peak, Mausoleus rode a golden chariot into eternity. "A little ostentatious for my taste," I decided, "but I like the Mausoleum anyway. It wasn't built out of fear for a god, but by a woman for her husband. Her love gave him immortality."

"It still couldn't bring him back," Rachel reminded me.

No, but at least she knew where he was at night. Silently I knelt. Should I pray to Isis or to Asklepios? Neither, I decided. Today it would be to Artemesia and Mausoleus, together forever . . . somewhere. Perhaps this pair of loving spirits would hear my plea.

On our way back down the hill, we browsed the shops. Among the crowded shelves of one tiny store, I discovered a collection of love poems. Signaling for Rachel to pay the eager clerk, I tucked the scroll under my arm. Perhaps I could emulate the poet's erotic style in a poem for Pilate. A returning ship could take it to him.

Once on board, I eagerly settled myself on deck with scroll, stylus, and tablet. The *Persephone* swung out from the dock, oars sprouting. A drum sounded belowdecks, and blades dipped on either side of the trim hull. It sounded again and they splashed the surface, three men pulling on each shaft. The ship glided forward, picking up speed as the drumbeats quickened. Gesturing to the slaves to take up their lyres, I reached for the scroll.

"So here you are, little dove!" Sempronia plopped down on the couch beside me. The tablet clattered to the deck, but she ignored it. "I searched the whole ship for you. We missed you at the landing too. Did you not remember that we planned to shop together? Plutonius hunted all over for a litter large enough for all of us, and when he returned, you were nowhere in sight. Where did you go?"

"Oh, I am sorry! I must have misunderstood," I apologized. "A litter wasn't necessary. Surely I told you that. After so much time on the ship, a walk was exactly what I needed."

"A walk! You walked? Plutonius would have been distraught if he had known you were walking alone."

"I was not alone. Rachel was with me."

"A female slave is scarcely protection, let alone companionship," Sempronia reproved.

"You worry far too much. It keeps you from more important things." I leaned over to retrieve my tablet. As a girl, I had been admonished by the priestesses of Isis to search for the goddess's face in every woman. I still made an effort, but found the task impossible with Sempronia.

"There's nothing I'd rather do than visit with you," she replied, settling back against the cushions.

Resigned to a lost afternoon, I eyed my self-appointed companion reflectively. Sempronia was well into her thirties, and her body was heavy, her face thickly covered with a pinkish-white powder. She enhanced her hair as well, it was several shades of yellow. Sempronia certainly was not the first to do that. Missing my mother desperately, why could I not find comfort in the older woman's eager attentions?

"My! Is this what you young girls fancy?" Sempronia's

fleshy arm reached across me to pick up the scroll. "Plutonius would never allow me to read such a thing."

"Indeed?"

"He would not think it proper for a Roman matron. Look at this, 'Her breasts, how smooth to my caress. How smooth her body beneath her bosom. How fair her thighs! We lay—' " She put the scroll down. "He would be shocked."

"Perhaps if you read it together. The poems are really quite lovely . . . evocative."

Sempronia giggled. "Not likely. He never reads poetry, not even this dirty kind. Military histories are all I've ever seen him look at. I'm not much of a reader either."

"I love reading."

"So I have noticed. Your nose is buried in a scroll most of the time."

Not that it has discouraged you any. "I've been reading about the miracle cures at Pergamum," I explained. "The god visits so many in their sleep. He's given sight to the blind, allowed cripples to walk, even raised the dead."

"Just be careful what you wish for," Sempronia warned. "You've heard about the woman who asked the god for a daughter? . . . You haven't? I thought *everyone* had." Sempronia appeared to inflate as she settled further into the cushions. "It seems," she began in a voice that carried the length of the deck, "that a woman went to the Asklepion and followed the priest's guidance. Sure enough, the god appeared in a dream and asked if there was anything she desired. 'I want to be pregnant with a daughter,' the woman told him. 'Is there anything else?' Asklepios asked. 'No,' she said, 'that is all I want.' "

"Did she get her wish?" I asked, curiosity overcoming my irritation.

"She certainly did, but . . ." Sempronia paused, prolonging the moment as long as possible. "Three years passed and she was still pregnant."

"How dreadful!" I exclaimed. "What happened?"

"Exhausted, the supplicant returned to the Asklepion. Once again the god appeared in a dream. This time Asklepios said, 'I see you are pregnant, you must have everything you desire.' "

"Did she ask to have her child?" I leaned forward eagerly.

"Yes, and according to the story, her pains came on so fast that her daughter was born right there in the sanctuary."

I laughed until tears formed in my eyes. "Thank you," I said at last. "It has been a while since I've enjoyed a joke."

"A joke? Surely you don't doubt that it happened?" Sempronia's pale eyes widened.

"Truly, I don't know what to believe. But I shall indeed be careful what I ask for. It would appear that Asklepios is a god with a sense of humor."

PERGAMUM, A CITADEL CITY, COMMANDED STUNNING views of sea and valley. Had the circumstances been different, I would have loved it. As it was, praying that my time there would be short, I went directly to the Asklepion's reception hall. The walls encouraged me, covered as they were with gold offerings, replicas not only of arms and legs, eyes and hearts, but male genitals, breasts, and even uteruses. In the room's center, an imposing statue of Asklepios rested on a column decorated with snakes twined about a laurel branch. Studying the fine-looking form, I was struck by how handsome the god was. More than handsome, his eyes, his mouth, his very essence radiated strength and compassion. Asklepios was the hero physician whom everyone longed for in time of need. Dear god, answer my prayers! I pleaded silently.

Galen, the priest assigned me, was a robust man with clear, unlined skin, bright sapphire eyes, and a ready smile. I guessed his age at thirty-five and was surprised to learn that he had recently celebrated his fiftieth birthday. Galen prescribed prayers, mud baths, massages, herbal teas, and long walks. His assurance impressed me. All the Asklepion staff seemed efficient and dedicated. The caliber of the guests—no one called us patients—reassured me too. Most were affluent and worldly, not the sort easily taken in by charlatans.

I began the regimen immediately, filling the remainder of the day with activity. That night I reported to the marble sanctuary where Galen led the way to a sleeping cubicle. The simple but inviting enclosure was screened from the others by silvery blue drapes pulled at night for privacy. The couch and its cushions, in contrasting blues, were covered in the same soft fabric. Heavenly constellations painted in gold against a dark blue ceiling created an air of serenity. Asklepios would appear to me that very night, I was certain.

But he didn't. "Perhaps you are trying too hard," Galen suggested the next morning.

"Calm down, enjoy yourself. People come to Pergamum from all over the world for rest and relaxation."

"Relaxation!" I wanted to scream.

"Claudia, Claudia," the priest soothed. "You must be calm."

"How can I be calm when every day is a day spent away from my husband? You can't imagine—"

"I can imagine, but I assure you that Asklepios will never come if you don't relax."

That afternoon I decided to visit the famous library. "We don't use papyrus," an attendant explained to me. "We have developed something better that we call parchment. Feel how pleasant it is to the touch. The library has more than two hundred thousand parchment scrolls."

"I trust I won't be here long enough to read them all," I commented to the zealous attendant.

"I have begun to fear the same," a soft, low-pitched voice interjected.

I turned to see a woman seated at a nearby table. When she smiled, I thought for a moment of Marcella. The two looked nothing alike—this woman's hair was the color of molten copper—yet both exuded the same warm luxuriance. "My name is Miriam," she introduced, adding, "Some call me Miriam of Magdala."

"I am Claudia. My husband, Pontius Pilate of Antioch, sent me here for a cure. What about you?"

"Not me, my . . . companion. His knees trouble him."

"It appears he has come to the right place. Everywhere I turn I meet one more surgeon, masseuse, or midwife. That's why I am here—I hope to make use of a midwife."

"Really? I have spent the past eight years trying to avoid the need for a midwife."

I looked at her curiously. A pretty woman, beautiful really, possibly a year or two older than myself. "I cannot imagine that."

"You are fortunate," she replied, making room for me on the bench beside her.

I learned that she had come to Pergamum from Rome. Noticing the sistrum about my throat, Miriam confided that she, too, was a devotee of Isis. I felt an instant bond and was eager to hear more, but before I could ask, Sempronia appeared insisting that she had something important to discuss. Thinking that it had to do with my treatment, I followed her from the library.

"Do you realize who that is?" she demanded.

"Just a pleasant woman."

"Pleasant!" Sempronia planted her plump hands on plumper hips. "She's one of the most notorious courtesans in Rome. General Maximus brought her from Judaea. Her parents had disowned her—some dreadful scandal. Since then she's gone from man to man, all of them rich. The latest—a senator, mind you—brought her here."

"How do you know that?"

"Everyone's talking. If you didn't spend so much time reading . . ."

By now I'd learned to ignore Sempronia, was adept at detaching my mind from her chatter. I thought of Miriam, cool and elegant, her green silk *palla* falling gracefully over a tunica the color of sea foam. On her long fingers and at her tiny, delicate ears large topazes flashed f ire. She looked expensive. Whatever Miriam did, she apparently did well.

Sempronia was still talking, shaking her finger. ". . . your reputation. What would your husband think?"

"He might hope I'd learn something new." Sempronia

stood open-mouthed as I went off to meet with the masseuse assigned to me.

In the next few days I spent a good deal of time with Miriam. She was warm and responsive, with a delightfully wry wit. Though usually reticent, I found it easy to share my feelings. Perhaps it was our shared faith or the vague resemblance to Marcella, perhaps merely that Miriam was a good conversationalist, well read, drawn as I to Virgil and the newer writer, Seneca. While her wealthy patron, Cato Valerius, soaked in the hot springs, we took long walks and attended the theater together. Literature and philosophy seemed to fascinate Miriam. Though her opinions were often humorous and perceptive, she rarely spoke of herself.

EACH MORNING, GALEN CAME TO MY SLEEPING CUBICLE. Smiling expectantly, he would ask, "Did Asklepios come to you?" Invariably I would shake my head. On the fifth morning, I ventured, "Maybe I am not worthy."

"That seems unlikely. Remember, it is not necessary that you actually *see* Asklepios. It is enough that you have a dream. I am here to help you interpret it and then aid in carrying out the god's wishes."

I shook my head helplessly. "All my life I have been plagued with dreams that I did not want. Now that it matters, why can I not have one?" I had begun the regimen with such hope. The health center's air of lofty purpose amid stylish surroundings had buoyed my faith. Now the passing days terrified me. I worried increasingly about Pilate. How much longer did I dare remain away from him?

"What shall I do?" I asked Miriam later that morning. "Without Pilate, I am nothing."

Her emerald eyes widened in surprise. "Whoever I am with, I am always Miriam."

"How can you say that? You of all people? I know who you are, what you do, the men you—you know. What if they no longer want you, what if they are cruel? You must be constantly needing to please."

"Only one man was cruel," she said with a slight shrug. "I left him. There are many eager for my favors. Pleasing men is what I do. In the part of the world where I grew up there are women who dedicate themselves to love. They are the sacred priestesses of the goddess Astoreth. It is their pleasure to give pleasure."

"But you can't go on giving—pleasure—forever."

Miriam smiled, obviously pleased with herself. "I have thought of that. Once I was alone and helpless. It will not happen again. My lovers are generous. I have put money away where no one can touch it. I have many good years remaining. When they are over, I will buy a villa by the sea and spend my days reading."

"I don't understand you at all. I cannot imagine such a life."

"I might say the same about yours."

One thing Miriam and I readily agreed on was our impatience with the Asklepion, though many guests seemed content to spend months lounging under shaded colonnades, conversing about their enemas and bloodletting. "What would you do if Cato wanted to stay?" I asked her.

"Leave him," she replied without hesitation, but added,

"Cato is a man of action. He is as impatient as we. Last night he said he was even ready to try the snake pit."

"Snake pit!" The hair rose on the back of my neck.

"He was joking, of course, but he *is* restless."

"What is the snake pit?"

"I don't know really. The attendants only whisper. It must be for incurables—mad people." She reflected a moment, staring out over the wild valley below, then turned to me. "Perhaps the serpent waits in the garden for everyone. Sooner or later we must all confront it."

What was she talking about? Snakes, lunatics, I quickly changed the subject.

The next morning Miriam announced that Cato Valerius had finally had a dream.

"Asklepios appeared to him standing before the Sphinx," she told me. "The priest believes the hot sun will be good for his joints. Tomorrow we leave for Egypt."

"I will miss you," I told her and meant it. How amazing that this strange woman with her scandalous ideas had become a close friend almost overnight.

"My dear, we will meet again. I know it," Miriam said.

I looked deep into her eyes and nodded.

WITH MIRIAM GONE, I THOUGHT OF NOTHING BUT PILATE. What was he doing and with whom? "I am going home," I told Galen the next day. "This is the seventh morning that I have wakened remembering nothing, absolutely nothing."

"You can't do that."

"Can't! What do you mean? Of course, I can. I *will*."

"Your husband wants you to remain. Your guardian made that quite clear."

A chill swept over me. "My guardian?"

"Plutonius, of course."

I lowered my voice, aware that others were listening. "We traveled here together, but I would hardly call him—"

"Your husband is anxious for an heir. He has placed you in Plutonius's care. It is his responsibility to see that you pursue every course."

"It would seem that I *have* pursued every course."

"Not quite." Galen hesitated. "There is one treatment we reserve . . ."

I recalled Miriam's words and gasped. "You don't mean the snake pit?"

"You have been listening to gossips in the bath. What do they know? Its cures are phenomenal, the soul as well as the body."

"If the patient survives. I won't do it," I cried out, not caring who heard me. "I just won't do it!"

CHAPTER 18

Asklepios

I screamed into the darkness. Strong, insistent hands grabbed me, lifted me off the bed. I opened my mouth to scream again, but heard no sound. Heart pounding frantically, I tried to struggle. My arms, strangely heavy, refused to obey. "No, no, no!" I moaned.

Waking later, aching and groggy, I winced. Bright sunlight streamed from a window across from where I lay. Feeling like a trapped animal, I looked from one unfamiliar wall to another. The small room was clean and white, cell-like in its austerity—one small window, a narrow bed, a chair and table, above them a little mirror.

I staggered to the window and was surprised to find myself high above the ground. Pergamum was a city of complexes. I easily picked out Asklepios's great central altar, then the library and theater. Rarely did the briskly moving figures below look up, and those who did appeared oblivious to my cries.

I beat on the heavy door until my fists were bruised. It was futile. My captors, soft-voiced men I had not seen before, came when they pleased, their guarded eyes never quite meeting mine. With their spotless white tunics and close-cropped hair, it was hard to distinguish one from another. Always patient, always polite, they told me nothing.

Certain that I had been drugged, I smashed the water pitcher they left me. Over time, as guards appeared and reappeared with new vessels of water, thirst overcame my fear. I was hungry too, very hungry. None of my possessions had been brought from the inn. There was nothing to read, no stylus or tablets on which to write. I kept track of the days by scratching a line with my fingernail on the table beside my bed. One . . . two . . . three.

On the morning of the fourth day I heard a bolt lift. My heart leaped. I caught my breath. The door opened slowly to admit Sempronia. Prurient curiosity had replaced her ingratiating manner. "My little dove! I am so glad to see you." Sempronia surveyed the tiny room, a benign grin pasted across her face. "It is quite pleasant here. I hope you have been comfortable."

I stiffened, not about to reveal my fear to her. "In prison?"

Sempronia's pink face grew pinker. "I hope you do not blame Plutonius or me."

"Who else should I blame? It was you who brought me here. Your husband suggested the trip to Pilate in the first place."

Sempronia backed away. I moved quickly, grasping her shoulders. "Do you know what they're going to do?"

"You have said again and again how much you want a child—"

"Would *you* do it?"

"I have three children."

"*Would you do it?*"

Sempronia looked away. "This is the most acclaimed Asklepion in the world. People come from everywhere to be healed. You were one of them," she reminded me.

"No one said anything about a snake pit. *You* never said anything."

"Plutonius wouldn't let me," she admitted, eyes cast down.

"Did my husband know as well?"

"I . . . I assume so." Sempronia broke free from my grip and backed away. "I should not have come. I only wanted to see if you needed anything."

"Needed anything! Well, yes, you might say I need a few things. Let us begin with Rachel. I want my slave. I want food and water that has not been drugged. I want my stylus and tablet, my clothes. Most of all, I want to leave."

Sempronia's eyes beseeched me. "No one planned on the snake pit. You are a dreamer—everyone knows that. Naturally, we assumed you would have a beautiful dream here, one that would empower you to conceive. We would all have a delightful holiday and then return to Antioch. Pilate would be so pleased—"

"That he would reward Plutonius with the wheat contract he's after," I finished for her. "But I didn't have that beautiful dream. I want to go home *now*."

"By Jupiter, woman, you are a Roman! Stop whining like a slave girl." I turned and saw Plutonius in the doorway. No trace now of the obsequious sycophant in his narrow, glinting eyes. "Your husband considers you quite remarkable. I believe his word was 'spiritual.' He was certain that Asklepios would appear to you." Plutonius shrugged slightly. "Unfortunately, that has yet to happen."

"Surely Pilate does not expect me to subject myself to—to—snakes."

"He expects you to do your duty." Plutonius folded his arms across a beefy chest. "As your guardian, it is my responsibility to see his wishes carried out."

I struggled to keep my voice calm. "I want to send a message to my parents."

Plutonius nodded as though considering. "Perhaps they would yield to your whims, perhaps not. Need I remind you that they are far away?"

Arms stiff, close to my sides, hands curled tightly into fists, I screamed in rage.

The door opened. Galen slipped past Plutonius into the tiny room. "It is best that you leave," he directed the couple. "My patient and I have much to discuss."

Looking relieved, Sempronia squeezed through the door. Plutonius hesitated, his eyes studying the priest. "You do understand the importance of this? The *Domina* Claudia can be both wily and persuasive when she chooses."

"The *Domina* Claudia and I understand each other very well," Galen assured him.

"I *thought* we understood each other," I said when we were alone.

I had never liked Plutonius or Sempronia. Now I hated them with all my being. I hated Galen too, for surely he had been conferring with them all along.

His calm, almost dreamy eyes regarded me. "You look tired."

"Of course I'm tired! Could you sleep if you knew that at any moment you might be dragged off to a den of snakes?

I am hungry too. What about the water? I am sure it's been drugged."

"There is nothing in the water to harm you," he assured me. "I am sorry that you are hungry, but a three-day fast is required before your treatment."

"Treatment! How euphemistic you are."

"Of course, it is a treatment. What else? Some have found the snakes to have miraculous powers."

"Those who survive them." Turning away from him I caught a glimpse of myself in the small mirror above the table. My face was thinner, but the new gauntness made my eyes all the larger . . . I looked back at Galen, lowering my lashes, softening my voice. "Surely you can intervene. You could save me, Galen . . . if you want to."

He stiffened. "My life belongs to Asklepios. I am a priest," he reminded me. "It is for the god to decide what form salvation will take. You shall know his will tonight."

WE STOOD BEFORE A MASSIVE MARBLE TEMPLE. I shivered in the night air, pulling my thin gown closer—a silk sleeping tunica. They might at least have allowed me a *stola*. A wave of dizziness swept over me as the priests crowded closer, so many of them. I felt weak, I could not breathe. As Galen opened the carved wooden door, I took a last look at the midnight sky. No moon had lit our way. A bad sign, I assumed, but Galen shook his head. "We cannot see the new moon, but it is there. Tonight is made for beginnings."

"No, please, no!" I shrank away from the doorway.

Galen held me firmly. "Don't make it more difficult for us or for yourself." He motioned to another priest. I tried to break free but the big man held me, his hands like a vise.

"You said you preferred to walk," Galen reminded me.

"Walk rather than be dragged? Of course, I am a Claudian!" I straightened my shoulders.

"Now, now, dearest Claudia," Galen chided gently. "You must realize that everything we do is for your own good." They were pushing now, propelling me into the temple foyer. Blazing wall torches illuminated the room. On the frescoed wall, centaurs romped across the skies. Directly before me was a statue of Asklepios. I fell to my knees. How could a compassionate deity subject me to this horror? "Asklepios!—dear god—" The priests pulled me to my feet.

"You will come with us." Galen's firm voice left no doubt as he and the other priests thrust me into a small, dank room. I realized now that the temple had been built over the entrance to a tunnel. A priest knelt before me, unfastening my sandals, pulling at them until I was barefoot. The marble floor was cold and slippery. The priests extinguished their torches. Pressing forward, they dragged me into the blackness.

I staggered often, clinging dizzily to Galen, faint from hunger as well as fear, as we moved deeper into the musty darkness. Sometimes I heard eerie, rustling noises. I wondered if I was descending into Hades. At last we stopped before a massive door. Chills ran through my body as I heard the bolt pulled back. Galen and another priest dragged me forward into a small, round room dimly lit by flickering lamps placed in high niches. At its center was a couch mounted on a low dais. A trough in the floor circled the room, but I saw no water there.

Galen lifted me onto the dais. My nervous laugh echoed in the still chamber. "Surely you don't expect me to have a dream here—now?" I asked.

"You may be surprised," Galen replied.

"What about the snakes?"

"There are no snakes. Look about you," Galen soothed while placing a pillow behind my head. It felt damp and clammy.

The other priests disappeared back into the tunnel. I clung to Galen, pleading, "Don't leave me."

"Asklepios knows best," Galen said, his eyes fixed on the wall somewhere behind me. He disengaged himself. "Just put your faith in him."

"I used to put my faith in Isis." I began to sob. "Now she has forsaken me. This is my punishment."

"This is a healing, not a punishment," Galen said, jaw tight. "I must leave now."

"Please, no!" I leaped off the dais and ran after him. The iron door closed and Galen was gone.

Throat raw from screaming, I looked about the room, an intricate pattern of entwined snakes covered the walls and ceiling. The same sinuous shapes squirmed across the mosaic floor. Could the term snake pit be merely figurative? If only . . . "I am descended from heroes," I said aloud, an incantation repeated again and again as I leaned against the door.

Lamps gave off an incense I had not smelled before, sweet yet earthy. I thought of lush, leafy vegetation. Somewhere in the shadows I heard a dry, sibilant sound. The twisting, writhing forms on the walls and ceiling made me giddy.

Something rustled, closer this time. Then I saw them. First one snake, then two, then hundreds slithered up from the trough. I screamed as one slid across my bare foot. Shrinking back, I stepped on another.

I ran back to the dais and climbed onto the couch. A large black snake glided upward from the floor, its head rising above the dais. It moved slowly toward me, sliding across the couch, then coiled around my ankle. I kicked frantically, but the snake's head slid upward. The sea of snakes filled the small room, quivering and coiling together, clustered about my couch.

"No!" I shrieked. "No!" Grabbing the snake I hurled it with all my might against the wall. The reptile fell limply to the floor. At least I had killed one, but no, the dead one was not dead. It rose again larger than before. Regarding me with glittering obsidian eyes, the serpent slithered back onto the dais. It was wider than a pillar, growing larger still. Raising its head higher, the snake's darting tongue touched my flailing leg.

Slowly the serpent rose until his eyes were level with my own. My nails dug deeply into the palms of my clenched hands. "Pilate! How could you do this to me?" I screamed.

The snake glided forward, wrapping its rippling coils about me. His force around me, inside me, subsuming me completely. The energy so powerful, my body pulsated. I could no longer breathe, no longer think of breath.

My eyes opened to dazzling, blinding light. A throbbing sound moved closer and closer, relentlessly beating, beating, beating, pulling me down, down, down into blackness. Waves engulfed me, immersed me in a bottomless well.

Falling faster and faster. Black water filled my lungs. I felt the life leaving me. I struggled, gasping. Nothing, nothing. Then the sweet sound of lyres, flutes, and sistrums. A hand so cool on my forehead. *Claudia, my chosen one, have you forgotten that I am always here?*

"Isis," I murmured, searching for the light.

The vision, the journey beyond knowing faded, moved on like a passing storm, leaving only blackness. New and opened, I thrust aside the old Claudia like a snake shedding its skin. My body floated, newborn out of ignorance into conscious knowing.

For a time I saw only blackness. Then somewhere in the distance a form appeared. It was *Tata*! He stood alone watching me, his face white and solemn. *Tata,* what is it?

"You have a duty, Claudia," he said at last. "You alone are left." My father turned, disappearing into the darkness. Somewhere far away, I heard Mother calling: "Marcus, Marcus. Wait! Don't go without me!"

THE WORLD ABOUT ME PITCHED RHYTHMICALLY FROM side to side, never still. Where was I? Steady throbbing echoed in my head. That pounding . . . what is it? I struggled to open my eyes.

"*Domina!* At last you are awake! We're on a boat. Galley slaves are taking us back to Antioch. Are you all right?"

"More than all right, Rachel"—a whisper all I could manage—"better than I have ever been." I wanted to say more, but could not. Wearily I closed my eyes and slept—who knew how long.

When I awakened, Rachel was again beside me. "Asklepios, did he come to you?" she ventured.

I nodded weakly.

"Did he hurt you?"

"He saved me. That was his gift. He gave me back myself."

Rachel frowned, puzzled. "And the child?"

"There will be no child," I said, struggling to sit up.

"But, *Dominus* . . . do you no longer love him?"

"Love? I know nothing of love, perhaps I never knew." I paused a moment, thinking. "I know about hope. I have fallen out of hope."

"*Dominus* could not have known about the snake pit," Rachel said, as she brushed my tangled hair.

"He knew, he had to know."

Rachel's hazel eyes watched me sympathetically. "Roman women obey their husbands," she reminded me.

"I know. Mother is most fortunate. For her it is easy. Few women love their husbands as she does—or have husbands like my father."

"You have changed." Rachel set the brush down and began to massage my scalp. "Did the god do that? You seem stronger . . . wiser. You see things as they are."

"Perhaps, but I have no intention of accepting what I see."

The undulating movement of Rachel's hands stopped. "What do you mean?"

"Mother and *Tata* gave me money before the wedding, each of them saying a wife should have something of her own without knowing the other had wished the same. There is more than enough to pay our passage to Rome."

"To Rome!" Rachel gasped, "What are you thinking?"

"I am going home to my parents. Let people talk as they will. It won't be long before they have something else to gossip about, someone else. Once I am home—really home—everything will be all right." I lay back contentedly, enjoying my new sense of confidence.

As the shipboard days passed and my energy slowly returned, I grew restless. The drumbeat that commanded the galley slaves underscored my eagerness to reach Antioch, sever my ties there, and get on with my life. Rousing myself at last, I asked Rachel to have my couch carried onto the deck. There I reclined for hours looking out at the sea. The waves frothed and sloshed at the ship's flanks, churning gray and deep. Passengers and crew tiptoed around me. Some were openly curious, others appeared almost awestruck. I suppose they had heard about the snake pit. I discouraged conversation even with Rachel. The only company I sought was that of Isis. I felt her strength now as never before.

Sempronia and Plutonius watched with anxious eyes. When the ship reached Halicarnassus, I saw Plutonius hand a scroll to an officer about to board a smaller, faster vessel anchored next to ours. No doubt he was making certain that his version of events reached Pilate first. How amusing, how unimportant.

I SAW PILATE WATCHING AS THE SHIP DOCKED IN Antioch. Before anyone could disembark, he boarded, shouldered his way past Plutonius and Sempronia. "I'm glad you're back," he said, his arms around me. "I missed you."

"Did you?" I asked, slipping out of his grasp. "Did you really?" I looked at him curiously.

The blue eyes I had once found irresistible were turned full force on me. "I understand you had quite an ordeal. I am sorry, truly sorry."

"An ordeal? You might say that. It was a very—how shall I say it?—enlightening experience."

"I am glad you feel that way." Surprise and relief were apparent on his face as he took me in his arms again. "There is something that I need to tell you."

An ugly dread swept over me . . . *the dream.* My heart began to pound as he cradled my head against his shoulder. "A letter came this morning from Agrippina."

Freeing myself, I stood back and looked at him. "It's *Tata,* isn't it? Something has happened to *Tata.*"

"I'm afraid so. Your father was condemned by Tiberius, condemned as a traitor and confined to his house to await trial. Everyone knew what was expected of him."

"Not suicide . . ." My constricted throat could barely form the word. "And Mother?" I took a deep breath, knowing already what he would say.

"She chose to die with him."

CHAPTER

19

The Handmaid of Isis

"What can I do, Claudia? Tell me, I want to help." I heard Pilate's voice as in a dream. "Let me take you home."

"Home?" I looked up at him. "You want to take me home? If I have a home anywhere in this world it is not with you." I pushed his arms aside and turned away, looking about in dazed bewilderment. Home was with Mother and Tata, but now they were gone, lost forever. How could I live without them? Where could I go? What was left for me?

"What are you talking about!" Pilate's eyes flashed angrily. "Your parents are dead. Your only home is with me!" He grabbed me again but I pulled back so hard that my *stola* ripped in his hands.

Just beyond the wharf I saw a battered chariot; the driver, an ill-kempt fellow, loitered nearby. Plutonius had come up beside us, seeking Pilate's attention. As my husband turned impatiently toward him, I ran to the chariot and climbed on.

"I'll pay you more than anyone," I offered. The driver's eyes moved over me, appraising. "Please," I begged, opening the pouch at my waist. "Whatever you want. Take me to—" I hesitated uncertainly. Pilate was striding angrily toward us. "Just go!" I screamed. "Get me away from here."

Pilate lunged forward, grabbing the reins. "Stop!" he cried, an impressive figure in his plumed helmet and scarlet cloak.

"No! Don't listen to him," I pleaded. "I have gold, you shall have it."

The driver looked at Pilate, then at me. He wrested the reins free, cracked his whip. The horses charged forward, almost jerking me off my feet. "Where do you want to go?"

Where? Where in the world could I go? And then I knew. The perfect place, the only place.

I braced my feet, clung tightly to the charioteer's waist, impervious to his smell, to the long, greasy hair that sometimes blew across my face. We galloped headlong through vast waterfront stalls, past porticoes and arches, markets and baths until, in the very center of Antioch, the chariot came to a stop. Looming before us in all its glory was the temple of Isis.

"You know that chariots aren't allowed here," the driver reminded me.

"Yes, yes, I know. Take this, take all of it," I said, handing him my pouch. "Consider it a gift from Isis to whom you have delivered me."

He helped me down and stood for a moment looking up at the temple. "A new life for you, is it? May Fortuna bring you luck."

I looked at him in surprise. "*You* have already brought me luck. Thank you." I turned and rushed up the wide marble stairs, fearful that Pilate might be close on my heels.

The temple swarmed with activity. Worshipers—in Egyptian kilts, Roman togas, Greek tunics—came and went from all directions. Proper-looking priests and priestesses in their fine white linen looked askance as I ran past them toward the inner courtyard. Someone must have summoned the mystagogue, for he stood as though waiting for me beside the great golden statue of Isis.

Dropping to my knees, I knelt before him. "Take me in," I begged, fighting back the tears. "My dear parents are gone. The marriage I wanted desperately is over. Only Isis remains. You must accept me as an acolyte."

Gently, the holy man raised me to my feet. "You *have* changed," he said, pushing back the tangled hair from my face. "I see the great sorrow that has befallen you. I also see that Isis has returned to your heart. You must continue to seek her truth, to meditate and to pray, but temple life—no. That is not for you."

"Just give me a chance to prove myself."

The mystagogue looked at me, a faint smile hovering about his lips. "You have no idea what you are asking. Everyday tasks have always been done for you. You scarcely think of them—if at all. Here you would have to serve others. I doubt that you are strong enough."

"If other acolytes can do it, I can."

"Most of them are freed slaves or foundlings. Rarely does a woman of your rank serve in the temple."

"Then let me be the exception. I will do anything you say."

"*Anything* I say? Do you promise that?"

"I do. Treat me as any novice."

The mystagogue shook his head doubtfully, but in the end agreed.

He took me at my word, too, giving orders that I was to be shown no favoritism. With no slave to assist me—I would not ask Rachel to share my exile—I had to learn to do for myself what had always been done for me. Simple things like dressing myself at first seemed impossible. My gowns—matching length with length, the folding and the fastening—were a mystery. There was a trick, I learned, of pulling the *palla* straight and anchoring it tight beneath my breasts. I had never before touched a hand to my hair; Rachel had spent hours on it. Now I struggled to tame the unruly curls, finally pulling them into a single thick braid.

Flavia, priestess of the *latrinas,* was my first taskmaster. With brows raised at the mystagogue, she led me away to a marble building that adjoined the baths. I bowed my head, held my nose, and entered. "Well, of course," she reminded me, "it is not as though we do not all come here several times a day. That's just it. We come here often. We are always grateful to find what we need when and where we need it and then we leave. Quickly."

She picked up a bloody menstrual rag, dropping it neatly into a wicker basket. "Some of us leave so quickly that we are unaware of the mess that we have left behind."

I discovered to my surprise that the priestesses were often less fastidious than the priests—I helped to maintain both *latrinas.* Priests and priestesses, like the rest of us, relieve themselves while sitting on wooden seats above a drain that discharges the waste into the main sewer, where it eventually makes its way into manure for the gardens. Despite the incense, nothing could cover the smell in either *latrina*; and, hard as I scrubbed, they never remained clean for long.

"What has excrement to do with Isis?" a young novice railed at my side.

"It is *all* an honor," Flavia reminded her. "Whatever our task, we do the goddess's work."

Mind numbed by all that had happened, I had scant use for philosophy. If I thought at all, it was of the task at hand. Sometimes I looked at my chipped nails and thought of Mother. "The worst takes its time to come and then to pass," she used to say. I cried for days, cried and scrubbed, cried and slept, cried and scrubbed again. The muscles of my arms and shoulders ached constantly; my knees were raw from kneeling. I was very, very tired, yet at the end of the day, alone in my tiny cubicle, I fell asleep crying for my parents.

One morning the mystagogue sent a message that Pilate was waiting impatiently for me in the anteroom. "Let him wait," I said, wielding the *latrina* sponge like a mallet. The next day the holy man himself appeared, urging me to hear my husband out. I shook my head emphatically. "Soon he will cease to ask. He will find another. She will come from a powerful family, one closely aligned with Tiberius, a family known to breed sons. He will want a divorce."

A month passed. To my surprise, Pilate's angry demands continued. I stood firm. There was nothing he could say that I wanted to hear. How could it be, I wondered vaguely, that the man to whom few dared to say no continued to return. The idea did not displease me.

Weeks went by until one afternoon a messenger announced that I had another visitor. This one I was eager to see—Rachel. I had missed her so much. Not only the things she did for me but what she was to me. My dearest, only friend. We rushed into each other's arms and then broke apart, standing back to look at one another. Rachel was Rachel. It was I who had changed and she let me know it. "You are a *domina*," she exclaimed, her eyes roving over my wrinkled *peplos*. "This is no life for you! What would your father think if he could see you here?"

"*You* worship Isis," I reminded her.

"But I am not a slave to her."

"I'm not a slave! I am an acolyte." Loose wisps of hair straggled down my neck. Self-consciously, I attempted to tuck them back into the braid. "This is the life I have chosen." I put my hand, so red and chapped, on her smooth one and smiled at the incongruity.

Rachel was not amused. "You need me to talk sense into you. You also need me to care for you. When are you going to stop this nonsense? When will you return to the life that you were born for, the life your parents wanted for you? You can honor Isis in your heart, you can come here to worship as much as you please, but—"

"Did Pilate send you here?"

"Yes, he did," she admitted, meeting my eyes squarely. "At first *Dominus* would not allow me to come. He expected you to just give up and come back, but today he asked me to tell you that he is sorry, that he never meant to hurt you."

"Do you believe him?"

"Yes, I do."

I looked beyond her across the garden to the *latrinas*. It would be so easy to go home, to pick up the threads of a life of leisure. I was sick of filth, weary of calluses and aching muscles. "Your place is in the world," the mystagogue had said. Tears welled up in my eyes. I hugged Rachel, burying my head against her *stola*. "No! Tell Pilate no." I turned and ran quickly from the room.

Perhaps I was good at cleaning *latrinas*, at least I never complained about them as the others did. After a time the mystagogue sought to promote me. "Planning meals for fifty priests and priestesses should be an easy task after all the large banquets you have overseen," he explained.

Straightening my sore back, I looked up from the toilet sponges I had been washing in a large stone trough. Mindless work brought solace. I was afraid to leave its safety. "If you wish to assign *culina* duties, let me peel vegetables or bring food to the tables," I said.

He pulled me around to face him, placing his hands on my shoulders. "Claudia, Claudia, the goddess does not expect this of you. If she wants someone to wait on her, there are many sweet serving girls to do it far better than you can. It is time that you went home."

"*This* is my home."

He shook his head in gentle exasperation. "Very well then, report to the *culina* tomorrow at dawn."

Each morning, before any food preparation began, the priestess in charge brought the ten of us serving maids together in the large whitewashed *culina*. A fire already blazed on the raised hearth, large stone tables were covered with stacks of onions and garlic waiting to be peeled, freshly slaughtered chickens ready for plucking. Silently we thanked Isis for the food we were about to prepare, meditated on our individual tasks, seeing them as part of a whole, and visualizing the successful outcome of our joint effort. I accepted the idea at first without thinking, but, as weeks turned to months, a sense of community stole over me and I took quiet pleasure in the accomplishment of shared tasks.

At first the others were critical of my fumbling—it was obvious that I would never be a cook—but no one doubted my effort. I volunteered for everything and did the best I could until a visiting priestess from Alexandria was seated at the head table. I was eager to serve her, hoping that she would have news of the high priestess who had befriended me years before. But how different this woman was from my original benefactor! The visiting priestess, unlike any that I had ever met, disdained to speak to a serving maid. When I bowed before her, she turned a haughty, beaklike profile to me, refusing to even glance at me. Later, as I approached her with a heavy platter of asparagus that I had harvested myself from the Iseneum garden, she looked contemptuous. "Ugh! *This* is asparagus?"

Rarely had I heard such a scornful tone—and never directed at *me*! Perhaps if she had not looked so much like Sempronia . . . The priestess's expression of smug superiority turned to horror as the buttered asparagus spears pitched onto her lap.

No one believed that the platter had just slipped. I was confined to my room for a month with nothing to do but meditate on Isis's scripture. How delicious, I thought, the first time I slept past dawn. Surprisingly, as time elapsed, I missed the *culina* ballet of which I had finally become a part. I thought almost longingly of the other acolytes grinding herbs on the stone *moratarium* or crushing wheat into flour on grindstones. For a time I even missed the smell of fish smoking in heavy iron pots over the fire. At least I had been a part of something. Fingering the sistrum I still wore about my neck, I prayed to Isis. *Where is my place in this world?*

The mystagogue dropped by often to lecture me. "Your behavior was a reminder that you are not meant to be an acolyte. Once you wanted marriage—wanted it desperately. Now you belong with your husband."

I sighed, wishing the holy man would leave me in peace. There was nothing to be said.

Then finally a morning came when I was eager to talk. I had had a bizarre dream and longed to share it with someone.

The mystagogue's bland expression changed quickly to one of interest as I related all that I could remember. "I was seated at a sumptuous banquet table. In Rome, I think. There were crimson draperies, heavy draperies, closing us off, and thick carpets. My parents, sister, and I were together again." I paused, trying to clear the lump in my throat. "It—it was all so wonderful, like old times. *Tata* had his arm about Mother. He offered her a silver chalice from which to drink. They were laughing, we were all laughing. And then the dream changed. I was a little girl again, but Marcella was a woman wearing white Vestal robes with her head covered. She climbed up onto the banquet table, scattering plates, silver, food, and flowers in all directions. Marcella started dancing, her feet white against the dark blossoms. She threw off her head covering and her hair fell long and curling just like it used to. Marcella danced faster and faster, the flowers crushed, bleeding across the cloth. The dance was—was wild. Her hair was flying; I saw her legs, her thighs! I felt frightened and turned to *Tata,* but he was gone, Mother too. I cried out for Marcella to get down but she would not . . . or could not. It was growing dark now. I could no longer see but heard Marcella calling from some black place. 'Claudia, Claudia, help me!'

"I woke then, my heart was pounding. What do you think it meant?"

The mystagogue sat down opposite me. "It does not matter what I think, what do *you* think?"

"I do not know. That's why I am asking you."

"What if you *did* know?"

"Whatever it means or does not mean, Marcella is far away in Rome and I am here. My life is in the Iseneum."

"Don't be too certain. Perhaps it is you who longs to dance on tables."

"Not likely. Tomorrow my confinement is over. I will be setting tables, not dancing on them."

As more months passed I moved from the kitchen to the garden. My back, shoulders, and legs ached in new places from bending and stooping between the long rows of eggplant and strawberries. The sun was hot, the flies persistent, and the fertilizer—well, I knew where *that* came from. I sought out Octavia, the priestess in charge of the garden, and persuaded her to teach me herb lore. I was fascinated and it was not long before I had created a niche for myself preparing potions. Mandrake for calming the nerves, wolfbane for relieving pain. I learned to make willow compresses to treat arthritis, became adept at mashing oak bark and leaves into poultices for festering wounds. This, I at last decided, was my calling; preparing potions was Isis's divine plan for me. Yet sometimes I wondered. Was there nothing more? Was this *it*?

I balked at preparing the love potions. "A lot of good they did me!" I protested to the mystagogue. I shoved the yohimbe and horny goat weed, so carefully ground, into a glass vessel containing olive oil and the essence of roses, violets, and lilies. "You should warn the poor fools."

"Much good my warnings did you, Claudia." His rare smile surprised me. "Love is the goddess's gift. It is meant to be treasured. The fault lies in obsession."

Obsession . . . of course. The more I had said the incantation, the more I had used the potion, seeking to win Pilate's love, the more obsessed I had become with him. It was I, not him, who was bound. How wrong—how foolish—it was to try to bend the will of anyone. What a price I had paid. Perhaps Pilate as well . . . If only I had taken the mystagogue's advice and left him alone.

The wise man watched me, his dark eyes intent. "You are free now from the obsession. Is it not time to use that freedom?"

"Use it! I have built a whole new life. I have dedicated myself to the goddess."

"But what of your husband, Claudia? He swears he would never have allowed you to be thrown into the snake pit had he known about it. He loves you and wants you back. He is a tribune now. Did you know that? Every week he comes here to distribute alms and receive word of you. He has given the temple a small fortune."

I looked at the mystagogue in bewilderment. "How can that be? It has been more than a year since I last used the potion or said the incantation."

"Is it so hard to believe the man loves you as you are, that there is no need for divine intervention?" When I stared at him doubtfully, the holy man persisted. "Your husband sees much in you that you have yet to recognize in yourself."

I turned my attention back to grinding herbs. "Whatever he sees or thinks he sees, he will soon see in someone else. It is only a matter of time."

"Perhaps," the mystagogue conceded. "But is that so important? He will always come back to you. You are a woman now, not a romantic girl. Isis has a purpose for you."

"Yes, right here!"

The holy man shook his head. "One year ago you promised to obey me. Now I am ordering you: *Claudia, go home.*"

ROME

in the thirteenth year of
the reign
of Tiberius (27 C.E.)

CHAPTER

20

Marcella's Choice

Pilate's family home on Aventine Hill, surrounded as it was by ancient gardens, magnificent pillars, and marble work, had that old patrician look. My husband's father had done well with his chariot business and who knew what else. Now, with his death, a large part of the fortune was ours and with it the house in Rome.

Lares familiares . . . spirits of the house. Welcome me, my troubled heart prayed silently as we entered. I bring no ill to anyone. I will fill your altar with flowers. I will light Vesta's fire. Grant me patience . . . grant me peace.

Close at my side, Pilate asked, "Do you like it?"

My eyes swept the room, taking in the mosaic floor, the exquisitely frescoed walls and marble ceiling. "What is there for me not to like?" I asked, moving through the atrium.

It was a palatial house with many rooms built onto a main rectangle, one off the other, the whole of it nestling in a lush garden. At the center, a slave waited. She bowed, then handed me a lighted taper. I knelt before the large stone altar beside the hearth. It was covered with family death masks—funereal likenesses of *Tata* and Mother among them.

I lit the home fire, thinking of all the women before me who had done the same. Vesta, Vesta, Vesta, I took you for granted until I had a fire of my own to tend. Now I know that it is you who binds us together. The empire is a family and you the constant reminder of its sanctity.

Though there was no escape from family obligation, the move to Rome might at least offer me a new beginning... Perhaps I sighed without realizing it, for Pilate looked up from the bill of lading he had been inspecting and asked, "What's the matter?"

"I feel old," I surprised myself by replying.

"Old at twenty-two. Poor girl, how will you feel at my advanced age?"

"Thirty-two looks well enough on you."

It did too. There were a few new lines around those amazing eyes, but the clipped military haircut became him well. Pilate had if anything grown more handsome in the six years since we had met. "Age doesn't matter so much for men," I said. "Some are even attractive at forty."

"Really?" He put down the bill of lading. "You have someone specific in mind?"

"My father."

"So that's what troubles you." He placed a hand on my shoulder. "I assumed you would like it here."

"So close to the man who murdered my parents?"

"Tiberius rules the world, Claudia. If I am to advance, I will need his support."

I looked about the sunlit room. Three hallways led beyond,

successive vistas of light and color, shaded passageways with black and white mosaic floors. "Your family home is splendid," I told him. "Aventine is the most fashionable neighborhood in Rome. If my parents were alive, they would be the first to remind me to be grateful for such luxury. But they are not alive."

"No, my dear," he sighed, "they are not, and nothing can change that." He picked up the bill of lading, went back to checking off items of furniture. "I thought you loved Rome; I recall your mother did."

"That's the trouble." I struggled with the lump in my throat. "This morning as we approached the city, I thought again and again of that other time: Germanicus and Agrippina triumphant, Mother ecstatic at being home, Marcella and I so excited, so very young, our lives ahead of us."

"Need I remind you that a great deal of your life remains? Soon you and Marcella will be together. A nuisance that she is off on retreat, but that won't last long."

"Yes, I look forward to her return—more than you can imagine—but today I am going to find Agrippina."

Pilate sighed again. "If your own judgment does not suffice, I shall have to be blunt: You will *not* see Agrippina. There is nothing more to be said." He picked up a ledger, subject closed.

This time I refused to be dismissed. "Agrippina has lost everything. First her mother—starved to death at Tiberius's orders on that wretched island and now"—I struggled to hold back my tears—"and now Nero and Drusus—"

"I know you miss them, Claudia. I am sorry."

"Miss them! They were brothers to me, wonderful men.

Each would have made a fine, honorable ruler. But now . . . Nero forced to commit suicide and Drusus—dear wonderful Drusus, always my protector—starved to death in the palace basement. Do you know that he ate the stuffing from his mattress?"

"These are difficult times. I grant you, Agrippina has been through a lot."

"And so have I—would you not agree? Have I not also been through a lot? Not only the great losses, the ones the world recognizes, but also the more private disappointments, the ones only you can know."

Pilate regarded me coolly.

I refused to waver. "Agrippina was a second mother to me," I reminded him.

"Very decent of her not to have contacted you, very discreet."

"That is why I must go to her."

"That would be awkward."

"*Awkward,* really?" I mocked him. "Awkward. How dreadful!"

"Does 'dangerous' suit you better? Do you think I want *you* starved to death?"

It took a few days to bribe the right servant, but eventually I learned Agrippina's whereabouts. Did Pilate imagine for a moment that I would not find her? Wrapped in Rachel's cloak, I stole out of the house, hurried down the hill to the main square, where I bargained for a litter. Inside, I settled down among the tired cushions, heart pounding. I had seen no one . . . but who might have seen me? The *delatores* were everywhere, notorious spies who pocketed one third of the estates of those against whom they informed. Dying of hunger would be terrible. But I had made the decision and had no intention of turning back. No longer able to contain my curiosity, I parted the heavy curtains and looked out. The neighborhood grew increasingly less alluring the farther we got from the Aventine.

Buildings crowded together, people crowded together. They cooked in the streets, laundered in the streets, haggled and fought, did *everything* in the streets. I closed the curtains firmly, but that couldn't block the raucous shouts, the loathsome smells. The litter twisted and turned. Where were we? I heard the runners I had hired shouting at beggars, beating off the more aggressive ones with their rods. My *stola* was plain but the gown beneath it . . . I wished I had worn something simpler. I opened the pouch at my waist; the dagger inside reassured me, a little.

Finally we came to a stop before a dark, uninviting building, a large rickety tenement built over a row of food stores. No wonder the head bearer had stared strangely at me when I told him the address. Now, helping me from the litter, he watched curiously as I looked uncertainly about. Motioning for him to wait, I pulled my *stola* closer and pushed open the unlocked door. Inside the dark foyer, the air was damp and foul. I saw no evidence of air vents as I ascended the narrow stairs. The walls were nothing more than cane and mortar. Judging from the stains and puddles on the floor, they could not be waterproof. Cats prowled the halls freely. I shuddered, thinking of their prey, but continued to climb, stopping to knock on every door. No one answered, though sometimes I heard hushed voices.

Of what were they afraid? Panting, I reached the sixth and final floor. One door remained. I knocked tentatively, heard footsteps. A slave answered, cleanly dressed but so shabby. Silently, the woman led me down a dismal hall to a small rectangular room. At least Agrippina had a slave, I thought, as the woman removed my *stola*.

"Who is it?" a voice called out. I would have known it anywhere, but not the tone. Frightened. "Auntie!" I cried. "It is I, Claudia."

Agrippina rushed out from behind a curtain—an Agrippina I could scarcely recognize. Cruel years had darkened the tawny hair, stolen the sparkle from her eyes. Agrippina's voluptuous body had thickened. She hugged me close, and then stood back to look. "Pilate chose well. You are a credit to a man of his ambitions. The way you move—that stunning gown, so exotic."

"I had the best of teachers."

"Those were happy times . . ."

"And these clearly are not." I looked about the dingy room. Clean, well ordered, but the furniture was worn. Secondhand, thirdhand? Where were Agrippina's gorgeous tapestries, her marble statues and Etruscan antiques?

"All gone," she said, as though reading my mind. "Tiberius confiscated nearly everything. What little that remained has been sold off gradually. I tried to ransom my sons—" She struggled to stifle her tears. "Claudia, you should never have come here. Pilate should not have allowed you. Your parents' only crime was loyalty to Germanicus. I wonder you do not hate me."

I put my arms about her, hugging her close, hiding the tears that stung my eyes. "My parents made a free choice. It is mine as well."

"You dear girl." Taking my arm, she led me to an intimate nook filled with family memorabilia. "I imagined that murdering my family would be enough even for Tiberius, but he is determined to frighten off every friend I have."

I settled myself on a rickety chair opposite her couch. "Have you seen Marcella? I can't wait for that retreat to be over. It has been so long—"

"Your sister has been wonderfully loyal. She was here just last week. I wonder she finds it in her heart to forgive that unfortunate matter with Caligula. How many times I have castigated myself for giving in to Livia." Agrippina's eyes filled with tears. "The Fates have been so cruel! Of my wonderful sons, only Caligula remains—that's only because Livia favors him. He lives with her now in the palace. I miss him dreadfully."

I restrained myself from commenting on the irony of the Fates' choice. Agrippina was so obviously miserable, this awful place . . . Impulsively, I leaned forward and took her hand. "Auntie, you have forgotten who you are. We don't have to act like rats chased into a cellar. I will have a banquet—a banquet like we used to have."

Pleasure transformed Agrippina's face. "It has been so long since the girls and I have been anywhere. What a treat to see your home. I have heard that it is very grand."

"Pilate's mother had a lot of money and enjoyed spending it." I shrugged, embarrassed, then added, "Mother would have loved it. I think of her often—"

"Try not to," Agrippina stopped me, "except to know how happy and proud she would be for you."

WHAT *WOULD* MOTHER HAVE THOUGHT, I WONDERED that evening when I told Pilate what I had done. My husband was furious. It was not enough that I had defied him by going to Agrippina's home, but a banquet . . .

"Are you out of your mind?" he roared. "Despite your abysmal connections, I have managed to forge a link with the emperor and now you do this. Are you trying to undermine any chance I have of moving ahead?"

"Pilate, please—" I began, trying not to cry. "They are my family—all that is left of it. Agrippina is so careworn, a shadow of her former self. If you could see her . . ."

"I don't want to see her! I don't want *you* to see her. How much clearer do I have to make that? *Do you hear me?*"

"Yes, yes, of course I hear you. I'm sorry you're angry, but—I *promised*. I told Agrippina that I would have a banquet like old times."

"Claudia"—he grasped my shoulders, his eyes leveled on mine—"it will *never* be like old times. We must move forward."

"But I gave my word. I said we would have it on Ludi Romani. I want to invite—"

"Ludi Romani—a harvest festival in the midst of the games! Are you out of your mind?"

"Pilate, please. Never mind Ludi Romani—just a simple party, only a few of our new friends."

"Our friends! With your relatives, we will have no friends."

"Just the family then," I pressed, "a chance for us to be happy and safe together, the way we used to be." I looked at him, imploring.

Pilate's expressionless face looked like one more death

mask. Finally he sighed. "Very well, Claudia, if it means so much to you. No friends, no outside entertainers. Only your aunt and her daughters . . . and your sister, of course. If anyone should get wind of this, at least there will be a Vestal present."

Relieved, I turned away, my mind already busy with plans. Pilate's hand on my shoulder stopped me, turning me about. "There is one thing more."

What now? My breath caught as I waited wordlessly.

"You have not been a wife to me since you left the Iseneum. Tonight you will share my couch."

I DEVOTED AS MUCH EFFORT TO THE SMALL DINNER AS I did to one OF Pilate's banquets. Thoughts of *Tata* and Mother rose unbidden again and again as I went over the details. I wanted Mother at my side advising, *Tata* standing tall and proud. I brushed the tears from my tablet and went on writing. It would be a grand affair, however small.

Each guest began with an individual head of lettuce, garnished with pickled tuna, rue leaves, and onion. Then came the main courses: oysters, stuffed wild fowl, followed by baked ostrich brains, a dish that Mother served often to *Tata,* who had loved it. Finally the desserts: platter after platter of confections borne by solemn-faced slaves, each carrying a delicacy more elaborate than the last. A highlight that warm autumn evening was snow brought from the northern mountains. Though most of it melted on the plate, the initial effect was spectacular.

Pilate had made it clear: no dancers, comic actors, musicians, or magicians. Fortunately a house slave played the lute quite well. Perhaps this was even better, for nothing interfered with our conversation. At first the reunion was bittersweet—who could forget the dead?—but, in time, joy at being together transcended even this. We no longer feigned gaiety. It was a splendid evening. Agrippina in her tattered finery was still regal and arresting; "baby" Agripilla, thirteen now, leggy and full of laughter; Druscilla and Julia, a bit thinner perhaps and simply dressed, were even prettier than I remembered them in Antioch. Still, it was Marcella who remained the family beauty. Her white gown and simple headdress drew attention to almond-shaped eyes, mysterious and wise, her voice still seductive, velvety, and slow, a mere request for salt becoming in her mouth a caress. Sadly a dalliance was unthinkable; lapsed Vestals were buried alive. Too dreadful to imagine.

Pilate surprised me. After his initial anger, he acquiesced to my plans with surprising grace. The bargain he had struck had, it seemed, satisfied him. At dinner, he was an attentive host to all but reserved his special charm for Agrippina. Pilate seated her at his right and selected tidbits especially for her. He solicited her opinion of the wine and directed the slave to play her favorite songs. I watched Agrippina blossom, sometimes showing flashes of the old carefree confidence. Isis bless him, I thought. He can be kind when he chooses. I had forgotten.

Too soon the party ended. Agrippina and the girls departed in our litter, slaves bearing torches to light the way. Pilate chatted with Marcella, expressing pleasure at meeting the sister-in-law he had heard so much about. She more than lived up to expectations, he assured her. Finally, excusing himself, he retired to his rooms. Marcella, allowed to remain with us for this one night, would share my apartment. I had looked forward to the reunion for so long. Now I felt suddenly shy. Could this remote stranger really be the laughing, impetuous companion that I had longed for all these years?

"Were you with Mother and *Tata* at the end?" I asked.

"Yes." She took my hand. "Has no one told you about that—about the banquet?"

"No!" I gasped. "What banquet?"

"It was a grand affair." Marcella spoke slowly, deliberately. "We who dared brave Tiberius's wrath to go—possibly one hundred who loved them well—were served the finest that money could buy. And the entertainers! They were magnificent—everything you could possibly imagine. Mother and *Tata* were wonderful, walking among us, smiling, chatting as though it were a wedding feast." Marcella stopped, struggling to hold back her tears. "Then, at the height of the evening, the slaves brought a finer wine than any served before, a rare and costly vintage brought from Gaul. *Tata* and Mother shared a toast, urged their friends to drink more wine and enjoy the revels, then said good-bye."

"You saw all this. Oh, Marcella, how terrible." I slipped my arms around her, fearing what must come next.

"They—they walked away smiling, hand in hand. In the bath, *Tata* opened his veins and Mother's while musicians played." Marcella was sobbing now and so was I. "Take comfort," she gulped, wiping her tears on the couch covering. "The banquet was so costly, there was nothing left for Tiberius to confiscate."

We cried together, held each other close for a time, unable

to speak. Grief united us, but was that all? So many years had passed since our girlhood. We were women now, following different paths. Very different. Lying together on a large couch as we had as children, I recalled long-ago nights when we had talked of high matters—the grand ladies we would become, the dashing husbands who would adore us. How certain we had been then of our destinies, how sure of our wisdom. Where was that casual camaraderie now, the easy words, the dreams, the secrets that once came lightly to our lips?

Marcella spoke at last. "Pilate is handsome. You must be happy."

"Very happy," I agreed. Could I tell a Vestal that my husband's lovemaking gratified my flesh, but left my spirit empty? After an uncomfortable silence, I ventured, "Do you find your duties challenging?"

"Indeed, yes. My apprenticeship is over; now I perform the sacred rituals, bake the *mola salsa*." Marcella had never been much for ritual; as for baking bread . . .

There was a longish silence and then she ventured, "You and Pilate did a brave thing—the party tonight. Your husband was wonderful to Auntie."

"Pilate can be the most charming man in the world when he wants something. I wonder what it is now."

"Perhaps it is you."

"But he already has me."

"As he would like to have you?"

I stared at Marcella. What could a Vestal know of married life? We fell silent again. Soon Marcella's breathing was even, but I remained awake. She was no happier than I, despite her seeming enthusiasm. Why did that frighten me?

I BREATHED A SILENT PRAYER TO ISIS AS I SAT DOWN TO breakfast the next morning. Give me back my sister. Plates of figs, dates, and assorted breads and cheeses covered a large table inlaid with ivory. "This is so good," Marcella said, spreading a wedge of cheese on a second piece of bread.

"It's an Egyptian cheese, Pilate's favorite," I told her. "I found it in a little shop on Velabrun Street, just down the hill."

"In Rome such a short time and you have already discovered Velabrun Street! Did one of your dreams lead you there?"

Hearing the old teasing note, I relaxed. "I have taken to dismissing Rachel with the litter and going off alone to explore."

"What does your husband say about that?"

"Pilate is far too busy to notice. We came to Rome because a well-placed contact here suggested that it might be advantageous for him. Perhaps you know the man—Lucius Sejanus?"

Marcella looked up from her figs in surprise. "Well placed indeed! Everyone knows the commander of the Praetorian Guard—he is the only one Tiberius trusts other than that hateful Livia."

"No wonder Pilate is happy." I paused a moment, then leaned forward, confiding, "I envy you."

Marcella threw back her head and laughed, a merry, bubbling sound. In her white gown without the head covering, she resembled a toddler playing dress-up. The hair once shorn to the scalp was a mass of close-cropped curls. "You"—she struggled to contain her mirth—"with all you have—you envy me?"

"First I belonged to *Tata,* now to Pilate. Should I outlive him, my son—if have one—or some other man if I don't, will be appointed to look after me."

"Only for your protection."

"*You* need not ask a man for anything." I felt my voice rising at the bewilderment I saw in her face. "If we divorced, Pilate could take our children. No one would expect any less."

"You don't plan to divorce Pilate?" Marcella's eyes were wide.

"Not anymore," I sighed. Why could she not understand? We sat silently for a time. "Men control everything," I reminded her. "Pilate could kill me and no one would challenge him."

Marcella leaned forward, her cheeks pink with excitement. "Only if you had a lover—do you?"

"Of course not! I am only saying that you, as a Vestal, have a life independent of any man."

"I pay a high price for that."

"Think how respected you are, how admired," I reminded her. "You preside at ceremonies. People of importance come to you to deposit their wills. You advise them. What you do matters. What do I exist for other than to please Pilate?"

"I should like nothing more than to please a man."

"Suppose you could not please the man you loved, not for long anyway. Suppose he wanted variety because it meant never having to be close to any one person. Suppose all that really mattered to him was power and influence. Would you still want nothing more than to please him?"

Marcella sighed. "It appears life has played a joke on us. I should gladly exchange the autonomy you admire for marriage—even if it is a lottery."

"Would you really, or do you simply believe that it would be different for you?"

Marcella shrugged. "Doesn't every woman imagine that she could make it different?"

The conversation ended abruptly when Pilate looked in on us before his morning appointments. It was time for Marcella to return to the Temple of the Vestals.

I SAW MARCELLA OFTEN AFTER THAT. SHE CAME TO OUR home for quiet family dinners and I frequently visited her at the temple. Occasionally we were allowed to go out together on short errands. We rode in the Vestal litter—luxuriously cushioned in snowy white silk. The exterior was white too, trimmed in gold and covered with flowers. Lictors with *fasces*, bundles of rods, preceded us wherever we went. There was always a great commotion. Once fighting broke out in the streets as people struggled to get a closer view of Marcella. Somehow a man stumbled and fell beneath the litter. Very bad luck for him! Everyone knows the penalty for such an infringement is death. But on another occasion we rounded a corner just in time to encounter a criminal being led to his death. In this case, a chance meeting with a holy Vestal meant reprieve. Of course, Marcella had to swear that the meeting was accidental—which of course it was—but the criminal, a murderer, I later heard, was set free.

It wasn't long before Marcella and I were chatting intimately as we once had. She was horrified when I described my experience in the snake pit, but refused to believe that Pilate had any part in it. It was clear that she liked and admired him. "You have a husband that any woman might desire," she pointed out, "and he loves you."

"If Pilate loves anything it is power."

"Ah! An attraction of opposites." She smiled knowingly. "I remember when we were girls. You were always so ethereal, off in another world someplace, just a bit . . . irrational."

"Pilate would surely agree, but what does he know?"

Marcella laughed. "So, you are not as impressed with him as he would like. I imagine he is a bit confused by you."

"I have no idea." I shook my head, unable to say more. "How do *you* know so much?"

"We Vestals see a lot. People come to us for more than wills. It makes them feel good to tell us their stories. They confess all kinds of things because they think we are so holy—above it all. You would be surprised what we hear." Marcella sighed, then quickly changed the subject.

December approached and with it Saturnalia, a celebration of the sun's rebirth. With the shortest day came the symbolic killing of winter. In early times a man reigned as Saturn until the season's end, when he was sacrificed for the good of the world. That was long ago. Now the death of Father Saturn was merely a reminder that the year was ending and it would soon be time to plant. An air of joy, optimism, and goodwill prevailed, manifesting itself in presents and parties, many parties. This was my first Saturnalia in Rome and I was quickly absorbed in the holiday rush.

A ceremony at the Temple of Saturn launched the season on December 17. Priests blessed the sowing of seeds for the year ahead. Slaves were given the day off so they could attend the free banquet. Shops and businesses closed so workers could take part in the festivities. Pilate and I, along with nearly everyone we knew, went about wearing freedmen's caps and greeting one another with the cry "Ho, Saturnalia!" Distinctions between slaves and masters were reversed. With the help of a caterer, I arranged a lavish banquet in which the slaves were honored guests, Pilate and I the servers. When at last we sat down, exhausted but pleased with ourselves, it was only after our temporary masters and mistresses had eaten their fill.

Pilate and I went to many parties together, sharing the same dining couch, something we hadn't done in years. One of the most gala events was a banquet at the temple of Mercury. I wore a gown of silvery blue silk brought by caravan from the far east. Around my throat was Pilate's Saturnalia gift, a star sapphire pendant. It was a magnificent stone. He said it matched my eyes.

Upon entering the vast portals of the temple, I glimpsed Marcella with two other Vestals. My sister's mischievous wink was our only exchange in the crowded confusion of the large gathering. The encounter didn't surprise me. The temples of Vesta and Mercury were side by side, a symbolic union. Vesta's round hearth was inside the home, while the priapic pillar of Mercury stood at every threshold. Her fire provided sanctity while his presence at the door welcomed fertility. Vesta's sacred flame warmed the home. Mercury was a guide to the larger world outside where wit, sophistication, and luck were needed.

I saw little piety in Mercury's priests; their party was the most licentious I had yet attended. Jugglers and acrobats performed naked in a crowded hall lavishly festooned with wreaths and garlands. Besides the flutes and lyres, a water organ pumped madly in time to drums while girls and boys in gauzy veils danced. Some of the guests also danced—on tables. Others reclined on them. I saw threesomes, foursomes, more possibilities than I could ever have imagined.

The wine, the proximity of our bodies lying together on the couch, the erotic movements of a few couples who had had the grace to cover themselves with *stolas*, and the sight of some who had not, inflamed me. The performance of my wifely duties had been perfunctory. Now, for the first time, I desired Pilate. "Why do we not go home?" I whispered in his ear.

His eyes lit with pleasure. "Why do we not find a place right here?"

My pulse quickened as I looked about at the well-oiled bodies gleaming in the lamplight. The thought of making love in a temple appealed to me, the ubiquitous statues of the phallic Mercury an unnecessary aphrodisiac. Was Saturnalia not a time to be outrageous?

Slipping away unnoticed, we found a remote room—perfect! Unfortunately, someone else had had the same idea. The couple, oblivious to all but each other, never saw us, but I saw them.

I stood frozen in the doorway.

The woman was Marcella.

CHAPTER

21

Vesta's Vengeance

The night was filled with horror as I lay sleepless, haunted by half-remembered dreams. Marcella alone in the fearful dark. Marcella screaming for help that would not come. Marcella *entombed*. I recognized now that signs had been shown me before but I had not recognized them. If Fortuna had decreed Marcella's destiny, her doom was sealed . . . No! It could not be. I would not let it be. There must be a way.

I was the first visitor admitted to the temple of the Vestals the morning after the Mercury banquet. Trembling with nervousness and fatigue, I urged Marcella to brave the Saturnalia throngs already crowding the street.

Once we were inside my litter, heavy curtains drawn, I confronted her with what I had seen. Like any woman in love, Marcella was only too happy to talk about it. She had met her lover, Quintus Atticus, a young knight from a prominent family, when he visited the temple in connection with his father's will.

"We loved each other on sight," Marcella told me, "but

nothing would have come of it if we had not chanced to meet again at the banquet. Do you not believe our union was blessed by Mercury?"

"Perhaps, but surely not by Vesta." I was furious; I wanted to shake her. "Do you not realize the risk? You know the penalty."

Marcella merely chattered on. "I took flowers to the Temple of Venus to thank her for this wonderful thing that has happened. I thought I would die without ever knowing what it was to love a man."

I gasped. "Are you insane? What will people think when they see a Vestal sacrificing to Venus?"

"I told everybody that it was for you, that I was praying that you would conceive a child. As a matter of fact, I did that as well." Marcella smiled, delighted by her own ingenuity.

"You were unbelievably lucky last night not to have been seen. The Saturnalia madness has overwhelmed you. Promise me—promise on Mother's honor—that you will never, never ever even think of doing such a thing again."

Marcella's eyes flew open. "I can't do that! I have already done it again. Early this morning we met beyond Mars Field. It was deserted. Everyone is recovering from last night's festivities."

I did not need the sight to know then that Marcella was truly doomed, that it was only a matter of time before she and Quintus were caught and punished, but I continued to plead with her.

Pilate was livid when I told him. "That damn fool girl! Doesn't she realize what she's doing to herself, what she's doing to all of us?" Not waiting for a litter, he hurried off to speak to Quintus, to demand that he put an end to the affair immediately.

Pilate's efforts were useless. In less than a month they were discovered. Several boys vying for equestrian status had gone early to Mars Field to practice jumping. One horse had taken a tumble, throwing his young rider into the same ditch occupied by Marcella and Quintus. Possibly the boys might have said nothing, but contestants were always accompanied by their mothers, women more competitive for their sons than the boys were themselves. Those harpies were not about to remain silent.

Now only Tiberius, acting as Pontifex Maximus, could save Marcella's life. I begged Pilate to intercede. Almost gently, he reminded me of the enmity the emperor had shown my parents, the obvious danger to myself.

"I do not care!" I protested. "I must see him. Surely you can arrange it."

"I can't. I *won't.*" I couldn't see Pilate's expression; he had pulled me tight against his chest, but the emotion in his voice surprised me. I realized that whatever could be done would have to be done by me.

That evening an unexpected opportunity presented itself when Lucius Sejanus, Tiberius's confidant and Pilate's patron, joined us for dinner. Both handsome and urbane, Sejanus was considered a ladies' man. He liked to flirt and he liked me. It was easy to arrange a few quiet moments with him. "Pilate tells me that an audience with the emperor is impossible, but somehow I feel that you . . ."

The next day an exquisitely carved ivory box was delivered to me, inside a message from Sejanus. Tiberius had agreed to an audience that very night. I knew better than to speak of it to Pilate. He could forcibly restrain me if he chose. Fortunately, some fellow officers called unexpectedly that evening. He was sitting with them in his *tablinum* when I stole out the back entrance. I refused to take Rachel with me, not wanting to involve her in whatever lay ahead. She reluctantly summoned a litter and I set off alone.

The palace, as always, swarmed with guards, but someone—Sejanus, or possibly Tiberius himself—had alerted them to my arrival. Their leader nodded a brusque greeting, then led the way inside. The palace was quiet, few sounds anywhere, only the slap of our sandals echoing on marble floors. Dizzy with fear, I entered the emperor's private chambers. The impact of the priceless art assembled there was stunning; so was the explicitly erotic subject matter. On one frescoed wall I saw Jupiter in the guise of a bull raping Europa. On another, as a swan, he ravished Leda.

As I studied the third, Jupiter annihilating lovely Semele with his thunderbolts, Tiberius silently entered the room. As his eyes swept over me, my heart thumped so loudly I was certain he heard it. Somewhere below us was the dungeon where Drusus had slowly starved to death, at last gnawing his own hands in desperation. Lately there had been rumors of the emperor's depravity, stories of women violated, wives of officers who had fallen from grace. Praying silently to Isis, I forced myself to meet his gaze.

The changes in Tiberius's appearance were shocking. Ten years alone could not account for the haggard face, the dull, bloodshot eyes. The large, bull-chested body was thick and bloated.

"So the little seer has grown into a beauty," he said at last. "I would not have known you but for your eyes. Do they still foresee the future? You did well for me at our last meeting."

"The circus was not our last meeting. There was another," I reminded him. "The ceremony marking my sister's induction into the Vestal order. It is because of her that I have come."

"Ah, yes, the lapsed virgin. You hope to plead her cause."

"Don't you feel that under these special circumstances—"

Tiberius raised a bushy brow. "Special circumstances?"

"She was not meant to be a Vestal."

"It would appear not," he said, lowering himself onto a couch.

"I mean"—I sat down opposite him—"entering the order was a mistake in the first place. She was overage."

"And, I hear, underqualified."

"Marcella was forced against her will to become a Vestal."

"Since when does a woman's will matter? A father decides what is best for his daughter."

"My father did not decide. Your mother did."

Surprise blotched Tiberius's face as he stared at me. Then quickly, so quickly I wondered if I had imagined it, his masklike expression returned. My words hung in silence.

It seemed an eternity before the emperor spoke. "You must love your sister dearly."

"Why else would I have come?"

"Then I am sorry for you."

"You have a choice," I reminded him. "Some other punishment—exile, perhaps, anything but death."

"She knew her fate. The penalty was ordained hundreds of years ago, at the birth of Rome itself."

"As emperor, you can change it."

"As emperor, perhaps; as Pontifex Maximus, never. Even if I wanted to save your sister, which I don't particularly, I could not. To ignore her violation, to show any sign of leniency, would undermine the foundation of the empire."

"Surely there is something—"

"There is nothing." He rose from the couch where he had been reclining and walked slowly toward me. Placing his hand beneath my chin, Tiberius tilted my head upward. Again I forced myself to meet his eyes. Another agonizing eternity. Finally he spoke, "Livia was wrong about you, wrong from the beginning. You are in no sense a mouse." Tiberius reflected briefly. "Very well . . . I will grant you a boon. Your sister will die, as decreed, but you may see her tonight and ride at her side tomorrow."

This was my last chance, I had to try. "Such a small lapse really, it's not as though she allowed the sacred flame to die. Must it be so cruel a death? Why not something quick? A sudden blow perhaps . . ." I hesitated, heart pounding. "You might permit her to take her own life."

"My dear, my dear"—he sighed wearily—"you know the penalty as well as I. Take comfort that it is a quiet death, a bloodless one. Quintus Atticus met his end by flogging."

Picking up a small scroll from his cluttered desk, Tiberius scratched a quick note that would be my pass, then handed it to me, his manner almost courtly. Was he mocking me? I could not tell, did not care.

My bearers took me directly to the Atrium Vestae, where an attendant led me to Marcella. Her room, though small, was comfortably furnished and brightly lit. There was a bouquet of violets on the small desk where she sat writing.

Marcella looked up in surprise at my entrance, knocking over the chair as she rushed to embrace me.

"I tried, I tried." My voice trembled. "Tiberius was implacable, nothing I said made any difference."

Marcella's eyes widened. "You went to Tiberius? Blessed Vesta! What were you thinking? You know what he's capable of. You know how he hates anyone even remotely connected with Germanicus and Agrippina. Only Fortuna herself saved you when Father and Mother died. If you had been living in Rome—"

"Pilate has said all that many times. It made no difference. Anything was worth a try and Tiberius did at least agree to let me see you. I expected to find you in prison."

"Why? Where would I go? There is no escape."

"I know that now."

"The other Vestals have been kind." Marcella gestured at the flowers. "They will miss me, I think. I was just writing you a letter. You would have received it tomorrow after—"

For the first time her voice wavered. "Quintus—I thought to write him too."

Sadly, I shook my head.

"Oh!" Marcella gasped, her face suddenly white. "Poor darling, he was so strong, so alive."

"You also, Marcella. You are more full of life's joy than anyone I know."

"But I was not living, not until I met Quintus. I made the best of things here, acted silly sometimes, played with the little girls, tried to make it all easier for them than it was for me. I showed some of the older ones a few things too, brightened their lives a bit." The impish smile I knew so well appeared for an instant. "But that wasn't living—not for me, not the way I was meant to live. We are not in this world to live safely. We are here to fall in love and break our hearts."

"And lose our lives?"

"If need be."

I looked at Marcella wonderingly. "You aren't sorry, are you?"

"I'm sorry we got caught. It would have happened sooner or later. I would have preferred later."

In just a few brief moments a Vestal, red-eyed from weeping, came to tell us that it was time for me to leave.

THE NEXT DAY I SAT BESIDE MARCELLA, WHO LAY ON A bier as one already dead. I held her hand as the funeral procession wove its way through Rome. A grim-faced Pilate rode beside our wagon on horseback as an escort. Agrippina, with her daughters, followed directly behind in a chariot. Fortunately Caligula and Livia were wintering in Capri, sparing us the further ordeal of their presence.

I expected jeers and cries of derision but the crowd was curiously silent, overwhelmed perhaps by the enormity of what was happening. Most stood solemn-faced as the procession slowly made its way to the Campus Scleratus, the Evil Fields, near the Colline Gate. Though glad our parents were spared this final horror, I knew they would have been as proud as I.

Spectators marveled at Marcella's courage as she lay quietly on the bier, face waxen, eyes clear and dry. The icy cold hand in mine remained steady. When at last we reached our destination there were no rites, no solemnities, not even a funeral dirge.

The oxen that had pulled our wagon stood stolidly as Marcella was lifted from the bier. She walked unaided, slowly but with great dignity, to a sunken tomb that had been freshly dug beside the gate. There was no opportunity for a final embrace, only a last look over her shoulder at me and beyond to streets wet now with early morning dew. The sun had just risen. It would be a clear day. Marcella's hand touched a large geranium bush growing against the stone wall. For an instant her fingers caressed the velvety softness of a leaf. Sick at heart, I watched Marcella turn and begin her descent into the tiny cavern. Inside, I had been told, was an oil lamp, a little food, and a small couch.

The entrance was quickly sealed, and the earth above moved to cover the vault, then tamped down. Soon there would be no trace whatsoever of the grave. The message was clear: a Vestal's life, the embodiment of the sacred flame, was snuffed out when she ceased to personify the goddess, then covered over with earth as one would extinguish smoldering coals on a hearth. It was as if she never existed.

I turned away, my arm drawn protectively across my belly. In the midst of all this horror I knew suddenly that I carried a child, a girl. I will remember you always, Marcella, I promised silently, and my baby will bear your name.

CHAPTER

22

My Second Mother

Black as night, black as death. It *is* death. I am buried alive . . . Screams, my screams. My fists beat against clammy sepulcher walls. "Let me out!" No one comes. No one will ever come. Hideous shrieks echo in darkness. Then silence. Silence of the grave . . .

Someone laughs. A giddy girl waves at me. It is Marcella, so pretty in her blue gown. Caligula pulls at her sleeve. Marcella long ago . . . in the palace, so exciting . . . a grown-up banquet.

"You're alive!" I gasp.

"More alive than you, Claudia." She pirouettes, arms like swan's wings ready to fly. "Go home! Go home! Go home!" That mischievous laugh again.

"I can't go home. I'm in your tomb."

"No tomb can keep you—or me. Open your eyes. Your life is waiting. Enjoy it. Enjoy it for me."

She is gone.

Faint sounds far away. Rachel? Agrippina . . . is that you? My eyelids are heavy. Too heavy to open. Another voice, stronger . . . Pilate? No, he would not come here. Still the voices. Why won't they let me be?

"Welcome back!" It was Agrippina above me. Her hands gently smoothed the covers. "We have missed you."

Rachel, too, was at my side. "It has been days since you said a word."

I struggled to sit up. "I knew somehow that you were there, but I was so tired . . . Too tired to speak, to know what was real or unreal . . . Pilate . . . I felt him too . . . He was kind."

"Kind indeed!" Agrippina exclaimed. "The tragedies that have plagued our family—and now this dreadful scandal! Another man would have divorced you."

"If that is his choice, I can always go to the Temple of Isis." Even as I spoke the words, I knew I didn't mean them.

As though my thoughts had conjured him, Pilate appeared in the doorway, immaculate in white, the narrow knight's stripe adorning the right shoulder of his tunic, his thick brown hair cut and combed in the short military style that became him well.

In an instant he had crossed the room, was leaning over my couch, his arms supporting me. Eagerly his eyes searched my face. "You've come back to us."

I saw the light cloak resting about his shoulders. "Yes, I have come back. Must you leave . . . now?"

"I can't stay. Something—something urgent has come up. Sejanus is waiting, but I won't leave you again," he promised.

He looked ill at ease, I mused drowsily. Strange for Pilate. I smiled, already feeling better. Where had I been? What had happened to me? Marcella's execution . . . so frightful . . .

I must not think of it . . . But Marcella's message . . . A dream, so real. *Your life is waiting.* Marcella never could stand long faces.

"I will look forward to your return," I told Pilate, kissing him lightly.

I AWAKENED TO THE SCENT OF ROSES. THE PALEST PINK, the richest peach—blossoms everywhere. Beside me, a cut-glass flagon of wine and another of water rested on a low ivory table with two golden cups and a silver plate of honey cakes. How perfect these past days had been.

I turned my head. Pilate was sitting beside me, his lips curved in a smile. Had he been watching me nap? I ran my fingers across his shoulders, feeling the skin, the bone, the smooth, warm muscle.

"You decide," he was saying. "We can go to Sejanus's banquet or dine here at home together."

I looked up, amazed at such a suggestion from the husband who preferred to go out every night, with or without me. "We have already accepted," I reminded him.

Pilate shrugged. "I can send a slave with our regrets."

I studied him from beneath my lashes. Lucius Aelius Sejanus, commander of the Praetorian Guard, was second only to Tiberius. To even consider forfeiting his invitation . . . Pilate was being kind. He must know how much I dreaded returning to society. I longed to take the opportunity offered me, but knew better. "We have dallied here much of the day," I said, stretching languorously. "It is time we were up and about." His relieved smile was my reward.

"Go now," I said, gently pushing at his chest. "I must get ready."

Pilate allowed himself to be banished. Within seconds Rachel arrived to draw my bath. As I splashed idly, she slipped from the room, returning moments later carrying a filmy confection of lavender and violet. "Isn't it time you wore this?" My breath caught at the sight of the gown. It was designed for a Saturnalia party that Pilate and I were to have given. A party that had been canceled.

"Why not?" Resolutely, I rose from the bath and allowed her to dry me. *Move on, move on. Life is to be lived.* It was as though Marcella stood at my side as Rachel slipped the violet underdress over my head. It was overlaid with lavender drapery sheer enough to allow the deeper shade to show through. To this Rachel added a third, even filmier layer of the palest mauve. Deftly, she twisted my heavy hair, securing it with gold clips, then knotting and coiling it so that only a few ringlets were allowed to escape.

"You remind me more of the lady Selene every day," Rachel said, dusting my hair with gold, which she had carefully extracted from a large glass vial.

"Not so! Mother was beautiful."

"She had a womanly glow about her, and now you have it too."

"If that be true, it is because I know at last that Pilate loves me. I am sure he does. During the day he sees only clients. The evenings he spends with me. There can't be anyone else. He has changed. Surely you have noticed."

Rachel knelt to slip my feet into court sandals, stitched and edged in purple. Her face was hidden as she laced the golden ribbons to just above my ankles.

I WAS STARTLED BY THE OPULENCE OF SEJANUS'S PALACE, only slightly less lavish than Tiberius's own. Standing beside Pilate as slaves removed our wraps, I struggled to compose myself. Except for a few short rides in my curtained litter, this was the first time that I had been out of the house since my sister's execution. How could I face the derision of many, the curiosity of all?

Senses reeling from the thick scent of Egyptian incense and flowers, I looked about the courtyard. A wave of nausea swept over me. Surely I was not going to be ill now! Resolutely, I took Pilate's arm. The hum of voices deepened as we moved forward past a brilliant fresco that depicted satyrs and nymphs at play. Pilate raised an eyebrow. The painting left nothing to the imagination.

Every inch of floor was covered with intricately designed mosaic tiles, every item of furniture coated with gold leaf. The sound of voices swelled to a muted roar as we passed through a gallery filled with dazzling larger-than-life statues of gods and heroes. At the entrance to the dining chamber, Sejanus strode forward to greet us. He had thrown off his heavy toga, as comfort and custom required at banquets, and wore only a scarlet short-sleeved tunic embroidered with gold leaves that matched his sandals. Sejanus looked splendid, but I sensed that he, like my father, was at his best in helmet, cuirass, and greaves, sword at his side, warhorse champing at the bit.

"Pilate! My most ardent supporter," he said, clapping my

husband's shoulder. His mouth lingered on my cheek a fraction too long, barely missing my mouth. Beyond his shoulder I saw some fifty guests reclining in twos and threes on couches carved in the shape of swans and inlaid with lapis and mother-of-pearl. As we advanced into the room, I walked between the two men, chatting lightly with Sejanus while my stomach churned with nervousness. One woman gasped. Another set her mouth tightly and fixed me with a reproving glare. Others merely watched with superior smiles. Was every guest sneering at me? I lifted my chin. How dare they scoff at me, how dare they pass judgment on Marcella? I wanted to throw something at them, something that would destroy them all and forever wipe out the sight of their gaping, curious faces. Instead, as Sejanus took my elbow, I looked up and smiled, pulling the corners of my mouth tight to keep the muscles from quivering. "What were you saying? I did not hear."

Sejanus grinned at me. "I said, 'Were I to have the opportunity, I should rather have you as my dinner partner than Venus herself.' Surely you and Pilate will join me?" He nodded toward the large couch at the head of the room. I took a deep breath and linked my arms with Sejanus and Pilate. Together we walked toward the room's center. As I reclined between these two powerful men I felt every eye upon me. At that moment rose petals rained down from nets suspended from the gilded ceiling.

Throngs of slaves served one course after another and drew flagons of wine from large basins of beaten gold banked by fresh mountain snow. "How have you kept it from melting?" I asked Sejanus.

"There's a lead-lined chamber beneath us. Apicata—my wife—designed it."

"Where is your wife?" I hardly dared ask. Was she absenting herself because of me?

As though reading my mind, Sejanus smiled. "She is wintering with our children in Pompeii. You will meet her soon."

On the couch beside us a man poured wine down his throat so fast it dribbled over his chin. The music, at first lutes and flutes, swelled to a frenzy as tambourines and cymbals, horns and trumpets were added. Windows, closed against the late winter chill, let little air into the room. It was hot, stifling, thick with the scent of flowers and aromatic oils that lithe young boys sprinkled on our feet. I felt another wave of nausea and forced it down. Not here, not now.

Pilate and Sejanus took turns playfully blowing the gold dust from my hair, laughing as it swirled to the floor where slaves scrambled to collect the tiny grains. I laughed too, beginning to relax. Then I caught sight of a woman watching us. She was tall and imposing, with swelling breasts and a small waist. Her hair was dark red, her skin clear and white, and her eyes a sparkling green that rivaled the emerald of her gown. Aggressively beautiful, she created an immediate impression of wild, untamable passion. I wondered at the hatred in that exquisite face, for she was surely the most spectacular creature I had ever seen. Puzzled, I returned her stare. As the evening progressed, the condemnation of the other guests had been replaced by interest in themselves. So why this intense hostility now from a woman I had never met?

Just then, Sejanus leaned across me to fill his jewel-studded cup; his arm moved lightly across my breasts. The woman's eyes missed nothing. That's it, I thought, the poor thing is in love with Sejanus. She is jealous. A flood of compassion swept over me. How well I understood the sick rage, the frustration and humiliation that mysterious woman must feel. How marvelous it was to be free of jealousy at last.

One morning I awakened to feel the baby stirring within me. Pilate's place beside me was empty. Bright sun streamed through the windows. I was certain that he had already breakfasted and was seeing clients. I could not disturb him, but wanted so much to share my pleasure and excitement with someone . . . Agrippina, of course. We had always been close, but now she was trying so hard to be the mother I had lost. I loved and depended on her more every day and was eager to share this wonderful new development.

My heart quickened with happy excitement as I jumped from bed. I was so anxious to be on my way that I didn't summon Rachel. Unwilling to wait for her, I pulled on my gown, twisted my hair into a clumsy knot, and rushed out into the warm spring morning. It was a gorgeous, glittering day, new buds everywhere. New life everywhere, I thought complacently. When my litter reached Agrippina's tenement, I was surprised to find imperial guards posted before the shabby door. "Where has the lady gone?" I asked the captain who barred my way.

"The emperor has taken her."

"Oh no!" I gasped. "Surely not." I shook my head, not wanting to believe the words. "Where are her daughters?"

"Gone, all gone." His eyes roved the streets cautiously, then returned to me. "You would be wise to leave as well." He looked pointedly at my belly. "Think of your health."

I turned back to my litter. A servant carefully helped me inside. "Take me home," I directed the bearers. "Hurry! Please hurry!"

Pilate was there when I arrived, the tension in his face easing at the sight of me. "I was going to send slaves to look for you. Have you heard about Agrippina?"

"Oh, Pilate, I was just there. She's gone and—"

He took me in his arms. "Now, now," he said, patting me gently. "I'll tell you what I know. Agrippina was invited to the palace last night, a command appearance. It was a banquet, Agrippina a guest, or so she was told. Tiberius offered her an apple. She refused—perhaps someone had warned her of poison. He became angry and ordered a guard to arrest her."

"Where is she? I want to see her."

"That is impossible. Besides"—Pilate pulled me closer, shielding me—"I doubt that she would want you to see her."

I stiffened. "What do you mean? What are you talking about?" I pulled away to confront him. Pilate's hands remained on my shoulders. "Agrippina should have known better," he said. "She resisted the guards, reminded them all at the top of her lungs that she was Augustus's granddaughter. She shouted that if anyone should be arrested it was Tiberius."

"In Isis's name, what was she thinking!" Fear, like a chill, raised small bumps on my arms. "What did he do to her?"

"You don't want to know. It would not be good for you or for the baby."

"Whatever it is, not knowing is worse."

"He ordered her beaten. They all watched."

My throat constricted. I forced the words out. "And then?"

"She lost an eye."

"No! Oh no! Agrippina—she was so beautiful, so very beautiful." Hands covering my own face, I turned away, sobbing.

"She still has her life," Pilate reminded me. "I will call Rachel. You must lie down."

I struggled for control. "How did you find this out?"

"Sejanus was here. He didn't want you to hear it on the street."

"Where is Agrippina now?"

"On her way to Pandateria."

"That wretched isolated island?"

"Perhaps she does not care."

"The people loved her so . . ."

"The guards took her early this morning in a closed litter. No one knew—but even if they had—" Pilate shrugged.

"She's gone then, like *Tata* and Mother, like Marcella. They are all gone. I have lost everyone."

"I'm here, Claudia"—Pilate took me in his arms—"and soon you will have our child."

CHAPTER

23

Titania

In the weeks that followed, I clung to Pilate's words like keepsakes, playing them in my head again and again. I had lost so many loved ones, beginning with Germanicus and the stillbirth of my first child at five months. What if I lost this child, too? The idea terrified me. I suffered sieges of nausea and on one occasion fainted. For a time swollen ankles kept me in bed. "It's nothing unusual," Rachel reminded me repeatedly. I listened gratefully, no longer thinking it strange that a slave had become my closest friend, perhaps my only friend.

Sometimes my changing body frightened me; at other times it brought a sense of wonder. I had felt from the beginning that my baby was a girl, and as the months passed, the certainty grew. I talked often to little Marcella, assuring her of my love, promising that I would always keep her safe. Finally, as the end of my term approached, the nausea disappeared and the swelling in my ankles abated. Feeling better made me restless. I wanted to get out, to ride through the streets in my litter and be part of the world.

"It feels like I've been fat forever," I confided to Rachel as she slipped a soft pink *chiton* over my shoulders. "At times I forget that I'm going to have a baby and think I'm just naturally huge. Pilate's been very kind and amazingly inventive, but I do miss being able to look down and see my feet."

"It won't be much longer," she said, hands on my shoulders, comforting. "Less than a month, I'd say."

"But I want to do something now. I'd like to go to the Forum Market. No," I amended, reaching for the contrasting bright rose *palla,* "I'm *going* to the market."

"You can't do that! *Dominus* would forbid it."

"Maybe—if he had the chance," I agreed, picking up my pouch. "But Pilate's with Sejanus this afternoon. We'll be home long before he returns."

"He will have me beaten for being party to it."

"Not likely, no one we know does that sort of thing to slaves, certainly not Pilate—and not to you."

"He could."

"He could, but he won't," I assured her. "What an idea!"

"Perhaps not," Rachel conceded, adding, "but we know it's dangerous for you."

"We know nothing of the kind," I argued. "I don't need Pilate's doctor to tell me that I'm fine. I know I am. I'm going out now—with a brave, smiling slave or none at all."

THE AFTERNOON WAS BRIGHT AND CRISP. I AMBLED happily from stall to stall, stopping at last at a booth displaying hundreds of vials of perfume. Opening one after another, I tried the contents of several. "I've worn sandalwood for so long. Perhaps I shall choose something new and different for after the baby is born. What do you think of this?" As I held the bottle toward Rachel, I saw a woman walking in our direction. "Will you look at *her*! She's gorgeous, but that gown would be more appropriate for a banquet than the street—especially in her condition."

Rachel looked over her shoulder, then quickly moved closer, so that she stood directly in front of me.

Pushing gently to get a better look, I found my slave surprisingly resistant. The woman, who carried a red parrot, cooed to it, oblivious to the stares of those about her, while slaves busily cleared a path. In contrast to the filmy black gown, the skin of her arms, shoulders, and an expanse of her breasts was chalk-white. Large emeralds sparkled from her throat and wrists. Like me, she looked to be in her eighth month but seemed scarcely aware of her bulk.

"Who do you suppose she is?"

"Titania!" Rachel almost spat the word.

I frowned slightly. "She looks familiar, yet I don't believe I know her."

"It is not likely that you would. She is a courtesan."

"Titania," I repeated the name, watching with interest. Whoever she was, Titania moved like a flame, beautiful and confident. And then I remembered a face glimpsed months before. Titania was the woman I had seen at Sejanus's banquet, the one who had watched me with such hostility.

"If she's a courtesan, why is she dressed in black?" I wondered.

"Perhaps for amusement. She had a husband, but they lived separately for years. For some reason he never divorced her.

Maybe she knew something he didn't want spread about Rome. Whatever the case, he died recently of a sudden fever."

"How do you know so much about her?"

Rachel shrugged. "Slaves talk. Titania's a legend."

"I suppose she has many lovers."

"Only a few important ones. She's become fabulously wealthy from those seeking her influence on them."

"That would make her powerful," I mused. As I studied Titania, she looked up and our glances caught. Titania's eyes slanted like an angry cat's as they moved to my belly.

I pulled my *stola* in protectively, but coolly returned her stare. Rachel must have summoned our bearers. I sensed rather than saw them, aware only of the challenge in Titania's green eyes.

"Your litter, *Domina,*" Rachel said.

"Why? Where are we going?"

"I'm taking you home. It's grown cold. You don't want to be ill now. Think of the baby."

Perhaps she was right. The sun still shone brightly, but I felt a sudden chill. Eyes never leaving Titania's, I allowed myself to be guided. It was a silly contest but one I did not intend to lose. As my litter was lifted from the ground, I continued to watch, forcing a faint smile until Titania was lost from view.

I LAY ON MY COUCH PROPPED UP BY PILLOWS PLAYING A board game with Rachel. "Ah, more luck!" Rachel lamented as I threw the dice. "You'll win this round too." She clucked her tongue despondently as I advanced my jade elephant another ten squares.

I sighed. "When is something going to happen?"

"Soon I think, soon."

"That's what you said an hour ago. Oh!" I cried out, arching backward. "Oh! That was a big one. Maybe it will be soon. Where did Selket go?"

"She's in the kitchen. I'll get her."

"Don't leave me!"

"I'm not going anywhere, just to the door to send someone for Selket."

"Of course." I let go of Rachel's hand, but smiled with relief a few moments later when Selket's bulky form appeared in the doorway. The woman's gentle touch and calm confidence had impressed me from the beginning. Now I congratulated myself once again for having insisted on a midwife from the Iseneum rather than the army surgeon urged by Pilate. Then another pain snatched the smile away and my breath with it. The board and pawns clattered unheeded onto the mosaic floor.

"Ah. Things are happening at last." Selket nodded approvingly as she bent over me. "Come, it's time for you to walk a bit."

"Help me to get her up," she instructed Rachel. Together they pulled me from the couch and supported me in a standing position. "We'll take turns walking her," Selket directed. "I will begin."

"Will it be long?" I asked after another spasm gripped me and then another.

"Now, now, you must not think ahead. Think instead that you have been in labor most of this day. It will go faster now. We will take good care of you."

"I wish my mother were here." I bit my lip, regretting the

weakness, and began to walk up and down the room. It was rapidly filling with slaves.

First Selket walked with me and then Rachel, then Selket again. "Talk to me," I begged when it was Rachel's turn once more."Tell me what the slaves are saying. What is the latest gossip? Tell me—oh! Tell me," I persisted when I could speak again, "about that woman, the strange red-haired woman. Ahh! What was her name?"

"Don't think of her." Rachel's arms tightened about me. "Do not waste time on her. She is no one to you."

"Titania," I managed to gasp. "I remember now. Tell me about Titania." I looked up to see Rachel exchange glances with Selket.

The walking ceased momentarily. Selket supported me while Rachel massaged my back. "Titania has not been seen of late," she said. "I suppose she's at home awaiting the birth of her child."

I shook my head, unable to focus on Titania or her child. Sometimes it was hard to even remember the child within myself. There was only the pain that went on and on without seeming to go anywhere.

The day passed and now it was twilight and still Selket did not say that I might lie down. I grew so weary that I could barely put one foot before the other.

It was not proper to want Pilate present for this most female thing, but I did want him, desperately. Finally the time came when I wanted him enough to cry his name. The slaves, even Selket, were shocked. I heard them murmuring among themselves. Then Rachel, stroking my back gently, said, "I will bring him now."

It seemed to me that she was gone for hours, but it could not have been long. When Rachel returned she was alone. "He was not in the house, *Domina.* Shall I send—"

"No, no! He is busy with his duties. Do not tell him—that I asked." I turned my head from side to side, gasping and biting my lips. At last I could walk no more, and Selket allowed me to lie down. Rachel remained at my side, holding my hands as the night wore on and nothing happened. "Ah, that's right, just a little more," she encouraged from time to time.

"I can't do it!" I cried, exhausted. "Help me, please help me!"

Rachel turned to Selket. "Surely there is something you can do. Some potion that you can give her."

"I have given her pennyroyal."

"And it hasn't worked. Her first child was stillborn," Rachel reminded the midwife. "*Dominus* wanted a surgeon. He will be angry if anything happens—"

Selket's usually florid face was pale, her light blue eyes heavily shadowed. "It is not my fault! Her hips are very small . . ."

"There must be something," Rachel insisted, her voice taut with anxiety. "There are all kinds of potions at the temple, I have seen them. You must have brought—" Her hand moved to Selket's basket of supplies.

The midwife pulled the basket away.

"I knew it! You do have something. Give it to her!"

"It's dangerous—sometimes—"

"Can anything be more dangerous than this? What if the baby dies? What if *she* dies?"

I saw them as though in a fog as wave after wave of pain

crested without breaking. When Selket at last held a cup to my lips, I turned my head aside. Pennyroyal and mint had tasted good at the onset of my labor, now I began to retch.

"Drink it, *Domina*," the midwife urged. "Try to swallow."

As my mouth opened once more to cry out, Rachel was ready and poured the liquid down. I fought back angrily, but then another pain grabbed me, another black tidal wave. When it receded slightly, I was aware of a soothing sensation in my parched throat. Slowly, almost imperceptibly, a dreamy relaxation stole over me, taking hold of me with increasing insistence, dragging at my mind and body, until I ceased to struggle and surrendered willingly. Engulfed in a whirlpool, I swirled at an ever increasing speed until I was lifted out of myself entirely and floated near the ceiling.

I saw Selket, eyes wide and frightened, kneeling beside a writhing body on the couch—my body. Poor, poor thing, I thought, and was mildly surprised to recognize myself. I felt no fear, only a delicious freedom from pain. I began to drift, floating back into some warm, pleasant world where there was no fear of death. Then I thought of Pilate and of our unborn child. Marcella! Must she die too? Oh, surely not, not before she had even lived!

Rachel was sobbing openly now. I waved my arms, struggling to communicate, but no one saw me. Would I always remain close to those I loved, yet so terribly far away?

Swept with longing, I looked about the familiar room, surveying each person below me, seeing them all with a new sharp-edged clarity. I heard each individual conversation distinctly. Words of concern, for the most part, words of sadness. No one expected me to live.

Two young slaves who had just entered with fresh water whispered softly, unnoticed by the others. Hovering above them, I heard each word distinctly despite the babble of other voices around them.

"She was a good *domina*," the younger one said. "You could not fool her, but she was always fair. I will miss her."

"I, too," the other agreed. "She was more than fair. The *domina* was kind, nice to be near. She knew what I was thinking sometimes and cared. We won't be so lucky again."

"Blessed Juno! What if he should replace her with the other?"

"He would never marry *her*!"

"I don't suppose, but he'll be fonder of her than ever now that she has given him a son. And who knows," the slave nodded toward the couch, "this baby may die with its mother."

"Fortuna can be so cruel. I heard both went into labor at about the same time. Titania hardly bore down and her child was born. She is a big woman, but look at our poor little lady."

Suddenly I was back in my body again, locked in flesh and pain. I felt agony beyond belief and then none. Somewhere far off I heard a baby squalling. My Marcella was alive.

I dozed, and when I woke Pilate sat beside me. He was concerned, he was tender, he even had excuses: urgent business on behalf of Sejanus had kept him from me.

He took my hand and kissed it. I looked into his clear blue eyes and wondered how often he had come directly from Titania's bed to mine.

CHAPTER 24

The Circus

Somehow, some way, I had to accept not only that my husband had a mistress but a son by her. What's more, every day Pilate ingratiated himself farther into the graces of the man who had killed my parents, exiled my aunt, and presided at the death of my sister. For a while it was enough to breathe, to merely float upon the surface. I had my baby and that was all that mattered.

Though propriety—and Pilate—demanded that I hire a wet nurse, it was I who bathed Marcella, I who dressed her and rocked her to sleep. Easy, joyous tasks. Marcella, so tiny, seemed the essence of femininity. The slaves marveled constantly at her sweetness and beauty. Pilate was enchanted by the way she smiled at him from behind her tiny fingers.

"She's flirting," he said. He had come to the nursery to find me. Now he bent over Marcella's tiny bed. "Another family beauty."

She does have Marcella's eyes, I thought, but said nothing.

The baby's small hand encircled Pilate's thumb. "We must keep her very safe," he said.

At least we agreed on something.

As my strength returned, I went each day to the Iseneum, often taking Marcella with me. Life had been so cruel. If only I could win some kind of promise from the goddess—not for myself but for my perfect, innocent child. Isis had an adored baby of her own. Surely she could understand my concern. I prayed often before her great golden statue while Marcella slept sweetly at my side.

"If Isis would just give me a sign," I said to the priestess kneeling beside me. "I have worshipped the goddess since I was a girl, yet one terrible thing after another has happened. All that remains is my baby."

"If you truly, truly believe then everything will be all right."

I turned to see a familiar face—wide, dreamy eyes, dimpled smile. Paulina Tigellius came often to the Iseneum. She was pretty, obviously indulged by a much older husband, but good natured and sociable. I could not help but smile at her spontaneity. I was lonely. Sharing a spiritual path with such an enthusiastic seeker might be pleasant.

It didn't turn out that way. Watching Paulina accept each sacred tenet without a single question, I came to wonder if she understood any of them. One day she confided that Decius Mundus, a high-ranking knight, was overcome with love for her. I knew Decius slightly. He was an intimate of Pilate's, attractive in a young unformed way and very rich. "He offered two hundred thousand sesterces to share my bed for a single night." Paulina tossed her head lightly, setting blond curls in motion. "How dare he! But Decius *is* handsome."

Decius wasn't much brighter than Paulina, I decided, and promptly forgot the matter.

Days passed and my anxiety grew. One morning I entrusted Marcella to a priestess and joined the temple slaves in scrubbing the steps leading to Isis's golden statue. If only the goddess would see my sincerity. "Protect my baby, protect my baby," I prayed silently again and again.

My normally happy baby began to howl. "She wants *you*," the priestess said, handing Marcella back to me.

"I cannot imagine what was the matter with her," I said to Rachel afterward. "She wasn't hungry, she wasn't wet—"

"Maybe the baby takes after her aunt. Would *that* Marcella have spent time in a temple if she had had a choice?"

Your life is waiting. Enjoy it. Enjoy it for me.

I WENT LESS OFTEN TO THE ISENEUM, RETURNING instead to a once familiar haunt, the Circe Bath, Rome's most fashionable. It was here that the newest tunes were played, the latest poems read, the spiciest scandals whispered. I listened idly to it all while being massaged and manicured; everyone agreed the Circe had the most adept and innovative bath attendants to be found.

One morning I arrived at the bath to feel the air charged with excitement. Mildly piqued, I looked quizzically at the two slaves who had begun to undress me. "Surely you have heard?" the older one asked as she knelt to remove my sandals.

"Suppose you tell me." I stepped out of my gown and turned slightly as the young slave wrapped a linen covering about me.

"The lady Paulina—Paulina Tigellius," the two said almost

in unison, then broke into giggles. "Shh," cautioned the older one, with a side glance at me.

I looked from one to the other, puzzled. As the slaves led me to the pool, I joined some twenty of the most prominent women in Rome. At their center, Sejanus's wife, Apicata, held court. Smiling, she made a place for me on the couch beside her. Though her husband had flirted with me from the beginning, it never seemed to bother Apicata. Perhaps, I thought, lying down beside her, such things ceased to matter after a while.

"It is the most shocking scandal," she explained, her round blue eyes sparkling with excitement. "Paulina Tegellius was seduced at the Iseneum."

Oh, Isis! My heart began to thump. This was more than gossip . . . I knew something terrible had happened.

Apicata went blithely on. "A priest from the Iseneum went to Paulina's home. He said the god Anubis had fallen in love with her and wanted her to come to him that very night. I am surprised you have not heard about it. Paulina was so flattered she went about telling everyone."

"Including her husband?"

"Saturnius was the first to know."

"And he let her go?"

"He was as proud as she and did some bragging of his own. Imagine having a wife so beautiful that even a god desired her. It's like Jupiter and Leda."

"Oh no!" I shook my head. "Anubis is an Egyptian deity who serves Isis. He is nothing like the Roman gods. Anubis is far too busy weighing souls, deciding who will have immortality and who will not, to waste time on silly women. Paulina is a devotee. She should have known that."

Apicata shrugged. "All I know is that when she went to the temple a feast had been prepared for her in a private room. Paulina was bathed and made ready for bed, the lamps were removed and the door closed. The god appeared to her in darkness."

I raised myself on my elbows. "Did she refuse him?"

"Hardly. She performed a night-long service for him again and again."

"What about in the morning?"

"He departed before dawn," Apicata explained. "Really, I cannot imagine how you missed hearing all this. Paulina told everyone. She spared no details, his ardor must have been insatiable."

I shook my head. "It was a hoax, a cruel hoax."

"If you guessed that, you are ahead of everyone," Apicata said. "What do the rest of us know of Egyptian gods? Until yesterday most of us envied Paulina's good fortune. Then, it seems, a young knight, Decius Mundus—do you know him? Yes? Well, this Decius accosted her on the street and laughed at her—can you imagine, *laughed* at her! 'Paulina, you've saved me 150,000 sesterces,' he said. When poor Paulina just looked at him, he explained, 'Call me Decius or Anubis, it makes no difference—the pleasure was all the same.' "

My stomach tightened at the outrage against Isis and her temple. "Surely the priests had nothing to do with it."

"Twenty-five thousand sesterces before and after the fact was a powerful argument for two of them. Too bad they will not have the opportunity to spend it."

A sick sense of finality swept over me. This was the very excuse for which Tiberius and his government had been looking. The cult of Isis was wealthy and threateningly female. I forced myself to ask: "What do you mean, they won't have an opportunity to spend it?"

"Saturnius took the matter of his wife's honor to Tiberius. Sejanus told me everything this morning. Decius has already been exiled, the priests will be crucified, the temple razed, and the great statue of Isis cast into the Tiber."

The temple razed! It was as though I had been brutally struck. I turned away, lest anyone see the tears. With the Iseneum gone, what solace remained for me? Where could I turn now for sanctuary?

I RARELY WENT ANYWHERE WITH PILATE AND MET HIS lavish gifts and other attempts at reconciliation with polite disdain. We did not discuss Titania. What was there to say? I was a wife to him in name only, arranging his entertainments, appearing in public with him when necessary, but otherwise avoiding his presence whenever possible. Instinct told me that as long as I did nothing publicly to anger him he would not divorce me.

Then one day Pilate asked me to accompany him to the circus, where we would join Sejanus and Apicata. I surprised us both by agreeing. Delighted, he honored my request that we go late to avoid the wild animal slaughter.

As we settled ourselves beside Sejanus and Apicata in their elaborate box, mid-afternoon sun shimmered richly on crimson robes, bright plumes, jeweled earrings and tiaras. Every seat in the great amphitheater was taken. Hundreds of commoners stood shoulder to shoulder in the gallery above.

Tiberius, resplendent in a diamond collar and a gold crown fashioned like a laurel wreath, sat close by in a raised, gilded box. I felt Pilate's pressure on my elbow. I would have to bow. My legs trembled as I did so. Slowly I forced myself to meet the emperor's gaze. Livia, at his side, watched me, mockery in her green cat's eyes. My stomach knotted as I bowed again. Oh, how I detested them both.

Just below were the Vestals, flanked on either side by senators with broad purple stripes bordering their togas, and senior military commanders in gleaming armor. Boys and girls in short red tunics made their way through the crowd, hawking cool drinks, roast meats, fruit, and wine. Four oxlike slaves dragged out the corpses, animal and human, while young boys raked the bloody sand and sprinkled it with heavy perfume. Drums pounded. Thousands of feet stamped, their impatient hammering like thunder. A more serious contest was about to begin, one that excited not merely the rabble but discerning connoisseurs. Wax tablets were passed from hand to hand as spectators scribbled the names of their champions and the sums they staked.

Sejanus shook his head. "What's the point? Holtan always wins."

"Holtan?" I had been idly chatting with Apicata; now I turned. "Long ago there was a gladiator—quite extraordinary. It isn't—"

"There is only one Holtan," Pilate said. "If you went to the circus more often you would know that."

"But Holtan has been in retirement," Apicata reminded him. "He only came today because Shabu challenged him—called him a coward in public. That slur, and perhaps the enormous purse that Tiberius is offering, brought him out. We will see if the great gladiator still has his edge. I may bet on Shabu."

"The Holtan I recall was a Dacian captive."

"That's the one," Sejanus assured me, "but he's come a long way since those days."

"Doesn't he own a gladiatorial school?" Pilate asked.

Sejanus nodded. "The best, and now he has opened a dining house in the Sabura. All it takes is the chance of running into the famous gladiator to send people flocking there. He has land holdings as well, vineyards, I believe."

Trumpets sounded, shrill, blood-chilling. Thousands of eyes fixed on a man dressed as Charon, the underworld's gatekeeper, as he raised his mallet. One. Two. Three times the great gong struck. The Gate of Life swung open, the massive gladiators strode in. Applause, an impatient storm, swept the amphitheater as the men, marching in proud military step, circled the arena, halting at last before Tiberius's box. There were twelve, most of them tall, all imposing. One had lost an ear. Another's nose was slit. They all bore scars, some still livid. A horn blew for silence as they raised their clenched right fists and chanted as one, voices slow, measured: "Hail, Caesar! We who are about to die salute you!"

I thought them splendid. Most particularly Holtan, whom I recognized immediately. Despite the scar that ran from one eye to his jaw, despite the flattened nose, I recognized his easy, leonine grace, his thick, shaggy hair the color of honey, the amber eyes that missed nothing.

Six of the twelve men carried short swords, the others held nets and tridents. Each pair would fight the other, the winner moving on to the next until only one pair remained. It began quietly. At first all were careful, deliberate, testing, and then drawing back like a dance, a feint here, a parry there, the movements stylized. Then, gradually, it became something more. Strike and counterstrike, they ignited like fire in wild, random rhythms. I watched only Holtan, who confined his parries to narrow, shallow strokes.

"Not much of a show there," Apicata commented, following my eyes. "I knew I should have bet on Shabu."

"Don't give up on Holtan," Sejanus advised. "He's conserving his strength—he will need it. I wager this will be his last match."

I gasped. "What do you mean?"

"He's a great fighter—no doubt about it—the best I have ever seen, but look at the other men. No question he could take one, two, even three of them—but all? At the very least he will be badly wounded, maimed."

Apicata shuddered. "Would he want to live in that condition?"

"Oh, stop!" I cried. "The match has hardly begun. He will win, of course he will. The odds were equally bad when I first saw him as a girl."

"Not quite," Sejanus said. "I saw that fight too. No one will ever forget it. But this one is different. These are the top gladiators in the world—Dionysus from Ephesus, Rameses from Alexandria, Hercules from Athens. That Ethiopian down there, Shabu, is a legend. Holtan can't beat them all."

But he must!

Every time Holtan changed position, his opponent, Hercules, followed. They moved together as if attached by a cord. It didn't take long. So much for Greece's finest. Holtan studied his next challenger, a hairy Scythian giant nearly twice his size. He stood quietly in place while his opponent charged him. At the last minute he stepped aside; the man, unable to stop his momentum, stumbled. In that instant, Holtan plunged his sword into the gladiator's side. Two down. All around Holtan other pairs struggled, bodies strained and grappled, breastplates clanged together, swords slashed into chests and bellies, dark streaks stained the sand. A slave dressed as Mercury walked discreetly among the fallen, testing each with a red-hot poker to make certain he was dead. Slaves dragged six lifeless bodies through the Gate of Death. The frieze of demons over its arch seemed less gruesome than the carnage below. Six gladiators now remained in the arena.

Holtan faced a nimble net man who darted toward him swinging his web with an awesome grace, then skipped backward, feinting and stabbing so quickly with his trident that I could barely follow his movements. Again and again the sharp-tipped tines clanged against Holtan's sword. Bleeding now from an arm wound, Holtan held fast. The crowd drew a collective breath as he advanced, forcing his opponent back, allowing him no room to maneuver his trident and overwhelming him with a rapid-fire series of slashes that left no time for recovery. It was over for Holtan's challenger. The crowd went wild.

I turned to Sejanus. "What do you think of Holtan now?"

Slaves sprinkled our party with violet-scented water that could not begin to mask the smell of blood and excrement wafting up from the arena. The boys and girls were back selling food and drinks. People were actually buying them.

"It's not over yet," Pilate reminded me. He nodded toward the arena where Holtan and the other survivor, the Ethiopian, Shabu, also a swordsman, circled each other. "He took a bad hit in his right shoulder. He looks tired."

"He *is* tired," Sejanus agreed. "He was lucky with that last butcher, but look at the size of this one."

My heart caught in my throat as Shabu lunged forward, sword flashing in a flurry of low, rapid strikes. Holtan jerked backward, meeting Shabu's thrusts with his shield. Sparks flared from the iron bindings. Holtan wavered slightly under the hammering but stood fast. Now Shabu directed a burst of short fast cuts at Holtan's head. Shield raised, Holtan retreated in a zigzag path. All his movements were defensive, while Shabu drove forward, impatient and aggressive.

"Holtan's done for," Sejanus said, holding out his wine cup. "Too bad. He was a great swordsman in his day."

"It is not over yet!" I exclaimed. My fingers caught at the tiny sistrum at my throat. Isis, please, I prayed silently.

Holtan stayed hidden behind his shield as Shabu attacked unopposed. I saw that his backward movements were bringing him closer and closer to the imperial box. Shabu lunged; Holtan turned, his sword slicing upward, hitting Shabu's weapon with a resounding clang. In one fluid motion Holtan's blade slid along Shabu's, a feigned attack on his right shoulder. It worked. Shabu moved his shield defensively. Holtan, seemingly unaware of the blood darkening his cuirass, battered his way into Shabu's defenses. The crowd, on its feet, bellowed like cattle.

Shabu kicked with his right foot, scattering sand in Holtan's face. Holtan was not so easily distracted. He advanced, tightly controlled rage increasing his swiftness and accuracy. Unexpectedly, Holtan leaped, arcing into the air, beginning a powerful cut in mid-flight. The two men crashed together, shield to shield.

"He doesn't look tired to me," I yelled at Sejanus. "He was only pretending."

I rose to my feet screaming with excitement. Pilate, Sejanus, Apicata—the whole world, it seemed—was crying out at my side. "Holtan! Holtan!"

And then Holtan's foot slipped on the intestines of an earlier opponent. He slid and fell hard on his back. I screamed as Shabu lunged forward, swinging his sword with all his might. Holtan rolled to one side, missing the blow by a hair. In an instant he was on his feet, the muscles of his leather-laced calves taut as he crouched.

The crowd roared with approval and delight as Holtan leaped forward and with both hands hammered his sword down in a stroke that nearly sliced Shabu in half. The Ethiopian monolith fell, crimson blood spurting like a fountain. Shabu jerked and quivered, plowing up the sand with his heels, then stiffened and lay still.

"By Jupiter, he's done it again!" Pilate exclaimed. He turned to me, smiling, "Your sight again, Claudia?"

I shook my head. My eyes were on the victor standing below. Smiling broadly, Holtan removed his helmet and bowed slightly to the emperor, then to the cheering throng. Did I imagine it, or was he looking at me?

AT THE PARTY THAT EVENING, PILATE SEEMINGLY IGNORED the women, instead closeting himself with Sejanus in a curtained alcove. I saw only Holtan. He stood between two imperial officers laughing at some private joke.

Apicata's eyes followed mine, "Extraordinary, wouldn't you say?"

"What do you suppose they are talking about?" I wondered.

"Women probably. Holtan's reputed to be successful in that arena as well. I would not call him handsome, but—"

"I would."

"Claudia! For handsome, look to Pilate. Your gladiator may have been attractive when he was young, when you made your famous prediction. He was scarcely out of his teens then, but now— Look at his nose! It's badly broken. And that scar. Imagine his body."

I liked imagining his body. "Scarred, of course, but think how he has lived, what he has experienced. I find the thought of it . . . exciting."

"Really!" Apicata looked at me curiously. "If you like that sort of thing. I shouldn't think you would."

Holtan strode across the wide marble hall, brushing aside several admirers who sought to detain him. Now he stood before us, his eyes on mine, smiling a silent greeting. Turning to Apicata, he bowed. "Your parties are the best in the world."

"That *is* a compliment," she conceded, "since I gather you have seen most of the world."

"I've not seen anyone like your companion—at least not in a long time."

Apicata laughed softly as she turned away. "I would watch out for Claudia. She is said to be part witch."

"Then tell my fortune, witch." He reached out his hand, palm up. "The wise women of Dacia, my country, tell fortunes by looking at the palm. Can you do that?" His manner was light but the eyes that watched me from beneath thick, shaggy brows were intense.

"My powers are much exaggerated," I said, tilting my head to meet his gaze. "But occasionally . . . a dream comes true."

"I would like that. I would like you to dream of me."

Your life is waiting. "Only Isis knows, perhaps I shall—some time."

I took his large, rough hand in mine, but felt only his warmth. My fingers trembled; I knew he could feel them. Beyond him, I saw Pilate emerge from his curtained alcove. His eyes swept the room, fastened on me. I dropped Holtan's hand. "What a pity! I can tell you nothing, nothing that all of Rome does not already know."

"But what of the future?" he persisted. "Do you see a woman there? Someone with dark hair that shines like polished mahogany when it catches the light? Someone with smoke-gray eyes like the sapphires from India? Do you see such a person?"

"Yes." I tilted my head once again. "I do see such a woman, but you should beware of her."

CHAPTER 25

Holtan

In the days following Sejanus's banquet, Holtan showed up everywhere—at the theater, the races, at parties and receptions. I felt his eyes on me, bold, appraising, in no way polite. I read his gaze as purely sensual, possibly threatening, uncomplicated by romance or even respect. That wasn't what I wanted. Or was it?

Like Pilate, he possessed an absolute certainty of his place in the world, but with a shady edge, the attitude of a man capable of surviving by any means. I watched him at a banquet, eyes languidly fixed on the senator who hung over his couch speaking so intently, and was reminded of a resting lion that might at any moment awaken with a compelling appetite.

Then three days passed and I didn't see him at all. On an impulse, I ordered my litter bearers to take me to Mars Field.

"Why?" Rachel asked. "You've never gone there before."

"Must I have a reason? Apicata says it's amusing to watch the new slaves learn swordsmanship."

"I have heard their instructors are among the best gladiators in the country," Rachel said, placing a dark gray *palla* about my shoulders.

I shrugged off the *palla*. "Not that old thing! I want the new one." I gestured toward a length of loosely woven wool, vibrant lilac, kitten soft against my bare shoulders.

When my litter reached the great field, I waved Rachel off and walked toward the stable. As a girl I'd often outridden Caligula, who fancied himself quite a horseman. I'd even held my own with Gaius. In Antioch, I'd ridden often, but one thing or another had kept me from doing so in Rome. Now I felt a surge of excitement, remembering with keen longing the glorious sense of a galloping horse, the feeling of being on top of the world. Perhaps a long ride on a spirited mount was just what I needed to banish the restlessness that plagued me.

In the large courtyard, slaves perfected their thrusts and parries under the watchful eyes of guards and trainers. They were a mixed lot, shiny black Nubians, some northerners with ice-blue eyes and skin fair as snow, a few from the Far East, sleek raven hair tied in one thick braid that whirled behind them as they lunged. Not all were agile. One boy alone showed real promise. I paused to join a small crowd that circled the youth.

"Shall I buy him for you?"

Startled, I turned to find Holtan standing nearby, his amber eyes alert and watching.

I laughed lightly. "You're joking. What would I do with a gladiator?" As he continued to study me, I felt my face flush. "He reminds me of someone, a boy I saw long ago," I remarked. "He, too, was very skillful with a sword."

"And very lucky."

"You are modest. This boy—is he also from Dacia?"

Holtan nodded. "A village near my home. He was brought in last week. You might find him a fine investment. I could have him trained at my school, then enter him in the arena for you."

"You are generous, but I could not. My husband would never allow me to accept such a valuable gift."

"He need never know. It could be our secret," he said, moving closer.

I backed away. "You think I would deceive my husband?"

His eyes were teasing, yet appraising. "I know you never have."

"I beg your pardon!"

"I know you never have," Holtan repeated.

"How can you know that?"

"I made it my business to find out."

Why was I not angry? Instead, I felt secret pleasure at his interest. "Your spies are very thorough," I said at last.

Moving on ahead of him, I entered the large stone building and looked about. The stable master, a stocky, red-faced man, approached us. "What does *Domina* prefer? We have a fair selection of ladies' mounts." He pointed to a chestnut mare. "She is gentle as a lamb."

"Perhaps, if I wanted to ride a lamb."

"She's a fine mount," Holtan said. "I know her owner."

"Do you keep horses here?" I asked him.

"A few."

"*Dominus*'s horses are the best," the stable master interjected, "but also the most spirited."

"I would like to see them."

Holtan nodded to the stable man who led the way to a wing lined with stalls. "You own all these?" I asked Holtan, who remained at my side.

"These are the ones I keep in Rome."

I looked from horse to horse. "I would like to ride that one." I pointed to a large stallion, his sleek ebony coat broken only by a white star on his forehead. He reminded me of a horse that I had owned as a girl and trained myself.

The stable master shook his head emphatically. "Oh no, *Domina* doesn't want that one."

"*Domina* does indeed," I insisted.

"That roan mare to the right of the entrance—ride her." Holtan said, taking my arm.

"Are you refusing to allow me to ride the horse of my choice?"

"The stallion's too dangerous. Saddle the roan and the stallion," he instructed the groom. Taking my arm, Holtan led me back out to the yard.

Soon we were joined by the stable man and a groom leading the two horses. Holtan stroked the mare's head. "She is a fine horse, plenty of spirit, you will enjoy riding her."

"Why don't you ride her?" I suggested.

"I would like to, but Poseidon needs exercise. The stable boys are afraid to work her."

I looked up at the stallion standing quietly beside me. "He's beautiful."

Holtan frowned. "He would not allow it. I am the only one who has ever ridden him."

I stroked Poseidon's muzzle. He watched me closely, but remained motionless. "Cup your hand," I instructed the groom.

Hardly more than a boy, the groom looked uncertain. As he hesitated, I kicked the mounting block into position. Pulling up my skirt, I grabbed Poseidon's saddle and jumped astride the horse. Taking the reins in both hands, I felt the enormous power of the beast. As I gave Poseidon a nudge, I saw the stable boy staring at my bare legs.

"Stop!" Holtan cried. "I cannot allow this."

"He seems gentle enough to me."

I had barely spoken when Poseidon broke into a trot,moving with smooth, quickening grace out of the enclosure. Holtan lunged forward to grab the reins, but the horse reared. The groom too leaped back. Riders in the exercise field scattered in all directions.

Oh, sweet Isis! What have I done now! I gripped him with my thighs as *Tata* had taught me long ago and lightened up on the reins. Poseidon set off at a full gallop, quickly crossing the old parade ground and heading toward open country. As he cleared one hedge after another, I could do nothing but stay low and hang on with all my strength. Thrilling to the ride, I shrieked with excitement. At last, as we reached a road paralleling the Tiber, Poseidon lengthened his stride and we were flying.

I had forgotten the freedom and exhilaration of having a great horse beneath me. Now I leaned forward on Poseidon's neck, entwining my fingers in his mane. Head back, I felt the wind in my loosened hair. Gradually I became aware of the sound of approaching hoofbeats. Glancing over my shoulder, I saw Holtan gaining on me. I pulled the folds of my *palla* down over my thighs.

"You might have told me how well you ride," he shouted as he drew nearer.

"You might have asked," I called back.

"Have you any other surprises?"

I smiled, feeling less fettered than I had in years. "Perhaps."

"WHERE HAVE YOU BEEN?"

Yanked from my reverie, I jumped as a hand pushed back the litter's curtain. Pilate's face was inches from my own, those cool blue eyes of his watchful, missing nothing.

"You care?" I asked coolly, but my heart raced as he took my arm.

"You were gone all afternoon," he said, helping me from the litter.

"Really?" I forced a shrug. "If you must know, I went riding."

"We used to ride together," he reminded me. He turned to Rachel, who walked behind us as we entered the house. "Did you enjoy the ride?"

I answered for her. "Rachel does not ride."

"Next time my groom will attend you. I do not want you riding alone."

"Nonsense! I grew up on a horse." I forced myself to meet his gaze. "Why were you waiting for me?"

"I have news, pleasant news. I've bought a villa in Herculaneum."

"Herculaneum! You never mentioned you were thinking—" I stopped, remembering.

"It was you who suggested it," he reminded me, "a place by the sea. You preferred it to Pompeii, said it was smaller, more leisurely. I expected you to be pleased."

I scrambled to regain my composure. "Oh, I am . . . of course. It will be very pleasant . . . later . . . Fall in Herculaneum would be lovely, or the winter months. Yes, let's go in winter. Perhaps Apicata and Sejanus will join us."

"What's the matter, Claudia?" Pilate turned to face me as we entered the atrium. "You were so anxious to be out of Rome. I agree with you, the place is a pesthole—barely spring and children are dying of fever. It's foolhardy to risk Marcella's health."

"Marcella," I echoed softly, my heart loosening. What had I been thinking? Was I mad? "Yes, a summer by the sea will do us all good."

"I'll make the arrangements," Pilate said. "This time next week, we will be on the road." With barely a nod he turned toward his *tablinum*.

As the heavy door closed behind him, I turned to Rachel, half sobbing. "How can I leave now?"

"It is the best thing that could happen," she nodded solemnly.

"How dare you say that!"

"Your husband does not miss a thing. He's suspicious. If I can feel it, you surely must."

"I haven't done anything," I argued defensively.

"You dare not. You know the danger. Within the law he could kill you. He would not even need proof."

"I will only see Holtan once, just once—alone. Pilate will never know."

I FOUND THE COLUMNED ENTRANCE TO HOLTAN'S DINING house impressive—what little I saw of it. Scarcely had I alighted from the hired litter before a slave darted from the doorway and hurried me through a side door. He bowed as though I were the empress herself. "My lady, *Dominus* is waiting for you upstairs."

"Waiting for me! How can that be?"

The slave shrugged. "The master said, 'When the lady comes, bring her to me.' "

"Really!" I had half a mind to leave, but instead found myself following him through the foyer to a stairway. It was small, rather dark, the stairs narrow and steep. I climbed a few steps and then stopped. Why was I risking my very life for a man who already took me for granted? I stood motionless, hand on the railing. Get out now. Quickly I turned and started down the steps.

"Claudia!"

I looked back over my shoulder. Holtan stood on the landing at the top of the stairs. In an instant he was at my side. "You *did* come!" he said, taking my hands in his. The warmth of his touch flowed through my body.

"It appears you expected me."

"Not expected—dreamed that you would search me out." Taking my arm, he led me up the stairs to a surprisingly spacious apartment. When I paused to look around, Holtan took my *palla* and handed it to the slave. "Bring wine, olives, some cheese," he instructed.

Directly before us was an atrium open to the sky, to the right his *tablinum*. I saw a desk cluttered with scrolls, behind it a balcony commanding an expansive view of the Subura rooftops to the hills beyond. "Do you conduct business here?"

"Some of it."

"This is all quite impressive."

I felt him stiffen. "You probably thought I couldn't even read."

"Well, yes. You came here as a young slave . . ."

He drew himself up proudly. "Claudia, I wasn't born a slave. My father was a prince. I had the best tutors money could buy. They taught me Greek and Latin, as well as swordsmanship. Life was good until the Romans came."

"I'm sorry, I only meant . . ."

"Let me show you the rest of my quarters," he said, nodding toward a hallway. We turned a corner and suddenly there I was—wide eyes, wild curls. I barely concealed a gasp when I realized what I was seeing. The entire room, floor to ceiling, was lined with metal polished to such brightness that it reflected our every movement. Window hangings of gold embroidered on scarlet matched the smallest stool and largest couch. Thick scarlet carpets scattered about the black marble floor muted our footsteps. A deity I did not recognize smiled down at us from the ceiling, his companions naked, full-breasted, round-hipped women in sensuous poses. I felt the room's savage, uncompromising challenge, its crude, boisterous beauty.

Perched tentatively on the edge of the couch, I imagined the women who must have lain there. I took a sip of wine, then another, and wondered if I could ever be like those careless, confident creatures.

"Years ago, I heard the story of your prediction," Holtan said, pulling me down next to him on the couch.

"The one about you?" I smiled, cocking my head slightly. "It surprised me more than anyone." We reclined for a time, looking up at the gods cavorting above our heads.

"Do you know what people are thinking?" Holtan asked. "Can you read minds?"

"I can read yours—now. It does not take the sight for that."

He leaned forward eagerly. "Did the sight tell you to come here?"

How young Holtan looked when he smiled. There were still traces of the boy I remembered. "I did not think it wise to ask."

Holtan's eyes were intent. "It's true then, your sight does tell you things?"

I shook my head. "I wish I could explain it. No sight guides me, but sometimes there's a kind of knowing when I feel in harmony with Isis—"

"She speaks to you?" Holtan encouraged.

"Not in words. But if I'm able to still my chattering mind, I feel her. I sense sometimes—don't laugh—I tried to explain it to Pilate once, and he laughed."

"I would never laugh at you." Holtan moved closer. "So, how *do* you feel?"

"Like Ariadne. It is as if I were Ariadne."

"Who?" He frowned slightly.

"A Greek princess who loved a hero." I looked up at him. "Not unlike you."

"What happened to them? Did they live happily ever after—the princess and her hero?"

"She saved him—saved them both—by teaching him to hold fast to a silver thread that guided him out of a black labyrinth. Sometimes I feel that I'm guided by such a thread—but so often I forget to reach for it . . ." I laughed, shaking my head again. "How silly this is!"

"Not at all. I don't know about the thread. I never felt that, but in the arena, I . . . am . . . Mars."

"I noticed the shrine in the atrium as I came in."

"In Dacia we had different gods. As a child I prayed to Wodan and Freya. Much good that did when the Roman legions killed my father, took me for a slave. Later, when I was brought here, I saw gladiators worshipping Mars. Is not one god as good as another?"

"Do you pray to Mars before entering the arena?"

"Pray to him? Mars is a force, not a being. I go through the motions to prove my Romanness, but it makes no difference whether I burn calves before his altar or piss on it. Sometimes I win by skill, by cunning, by tricks, but most of the time, I win because Mars is in my gut. Do you understand?"

I nodded, remembering Holtan in the arena. It was this passionate force that had drawn me. His eyes were on mine, a half smile on his lips. I looked away only to confront myself. How many women had seen their forms reflected on these mirrored walls? Did it matter? This was for me. Only once, only now.

Holtan reached out, his arms sliding about my waist, slowly drawing me toward him. His words of endearment had a comforting edge of roughness as I raised my mouth to meet his. Holtan held me gently at first, but soon his deep kisses brought heat to my veins, and as I eagerly sought his mouth, he strengthened his hold. My hands roamed over him of their own accord, reveling in the feel of taut muscles while searching for the fastenings of his tunic. He pulled back, smiling at my boldness, then eased the *chiton* from my shoulder. His mouth followed the silken fabric as he slowly slid it down my body, gradually exposing my breasts, my belly, my thighs. I felt myself arch up toward his mouth and cried out with pleasure and when he came back up, his face was serious. *"My sweet Claudia!"* he whispered, softly kissing my eyes, my cheeks, as if I were the most fragile creature alive. Hot honey oozed through my body as slowly, carefully, he entered me. I clung to him as his movements became my own, all boundaries between us ceasing to exist.

Later, much later, I lay still, savoring his weight against me. "Don't move," I murmured as he started to raise himself.

"I'll crush you."

"I like being crushed by you. Promise you won't move."

We laughed softly, gazing at each other. Holtan kissed me gently. I nuzzled his neck and he held me tenderly for long moments in a rich silence broken only by an occasional muffled word of love. How was it possible for two people to be so close?

Later, much, much later, I pulled free and rose from the couch. Looking down at the man who, within a few short hours, had become not only my lover but someone who understood my deepest feelings, I forced myself to speak. "I can never do this again."

Holtan stood before me, his hands on my shoulders. "I know."

CHAPTER 26

My Choice

"Hurry! They're waiting." Pilate stood impatiently in the archway while I paused before the mirror. His eyes swept over me. "Red is very becoming to you, my dear. I'm surprised you don't wear it more often."

Why was I wearing it now? Why was I once again playing the perfect wife, when I wanted nothing more than to sink into my couch and dream of all that had transpired that afternoon? Instead, here I was, headed to some unknown destination where I would be forced to smile and laugh and talk as though my entire world hadn't changed forever. Why had I not pleaded a headache earlier when I had the chance?

Too late now. Sejanus and Apicata's litter already waited outside. As I followed Pilate to the courtyard, I gasped in surprise at the purple-and-gold-striped canopy shimmering in the torchlight.

"What do you think?" Apicata pushed back the silken curtain, waving merrily. "Is this not the grandest litter you have ever seen?"

It was surely the largest. Fourteen bearers, seven on each side, stood at attention, waiting for us to join their master and mistress.

"Very impressive," Pilate said to Sejanus, who had parted the curtain to wave his greeting.

"Come see the inside," Apicata called out. "That's the best part."

A bearer rushed to put down a silken rug before the entrance to the litter. I stepped in, followed by Pilate. Sejanus and Apicata reclined on a satin couch that could easily accommodate eight. Beside them a young slave girl waited to serve wine and sweetmeats. I saw racks of scrolls, games, and musical instruments.

"It arrived just this morning, a gift from Tiberius," Sejanus told us. "What do you think?" he asked, turning to me.

"I have never seen anything to compare with it," I assured him. The slaves hoisted the litter onto their shoulders and a moment later we departed, heading down the hill at a steady trot.

"We have a surprise," Apicata announced. "Especially for Claudia." Her face looked guileless enough, but I felt a tiny warning chill. Once I reached to open the curtain, but she stopped me. "Now, now! We will be there soon enough."

I took the wine offered me and waved away the water pitcher, feeling the need to drink it straight. It was the finest, of course. I had a bit more than usual and began to wonder why I had been apprehensive. Surely, whatever Apicata planned was only meant to please me. Perhaps the outing would remove a little of the bittersweet longing for what could never be again.

"I thought I knew where we were going—the Forum Market—but that last turn confused me," Pilate said.

"Not much further," Sejanus assured him.

The mystery nagged at me. "Have I ever been where we are going?" I asked.

"Not likely, though I am certain you have wanted to go."

"Could it be the animal market? I have heard the young cheetah cubs can be trained . . ."

"Not this time, Claudia, you will just have to wait." Apicata's eyes danced mischievously.

The street sounds grew noisier, the pace slower. The large silver water carafe sloshed in rhythm to the bearers' heavy tread. I drained my wineglass quickly lest I spill it on my gown. Often I heard Sejanus's bodyguards call out, "Make way! Make way!"

Where are we? I wondered. Another turn, the slaves' movements were slower now, more deliberate. The streets must be crowded. At last, we stopped.

The litter was carefully lowered to the ground and a slave parted the curtains. Sejanus and Pilate stepped out, then Apicata. Pilate reached in and took my arm. As my eyes came to rest on the entrance before me, I stumbled against him. What kind of bizarre nightmare was this? We were standing before Holtan's dining house. Would I have to face him on the arm of my husband?

"Here we are!" Apicata said with a flourish. "Surely you have heard of the Sword and Trident. Everyone's talking about it."

My eyes searched her face. Did Apicata know? She looked back, obviously pleased with her choice, wide eyes seemingly ingenuous. Was it merely an unfortunate coincidence?

The same slave who had admitted me that afternoon rushed forward to greet us. Great Isis, what if he says something? My heart raced with panic, but the man's air of professional geniality never wavered as he looked from one of us to the other, smiling broadly. Bowing low, he gestured for us to follow. This time it was the main entrance.

We stepped into the foyer, moving straight ahead into a large banquet area. The air was heavy with perfume, spices, leather, and sweat. I could barely breathe. The large torch-lit room was filled with couches, all of them occupied—sometimes four people reclined together. "Perhaps we should go?" I suggested. "There's no place for us here."

"There is always a place for a party as distinguished as yours." With a flourish, the slave pulled aside a crimson curtain. Before us was a raised alcove with two wide couches covered with pillows on either side of a low brass-topped table. This choice recess faced the room's center. Behind it was an archway. With the drapes drawn, guests could come or go discreetly. With the drapes open they looked directly out at four women dancers—fair-skinned, golden-haired. They wore ruby-studded girdles and nothing else. Prominently displayed on wall behind them was Holtan's *rudis,* the large wooden sword traditionally awarded a gladiator who had won his freedom.

I took Pilate's arm as we stepped into the gilded enclosure, flashing what I hoped was a delighted smile at Sejanus. "What an exciting idea!"

"We thought you would enjoy seeing your favorite's lair."

"My favorite?"

"You did, in a sense, discover Holtan. Besides, I made a fortune on his last win. Might as well spend a little of it here."

"*Dominus* is very kind." Holtan's large body filled the archway behind the alcove. "It is an honor to have such distinguished visitors." I was afraid to look at him, but forced myself. I saw a smiling face. For an instant his amber eyes sought mine. Then he stepped back to admit a slave bearing a flagon of wine and four glasses on a silver tray. "This is a special vintage. I hope you will like it."

Holtan poured the wine himself, handing a glass to Apicata and then to me. For an instant our fingers touched. I willed my hand to remain steady.

Pilate took a sip and then another. "Excellent Falerian."

"It comes from my vineyard near Stabiae."

"Stabiae?" Pilate studied him. "What a coincidence—my wife and I will be traveling near there three days from now. We've—"

"Sorry, my friend, not so fast," Sejanus interrupted him. "It seems Tiberius has other plans for you, for both of us. I have yet to tell you. He wants—"

Sejanus's voice faded. I saw only Holtan, his heated gaze skimming over me. I trembled. Be careful, careful now. I forced my mind back to the conversation.

"I'm sorry to delay your holiday," Sejanus said, rising from his couch and seating himself beside me. Taking my hand, he stroked it lightly. "Surely you'll allow me to steal your husband for a short while?"

"Oh! He's going away. Not again." I heard myself say the words, almost as though I meant them. I felt Pilate's cobalt eyes watching.

Sejanus went on, explaining, "Tiberius's business will take us to Syracuse. A month, that's all, then he can join you in

Herculaneum. I've found that absence is good for the heart." Casually, he turned to Holtan. "Don't you agree?"

"Help me, Rachel, you must help me," I said, looking up from my sleeping baby. We stood beside the small couch, watching Marcella. How could anyone so tiny be so all-important? I wondered not for the first time.

"She is beautiful," Rachel said, leaning over to straighten Marcella's coverlet.

"She is the whole world to me."

"Yes . . . a woman would be mad to risk the whole world."

We met two or three afternoons a week.

Holtan's plan was simple. Leaving Marcella with her baby nurse, I left home dressed as usual. Traveling in my own litter, I stopped at an obscure trattoria where Rachel waited. She donned my garments, put on a dark wig that matched my hair and left by the front door. I, in my own disguise, heart beating wildly, went out another exit, then hired a litter or walked to the lodgings that Holtan had arranged for the day.

Once, I wore a coarse brown tunic and tucked my hair into a freedman's cap. Another time I swathed myself in a heavy toga, draping its purple-edged folds about my head. Alone together, our fears abating, we'd laugh heartily at my disguises. Holtan would turn me about while I mimicked the speech and manner of whoever I was supposed to be.

"Do you like me as a blonde?" I asked Holtan on the day I wore a magnificent skein of golden curls.

"I like you best as you are."

"Who is that? I am no longer sure."

I turned to look at the meal Holtan had ordered. A delicate white linen cloth covered the table, at its center a bouquet of pale peach roses. There were oysters still in their shells, barley soup laced with mead, sweet leeks on endive, a stuffed pheasant, and strawberries in fresh cream.

"Oh! Everything I love," I exclaimed, hugging him. "You always know what I like best."

The apartment that Holtan had rented for the afternoon, though small, was bright and cheery. I had been breathless from climbing the many stairs, but when I reached the top there was Holtan waiting on a small balcony. All of Rome lay before us. In that instant we owned the world.

We enjoyed the good food and wine, absorbed in each other, laughing and talking. The next thing I knew, the sun, high when I arrived, had faded.

Suddenly it was dusk, though not yet dark enough to light the small wall torches. Once more our idyll must end. I pushed myself up on one elbow from the couch where we had been lying. As I looked down on him, my throat swelled and began to ache. "I can no longer do this."

"No, you cannot—never again." Holtan turned to look into my eyes. "I am ashamed to have let you—to have encouraged you. The other day when you didn't come—all I could think of was that Pilate had come back early, had caught you—"

I leaned down, sought his lips and kissed them.

"He could have you killed," Holtan said at last.

"If he chose. More likely he would have me banished—forbidden to see my child." My voice quavered. "I could not endure that." After a pause, I continued. "There is Livia, too. She has returned to Rome. I saw her at the theater last night, those dreadful green eyes of hers watching me. Livia is capable of anything."

"There's no family friend who would stand up for you?"

"Not anymore. They are all gone."

"And your faith—Isis? Could you seek sanctuary?"

"You'd like that, wouldn't you?" I asked, lightly teasing. "You would like me sequestered from the world."

"Better than with Pilate," he admitted.

"There is no sanctuary for me since Tiberius burned the Iseneum. I have nowhere to go, not even for counsel."

Holtan pulled me to him, then pushed me away. "I must leave here, go so far that I will never be tempted." He rose from the couch, reaching for his tunic. "The Parthians are clamoring for a match."

"Oh no!" Dread swept over me as I looked up at him. "I thought you had given up fighting for good."

"You know what will happen if I stay in Rome. How long will it be before we are discovered? It frightens me how powerless I am against the desire to be with you. I cannot allow you to risk more than you already have."

I stared at him wordlessly, feeling as though the sun had been banished and I condemned to a twilight world. "Pilate's absence made it easy for us," I acknowledged at last. "We have been very lucky, but soon that will end. I had word this morning. He and Sejanus expect to sail from Sicily next week. I am to meet him at our villa in Herculaneum."

"So near *my* villa. Are the gods tormenting us?" Holtan was standing now, pulling me to my feet so that I faced him.

"There is fever in Rome. I worry about Marcella. Pilate reminded me again of how good the sea breeze will be for her."

"By all means, do not refuse him, but meet me first. Let's have a few days together before he returns."

"A few days! Are you mad?"

"One night then."

"What are you thinking?"

"My villa's just outside Stabiae. They say the sirens lured Ulysses there. You would like it. I *know* you would like it. Come and lure me."

"Like it! I would love it." I shook my head sadly. "You know it is impossible."

"Nothing is impossible. Send Marcella with Rachel to Herculaneum. They will be well guarded. I will have my best men hidden around them all the way. Stay behind, say you have a few last-minute things to do in Rome—the house to close, one more party to attend. Women are always adept at such excuses, surely you can think of something."

"Surely," I mocked him, then added, "You *are* mad."

"Claudia, it's our only chance to have a night together. When you return to Rome in the fall, I will be gone."

Frightened tears stung my eyes as I realized what he was planning. "Why risk your life in the arena when you have everything that anyone could ever want?"

"Everything? You think that? Whatever I have is nothing without you."

My mind raced. *Your life is waiting.* What a price my sister had paid. Was I ready to risk my life for love? I looked at Holtan and knew the answer. Today he was at the top of his form, but in every major city, there were twenty gladiators determined to best him, wild to establish themselves by killing the champion. One mistake, one false step—

"Tell me," I asked, my voice dropping almost to a whisper, "that one night with me . . . what would you do for it?"

"Anything," he said, pulling me close. "Anything you ask."

CHAPTER 27

The Last Rendezvous

The night was hot. I wore only a loose white tunica, open wide at the neck and sleeves. Leaning forward, clinging to my horse's mane, I drove him faster. Far below me, a string of seaside villas glittered like a priceless bracelet, stretched as far as I could see.

The rough, mountainous route I chose kept me off the main thoroughfare where I would be seen, yet even on these wretched roads I sometimes had to hide behind boulders or among clumps of trees to avoid other travelers. Or were they merely travelers? Peasant women rarely traveled unattended, and here was I, alone, riding a fine-looking horse.

A man stepped out onto the road and attempted to block the way. He grabbed at the reins, but I spurred my mount onward. After a few paces he gave up. Trembling with fear, I pressed my knees against the horse, urging him on. Holtan so near now, soon we would be together.

Emerging from a clump of trees, I looked down, scanning the lights below. Stabiae! Time to cut down to the sea. Letting the horse pick his way carefully, I wound down to the paved road that skimmed the cliffs, one sharp curve following another. A full moon hung low over the sea as my horse rounded yet another bend. At last the massive outlines of Holtan's villa loomed before me. Unlike the other seaside homes I had glimpsed, it was built fortresslike out over a cliff. As I approached the high terra-cotta wall, an arched gate opened. Torch-bearing slaves rushed forward, lighting my way through fragrant gardens, past statues, fountains, across a mosaic terrace alive with leaping dolphins.

Holtan ran toward me, a radiant smile lighting his face. My terror melted at the feel and smell of him as he lifted me from the horse's back and carried me inside. "My darling, my foolish wild one," he murmured into my hair. "Could anyone have followed you?"

"Does it matter now? I am here."

Holtan spoke to his steward, orders I didn't catch. Turning to me, he smiled again. "Wait till you see what I have prepared for you." I moved closer, comforted as always by his rough-edged voice. Taking my hand, he led me down a corridor—a blur of white marble and bright frescoes—then flung open a door.

My breath caught. "Do you like it?" Holtan asked. His eyes searched my face.

I looked beyond him to a fresco that dominated the far wall: The classic Venus rising from the sea. But the wide gray eyes and curly mane were my own.

He smiled at me. "She *is* your ancestor."

"A family myth I never believed."

Holtan regarded me solemnly. "I believe it." His hand moved lightly down the small of my back.

There was so much to see. Polished moonstones set into the walls reflected a forest of crystal lamps suspended from the ceiling. Their glow rippled like a mirage. Sheer draperies, a sea spray of blues and greens, and a sensuous mass of silken cushions created an oasis of peace and harmony. I looked up at Holtan. "Everything is perfect—the feeling of the room—my favorite colors—how did you do it?"

His face relaxed into a broad grin. "My men and I—we only finished this afternoon."

"But my likeness. How did you do that?"

"Did you not see the artist when you were in my dining house?"

Happy tears stung my eyes. In this magnificent room I would play a game, imagining for however short a time that we were married. Unable to trust my voice, I took Holtan's hand, kissing a hardened scar on his palm. My eyes strayed to the fresco above the bed. Another classic image imposed itself from memory. Venus and Mars snared in a golden net, captured by the goddess's jealous husband, and revealed to all the gods in the very moment of their union. But Pilate could not know. I had sent word that I was staying an extra day to oversee improvements to the *culina*. Surely he was too busy with some new mistress to even think of me.

Holtan slipped his arm around my shoulders. "Our bath has been drawn."

Having ridden far and fast, I could smell the musk odor of my horse's flanks still clinging to me as we entered an adjoining room. Steam rose from the circular pool. I relished the thought of soaking away the grime of the journey.

Holtan paused before a marble table where a silver wine service gleamed. "Would you like—?"

I nodded, throat parched from the long ride, watching his large hands unexpectedly deft as he poured equal parts of claret and snow-chilled water into two iridescent goblets. He handed one to me. "A honey cake?" he asked, raising the platter toward me.

I shook my head, pulling at the clips that bound my tangled hair until it tumbled loose. "You make a fine steward." I smiled at him over the rim of my glass.

"I like doing things for you."

"And I for you."

He watched me as I sipped. The wine was rich and full bodied with a subtle taste I could not place.

"It's the volcanic ash in the soil," he said, answering my unspoken question.

I reached up, tracing the cleft in his chin. "Rare wine a volcano's gift? Not unlike my life." After devastation had come the greatest gift. I had lost so many loved ones, yet here I was enjoying this moment as no other. Draining the goblet, I placed it on the table and quickly slipped out of my tunica.

Holtan dropped to his knees. Voice husky, he whispered, "Too fast, let me do that." The glaze of mosaic tile felt soothing underfoot as he removed my sandals. I ran my fingers lightly through his thick blond hair. Then I stood, allowing his hands to caress my body before I slid into the pool. Smiling with easy satisfaction, he shed his clothing and plunged in after me, splashing warm water across the tiles.

Above us a vaulted ceiling painted with dolphins and sea sirens floated and billowed in the light of a golden candelabrum.

I looked into Holtan's amber eyes, my fear and fatigue replaced now by anticipation more intoxicating than any wine. We could wait no longer. Slippery from the bath oils, we slid from movement to movement, into and around each other, until our merging bodies became all—the air we breathed, the wine we tasted, and, at last, the couch we lay upon.

A scream shattered the silence. Heavy pounding and splintering wood in the next room. Holtan leaped up, his goblet crashing on the mosaic. Shards of glass, rivulets of wine spilled like blood across frolicking nymphs and satyrs. Frantically, I reached for a towel, wrapped it around my body with shaking hands. Was it Pilate?

I turned slowly to confront a phalanx of soldiers, swords drawn. They parted to reveal an even more deadly intruder. "Livia!"

She stepped forward, a slender purple column, formidable as always. The empress tilted her head to one side, surveying me. "Claudia, you never cease to amaze me. Who could imagine that such a quiet one would have as her lover the mightiest gladiator in the empire. And you, Holtan"—the empress turned to him—"you, who might choose any woman, what do you see in this spare little thing? Has she bewitched you? Shall I charge her with sorcery as well as adultery?"

Holtan's hands clenched. "Leave my home. Leave now! Guards!"

"No use calling, Holtan. My soldiers found them easy prey."

I caught my breath as Holtan moved threateningly toward her.

Livia merely smiled. "Boldness has served you well, Holtan. So many victories. Even my son admires your prowess. It would be a pity to see Tiberius disillusioned. He can be extremely resourceful when dealing with fallen idols. Only recently he ordered priests from the Temple of Isis crucified—no doubt friends of yours, Claudia."

Livia appraised the room, her patrician nose taking in the scent of oils and fine wine. "You have come far for a slave, Holtan. Are they all like you in Dacia? So strong, you northern barbarians. But you have been lucky as well."

She's toying with us the way a lioness amuses herself with prey, I thought, as Livia's eyes shifted back to me. She looked older than the last time I had seen her but no less deadly.

"Fortuna has been generous with you as well, Claudia." Livia's hand, blue-veined and weighted by rings, traced a figure of Mars inlaid in ivory on the Etruscan table beside her. "Fate appears to have left you untouched. Does your 'sight' reveal what I shall do about that?"

"Would I have come if it had?"

The empress smiled, her glittering eyes amused.

"Well, well, well—" Caligula stood in the doorway, the corners of his Cupid's mouth curling as he took in the scene. His smile broadened as he turned to Livia. "I wondered why you left so suddenly and with such a heavy guard. Aren't you going to invite me in?"

The empress turned, her stiff movements regal still. For an instant I caught a look of surprised annoyance as she faced him. At Livia's nod the guards yielded, allowing Caligula to strut into the room. He was in full uniform with breastplate and crested helmet.

"Do forgive my intrusion," he purred. "It is always a pleasure to see you, Claudia . . . and now to see so much of you. We don't meet often enough these days." Caligula gestured to a guard to pour him wine. Drinking slowly, with obvious enjoyment, he nodded to Holtan. "Very good Falerian. I heard you had the best vineyard in southern Italy." His heavy-lidded eyes shifted back to me, resting on my naked thighs. "Seeing you like this, my dear, so casually dressed, takes me back to our childhood, those carefree days on the Rhine." His gloating eyes looked fevered.

I shuddered, remembering the hapless barnyard creatures he had tormented when we were children. Meeting his speculative glance, I made no attempt to disguise my loathing.

Unperturbed, he continued to taunt me. "You and Marcella were charming playmates. A pity about Marcella. She was lovely, so spirited, so affectionate . . ."

Caligula's eyes slid over Holtan's body, barely concealed by the towel hastily thrown about his waist. "Ah, I am in luck! Life with great-grandmother is quiet, not much excitement there. How fortunate I am to discover a celebrity in an arena of a different sort."

Holtan lunged forward, taking him by surprise. Caligula, despite his armor, was no match. He shrieked like a girl as Holtan grabbed the sword from his belt. Pinioning Caligula's arms behind his back, Holtan used him as shield, brandishing the sword before them at the Guards.

"Run, Claudia," he cried. "Get out!"

I darted toward the door only to face more soldiers. One grabbed me. The others, swords drawn, rushed Holtan. He held them at bay. Caligula struggled free only to slip on the wet floor. Cursing violently, he pulled himself up, reached for a sword, and started toward Holtan.

As the guards moved in, pushing the circle tighter, Caligula cried out: "No! *I* want him." Four of the guards secured Holtan as he advanced.

"You cannot!" I pleaded, struggling with the soldier who held me.

"Oh yes, I can. He's mine."

"He will die when I choose," Livia said coolly.

"Grandmother!" Caligula pouted. "He belongs to me."

"I shall decide that. Now get out! I have had enough of you for one night."

Caligula, his face mottled with anger, stalked out.

Livia turned toward me. "And now, Claudia—" The guard's grip tightened.

This is it, I thought. Somehow I had always believed that rules were made for others. Now, when it mattered most, Fortuna had deserted me. I felt the cold dagger on my throat, closed my eyes, stiffening with fear. I would not scream.

"Put on your clothes, Claudia," the empress ordered. "You are coming with me."

CHAPTER 28

The Villa of Mysteries

It was hours since Livia had spoken a word to me. Arms and legs tightly bound, I sat across from her in the royal carriage awaiting her command. Again and again, visions of Holtan as I had last seen him, helpless and bleeding, tormented me. What were they doing to him? Was he even alive? At the empress's insistence the curtains had remained closed, but I sensed we had been traveling for some time through open country. Where were we going? What awful death had Livia planned for me? I thought again and again of Holtan and Marcella, longed to hold them one last time.

At last, the carriage slowed. I heard voices, but couldn't make out the words. Our wheels rumbled over paving stones. I heard flutes, drums, merchants' cries, and beggars' wails. Food sizzled nearby, delicious smells. How long since I had eaten? Livia's eyes were shut, her mouth slightly open. I wiggled across the seat, pushing the curtain open with my shoulder. We passed a market, a public bath, and a small forum. It could be any Roman town, but which? The carriage rounded a corner. Before us was a splashing fountain, beside it an outdoor restaurant. Now I knew! Pilate and I had stopped there on a summer holiday. Livia had brought me to Pompeii. But why?

Livia's eyes snapped open. "Close the curtain!" she demanded. "Faster!" she cried, banging the carriage's ceiling with the gold knob of her cane. "Faster!" The horses' steady trot quickened. People in the street jumped back. We were flying.

I turned to face her. "Won't you at least tell me what you have done to Holtan?"

"Your lover is on his way to Rome. I have decided to turn him over to Caligula."

"You would not dare! Holtan is far too popular. The people wouldn't stand for it."

Livia laughed. "Did popularity help Germanicus or your dear auntie Agrippina? The people have notoriously short memories—as do you."

"You think you're so powerful! There's something you want—I *know* it."

The mocking expression in Livia's eyes flickered for an instant. "Indeed? Now what could that be?"

"I don't know, but it has to do with me."

"How very perceptive of you. Of course I want something. Why else would I have allowed you to live—and allowed your child to live? Remember, my dear, you are not the last of your line."

Marcella too! Oh, Isis, no! I struggled to appear calm.

Livia smiled, her eyes gloating. "I have watched you for some time, observing the progress of your little affair—"

She paused again reflectively. "You thought you were so clever with your disguises, your little love nests. You never dreamed that I . . ." She was sneering now. "It was amusing at times."

"How dare you!"

"My dear, I dare anything that suits my purposes. Now it's *your* turn."

A warning chill raised bumps on my arms. "What are you talking about?"

"You are the intuitive one. *You* tell me; that is why I have brought you here."

The carriage came to a stop. I was certain Livia could hear my pounding heart. She watched me appraisingly as a hunter might a trapped animal.

"Your little dalliance with Holtan would have been of no earthly interest if it had not reminded me of your prediction years ago. A lucky guess, I thought at first, but since then there have been rumors. Those dreams you have . . . Some say you are a witch."

I waited, refusing to take her bait.

Finally, Liva continued. "My life has been full. I have everything I could want, except . . ." She paused, regarding me speculatively.

I returned her stare, aware suddenly of how frail Livia looked. How old was she? Sixty? Sixty-five? The lines about her eyes and mouth, the crepey neck. No amount of artifice could hide them forever. Of course! "Except immortality. You want to live forever."

"Very good! But you are wrong if you imagine that I want to live on in this worn-out body. The priests have assured me that

I will be made a goddess. Is it not fitting that I reign in heaven beside my husband, the Divine Augustus?"

I shrugged. "What has that to do with me?"

"You have powers. You see the future."

"You exaggerate any ability that I might have. I can't—"

"Oh yes, you can, for you yourself are about to die. Perhaps, if Fortuna wills it, you will return to tell me what you have seen."

"Oh, my goddess, no!"

"Oh yes, my dear, yes. Pray long and hard to your Isis, for you are about to enter the Villa of Mysteries. *If* you survive the ordeal and, more important, *if* you bring back the knowledge I seek, your baby will live."

I forced myself to look straight into her malevolent eyes. "And Holtan?"

"My dear, you are hardly in a position to bargain."

"Holtan, too, or I will surely die and you will learn nothing. Promise on your honor—on the honor of the goddess you hope to become."

"You are a cheeky one! But yes, Holtan too. Now get on with it."

A slave pushed aside the curtain. At a nod from Livia, he cut my bonds, then pulled me roughly from the carriage. I looked up at Livia. "You are not coming?"

"I must first discipline Caligula. He was a naughty boy to follow me against my orders. I cannot allow that. But never fear, you will feel my presence. Be certain of it."

Two guards who had ridden behind us leaped from their horses, positioning themselves on either side of me. "Take her!" Livia commanded them. With a firm hand beneath each elbow, they half dragged me onto the portico. As we reached the top, the door opened and a woman stepped into view.

"You have her now," Livia said. "You know what to do."

The woman bowed to the empress and the carriage rolled on. "I am Portia Proxius," she said to me. Her extended hands were delicate, too small for the heavy rings she wore. "We have been waiting for you."

"This is your home?" I asked, looking curiously at the small, elegant figure. "Livia called it the Villa of Mysteries. I have heard strange rumors . . . women have disappeared from here . . ." I hesitated, trying to reconcile Portia in her filmy gray *stola* with the bizarre stories whispered about the villa.

She pushed back a dark, glossy curl, slightly tinged with silver. "Surely the empress told you about us. She is our patron." Portia opened the door wide to admit me.

I looked at her with surprise. "Livia comes here? "

"Sometimes, when affairs of state permit. Many of her closest friends are part of our group. You may recognize some." She gestured toward the atrium before us where a group of women silently watched.

"Claudia has joined us at last," Portia announced. The women greeted me, their manners impeccable, yet curiosity, perhaps even appraisal, shone in their eyes. I had a nodding acquaintance with several—a few senators' wives, the owner of a large greenhouse filled with rare plants. I had rented garden slaves from her only a month before. What were they doing here?

One woman sat alone in a leafy corner of the atrium. The scroll she had been holding slipped unheeded to the floor as her eyes met mine. What eyes! Deep green, set wide apart. For an instant I thought of my sister. The two looked nothing alike . . . yet there was something . . . I had seen this woman before, but where?

She rose slowly and walked toward me, a slim hand extended. "I am Miriam of Magdala. We met at the Asklepion in Pergamum."

"Of course!" I stepped forward, taking her hand, remembering the worldly woman who had livened those dreadful days. "It has been a long time, more than three years—so much has happened since then."

Miriam nodded. "For me as well."

"It is too bad that you cannot spend the remainder of the day chatting in the atrium with us," Portia apologized crisply, "but you know the rules."

"I know nothing." My fears increased at the pity I read in Miriam's limpid eyes.

"I should have thought the empress . . ." Portia took my arm. "You will know everything in time." She led me away from the atrium's brilliance, down a shaded passageway. The black and white floor tiles swam crazily before my eyes as we passed a *tablinum* guarded by a bronze bust of Livia.

Portia opened a heavy door at the end of the hallway and held it for me. Reluctantly, I stepped inside. The room, hardly more than a cell, contained a narrow cot with a small table and chair. The only adornment was a large statue of Dionysus. How strange in such an opulent house. "Are all your guest rooms this spartan?" I asked Portia. "Perhaps I might have something to eat? It is afternoon, and I have had nothing since yesterday."

"I am sorry on both counts, but you know the rules."

"Stop saying that! I *don't* know the rules. Who are you?"

"The mistress of the ritual."

"What ritual? Who are those women?"

"Ladies from the highest classes, like yourself," Portia assured me.

"What about the red-haired one? Miriam? Who is she?"

"How astute you are! Miriam is a bit different. She is a courtesan."

"You knew that and invited her?"

"Of course, we know the backgrounds of all our devotees. She is of the very highest order, somewhat similar to your husband's favorite. What is her name . . . Titania."

"If your purpose is to humiliate me—"

"Not at all." Portia touched my arm lightly. "I merely meant that women like Titania and Miriam are welcome anywhere. Both are wealthy and well connected, but that, of course, is where the similarity ends. Titania cares only for powerful men. Miriam is quite different. She is philosophical, a patron of the arts, some might even say spiritual."

"Then why did she become a harlot?"

"Oh, that is harsh. Is her life so different from your own? Miriam at least has independence."

"Then what is she doing here? What are any of you doing here?"

"We are as we seem . . . women with the means and inclination to attain power beyond earthly imagination."

My throat constricted. I could barely speak. "What do you want of me?"

Portia's dark eyes glittered as they swept over my body. "Tonight you will be the bride of Dionysus."

I lay on a narrow cot. Before me was a statue of the god, his handsome face veiled and unveiled by smoke from the pungent incense burning at his feet. Head reeling from the heavy fumes, I felt infused by Dionysus's life-giving, seminal moisture, pure, mindless, liberating.

Dionysus brings wildness; a faraway voice warned of terror as well as ecstasy. The god's frenzied devotees tear animals apart. In their madness, sometimes they devour each other. Was I to be their victim? Pulling myself off the cot, I pounded on the door with all the vigor my strangely languorous hands could summon. What was the matter with me? In the distance I heard approaching footsteps.

"Yes, *Domina,* we are coming," a voice assured me. A moment or so later I heard the bolt scrape and the door swing open. Two female slaves bowed low before me. Each carried a thyrsus, a kind of wand with a pinecone wound into the staff. I had seen it pictured in countless frescoes. Were they maenads, handmaidens of Dionysus?

One slave stepped forward. "If it pleases the goddess, we have come to prepare you."

"If it pleases the goddess?" I echoed, the words slow to my tongue.

Portia, standing behind them, beckoned. "We honor you tonight as Ariadne."

"Ariadne!" My legs went limp. I would have fallen had it not been for the slaves. All my life I had cherished a connection with Ariadne. What cruel irony was this? I struggled to keep my voice steady. "What do you mean?"

"There is no need for you to understand," Portia murmured.

"It is enough that you *are* Ariadne and will soon join your divine lover. Come, my dear."

Kithara music filled the passage. Golden candelabra shaped like many-branched trees had been set in wall niches along the corridor. Every surface of the hall gleamed luminously. I leaned heavily on the slaves who led me to a marble bath where they removed my clothing. Slipping into the water, I saw the likeness of Dionysus smiling down from the ceiling.

The women's hands, gloved in sponges, caressed my naked body. I raised an arm to wave them off, then languidly dropped it. I had lost the will to resist. Their insistence, the pressure of the soft sea sponges, the trickle of soapy water down the valley of my breasts was surprisingly pleasant. Too soon they helped me from the bath, patting me dry with soft linen towels. The slaves covered my body with gold dust, anointed my thighs and breasts with sandalwood. As if in a dream, I felt the sheerest gossamer slip over my head. Examining the delicate fabric, I saw hundreds of tiny brilliants. "They look like stars," I heard myself say in a strange, breathless voice.

"They *are* stars." Portia purred like a tender mother. "Tonight you are the Queen of Heaven."

I shook my head to clear it. "Ariadne's lover abandoned her. Some say she died."

"But she returned transformed," Portia gently reminded me. "Ariadne's *mortal* lover abandoned her—as so often happens—but Dionysus came for her as he will come for you." Portia placed a bridal crown of myrtle on my head. "You, too, oh, lovely one—daughter of mighty Minos—shall reign as a goddess and know all that a goddess knows."

She guided me down the hall. A door was thrust open. My breath caught at the sight before me. Women wrapped in panther skins crowded the room. Many struck cymbals, pounded drums, or blew flutes. Others, twined with garlands, danced and sang. I could not understand the wild and blurry words, nor did I recognize the celebrants, for they wore masks. Above their swaying breasts and smooth shoulders were the heads of lions and leopards.

They surrounded me, twisting and writhing, weaving one circle, then two and three. As they drank freely from wineskins passed among them, the women's cries grew louder. The music, the wine, the excitement of the dancers was infectious. Someone offered me a cup. "Drink the wine of Dionysus." As I savored the contents, unlike anything I had ever tasted, my fears melted. I am a force of nature, I am the sap running in a tree, the blood pounding in the veins, the liquid fire of the grape. Was this not how life was meant to be—drinking the sweet red wine and smelling the rich, musky fragrance of the women pushing in around me?

The dancers whirled, twisting this way and that, taking the wine into their mouths and spraying it between their teeth into a thin mist. It stuck to me, enveloping me, mingling with the pungent smoke from many tripods scattered throughout the room. Head swimming, I glimpsed two new figures and strained to see more clearly. They carried a large wicker basket and were walking slowly toward me.

Someone held a small bowl on a tripod before me, forcing me to inhale its acrid fumes. My lungs filled to bursting. Sensations of every kind assaulted me. Each sound, each sight intensified almost beyond bearing. Every pore tingled and pulsated with a life of its own. I screamed as colors I could not name exploded before my eyes in grotesque shapes. Each part of me pulled in a different direction. My patrician status, the power and privilege, however fleeting, that feminine grace and beauty brought me were ripped away until I was stripped of every defense, every trick, every shred of personality. Finally only my trembling soul remained alone and vulnerable. Holy Isis, be with me. If I must endure this death, let me use it to save my loved ones.

The basket lay before me, lid open. I saw the leather rod with straps at one end. My heart was ready to explode. A masked woman tied the straps about her waist. I shrieked and struggled to free myself as the tall, muscular figure advanced toward me. Women surrounded me, holding me fast while others swiped at me with small leather whips. At first the strokes were short and stung like light rain, but soon they came harder and faster. I struggled frantically as they dragged me toward a couch.

The woman with the rod climbed on top of me. Or was it a woman? Dionysus's spear of fire seemed to be everywhere, over and around me, assaulting me, enveloping me, dominating me. The singing and the music grew even louder, drowning out my screams until after a time even I no longer heard them. Again and again I was consumed by the god until I was finally one with him. I heard the rushing waters of the Styx, saw white-haired Charon waiting. The forms of so many that I had loved waited on the other side, but not Marcella and Holtan. They were here in this world. "No!" I cried, but the sound was no more than a whisper. "I don't want to die, I don't . . ."

MUCH LATER THE MUSIC SLOWED, ALTERING SUBTLY UNTIL it had changed to a soft lullaby. Gentle hands ministered to me, slipping away the ripped gown and replacing the soiled covering beneath me with a fresh one. Deft fingers washed away the wine and blood from my bruised body and carefully dressed me in a satin gown studded with seed pearls and richly embroidered in a pattern of golden stars. Propped up by silken pillows, I watched as one by one the women removed their masks. Covering their nakedness now with luminous robes, they knelt before me.

"It is time, Great Ariadne, to tell us what you see."

I turned my head. It was Portia who spoke, a very different Portia. This woman regarded me with reverence as she slowly advanced. In her hands was a silver bowl, which she placed on a small table before me. Portia's voice was hoarse, hardly more than a whisper, as she asked, "Will the goddess share that which she sees?"

I looked down at the bowl. It was filled with clear water. Just water. But as I continued to stare into its depth, the liquid swirled. Visions slowly appeared, only to fade again. They made no sense, yet filled me with apprehension. I pushed the bowl away. I would not do it. Unheeding, the women pressed forward, jostling one another in their eagerness.

They had forced me into this, why should they not face the consequences? "You won't like what I see," I warned.

The women ignored my words, jostling each other, murmuring impatiently among themselves. Portia held her place in front.

I looked again into the bowl, studying the shapes I saw

drawing closer, clearer. "Your husband has been posted to Germania," I told her.

"Yes, yes, everyone knows that."

"Perhaps. But everyone does not know about the chieftain's daughter. She is blond and very beautiful. Their alliance is political, but he will come to value it for other reasons. Your husband will never return to Rome."

"That is impossible!"

"He will *never* return to Rome."

Turning to another, the master gardener, who had pushed her way to the front, I said, "You want to know about your daughter, your only daughter."

The woman nodded eagerly.

"She will conceive. She will have a son, a beautiful, healthy boy, but she herself will die."

Another woman crowded in beside her. "Can you tell me about my house here in Pompeii? I have been offered a good price. Should I sell it?"

I felt a wave of heat, the breath sucked from my lungs. "Yes . . . yes!" I gasped. "Something terrible will happen here. Take your family. Leave this place."

Miriam stood before me now, eyes large. I struggled with a vision, trying to understand. Bizarre, frightening. What did it mean? My sight was already fading. "You think there is nothing left for you in Galilee, but you are wrong. You must return. Go home. There you will find your greatest love, a man unlike any other. I see much joy for you. I see a crown . . ." I broke off. Was this man a king? Then why a crown of thorns? What did it mean? What should I say to her? "Miriam, go now!" I gasped. "Your time with him is short."

Miriam caught her breath. "Claudia, what do you mean? How will I know him?"

The others pushed forward, each with a question. Whatever the gift's source, it would soon be gone. Surely, I reasoned, I have earned the use of this power for myself. Closing my eyes to the pleading faces, I looked into the void. For one awful moment, I saw nothing. Then, at last, Holtan's form appeared before me.

But was it Holtan? Gone were the power and grace I knew and loved so well. I scarcely recognized the strangely shrunken body lying before me. Why the haggard face, the pain-filled eyes? I saw no wounds, but surmised they must be terrible. Holtan's lips moved. I struggled to hear.

"I had—had to see you—Claudia," he gasped in a raspy whisper.

CHAPTER

29

The Goddess Livia

The Villa of Mysteries was quiet now. One by one the others had slipped away. Numb with fatigue, I sat with my back against a marble column, feet dangling in the lily pond.

"May I join you? I have come to say goodbye."

Startled, I looked up, squinting in the morning sunlight. I had dozed off. Now I saw Miriam, a slim figure in a russet *stola,* standing in the archway. She was dressed for traveling. "You must be returning to Rome?"

Smiling, she shook her head. "No, I am going to Judaea. Perhaps I will find my lover there, the man you saw in your vision." She drew closer, her eyes on mine. "Tell me, Claudia, how will I know him?"

I struggled to recall the image. "He has a wonderful face . . . eyes that reach into one's very soul." Eyes that reach into one's soul. Had I seen those eyes somewhere else? *That face* . . . Impossible, this was Miriam's life, not mine. I struggled to recapture what I had originally seen for her the previous night. It had all been so confused. There was joy . . . but also . . . oh no! I paused, hesitant to say more. "I see great love for you, but also sadness."

Miriam smiled ruefully. "I have never experienced great love. Perhaps it is worth some sadness." Throwing back her mantle, Miriam sat down beside me. "Did you see something for yourself last night?"

"Yes." My eyes filled with tears. "The one I love . . . I saw him clearly. He had come to me . . . from far away, I think . . . but," my voice sank to a frightened whisper, "*he was dying*."

"The man was not your husband."

"No, not my husband."

"What will you do?" Miriam asked, her eyes compassionate as they studied me. "What *can* you do?"

"I have been thinking. If I never see him again . . . that terrible thing won't happen."

"Is that possible? What Fortuna has written—"

"I will not believe that!" I exclaimed, kicking at the water's placid stillness. "I can change what is written. I *must* change it!"

"Then may Isis grant you strength."

"And you, as well."

We clasped hands, looking deeply into each other's eyes. When I looked up, I saw a tall Nubian garbed splendidly in gold. He bowed to me from the doorway. "The empress bids you join her."

"Take care!" Miriam warned softly.

I squeezed her arm reassuringly. "I have been to the banks of the Styx itself. Surely I can handle Livia." Almost sauntering,

I followed the slave to the *triclinium* where the empress breakfasted alone.

"Good morning, 'Ariadne.' " Her eyes slanted maliciously as she gestured toward a walnut and ivory chair beside her couch. "So you survived your nuptials. Not everyone is so fortunate."

Fortunate, indeed, I thought, watching Livia dribble cream over her figs. How little she knew. "I thought you would be there."

"I was there."

"I did not see you."

"But I saw you. Quite a performance."

My chair scraped across the marble tiles as I leaned forward. "You cannot imagine the gift you have given me." I met her gaze coolly. "I am very grateful."

"Oh, for Jupiter's sake!" Livia exclaimed, eyes blazing like emeralds. "What have you to tell me?"

"I am surprised you did not ask last night with the others."

"I am the empress, you stupid girl! Tell me now, will I be a goddess or not? What did you see for me?"

I had seen nothing related to Livia, yet the lives of Marcella and Holtan depended upon the right answer. The empress was shrewd; I would have to make it good. Isis help me!

I took a deep breath and closed my eyes, intoning: "Your name will live long into the future." Another breath. "In fact . . ." The sacred space eluded me; I saw only blackness. "In fact . . ." I paused again, the lie that I had prepared frozen on my tongue. What could I say to her? There was nothing . . . and then, to my amazement, a shocking image took shape. "Much of the Palatine is in ruins. People wandering through the rubble wearing strange clothing and speaking languages that I have never heard. They walk about looking at crumbling walls and pointing their fingers at . . . at nothing, really. There's nothing to see but fallen columns, piles of debris. Part of it may be the forum, but I am not certain . . . So little remains . . ."

"But what about me?" Livia urged impatiently.

"These strangers seem to know you," I continued slowly. What was I seeing? My world, all that I knew and cherished had crumbled to nothing. "There is a sign with your name and an arrow pointing the way to your house. It too is a ruin, but better preserved than the rest. People go there and stand, almost in awe, looking at the mosaic on your floor. Why that should be, I cannot imagine, since it is very faded."

As I strained to make sense of what I saw, the vision slowly faded until it was gone. What dreadful thing had I been shown? I opened my eyes to find Livia smiling delightedly. "That settles it! Of course I am to be a goddess. What else could it mean?" She leaned back expansively. "You have done your job well. I shall allow you to join your husband in Herculaneum. You may tell him that you have been my guest these past two days." She dismissed me with a glance and reached again for the cream pitcher.

"But my baby—Marcella—is she all right?"

Livia shrugged. "So far as I know. She is with your husband."

I drew a deep breath. "And Holtan?"

"Unharmed. I shall release him when I return to Rome." Livia turned her attention to the figs, islands in a sea of cream. "Oh yes, there is something else." She looked up briefly. "Last night I received a message. Pilate's son by that alley cat Titania has died of a sudden fever. No doubt your husband will look to you for comfort. I never thought him overfond of Titania, but the boy, that is another matter. I hear he was a handsome lad—took after Pilate."

She paused to spread honey on a slice of bread. "I shall have a word with Tiberius—see if he can arrange something for Pilate. Something outside of Rome. I am weary of seeing that face of yours at banquets. Your gray eyes annoy me." Her head nodded perfunctorily; I was released.

With Isis's help I had managed to survive Livia's capricious cruelty. But what awaited me in Herculaneum?

OUR NEW VILLA—LIKE HOLTAN'S—HAD A DOUBLE portal, heavily studded, bronze-hinged, firmly bolted. I waited like any outsider while the groom that Livia had sent with me pounded forcefully. Almost at once the door was opened by a porter I did not know. Fair, tall, and broad, probably a Thracian. He studied me uncertainly.

"This is your *domina,* you fool," Livia's groom snapped.

The porter backed away, wide-eyed, bowing profusely. Another unfamiliar face appeared, tall with close-cropped gray hair and an air of quiet authority. "I am Hieronymus, your new steward," he said, bowing even lower than the flustered porter, who was sent in search of Pilate. I hurriedly dismissed Livia's groom, sending him back to her. The less the empress knew of my affairs, the better.

The steward led me down a marble corridor toward a sunlit atrium. Feeling like a stranger in my own home, I looked beyond him into the interior, perhaps a hundred feet or more of successive vistas, light and shadow. I had not expected the villa to be so large. Perhaps, I speculated, Pilate intends for me ogave way to sympathy. It was unthinkable to lose a child. I lifted my hand, touched his face for an instant, longing to comfort him. There was so much to say, yet none of it could be said. "I am tired." I excused myself. "The Mysteries . . ."

"You look exhausted. The empress must have been demanding."

A WEEK PASSED. PILATE SAW FEW CLIENTS AND REMAINED at home. I felt his thoughtful eyes and was grateful that the Mysteries were secret even to husbands. Then one morning I stepped out onto a balcony and found Pilate staring at the sea. It was a gorgeous summer day. Blue, blue, blue everywhere. Turquoise, indigo, sapphire. Crystal shallows, deep waters, distant sky. Our new villa, with its back to the hillside, its face to the bay, had been built for this sublime panorama.

My eyes traveled to a loosely wrapped scroll that he tapped idly against the wall. It bore the imperial seal. My pulse quickened. "What is it?"

Pilate handed the scroll to me. "See for yourself."

Hurriedly, I scanned the column of script. "What is this? You are to be governor of Judaea!" I exclaimed, looking up at him. "Your first command! I am so happy for you, so proud of you."

Pilate shrugged slightly, frowning. "Judaea has always been a trouble spot, the thorn in Tiberius's side."

"Then it is an opportunity to show him what you can do. Judaea is Rome's bulwark against the Parthians. The emperor has confidence in you or he would not offer such a challenge."

"I am glad you see it that way. Many find Judaea's mountains and deserts attractive. I hope *you* will. Jerusalem is ugly, I hear. The palace there hasn't been renovated in sixty years—not since Antonius and Cleopatra's state visit. Except for official inspections, we need never go there. The provincial palace in Caesarea will be more to your taste. It's considered a showplace. Of course, you can make whatever changes you like to either—"

I stepped back. "I hadn't thought to accompany you, I—"

Pilate lifted my chin, tilting it so our eyes met. "It *is* my first command. I want you at my side, sharing it with me." His cool eyes searched my face. "Even Tiberius thinks it best that you accompany me. Look"—he pointed toward the bottom of the scroll—"the emperor mentions your 'unique instincts.' "

It had not taken Livia long to put her plan in motion. A word to Tiberius and I was effectively banished. Must she always have her way? My thoughts turned to Holtan in Rome. Judaea was the other side of the world. How could I bear to leave him? I couldn't. Then I recalled my vision, saw Holtan's anguished face as he whispered my name. If separation was the only way to ensure his life . . .

"I must have time," I said at last. If only I could stay on in this lovely house, never seeing Holtan, but at least knowing that he was near.

"Not much time, Claudia."

THE FOLLOWING DAY I RETURNED FROM A WALK ON THE beach to find Livia waiting in the *nymphaneum*. Whether by chance or design, the couch the empress reclined upon was beneath a statue of Priapus, guardian and motivator of fertility. The villa's previous owners had rubbed the crown of his huge marble phallus shiny smooth with their passing hands. Had it brought them luck? I would need more than that if Livia decided to tell Pilate about Holtan.

She wasted no time with greetings. "You betrayed me!" she accused. "You have made no plans to accompany Pilate to Judaea."

"How do you know that?"

She shrugged impatiently. "How do I know anything? Don't waste more of my time. This is a splendid opportunity for your husband, exactly the chance for which he has been conniving. Too bad Herod the Great is not alive—a delightful man, very popular in Rome. Once the entire senate stood to applaud him . . ." She paused, lost in thought. "Yes, Herod was a clever one—holding off the Parthians, all the while keeping that barbaric country of his own together. No one has done a decent job since. Of course, his family life was a bit strange. My dear husband once said that it was safer to be Herod's pig than his relative."

"I don't understand."

"Judaeans have some foolish proscription against eating pork."

Where was this leading? "But Herod?"

"He was obsessed with the idea that one of his many sons might seize the throne. Before it was over Herod killed some forty family members—many of them his own children." Slamming the table with her fan, Livia turned to face me squarely. "Enough chatter. I find your ingratitude foolishly dangerous."

I shivered despite the dazzling sunlight, but kept my voice steady. "You of all people know how complicated the situation is."

"Indeed. Then I shall uncomplicate it." With a snap of her ringed fingers Livia signaled a passing slave. "Fetch your *dominus* at once," she commanded. Turning to me, the empress smiled. "No doubt Pilate finds your reluctance puzzling. I think it is time we enlightened him."

"No! No, there's no need for that."

"Too late, my dear. A pity that you will never see your daughter again, and, as for your precious Holtan—I will have him flogged to death. It will take a long time for a man that strong to die. Perhaps we can arrange for you to watch."

I stood facing her, my hands gripping the back of a bench to support my trembling body.

"Please," I begged, my voice a hoarse whisper. At that moment, Pilate entered the atrium.

Livia smiled benignly at him. "Your lovely wife and I have been discussing your appointment. I believe she has something to tell you."

PART IV

CAESAREA

in the sixteenth year of
the reign
of Tiberius (30 C.E.)

CHAPTER

30

In the Temple of the Lord

As the *Persephone* swung out from the harbor, she seemed to sprout oars, twenty on either side of her sleek hull. The luxury cruiser, Sejanus's parting gift to us, had been painted purple in my honor. Belowdecks a drum rumbled and the blades dipped. More thunder and they splashed the surface, two men pulling on each shaft. The ship glided forward—slowly at first, then picking up speed as the drumbeats quickened. Too soon the Bay of Neapolis slipped from view.

Day after day I sat under a rippling awning staring out at the twin blues of sea and sky.

The smooth voyage gave me too much time to think. Was Isis laughing at me? Had she been laughing all along? Once I had prayed so earnestly for Pilate's love, zealously repeating her incantation. Had the goddess heard my prayers and granted the object of my desires, or had it all been merely a girlish fantasy gone wrong? Pilate did, indeed, want me as his wife, yet what did that matter? Our union seemed so foolish, so misbegotten, now that I had tasted real love. What need was there for potions and incantations? Holtan and I had known from the beginning. I smiled sadly, thinking of Isis and her Osiris. Their love seemed very like our own.

One day Rachel joined me at the railing. Reminded of yet another sorrow, I turned to her, forcing a smile. "You must be very happy, returning at last to your homeland."

Rachel shrugged, her face turned away toward the sea.

"Pilate and I spoke last night. He—we have decided to free you. It is only right that you return at last to your family. Pilate will present your manumission papers at a ceremony. It will be rather grand—Herod Antipas and his court, possibly a few of those high priests, the Sanhedrin. Your family, of course, in the places of honor."

"I have no family," Rachel said, turning to face me. "They are all gone—dead." She started to move away, but I caught her arm. Held it. "I thought your father was an adviser to Herod the Great."

"He was a most trusted adviser, but he was also a Pharisee and a patriot. Father hated Herod's garish shrine. He believed the *world* was God's temple and thought that men should be their own priests. Herod would not hear of such talk. The Temple was his proclamation: 'See how good I am, see how grand.' "

I shook my head impatiently. "That is merely philosophy. Your father was a member of the court. One doesn't reach such a position without compromise."

"He would have been the first to agree with you," Rachel said. "Father was an idealist but not unworldly. He understood

Herod's need to reassure the fundamentalists at home and still show the world that he was more than Rome's client king."

I nodded. "It would seem that he achieved his goal. Jerusalem's Temple is the biggest in the world. Even in Rome, they say, 'He who has never seen Herod's Temple has never seen anything beautiful.' "

"Beautiful, yes," Rachel agreed. "But the abomination he added—"

"I don't understand—"

"My father was an orthodox man. He put his faith in the Law, he *lived* the Law. The Second Commandment is clear: no graven images. Over the years Judaeans have learned to live with them. Pagan images are everywhere—in public baths, theaters, civic buildings—but when Herod placed a huge eagle with outstretched wings over the very temple itself . . ."

"An unfortunate impropriety," I agreed, but reminded her, "He *was* the king. If that's the worst he did—"

"Yes, yes, Father recognized that. Unfortunately, my brother, Aaron, did not. Father's closest friend was Aaron's teacher, a devout Pharisee who came often to our home, talked late into the night. Aaron was fourteen, eager to be a man, listening to every word. His teacher was incensed by the eagle and spoke of tearing it down. Father was horrified. He warned the firebrand, reminded him that Herod was dying, each breath an agony. 'Be patient,' Father admonished and thought no more about it.

"Then one morning the Pharisee scholar delivered a lecture on the wages of sin. It was sin, he said, that caused Herod's illness, sin that burned and gnawed at his bowels. The time had come to remove the eagle no matter what the risk. Aaron was just young enough, idealistic and foolish enough, to rally to the cause. He and some forty other boys ran to the temple, scrambled over the walls, and chopped the blasphemous eagle to pieces."

Rachel's voice was cool and calm, almost as though it had all happened to someone else. "Of course, they were thrown into prison. We prayed that Herod might die before they could be sentenced, but Yahweh wasn't listening. Perhaps we merely amused him—like some board game played by ants. My father was hacked to pieces by guards as he knelt at Herod's bedside begging clemency for his son. Soldiers threw Mother from the tower when our home was taken. One of Herod's last acts was to sell me into slavery. He lived long enough to watch the boys, Aaron among them, burned alive."

"Rachel, Rachel, dear." I held her stiff body in my arms. "I am sorry, so sorry. I knew nothing. You never told me. What can I do for you now? Are you afraid to go home—afraid of Herod's heirs? Do not forget that Pilate is now the foremost man in Judaea. We can still free you, send you anywhere you care to go."

"Herod was a madman. Only two sons remain, Antipas and Philip. Surely they praise Fortuna every day for their own lives. They would scarcely remember a screaming child. I have nothing to fear in Judaea, and no wish to be anywhere but with you."

On the morning of the fifteenth day at sea, I spied Caesarea sparkling in the distance.

Pilate stood beside me as we approached, his long, elegant fingers drumming impatiently on the rail. Sounds of the city floated toward us as ships and buildings drifted into view. I had been told that Caesarea was one of the most beautiful cities in the world. Glancing up at the exquisite temple to Caesar that overlooked the harbor, I believed it. Houses, white for the most part, spilled down palm-shaded terraces toward the docks. People waved from windows, crowded balconies. As the *Persephone* sailed into the harbor, a cheer went up from the shore. Flowers, bright blossoms everywhere, drums and flutes, red-robed ministers lined up to welcome us.

The gangplank swayed over the water, crush and noise, bags and boxes at the ready. Since I was a child, the prospect of new places had filled me with wonder and excitement. Now, so far from Holtan, I felt only despair. Rachel brought Marcella out on deck. My child squealed, holding her arms out to me, but it was Pilate who took her. "This is Caesarea, my little one," he said, holding Marcella up to see the spectacle before us.

Looking at me over our daughter's curly head, he added, "We will all be very happy in Judaea."

If material possessions could make for happiness, we had them in abundance. Our palace was grand. My apartment was large, with rooms overlooking the sea, balcony after balcony, each a hanging garden. I dedicated the largest to

Isis, making a shrine of it with flowers and soft rugs surrounding her statue. Every day I meditated there, but not for long—my social schedule left little time. With a dining room large enough for one hundred couches, Pilate expected me to entertain often. By now I did it easily. Banquets for three hundred were not uncommon. I thought often of Mother. She would have adored my life. I was merely grateful to be kept busy.

Caesarea, built by Herod the Great as a tribute to Julius Caesar, tried hard to be Rome and in many ways succeeded. The city boasted a marble theater that would hold five thousand people and one of the largest amphitheaters in the world. Pilate officiated at state rituals in Caesar's temple. The statues to which he raised his eyes were those of Augustus, Jupiter, and Roma, comforting images of home. I saw more Romans, Greeks, and Syrians on the streets than Jews.

If all of Judaea had been like Caesarea, Pilate's job would have been easy. Unfortunately, nothing could change the fact that it was the Hebrews that my husband had been sent to govern. His entire future depended on it.

Pilate's first action was to dispatch a small troop of soldiers to Jerusalem with orders to display the Roman eagle standards before Antonia. Such a small thing. Antonia was a Roman garrison. The eagles had not been taken into their temple. I was as shocked as Pilate by the reaction.

The Jews were aghast at the intrusion of "graven images" into their sacred city. Within two days, more than a hundred of them journeyed by foot over mountains and through valleys to prostrate themselves before our palace in Caesarea. Shivering in the fall chill, they swayed and moaned, praying that the governor would be moved to take down the accursed eagles. In the face of Roman soldiers with swords drawn, the supplicants remained day after day. Pilate watched from the palace, growing increasingly uncomfortable with their presence.

"Shall I call out the soldiers?" he asked me at last.

"You can't kill people for sitting! But I am sick to death of their wailing. Why not just take down the standards? Tiberius told you to 'keep them happy and peaceful.' Surely giving in to this one peculiarity won't jeopardize Rome. The Jews will be happy, we will be peaceful. Do it—for me."

I was pleased when Pilate complied and I stood beside him on the palace balustrade breathing a sigh of relief when he gave the signal. After six days of passive protest, the supplicants went home, their mission accomplished.

"I don't understand these people," Pilate said as we watched the dust settle after the departing caravan. "The Jews *asked* Rome to come here and settle their problems."

"I know, but that was long ago. *Tata* told me about it when I was a girl. His grandfather served here under Pompey. He died trying to settle their disputes. But," I hesitated, "that was a long time ago. The people who invited Rome are dead."

"Their descendants should be grateful. We guarantee their peace. No more fighting among themselves, one faction constantly at the throats of another. They have their own courts, their own religion, collect their own taxes—"

"We tax them, too," I reminded him.

"Of course. That's the price of a stable government. Should we be expected to give up this splendid buffer against Parthia? The Jews will just have to live with Rome. Everyone else does."

In the spring, Pilate asked me to accompany him to Jerusalem on his first inspection tour. Curious about the fabled Holy City, I agreed. The road to the ancient capital sixty miles to the southeast was a fine one built by legionnaires, who had marked the way with Roman milestones. In Caesarea we had been popular, with cheering crowds everywhere. Now, the farther we got from the coast, the more I sensed antagonism. Nothing overt, but sullen glances; and once, as we neared the outskirts of the city, I heard angry muttering. I had traveled far with Germanicus and never experienced anything like it. What was the matter? Aware of Jerusalem's antiquity, I had anticipated a cosmopolitan center with a sophisticated worldview. What I found was a dreary desert garrison filled with narrow-minded, argumentative people who barely bothered to conceal their hostility.

Nevertheless, the city had one attraction that was world famous. Everybody who had ever been to Jerusalem spoke with awe of the Temple. As our caravan approached the citadel, the mammoth structure, framed by massive walls and porticoes, took my breath away. The whiteness of its stone was so brilliant that the Temple looked like a mountain covered with snow. I wanted to see the inside, but Pilate was adamant. He perceived Jerusalem as a breeding ground of unrest. "Stay inside the palace," he ordered. When I looked up at him in surprise—I had not heard that tone in a while—his voice softened. "You'll have plenty to do there. Let the city come to you."

Settling into the residence that Herod had redecorated for us did keep me busy. It was a white-marble wonder with agate and lapis lazuli floors and splashing fountains. The vaulted ceilings were painted gold and scarlet, the silver inlaid furniture encrusted with jewels. A little overdone, Pilate and I agreed, but what could you expect from barbarians? These people were so—so—flamboyant. Fortunately, we would not have to spend much time in Jerusalem, and I did enjoy the view. The hillside palace commanded a splendid outlook of the city on one side and tree-shaded gardens on the other.

Early one morning I watched with Rachel as the city's gray stone buildings slowly emerged from the blue-black shadows of night. The entire east side of the city appeared to be engulfed in flames as the first rays of dawn struck the burnished gold plate atop the sanctuary columns. "You must admit it is splendid," she said as the rising sun gilded the Temple's dome. "When I lived here as a child, Herod was still rebuilding it. Pompey's armies . . ."

"Splendid, indeed," I hurriedly interrupted her, feeling a tinge of Roman guilt for the earlier destruction. "Pilate said it took a thousand priests overseeing ten thousand workers to complete the job."

Rachel merely shrugged. "The Temple is everything in Jerusalem."

Everything, indeed. That settled it, I was determined to see this marvel for myself. Without saying anything to anyone, I slipped out one afternoon and hired a litter. It was a long ride down one hill and up the next, the bearers grunting all the way. As we neared the Temple Mount, I noticed an unpleasant odor and thought of Agrippina's makeshift hospital in Germania. So terrible, but this was worse. I had never smelled anything like it. At last the litter was lowered to the ground. I pulled the curtain and looked out. The front of the Temple was certainly impressive—huge white slabs of polished marble and lavish gold plating that glittered in the sun. But, oh, the smell! Large troughs at the side of the building overflowed with blood and entrails that drained out into the street and down the hill.

"Are you getting out or not?" a bearer asked impatiently. We were at the entrance, people were staring. I stepped out, handed him a coin, and hurried inside the massive doors.

The Courtyard of the Gentiles is famous, of course. Everyone talks about it, but nothing could have prepared me for the reality. Porticoes and marble columns were everywhere, the effect not only elegant but immense. But the noise! The din was unbelievable, unlike anything I had ever heard. Thousands of feet shuffling across the vast stone courtyard. Animals, lowing, cooing, bleating, bellowing—hundreds of creatures, large and small, lambs, bullocks, goats, chickens, doves. Voices in a dozen different dialects counting coins or begging alms, shrill cries of money changers. "Goats! Goats! Buy your goats here!" "Unblemished animals! Mine are perfect!" "Lambs! Lambs are best! Pure and docile!" "Is your currency clean?" a man asked, grabbing at my arm. "You cannot bring unclean money into the Temple. Exchange it here." "He is a thief!" another cried, shoving his way toward me.

Glad that I had dressed conservatively in a black *stola* of Rachel's, I pulled it tightly around me and pushed forward. In the distance I saw a broad flight of steps. If I could get above the confusion—the pushing, shoving pilgrims, the raised arms of the beggars—I might gain some perspective. I was jostled this way and that by money changers who importuned me every step of the way, but at last I reached the base of the marble stairs.

Breathing a sigh of relief, I began to climb. When I stopped at midpoint to rest, a surprising sight met my eyes. On the landing above me was a door, but on either side of it were signs in Greek, Latin, and Aramaic warning that entry beyond this point was restricted to Jews. Gentiles who attempted to enter would be put to death. Well! I was annoyed and disappointed, but the message was clear. I had risked enough already. Reluctantly I turned and was about to descend the stairs when all of a sudden the entire Temple reverberated with the sound of trumpets. Looking down I saw the crowd part as a procession of priests crossed the courtyard. They were an impressive lot in their brocade robes covered with jewels and hemmed in gold. With great solemnity they approached a large altar where a calf was tied. The terrified creature bleated piteously. Impervious, the high priest raised his knife. I saw the blood rush forth, heard the sigh of onlookers who gathered to witness the ceremony. More trumpets blared. Everywhere people were prostrating themselves on the stone floor while metal cymbals clashed above them. I could not get out fast enough.

No one had missed me—or so I thought. I looked in on Marcella, busily constructing her own citadel with clay blocks while a watchful slave beamed encouragement. Pilate, too, was occupied, closeted with petitioners in his grand *tablinum*. The afternoon passed quietly. As the sun began to set I put aside the banquet menus I had been studying and went to the highest parapet in the palace as had become my habit. Leaning against the railing, I watched purple shadows steal over the city. As always, I thought of Holtan. Where was he? What was he doing? Did he think sometimes of me?

CHAPTER

31

Caiaphas

Dark eyes, filled with anguish, beseeching me. What have I done? What must I do? A crown of thorns cuts into his brow. I run from the bloody visage, plunging headlong into a garden. Broad, leafy trees offer sanctuary. No! *No!* The trees are turning to crosses. They surround me, weeping blood. The forest floor runs with it. I try to flee. Crosses are everywhere, so many of them. Something holds me, traps me.

I struggle to remember what has frightened me. *The face.* Half remembered from another time. I lay on a great couch with lion's feet and silken coverings. My couch. Tossing this way and that, I struggle, pulling free, only to realize that it is Rachel who holds me. Pale sunlight fills the room, the face is gone, the crosses. "I'm all right," I tell her. "It is only another nightmare." *Only.* I sigh, the world once again as I know it.

"You could be facing far worse than dreams." Rachel pulled back the tangled covers. "You did a foolish thing yesterday."

"I went to the Temple alone because I did not want a lecture on what I should and should not do," I said, sitting up.

"*Domina* needs a lecture. The city is filled with dangerous factions. The Sadducees, the Pharisees, the Essenes, the Zealots—the only thing they hate more than each other is Rome. Suppose they had recognized you, suppose—"

"Yes, let's talk about suppose." Pilate had entered the room as we were speaking and stood above me now, livid with anger. "I forbade you to go to the Temple."

"I am not a child to be forbidden anything." I stared back, angry as he. How I hated this place!

Rachel slipped in close, standing protectively at my side. "*Domina* has only just awakened. She has had a terrible dream. She is not herself."

"Not herself indeed. Did you imagine that I wouldn't find out that you left the palace without guards, that you went alone to the Temple of all places?"

"Was that such a sin? Everyone talks about the Temple. I simply wanted to see it for myself."

"But what if *you* had been seen! They might have held you hostage. I am the governor, for Jupiter's sake. It is I who would have had to decide, would have had to choose between jeopardizing Rome by meeting their demands or standing by while they wreaked their vengeance on you."

The anger disappeared from Pilate's eyes as he looked down at me in my twisted shift. "You must promise, Claudia." He placed his hands on my shoulders so that I faced him directly. "Nothing of this sort can happen again."

"The last thing I want is to cause you more trouble," I

said softly, pulling my tangled hair together. "But we know you would always choose Rome."

"Don't force me to choose," he said, voice thick. Turning swiftly, he was gone.

Before I could answer, trumpets blared a loud, clear blast that floated across the city from an upper terrace of the Temple. A priest's ritual knife must be slashing the throat of the first sacrificial creature of the day. I trembled, remembering the cries of doomed animals, the acrid smell of warm blood. "Do not worry, Rachel, I will not go to the Temple again. It is a house of slaughter. The shouting, too, is dreadful."

Rachel looked puzzled, then laughed. "Oh, the money changers! All Jews must pay homage at the Temple at least once in their lives. Those who can, go often. The money changers are there to serve them."

"So I have noticed. A whole army stands ready to take their money. All that wrangling cannot be conducive to prayer."

"The bargaining gets noisy," Rachel admitted as she slipped a robe over my shoulders. "Everyone who wants to pray in the Temple must sacrifice an animal, which can only be bought with Temple shekels. Someone has to change the money."

I wrinkled my nose. "You cannot escape the smell. The whole city is permeated."

"Well . . . sometimes when the wind blows a certain way," Rachel conceded, adding, "Romans also sacrifice animals."

"*One* animal, for a special occasion," I granted, "nothing like this. All that waste, the blood—"

For a time we stood silently on the terrace, watching the sun rise over the Temple. Finally, I asked a question that had plagued me. "What about the upper floors? The signs forbid Gentiles . . ."

"Women are forbidden as well."

"Really! No wonder you worship Isis."

"Isis reveres animals. But here, the Sanhedrin—the high priests—believe that ritual is the glue that binds the Jews as a people."

"Surely there is more to faith than killing animal after animal, hour after hour."

Rachel's brows furrowed. "I am not the only Jew who questions the practice," she admitted. "One prophet cried out against it. We learn his words as children: *'He hath shown thee, Oh man, what is good and what Yahweh doth require of thee, but to do justly, to love kindness, and to walk humbly with thy God.'* "

I sighed, thinking of how far the Temple and its hundreds of dependents had strayed from that ideal. After a time Rachel ventured, "*Domina* must agree that the Temple is beautiful?"

"It is very *grand* but . . ." I stopped, not wanting to wound her civic pride. The lack of statuary seemed an odd eccentricity, but I was far more concerned with the city's sanitation. Located high in the hill country, far from any lake or river, the whole city depended on rainwater held in crumbling cisterns.

That night I brought the matter up with Pilate.

"Roman engineering could easily solve the city's water problems," he agreed almost eagerly. There had been no more discussion of my foray to the Temple. I was sorry for the distress I had caused him. I must do better.

"An aqueduct would benefit everyone," I suggested.

"Representatives from the Sanhedrin are coming here tomorrow. Their Temple treasury holds a fortune. Besides tithes and offerings, every man in the country pays a half shekel a year. They can easily afford an aqueduct."

The next evening, reclining beside me on our dining couch, Pilate described the day's events. To his amazement, the council refused. "Not one shekel," their high priest had announced.

Pilate had been adamant. His soldiers marched straight to the Temple compound and confiscated the necessary funds. Turning to me with a satisfied smile, my husband concluded, "If I am known for nothing else, it will be for bringing a proper water supply to this sorry town."

PILATE DID HIS BEST IN ALL THINGS. WHEN I ALLOWED him to share my couch, he was eager and passionate, but I felt nothing. Might these joyless moments result in another child? I sometimes wondered. No answer was revealed. After a time I speculated that Marcella's birth had injured me in some way. Perhaps there would be no other children. So be it. Marcella was my solace. Merry and mischievous, the child, nearly three, reminded me more of my sister with each passing day. I must guard my baby carefully, I thought often, all the while warming myself in the glow of her childish enthusiasm.

At times day-to-day life seemed almost bearable, and then something would invariably draw me back to Holtan. A rare letter from Apicata tore at my heart. She had glimpsed him at the theater surrounded by admiring women. At least Holtan is alive, I reminded myself, but nothing could stop my longing. I remembered with painful clarity all the things I loved about him: the warm timbre of his low-pitched voice, the odd amber color of his eyes, the texture of his sun-bronzed skin. I ached with longing for even a few brief minutes with Holtan.

As for Pilate, he was changing before my eyes. The husband who sought my company with increasing frequency seemed bewildered and frustrated, sometimes even frightened. He had only a small military presence in Judaea—merely five cohorts and one cavalry regiment. Should a serious uprising occur, he would have to appeal to the legate in Syria for help. Often he solicited my advice. Invariably it came down to one question: How could he placate the Jews and still maintain Roman sovereignty?

As I had no knowledge of Judaea, my impulses were intuitive, always returning me to the Sanhedrin. "They are the key," I told him one night as he lay beside me. "They control the Temple and the Temple rules the city."

"Can't you say more than that?" he asked impatiently.

"The sight does not come on command!" I answered, my voice edgy as his.

Receptions and banquets filled my life. Tonight, with a scroll by a new Egyptian writer, I had looked forward to a quiet evening. Then Pilate surprised me with a visit. Usually he went to sleep afterward; tonight he wanted to talk.

"But you do . . . sometimes know things," he prodded. "Try now. Try because I want you to."

Stifling a sigh, I pulled myself up, focused my eyes on the flickering lamp beside me. I breathed deeply, stared into the flame. What right had I to ask Isis anything when I had been so lax in my devotions? Yet this was not for me . . . it was Pilate who sought guidance. In this uneasy city he needed all the help the goddess could give him. The lamp flickered but I saw nothing. Please, please, Isis, tell me something that will help, something that may bring peace to a troubled man and the angry country that he must govern. Probing inwardly, I waited until at last images slowly began to appear. What did they mean? Help me, Isis, show me truth. "There is a man . . ." I said at last. "His name is Joseph . . ."

"Jupiter!" Pilate exclaimed. "They're all named Joseph!" Watching me intently, he pressed, "What does he look like?"

"A large man, but with a narrow face . . . thin lips. Not much older than you, but he is proud . . . arrogant."

Pilate stared at me, almost in wonder. "You're describing Joseph Caiaphas. A most ruthless man, I've discovered. He became high priest by marrying the former high priest's daughter. Now his power is second only to mine. What can you tell me about him?"

I stared into the flame. There were so many shadows, shifting forms. What did they mean? This Caiaphas, the mighty priest . . . "Power is everything to him, more than his people, more even than the god he serves." As though from some great distance, I heard myself warning Pilate. "Beware of him. He will try to use you."

Just beyond Caiaphas, another form came into view. "Oh!" I gasped softly. There was something so familiar . . . If only I could see him more clearly. I turned to my husband. "Caiaphas is an evil man, but there is someone else . . ."

"Another enemy?" Pilate leaned forward, grasping my hand.

"I cannot see him, he is just beyond my sight, but I feel that he is not an enemy. There is kindness—more than kindness. Someone who could . . . change the world. He is nothing like

Caiaphas . . ." Foreboding gripped my heart. I knew without knowing that the shapes I barely saw held significance far beyond our lives. Pilate and I were as nothing in this grand scheme, yet I sensed a terrible drama waiting to engulf us. As the hidden form moved toward me, I saw the crown of thorns.

"Oh, Pilate, stay away from him!" I pleaded. "You must avoid that man at any cost. There will be trouble, terrible trouble. Your good name will be . . . mixed up with him in some awful manner. Stay away from him. You must not be involved in any way between Caiaphas and this stranger."

My husband watched anxiously, fear in his eyes. "Who is this man who would change the world?" Pilate shook his head impatiently. "He sounds like just another one of those maniacal zealots."

"I don't know who he is." I was almost sobbing.

"Then look—look deeper!"

The visions were shifting. I struggled to make sense of them. Despite the sultry evening, a chill raised bumps on my arms. A man alone, praying in a garden. Swords. A cross. No! I had seen enough of death. I turned away. "All I know, Pilate, is that a dreadful tragedy lies in wait for that good man and you are in some way part of it."

"But who is this man?" Pilate persisted.

Slowly the vision faded, and I was left only with a vague impression. "I . . . think he is a Galilean." I was exhausted, all my force gone.

"I might have known! They're nothing but trouble. Even here in Jerusalem, where the Temple hierarchy keeps people in line, the Galileans are rebellious—always searching for a messiah. They question everything, even their own god."

I tried to reassure him. "Are they not just a simple country people?"

Pilate shook his head, frowning. "Not really. Nazareth is on the caravan route between Alexandria and Antioch. Galileans hear the latest news before Jerusalem."

"But I am told they are mostly fishermen."

"Don't imagine them as a few men in little boats fishing for dinner. Most of the dried fish for our garum sauce comes from Galilee. They supply much of the world."

I nodded absently, calmer now, my thoughts far removed from fish. Once Pilate's concern for my opinions would have made me the happiest woman alive. Now it saddened me. The only attention I longed for was Holtan's, and he was far away.

CHAPTER 32

Herod's Palace

When Pilate announced a holiday in Tiberius, I winced. "A city named for the man I hate most in the world!"

"It's an official visit, I want you with me." His voice softened. "There's something more. It will please you and so will the town. You have my promise."

To my surprise, he was right. Devout Jews professed to fear the city, for it was built on the site of an ancient graveyard. Partly to overcome their aversion, partly to show the world what he could do, Herod the Great's heir, Herod Antipas, had created a showplace.

When our party reached the sparkling new enclave built on the shores of Galilee, I looked about in wonder. Tiberius was a city of great beauty with broad streets, splashing fountains, and marble statues. The pavements glistened. I could smell the raw odor of fresh-cut building stones and above us the sky, not yet shaded by canopies or trees, shone bright blue. "I have never seen anything like it!" I told Pilate. "The bath, the forum, the theater, even the marketplace—they are all so clean."

"Herod spared no expense," Pilate explained. "He can afford it. He taxes his people to the limit."

Pilate too had spared no expense. His surprise gift to me was a splendid seaside villa that reminded me, as he knew it would, of our first home in Antioch. I marveled dutifully over the frescoed walls. Nymphs, satyrs, cupids frolicked in joyous abandon. My husband was trying to regain my heart.

"Do you like it?" he asked, his eyes on mine. "The colors—"

"Jupiter's palace could not be livelier or more grand." Forcing a smile, I surveyed my apartments. A profusion of pinks, purples, and soft oranges reflected the riotous blooms outside, softening the effect of the high vaulted chambers. It should have been a happy room. I hated it. "Charming," I murmured, moving away from him onto the parapet. Below me was a graceful marble path twining through terraced lawns to the water's edge where an ornate barge awaited our pleasure.

Pilate followed me out onto the parapet. "We spent many happy hours on a barge like that," he reminded me.

"A long time ago."

"Not so very long." He took my hand. "The barge will be waiting for us when I return."

"You are going away?" I tried not to sound relieved.

"Yes, I must, but not for long. I've business with Herod. There's been another demonstration in Jericho, something must be done about those Zealots. There's one—Barabbas—who incites them to insurrection. Barabbas won't rest until the last Roman is out of here—foolish man. We'll get him this time."

As the fading sounds of Pilate's chariot echoed down the road, I felt a reprieve and almost ran from the house that had begun already to feel like a prison. "Take me out on the lake," I ordered the slave master waiting beside the boat. "Have them row as fast as they can."

"Where to, *Domina*?" he asked, assisting me into the craft.

What did it matter? "To—to the next town, any town."

"The next town is Magdala, *Domina*."

Magdala? Was that not Miriam's town? How had it turned out for her? I wondered absently. Had she found the man I had seen in my vision? Perhaps they were together now. Maybe I could find them.

Within moments the barge was under way. I lay back on silken cushions, listening to the rhythmic sweeps of the oars. My eyes shifted restlessly from one lavish villa to another.

Encircled by mountains blue as sapphires, the lake possessed a startling beauty. I thought of Holtan as the line of lakeside villas gave way to groves of olives, flocks of sheep, and lush vineyards. Though it had been more than a year since I had last seen him, the memories remained vivid as ever. Again and again he smiled as the triumphant boy gladiator, holding out his palm for me to read at Apicata's banquet, splashed beside me in his pool. He was never out of my thoughts, no matter how hard I tried to forget. The yearning was so great, sometimes I wished that I might die. How much longer could I go on living with one man and loving another?

Lost in thought, I scarcely noticed the landscape change. Isolated, tumbledown shanties now dotted the shoreline and a stench filled the air. As the outskirts of town slowly took shape, the odor grew more pervasive. "What is this place?" I asked my steward.

"Magdala, *Domina*."

"Ugh!" I exclaimed, wrinkling my nose. "Why does it smell so terrible?"

"Fish-drying platforms, *Domina*. The catch is brought here from all over the lake to be dried and salted."

Nodding absently, I reached for my pouch and extracted a small perfume vial. The excursion had gone sour. What point was there in going on, what point was there in anything?

"Turn around. We will return to Tiberius," I directed, holding the vial to my nose.

As the slaves slowly brought the barge about, my glance traveled along the dock where fishermen's nets were spread, a damp mass of woven cords and twine. Many of the fishermen had pulled off their sodden tunics, their body smell competing with nearby platforms where flayed fish dried in the sun.

Just beyond, I noticed the slender figure of a woman standing alone near a row of massive amphoras awaiting transport. Curious, I looked again at the long silky hair bright as copper in the sunshine. Could it be?

"Stop!" I ordered my men. "Take me to the shore." When the barge reached the shallow water, a slave lifted my friend across the small waves and into the boat. I hugged Miriam eagerly, then held her back at arm's length. "I hoped I might find you here, but I must say Magdala comes as a surprise."

Miriam shrugged. "It is not so bad once you are accustomed to it."

"Accustomed to it!" I looked about at the fish-drying

platforms. "If garum comes from this, I will never look at fish stew again."

"It does," Miriam nodded vaguely. She seemed strangely subdued, not as excited as I would have expected by the surprise encounter. Standing beside me at the railing, she looked thinner than I remembered. "People once grew rich catching and processing fish here. That is my parents' home." She pointed to a large villa dominating the hill high above town.

"Very grand."

"It *was* grand. The courtyard has some of the most beautiful mosaics that I have seen anywhere—though you might not care for the subject matter. Fish, fishermen, boats—a shrine to the business that made our family fortune."

"Why do you say was—*was* grand?"

"Herod Antipas takes a third of everything—grapes, barley, olives, livestock, and, of course, dried fish—that's after the Temple's ten percent. Every day I hear of someone who has lost a family farm or business. Tax collectors confiscate them when the owners can't pay. All that my parents have left is a villa crumbling to ruin."

Herod's taxes, Temple taxes, and, finally, Rome's taxes. What could I say? Changing the subject, I ventured, "It must be wonderful to be with your family again."

Miriam looked at me questioningly. "I thought my story was known to all." When I shook my head, she lowered her eyes.

"Tell me as much or as little as you like," I said, gesturing for her to sit beside me under the purple canopy.

"Years ago my family arranged a marriage for me," Miriam explained in a tight, controlled voice. "They were pleased; my betrothed's people were wealthy and prominent. I was happy too; he was young and handsome. I counted myself fortunate until the wedding caravan taking me to Jerusalem was set upon by bandits. Their leader beat me, forced me. It was the last thing my brothers saw . . ."

Miriam took a deep, shuddering breath. "The brigands were arguing over who would be next with me when a troop of Roman soldiers appeared. They killed most of the bandits and drove off the rest. Theodosius Sabinus, their centurion, offered to send me on to Jerusalem with an armed guard but my father would not hear of it. A wedding was unthinkable. My parents turned from me. I had disgraced them."

I put my arms around Miriam. "How terribly unfair. What did you do?"

Miriam turned away, staring out over the lake. "There was nothing I could do. No one spoke up for me. The centurion signaled to one of his men to put me in a wagon and we started off. I was terrified. I had never been more than a mile from home. Hours later someone lifted me out. I stood, bruised and bleeding, on the threshold of Theodosius's villa in Caesarea. Everywhere I looked I saw frescoes—nymphs, satyrs. Did people really *do* those things? Would the Roman expect me to do them? I shuddered as he approached me, but when he raised his hand it was merely to examine my bleeding head wound. A nod from Theodosius and two female slaves led me to a beautiful room overlooking the sea. It was mine, they said. They brought food, bathed me, dressed me for bed, and left."

The purple canopy flapped lazily in the breeze as we floated downstream. Spellbound I watched Miriam as her story unfolded.

"Every night I lay trembling, waiting for Theodosius to call for me. The Romans were brutes—everyone said so. I thought of casting myself into the sea, but lacked the courage. Then one night Theodosius called me to the *triclinium*. It was a pleasant place—bright frescoes depicting sea nymphs at play, the fourth wall open to the sea. White spray splashed against rocks below us while musicians played. Theodosius explained that he had been away the past week. Speaking pleasantly, as though I were a guest in his home rather than a captive, he apologized for neglecting me. Was the room to my liking, how was the food? He did not ask me to share his couch, gesturing instead to the one adjacent.

"As we feasted, Theodosius asked questions about my life in Magdala. Was I much saddened by the loss of my husband-to-be? I confessed that I had seen him only once from a distance. 'Ah, an arranged marriage.' He smiled a little sadly. After a moment, he explained that he and his wife had allowed their oldest daughter to select her own husband. 'Friends advised against it,' he said. 'Now I wonder if they might have been right.'

"Theodosius spoke often of his wife and children in Rome. By the end of the evening I no longer feared him. The business between a man and a woman was not unpleasant. Theodosius thought I had a talent for it. He counted himself lucky, but now I realize that I was the lucky one. Pleasing a man on his couch was easy, but Theodosius also wanted a companion. He had me tutored in Greek and Latin, introduced me to philosophy and literature. By the time his tour of duty was over, Theodosius had grown fond of me. I returned with him to Rome. There were problems with his wife—

inevitable, I suppose—but many were eager to take his place as my 'protector.' "

"Perhaps," I ventured, "you are better off . . ."

"I have always thought so."

"But now," I said, looking back at the hills of Magdala, "you have reconciled with your parents. How happy you must be."

Miriam shook her head. "You do not understand our ways. Because brigands had ruined me, my parents sat with ashes on their heads for three days as though I were dead."

"But that was so long ago. Surely now—"

She smiled wryly. "Now *should* have been perfect. Rufus, my latest protector, died two months ago of a fever. He left no family. His estate went to me—all duly recorded with the Vestals." Miriam sighed wearily. "I returned to Magdala filled with joy, thinking of all that I could now do for my parents. As I climbed the hill, I imagined that we could go back to the way we were—a happy loving family."

Her large eyes filled with tears. "Their one remaining slave, my old nurse, would not even allow me into the atrium. I pounded until finally a face appeared at an upper window. It was my mother—*my mother*—she—" Miriam broke off sobbing. "She gave orders. *I could hear her.* 'If that whore shows up here again, stone her.' "

Again, I put my arms around Miriam, and stroked her back. "My dear, my dear, what can I say?"

"There is nothing that anyone can say." She pulled away, wiping her eyes, and looked at me. "Claudia, I have liked and admired many men, but loved none. At the Villa of Mysteries, you prophesied that I would find my true love here in Galilee. Instead, I have found only despair. My parents would rather I had died in the desert than live the only life open to me. The people in Magdala who praised and petted me as a child now view me with contempt. I should return to Rome, pick up the threads of my life. Every day I think I will make the arrangements, but sometimes I am too exhausted to even rise from my sleeping couch. It is as though a devil sat on my chest."

I nodded, recognizing her depression. "Not one devil—at least seven. When I lost my first child and later when my sister was executed, I, too, lay day after day upon my couch. It was as though I lived always in twilight. People spoke to me but I would barely hear them, did not want to hear them."

"Yes, that is how it is." She nodded. "This is the first day I have ventured out of the inn. A slave had to do everything for me. I could hardly step into my sandals. Walking to the sea was so hard, I had to stop several times. It seemed so far."

"That settles it!" I exclaimed "You are coming back to Tiberius with me. My men will get your things. You must stay at our villa."

Miriam smiled wanly. "I would not be very good company."

"I am not inviting 'company,' " I said, giving her a little hug. "For once you need please no one. Sleep, read, lie out on the terrace under the sunshade. No one will bother you. When you are ready, I will be there. We can explore Tiberius together. It is a beautiful city."

"That sounds very pleasant . . ." Miriam considered for a moment, then shook her head. "Perhaps later. There is someone I must see first."

"Who can it be?" I asked.

"A holy man, many say a prophet."

"That does not sound like you."

"This man is different. Everywhere I go people talk of him, some even believe him to be the messiah. Surely a mystic who has cured madmen—raving lunatics—can raise the awful blackness that surrounds my soul. The old life now seems meaningless. What am I to do with myself?" Miriam looked at me, her large green eyes rimmed with red.

"Go to your holy man," I surprised myself by saying. Unlikely as it sounded, her pilgrimage felt right to me. "Come to Tiberius afterward. Who knows, if he helps you, perhaps I will go to him myself. I would do anything to be rid of the awful dreams that torment me. They grow worse with every passing night."

I THOUGHT OFTEN OF MIRIAM IN THE MONTHS THAT passed, worried about her. Then came a diversion I could never have imagined. It began with an invitation. Herod Antipas was celebrating his birthday with a banquet. I had met the flamboyant puppet king briefly in Caesarea and was curious to see his new palace in Galilee, more curious to meet his wife. Tales of Herodias had even reached Rome.

HEROD'S PALACE WAS, I WAS AMAZED TO DISCOVER, larger than Tiberius's. Each room possessed a violent, almost savage quality of its own. No human being had a chance of feeling important among the wild animal skins, crimson drapes, mirrored ceilings, and surging fountains. Pet cheetahs roamed at will, making me particularly uneasy, yet I saw that Herod and his queen delighted in the crude, boisterous beauty that surrounded them.

Herod was a large man with massive shoulders and a thick black beard, oiled and curled. His dark face with its ringleted mustaches was an obsequious mask. He kissed my hand not once but three times. I did not like him.

"We were afraid you would never leave Caesarea," his queen said, taking my hand from him and clasping it to her large breasts. "The capital is grand, of course, but we need your beauty in Galilee."

"You are very kind," I murmured. I studied Herodias. Her startlingly blue eyes and full, voluptuous lips might easily turn a man's head. I could see why Herod had risked so much to have her.

"Can we not share a dining couch—just the two of us?" she suggested. "At least for part of the banquet. Let the men talk their boring talk on their own couch beside us. I want to hear about you."

But it was Herodias who did the talking. Ignoring the hundred or so other guests, ignoring the procession of dancers, singers, snake charmers, and fire-eaters who performed before us, she chattered endlessly. Fortunately, the queen's deep, throaty voice was pleasant to listen to. She had lively opinions on everything: the Roman court, fashions, child rearing—most particularly her own eldest daughter, Salome.

"It is difficult to believe that you have a daughter ready for marriage," I said when Herodias finally paused for a sip of wine.

"Oh, I do indeed, you will see her later. Salome's going to dance tonight as a special treat for her stepfather."

"Do you and Herod have children together?"

"No." Herodias pouted. "The Jewish bigots say it is a punishment for our 'sin.' They are so narrow-minded, so unfair. It is nothing to them that Herod divorced *his* wife. A man can do that any time he pleases, but when I divorced my husband, Herod's half brother—a wretched man, nothing like Herod—they called me a Jezebel. Is that fair?"

"No, it isn't," I agreed. "But is your husband not also your uncle?"

Herodias sighed impatiently. "I suppose it is a bit unconventional, but we are the ruling family. Surely we have a right to do as we please."

"Most rulers do," I agreed.

"I am so glad you understand. Who cares about an old law written hundreds of years ago! We live in the present. No one else would care either if it were not for that wretched rabble-rouser."

"Who do you mean?"

"Surely you have heard of John the Baptizer?"

"No, I have not," I said, shaking my head.

"He is a wild creature out of the desert with dirty, unkempt hair, but people flock to him. They leave their boats, their vineyards, their sheep—everything. How can my husband run a country like that? I urged Herod to arrest him, but his advisers feared a revolt. 'John is a good man,' they say. 'He poses no real threat.' So there he is, day after day, bathing people in the middle of a wilderness that my husband hopes to colonize."

"Surely that is just a fancy. People are so quick to follow anything new; bathing people is certainly novel, but before you know it, they will be off to something else."

"That is what Herod said for a while—he is so tolerant. But then this dreadful John person began to speak out about me. About *me*!" Herodias's eyes flashed as she set her wineglass down with a thud. "Herod has been remarkably forbearing, but I cannot allow my good name to be sullied in that way. Surely you can understand?"

I felt the beginning of a warning chill. "What did you do?"

"John is here now in the palace dungeon, awaiting trial. Herod is thinking a scourging followed by exile, but that is far too lenient. I would like to drown him in his own bathwater."

Again the chill. My hand trembled slightly as I took the wine goblet offered me by a fair-skinned boy with painted cheeks and a mincing gait. Just then the jugglers who had been entertaining us bounded off. For an instant, the torches dimmed. Drums rolled and then musicians began to play music that I had not heard before.

"Ah, my daughter, Salome." Herodias pointed proudly.

Lights flared as a young woman, sinuous and perfect, appeared. The resemblance to Herodias was unmistakable. As the nubile dancer spun before us, her diaphanous costume flared like the petals of an exotic flower. Dipping and swaying to the voluptuous rhythm, Salome moved closer. Then just as Herod, who had been lying with Pilate on the couch next to ours, leaned forward to pull at the filmy folds of her gown, she slipped gracefully away, teasing him.

The tempo slowed as Salome's body undulated, her feet scarcely moving, in a love dance, a voluptuous poem of amorous adventure portrayed almost entirely by her torso, arms, and hands. I felt Pilate's eyes on me, turned and read his expression easily. He will want me tonight, I thought, and looked away. Those times could not be avoided, but how I dreaded them.

Soon it was impossible to think of anything but the erotic movements before me. It was the age-old story of courtship, conquest, and fertility. I longed for Holtan as my own body began to quiver. My cheeks grew hot, my pulses throbbed with the music, a wailing, sensuous beat that bespoke a woman's eternal love for her man.

Slowly, very slowly, Salome dropped one of the red veils that covered her. As the audience gasped, another veil slipped to the floor and then another and another. The kithara quickened, great sweeping strokes filling the room with throbbing bursts of sound. Gleaming cymbals crashed together while drummers added their thunderous rhythm to the sudden rush of sound.

I glanced at Pilate; curiously his eyes still rested on me. Meeting my gaze, he raised his glass and smiled. Had he seen my passion? Did he imagine it was for him? I turned away. Drunken guests pounded on the tables beside their couches as the dance moved to its climax. Salome dropped her final veil and danced before them clad only in a small girdle of gold held in place by delicate chains drawn about her hips.

"The girdle! The girdle!" men shouted, more and more insistently. Strings and flutes wailed a sensuous rhythm against throbbing drums.

Sparks of light glittered in the torchlight as Herod beckoned to her. "Whatever you ask for, Salome, I will give to you, even half my kingdom."

Pilate and I exchanged quick glances. Herod had no kingdom to give without the consent of Rome.

Salome moved to the couch shared by Herodias and me. "What shall I ask for, Mother?"

Herodias whispered a few words that I could not catch. The girl gasped. For an instant Salome's face turned pale as she stared at her mother. Herodias whispered something more. A smile spread over Salome's full lips. Her hands flashed down across her hips and came away bearing the fragile girdle in her fingers. She paused for an instant, then tossed the golden bauble to Herod.

The room fell silent as the dancer moved to Herod's couch and slipped gracefully to her knees before him. Salome's thick hair cascaded over her shoulders, dark and glossy as a raven's wing against the delicate pallor of her skin. She slowly raised her head to meet her stepfather's eager eyes.

"One thing and one thing only," she said in a soft, husky voice very like her mother's. "Give me the head of John, the one they call the Baptizer. Bring it to me here. Bring it to me now on a silver platter."

CHAPTER 33

Astoreth's Handmaiden

Thoughts of Miriam haunted me. Had she found her holy man? Had he been able to heal her? Where was she now? As weeks passed, my concern mounted, I returned to Magdala, waiting in the boat while my slaves went from door to door asking after her. They came back empty-handed. The townspeople claimed not to even know Miriam.

Unwilling to settle for that, I got out. Picking my way over the discarded fish heads and tails, I approached a group of men who sat mending their nets by the wharf. Though they couldn't or wouldn't tell me anything of Miriam, I saw the anger and scorn on their faces at the mention of her name. They would have stoned *me*, had they dared. Well, why not? Was I not also an adulteress?

I RETURNED HOME HEAVYHEARTED. RACHEL, WHO HAD come down to meet my barge, listened gravely as I told her about Miriam. "The ways of Galilee and Judaea are harsh," she agreed. "They are men's laws made to govern women."

"Cruel, vindictive men," I agreed as we entered the villa. "If only I could go to an Iseneum. I want so much to talk with a priestess."

"Tiberius has no Iseneum, but there is a temple with priestesses who would understand the *Domina* Miriam very well. Perhaps they could even help."

"Priestesses?" I echoed incredulously. "A goddess is worshiped *here!* Everything in this land is so—so masculine, so unforgiving."

Rachel gestured for me to lower my voice. "Anna, the new Syrian kitchen maid, told me about a temple to a very ancient goddess. Many still worship her. I will take you to her sanctuary tomorrow . . . I think it best that *Dominus* not know." She gestured toward the *triclinium*. "He is waiting for you now."

As I entered the room, I saw Pilate reclining on a couch, his brows knit in a deep frown as he studied the scroll before him.

"More trouble?" I asked, seating myself at his side.

He reached for the wine goblet on the ivory inlaid table beside him. "The times are uncertain. Barabbas and his *Sicarii* are hiding in the hills."

"The dagger men!" I gasped, thinking of the weapons they carried, small and curved to easily fit the hand. The knife had earned the assassins a name as well as a reputation. "I thought you had trapped Barabbas."

"We had him once, but he got away. It won't happen again."

Pilate patted my shoulder reassuringly. "I'll see him crucified if it's the last thing I do. In the meantime, we'll remain here till things calm down."

"Have there been more demonstrations?"

Pilate's brows came together again in a heavy frown. "The people are angry about the way Herod handled that Zealot."

"I should think so!" Would I ever forget the severed head with its great staring eyes frozen in horror, the fresh blood pooling on the silver platter? "They say John the Baptizer was a good man."

Pilate agreed. "He was radical, but posed no threat, just another of those would-be messiahs who appear out of nowhere to stir up the Jews, make their priests nervous, and add to my burdens. There've been so many, it's hard to keep track." He laughed mirthlessly. "I hear this one was a fiery orator with a penchant for dunking people in water before converting them to his own brand of Judaism."

"That hardly warranted a death penalty."

"Herod was weak, allowing those women to manipulate him." Pilate frowned. "Ill advised, as well. The last thing we need here is a sacrificial victim—but try to convince him of that. Herod's more like a child than a representative of Rome."

"Speaking of children—" I drew his attention to a wide-eyed Marcella standing in the entryway.

There was no more talk of severed heads.

The next morning Rachel and I set off in a litter. As we reached the city center she pulled the curtains back and looked this way and that, searching. Once again I was struck by what a lovely city Tiberius was with its lofty statues and charming public *nymphaneums*. As we rounded a corner, a great statue of the emperor loomed above us. I winced despite myself. Evil man!

"Let us get out here and leave the litter," Rachel suggested.

"You are very mysterious," I protested, signaling for the bearers to stop.

"Anna said the temple was down the hill from Tiberius's monument," Rachel said, once we had been assisted from the litter.

We wandered along a winding street, turned a corner, and there before us was a red building with golden columns. "Whose temple is this?" I wanted to know. Rachel merely smiled secretively and led the way up the marble steps.

We entered, passing through the dark foyer lit only by a perfumed oil flame. The chamber beyond took my breath away. There among hundreds of blazing candles were frescoed walls, mosaic floors, and dozens of statues all depicting a strange goddess I had not seen before. "Who is this?" I asked, looking at Rachel in surprise.

"Astoreth. Though not Isis, she is *of* Isis. Astoreth is the divine female, the bringer of fertility."

My eyes traveled about the brilliantly lit room. "Astoreth," I repeated, liking the sound of the word. Astoreth's loins were broad, the essence of fecundity. Her breasts were bountiful, her hips round. I thought of Yahweh's thin-lipped priests, remembered the men on the wharf in Magdala who had refused even to speak of Miriam. "It scarcely seems possible that such a—a robust goddess could exist here."

"Priests and prophets have tried for centuries to banish

Astoreth, but she is too strong for them. Even Solomon built a temple to her."

"But that must have been hundreds of years ago," I reminded Rachel.

She shrugged. "This temple is brand new. In a land of farmers and shepherds, fertility is everything."

"I think it is more than that." A dim memory tugged at my brain, something that Miriam had said long ago . . . *It is their pleasure to give pleasure.* "Did men not worship Astoreth by—by making love? Did they not pay for that love?"

"Yes." Rachel nodded. "Astoreth's priestesses are sacred prostitutes."

"*Are* prostitutes! They still do that?" I asked incredulously.

"Indeed we do, though prostitution is hardly the word I would choose," a soft feminine voice interjected. I turned at the sound. "We who serve Astoreth do so with our bodies. Our pathway is no less divine for being physical."

A woman in a blue gown had entered silently and now stood beside me facing the altar. Though her long, rippling hair was white, her body—which I could see clearly beneath a transparent gown—was firm and shapely.

"I am Eve, high priestess of Astoreth's temple. How may I help you?"

"Surely it is the men who are helped here."

Eve smiled. "You would be surprised. Women also pray and make offerings." She nodded in the direction of two large side altars covered with round cakes. "These were brought only today by supplicants who seek Astoreth's blessings. Many want to gain or hold lovers. Others wish to conceive."

I studied the priestess curiously, trying to guess her age.

The intelligent eyes were lit with humor as they returned my gaze. The priestess's skin was smooth, well cared for, but the bright lamplight revealed fine lines about her eyes and mouth—smile lines. I thought for a longing moment of my mother.

"I have served the goddess for twenty-five years," she said, as though answering my unspoken question.

"For you, it appears to be a good life."

"A very good life," she agreed, straightening a bouquet of marigolds on the altar. "Service to the goddess may last a year or a lifetime. That is up to us. Some choose to bear children and raise them here in the temple. Many priestesses are daughters of priestesses."

I was deeply shocked. Her words were contrary to all that I had observed in Judaea and Galilee. With the exception of Herodias—who could scarcely be counted—women's lives seemed highly circumscribed by tradition—traditions that men had established long ago and still sternly enforced. "But," I argued, "Yahweh—his priests—they cannot accept—"

"A woman making her own choices and enjoying them? No, that is rarely popular with men—even those who are not priests."

"Domina." Rachel looked concerned. She was pulling gently at my arm. "*Dominus* would not like . . ."

Eve and I exchanged glances, both of us laughing. "Indeed he would not," I agreed.

"Why have you come to us?" the priestess asked.

"By chance. I am a follower of Isis."

"Ah, Isis," Eve nodded. "The great goddess over all. In the end, she is the one." The priestess studied me silently for a moment before speaking again. "There is no such thing as chance. During her long journey in search of Osiris, Isis was a prostitute. She has sent you to us now for a reason. I feel that you are troubled."

"Yes," I admitted. "There is someone—a friend—who once spoke much as you do. She is a follower of Isis who lives in a cruel world, not in a temple. Miriam was punished—punished terribly—for nothing more than accepting the path that had been forced upon her. Now she has disappeared and I am frightened for her. My slave," I nodded toward Rachel, "brought me here. She knew you would understand. Is there anything . . . ?"

The priestess had been listening, nodding attentively. Now she threw a few grains of incense on the large copper brazier before the goddess. "Come," she said, taking hold of my hand and Rachel's, drawing us toward her. "Let us kneel. We will pray together."

As we rode home in the litter, I felt Miriam's presence close to me. She was safe and happy. *I knew it.* It was no surprise to find her at home sitting in my atrium. She was the old Miriam, too, a confident smile hovering about her full lips, the emerald fire back in her eyes.

"Astoreth must be a powerful goddess," I said, slipping off my mantle and sitting down to take her hands in mine. "One little prayer and here you are."

"Why not? Astoreth has always served me well. She is the aspect of Isis that I most adore."

I laughed lightly at her mock seriousness. "Somehow I

knew that!" The twinkle was back in Miriam's eyes. I liked that, but something else about her puzzled me. Miriam had in some way changed. What was it? Her hair was again smartly coiffed, large pearls visible among the curls, b ut her gown—though cut to perfection and of the finest linen—was simple. Simple and white. "You look a bit like a Vestal," I said at last.

Miriam tipped her head back and laughed, the low throaty sound I remembered.

"A Vestal! Quite the opposite," she said at last. "I am very much of the world as always, but now something wonderful has happened. My world has changed. Soon the whole world will be changing. That is what I have come to tell you. I have met *him*—the man that you foresaw for me in your vision."

"For some women all it takes to set things right in their lives is a man, but I would never have thought that of you." I studied Miriam closer. She fairly sparkled. I had never seen her more beautiful. "I must admit, you look like a different person."

Miriam smiled happily. "I *am* a different person. I have met the messiah and he has healed me."

It was as though a sliver of ice pierced my heart. "Miriam, Miriam. The last messiah I encountered was a head on a platter."

Her face paled. "You mean John the Baptizer. He was the holy man I told you about, the one I sought. I followed him to the river Jordan, hoping that he would heal me, but when I reached John's encampment he was no longer there. Herod's men had taken him away. A great tragedy," she said, shaking her head sadly. "Some mistook him for the messiah," she went on to explain, "but they were wrong. John was a great prophet sent to prepare the way for the true son of Yahweh."

"I'm frightened for you," I said, leaning forward, my voice lowered. Anyone might be listening. Who knew these days? "Everybody in this country loves the idea of a messiah, yet no one wants to be confronted by the reality. The priests in Jerusalem are rich and powerful. The last thing they will tolerate is a challenge to their authority."

"I am too happy to argue about anything. The messiah has shown me a divine plan, I know it in my heart." Miriam smiled, leaning back against the cushions. "I have chattered long enough—tell me about you. The last time we met I was so full of my own woes that I did not even ask. Do you like Galilee? Are you happy here?"

"Happy?" I repeated, rising from the couch and looking out toward the lake. "What is happiness? I thought I knew once. I used to think, if only Pilate would be faithful—then I would be happy. How silly that all seems now. Pilate has changed in the past year. I doubt that there have been any other women. Amazing, is it not?" I sighed, forcing myself to continue. "It is I who am the adulterer. I lie in his bed recalling another man's kiss. Sometimes at night I even pretend that Pilate—"

Miriam got up, moved to the balcony beside me.

Reluctantly I turned to meet her eyes. "I am ashamed that I miss Holtan so much. Sometimes I feel that even a few hours with him would be worth any risk, any sacrifice."

"You will find your way, I know it," Miriam assured me, clasping my hands in hers. "In the meantime, I have come to invite you to a wedding—mine."

CHAPTER

34

The Wedding

Pilate had grown increasingly fond of Galilee. He was drawn north to the rugged mountains, a desolate area inhabited primarily by panthers, leopards, and bears. Herod's courtiers frequently hunted there. Sometimes my husband took a small contingent of officers and went with them. I knew that Isis was smiling when Pilate announced another such excursion, for it solved the problem uppermost in my mind.

I feared for Miriam, so vulnerable in her joy. Although I was powerless to alter the path she had chosen, I must at least be at my friend's marriage. Yet how could Pilate's wife attend the wedding of a former harlot and a self-appointed messiah? Messiahs and the controversy they caused in a contentious land had become the bane of Pilate's existence, and Miriam's background was a social embarrassment to the governor's lady. But with Pilate far away . . . a peasant woman might go . . . two peasant women . . . of course!

My plan was simple. Rachel and I traveled on horseback

due east to Sepphoris with a small contingent of guards. When we reached the hostelry—a palatial affair with an obsequious staff that welcomed me as though I were Livia herself—I surprised my honor guard with a holiday. "I want to explore Sepphoris at my leisure," I explained. "Go back to Tiberius and return for us tomorrow."

The soldiers stared at me as their leader protested: "*Dominus* would never permit . . ."

"You dare to know the governor's mind!" Tone softening, I explained, "One of Herod's conjurers has promised to show me a rare herb to soothe my husband's headaches. The wizard is a jealous man. He will refuse if he imagines that you are spying on him. Leave now," I ordered, "and no looking back!"

Rachel shook her head as the men rode off. "What a storyteller you are! Yahweh should strike you dead."

"I am sure he would," I agreed, "if I believed in him."

"*Dominus* cannot be dismissed so easily," she reminded me. "The risk, the occasion itself—everything about this is wrong. He will be furious when he finds out."

"*If* he finds out. With Isis's blessing he will not." I sighed impatiently. For weeks I had been the good wife, going only where Pilate wanted me to go, seeing only the people he wanted me to see. Miriam was *my* friend, I loved her and wanted to support her decision—whether I agreed with it or not. Beyond that, something told me that I should go to Cana, that I was meant to go.

I shrugged, mind made up. "Even if Pilate does find out, what can he do? Order away a memory? Hurry, let us change our clothes."

We dressed simply. I wore a gray cotton tunic with a blue-

and-white-striped mantle. My only jewelry, tucked well out of sight, was the golden sistrum the priestess of Isis had given me long ago. Eschewing the carriage offered us by the innkeeper, we rode donkeys. "No one will ever recognize us," I assured Rachel. The donkey I had chosen nuzzled my shoulder. Such a gentle beast, a far cry from the spirited horses I ordinarily rode. I stroked his ears.

SEPPHORIS WAS A BUSTLING CITY. FOLLOWING HEROD the Great's death, it had been a rallying point for Zealots seeking to overthrow both Rome and the Herodians. Retaliation had been swift. Roman troops from Syria swept through Galilee routing out dissidents and burning Sepphoris to the ground. A few years later Herod Antipas had rebuilt the city as an administrative capital. It looked very prosperous—and very Roman. In the public *nymphaneum,* water gushed from the nipples of Venus. Above the entrance to the public bath stood a nude statue of Apollo. Twin images of a drunken Dionysus flanked the stairs to the theater. "The Jews must hate it," I commented to Rachel as our donkeys plodded behind carts and chariots.

"They have more to worry about than artwork," she responded. "Herod's spies are everywhere, making certain that no one shirks his taxes."

ON THE ROAD TO CANA, A MORNING'S RIDE TO THE north, we passed tiny villages, farmers and shepherds living in stone homes built in clusters. The houses, surrounded by an inevitable patchwork of small pastures and fields, looked like they had been there forever.

Just outside Cana we heard drums and flutes. As we followed the cheerful clamor through the small town, the resonance of music and laughter led us up a hill past a carefully cultivated vineyard. At the top, encircled by an olive grove, we found an attractive villa bigger than any dwelling we had seen since Sepphoris. Rachel and I followed a small group through the main gate to a large courtyard. For some reason I had imagined Miriam's messiah as a poor peasant. Apparently that was not the case. The colorful plantings, splashing fountains, and intricate mosaic pathways indicated a wealthy family.

Despite our simple clothing, servants hurried forward to help us dismount. As our donkeys were led off to be watered and fed, I glanced inquisitively about. Weddings draw women like moths to a flame, or so it has always seemed to me. They laugh, giggle, rush here and there, bright eyes alert to their own advantage. This occasion was a marked exception. Tight-lipped guests gossiped in corners, their eyes critical, some even malicious. "The king and the whore, what a pair!" one young woman laughed loud enough to be heard. "What a fool to choose *her* when he might have had anyone." The others giggled among themselves, straightened the bright roses in their hair and drifted off to other groups. The very air felt charged with their resentment.

A somberly dressed woman came toward us, moving with quiet elegance. "Welcome to my brother's house," she said, her voice oddly toneless.

Before I could say anything, Rachel stepped forward and introduced us. "I am Rachel. This is my sister, Sarah."

"I am Mary, the bridegroom's mother," the woman replied, extending her hands to each of us.

"Mary?" I repeated. In the past year I had acquired a working knowledge of Aramaic. I understood her words well enough, yet wondered at the reserved manner. Mary was tall. I thought of a slender willow tree stirring in the breeze. Clearly she was a gentlewoman, the mistress of a fine house.

"You know my son?" she asked.

"We have not yet had that pleasure," I explained. "We are Miriam's friends."

"Really?" Mary looked startled. Perhaps she wondered what two peasant women were doing there. I stared back. She was a pretty woman with dark hair just beginning to gray; but looking closer, I saw that her wide brown eyes were red and puffy. It did not bode well for the bride-to-be.

"I am eager to see Miriam," I said. "Where is she?"

Mary nodded to a young woman carrying a pitcher of wine. "Leave that on the table and take our new guests to the bride."

The servant girl led us inside the villa past comfortable couches, exquisitely carved tables and chests. I caught glimpses of frescoed walls and statues—no likenesses of gods or humans, to be sure, but animals aplenty. None of this was what I had expected. What sort of messiah lived here?

I found Miriam sobbing quietly in an upstairs *cubiculum*. Leaning over her was a small, blond woman who stiffened at the sight of us. Miriam jumped up from the couch where she had been lying and rushed forward to embrace me. "Oh, Claudia, you *did* come! How good of you. I know the risk you took . . ."

"Isis protects me," I assured her, smiling, hoping it was true. "Tell me, dear, what's the matter?" I asked, hugging her tight. "Why are you crying?"

"There is no one from my family present and none of my friends from Rome would dream of coming. I thought this would be the happiest day of my life, but everyone hates me. Have you ever seen so many sad faces?"

"Let's do something about yours," I said, leading Miriam to an ivory-inlaid chair before a large mirror. "Your future mother-in-law doesn't look particularly happy," I had to agree, stroking the tangles from her hair.

Miriam smiled wryly. "Every rabbi is supposed to have a wife. Mary has prayed for fifteen years that her son would marry. Now that he has chosen me she believes the most high has played a very bad joke on her. It is all a terrible mistake, she says. Her son deserves a better wife than me. Mary says that a dazzling being appeared to her before my betrothed was even conceived. He called her 'Blessed among women' and said she had been chosen to bear the son of Yahweh."

"Really! I wonder what her husband thought about that? What does your betrothed say?"

"That no one will ever understand anyway and not to worry about it."

"When Mary knows you better . . ." I ventured hopefully, reaching for a basin of water. Miriam's eyes must be bathed. I signaled to Rachel.

"That is what Jesus says."

"Jesus," I repeated the word. "So that is his name. Thus far you have called him only 'the master.' When I was very young

I was obsessed with my husband. I adored him, yet even then would never have addressed him as 'master.' "

The blond woman who had been attending Miriam turned, studying me closely. "But the governor is not Jesus," she stated matter-of-factly.

"You know my husband?" I asked curiously. "Who are you? Have we met?"

"I am Joanna, wife of Chuza, King Herod's steward. We met briefly once. You and your husband were at the banquet . . . that awful banquet."

That awful banquet. "Yes, of course, I remember you now," I said, but did not. The day of John the Baptizer's death was an ugly blur. I had blocked out all that I could. Now to be recognized, particularly by someone connected to Herod! It was bad luck. Forcing a smile, I stepped forward to take Joanna's hand.

Rachel moved between us. "It is best that *Domina*'s identity remain secret. She came here without her husband's knowledge."

"I understand." Joanna nodded. "My husband does not know that I am here either. He is Herod's man through and through. Chuza would have done anything to prevent me from following the messiah."

"Who *is* this Jesus?" I wondered aloud.

"The king of the Jews," Miriam answered, a proud smile hovering about her lips.

"The *king*! Herod Antipas is king."

"Herod Antipas is a usurper!" Joanna broke in. "His father, Herod the Great so-called, was not even Jewish. He was a converted Edomite. The Romans have ignored the rightful rulers of Israel in favor of a puppet king they choose themselves."

"Is that true?" I asked Miriam.

"Everyone knows it," she assured me. "It is Jesus who is the Christ, the anointed one. He is descended from the royal line of David on his father's side and the priestly order of Aaron on his mother's. Judaea, Galilee, Samaria—all the lands of Israel—are rightfully his, but he cares nothing for that. He says that Yahweh's children are equal with no division between male and female, *dominus* or slave. Jesus' true kingdom is in heaven."

"Pilate will be relieved to hear that!" I knew not whether to laugh or cry. "Do you realize how serious this is?" I took Miriam's hands in mine. "A religious leader might be tolerated but a political one—never! Do you imagine for a minute that Pilate—that Rome—would permit the removal of their appointed ruler?"

"Claudia, Claudia, calm yourself." Miriam's arms encircled me soothingly. "It is not at all what you think. Jesus was sent into this world to save men's souls. He has come to fulfill a prophecy with no desire to rule our bodies. He wants only for us to love one another. He is so full of love himself, it brings out the love in me—in everyone who knows him. There is no one like him."

The tears were gone. Miriam was her old confident self as she smiled up at me. "I will be at Jesus' side, his beloved companion, and"—she paused, smiling—"my money will further his ministry."

I looked at Miriam in amazement.

"Why should that surprise you?" she asked. A gentle air of

pride lighting her face, she confided, "It is fortunate that my dowry is large for we will have need of it. More and more followers come every day. They leave their parents, their wives, even their husbands behind—as Joanna has done. They want only to sit at the feet of Jesus, to walk in his footsteps. Someone must see that they are fed and clothed."

"But," I ventured, looking about the well-appointed room, "it appears that Jesus' family is quite well off."

"Cleophas is a fond uncle, but not a follower. Indeed, his tastes are rather Roman—perhaps you have noticed. Jesus merely laughs at the family differences. It is difficult, he admits, to be a prophet in one's own land."

"He has no money of his own?"

"Jesus' father was a builder. He and his workers rebuilt half of Sepphoris, but long ago Jesus gave his share to his mother and brothers. I would that Jesus could be content with what must have been a very good life, but that is not his path. Jesus says, 'Take no thought for the morrow,' but someone must. That someone will be me."

I hugged Miriam quickly lest she see the tears that stung my eyes as I imagined the heartache awaiting her. "Isis's blessings on the path that you have chosen," I whispered. Hurrying from the room, I left Rachel and Joanna to prepare the bride for her vows.

Once downstairs, I noticed Mary, who wandered listlessly from guest to guest, her manner more appropriate to a funeral than a wedding. Some women even put their arms about her, openly consoling. Poor Miriam.

Across the courtyard a group of men in simple white tunics sat with a man I assumed must be the bridegroom. They joked, slapped him on the back, the traditional masculine teasing of a man on his wedding day. The bridegroom laughed heartily, teeth startlingly white against his sun-browned face. Perhaps feeling my gaze, he stood up, detaching himself from the others, and approached me. The bridegroom was tall, with long, beautiful hands that he extended in greeting.

Smiling down at me, he said, "Once again I tell you, truth cannot be hidden by a simple gown."

Puzzled, I studied the face before me. Dark, intense eyes . . . eyes that seemed to . . . look into my soul. "It was in Egypt!" I exclaimed. "We met at the Iseneum. You told me your name then, but I had forgotten. Miriam's Jesus!" How familiar he looked, as though I had known him all my life. Why had I not recognized him? Then I realized, "You had no beard then."

"I was a boy . . . still searching."

"And now?"

A smile lit Jesus' face as he nodded. "I have discovered my *abba* in heaven. He was always there but for a time I knew him not."

"Your *abba*?" I asked. "What does *abba* mean?"

"It is much like your word '*tata*.' "

I looked at Jesus in surprise, "You feel so close to Yahweh that he is like your own father?"

"Yes." He nodded. "A very loving father." He smiled reassuringly. "My own people know him not. It is for me to show them the way back."

Before Jesus could say more, Mary appeared beside us, tugged at his sleeve, admonished, "There is no more wine!"

Jesus shrugged. "What has that to do with me?"

Clearly he did not want to be interrupted. Perhaps there was more that he wished to say to me, but Mary was not to be put off. "It has everything to do with you!" she said. "This wedding is your choice. These are your guests."

When Jesus merely smiled, Mary beckoned to a group of servants. "Do whatever my son tells you," she instructed them.

They looked questioningly at Jesus, who pointed to six large stone jars resting by a far wall. "Fill each of these to the brim with water."

I watched incredulously as the bewildered men followed his directions. Jesus thanked the servants with a pleasant smile and bade them draw water from the jars, then take it to his uncle Cleophas. Mary's jaw dropped. What kind of joke was this?

Turning back to me, Jesus took my hand. "You will see me again," he said before leaving to rejoin his friends. Jesus' manner was kind, but there was something unsettling about him. I thought back to our first meeting more than ten years before . . . a wise young man, gentle but confident, seeking his place in this world . . . or beyond it. But there was something else, something more. It was as though I possessed another memory, something ugly, frightening, that I could not quite recall.

"So you do know my son." Mary was still standing close by, her gaze now fixed on me.

"Not really. It was merely a chance encounter long ago."

Mary's melancholy eyes regarded the assembled guests. "An encounter," she repeated softly. "That is all any of these people are to me—except for a few relatives who took pity on my shame—my old uncle, Jesus' brothers and sisters. Those others . . ." She looked sadly at Jesus' table companions. "'Disciples,' he calls them. Small wonder we ran out of wine. Who knows where they come from! Some are illiterate fishermen, boys really, scarcely half his age. Another is a tax collector. A tax collector, mind you, in my brother's house! Jesus insists that he be welcomed like any other guest. Women, too, have begun to follow Jesus. Rabbis don't address their sermons to women! We are seated separately behind a curtain. Now Jesus invites everyone—men and women—to sit before him." She looked suspiciously at me. "I suppose you are a new one."

I shook my head emphatically, thinking once again of the Baptizer's tragic fate. "I assure you I am no disciple. I came only to be with my friend Miriam. Believe me, I would steal her away from here if I could."

"Then we are agreed on one thing. Last night he told me that this Miriam person will one day sit at his right hand in the house of Yahweh. Have you ever heard such blasphemy! It is all so terribly wrong. A woman such as that should not be his queen."

Tears coursed down Mary's pale cheeks. Instinctively I moved to shield her from view. Taking Mary's hand, I led her to the stone bench where I had been sitting. "Mothers are often sad when their sons marry," I reminded her.

"No, no, you do not understand. You cannot understand. Long ago I had a vision. It was revealed to me that Jesus was born to fulfill a prophecy. His is a wonderful destiny, but also a terrible one. No mother should feel such sorrow, bear such loss." Mary buried her face in her hands.

I put my arms about her, stroking her back until she was

still. At last Mary disengaged herself, slipped a linen cloth from the pouch at her waist, and dabbed at the tears. "Do you have children?" she surprised me by asking.

"Yes, one. A little girl."

"That is nice," she said. "Promise me that you will enjoy every moment with her. The time is so short." She sat silently for a while, seemingly lost in thought. When Mary turned her gaze on me again, her expression was apologetic. "You must think me a terrible hostess, unburdening myself to you, a stranger."

"Sometimes I think it easier to talk with strangers. Your secrets are safe with me."

"Yes." Mary looked into my eyes. "I know that."

We were silent for a time and then Mary spoke. "Do you ever think that . . ." she hesitated, began again. "Do you think it possible that visions can be false, that bad things do not *have* to happen?"

"I have often hoped so."

When Mary said nothing, I ventured at last, "You will learn to love Miriam. She is a wonderful woman, wise and kind and full of humor."

Mary shook her head in disagreement. "Surely you must have heard that her family cast her out."

"Is there any family that does not have a scandal hidden somewhere?"

To my surprise Mary's face turned white. "What do you mean? What have you heard? We are a fine family! I have done nothing wrong! People don't understand—"

Just then the flutes and drums sounded. Miriam emerged from the house. She wore a gown of the sheerest linen, the color of rich cream, exquisitely fashioned, but simple. Her only adornment a crown of white flowers twined with olive leaves. The assembled crowd turned toward her, their expressions curious, appraising, often openly hostile. Seemingly oblivious, Miriam moved forward, swaying gracefully as she approached an arched canopy at the back of the courtyard. Jesus was led to her side by his companions. A few of the men didn't look much happier than Mary. I wondered if they were not a little jealous of Jesus' love for Miriam. I thought longingly of Holtan, remembered the adoration of Marcella and Quintus, of Mother and *Tata*.

Beside me, Mary struggled to control her tears. I signaled to a passing servant to bring water. In his place a portly, well-dressed gentleman approached, introducing himself to me as Mary's brother. "I am Cleophas," he said, putting a large jar down on the table beside us. Red-faced from the effort but smiling, he filled our cups from the jar. To my surprise, it was not water at all but a rich red wine.

I accepted the cup curiously. "I thought you were out of wine."

"Taste it," he replied, smiling even more broadly. "Everybody I know serves his best wine first and then brings out the poor stuff, but our Jesus has kept back the good wine until now."

Miriam and Jesus stood together under a silken canopy, sipping from cups that had been offered them. As the flutes began again Miriam circled Jesus in a slow, twining dance—one, two, three, four, five, six, seven times around.

"The bride binds them together, creating a family circle," Mary explained to me. "Such a tie cannot be broken," she added sadly.

The music faded as Miriam stepped forward. Addressing the assembled group, she spoke softly, yet all could hear:

> "I am the first and the last
> I am the honored one and the scorned one,
> I am the whore and the holy one . . ."

The assembled group gasped. What kind of wedding vow was that? I doubted that any of them had ever heard the sacred words of Isis, yet how perfectly they fit the moment. A shiver ran through my body. *An earthly union of Isis and Yahweh.*

"You are my beloved, you are my bride," Jesus replied, pulling Miriam to him and kissing her full on the lips.

A man stepped forward, black-bearded with fore curls dark as the robes he wore. Kneeling before them, he placed a clay drinking cup on the ground. Jesus kissed Miriam once again, then ground the cup slowly beneath his heel.

"What does that mean?" I asked Rachel, who was now standing beside me. Mary answered. "It is a reminder of the fragility of life, a reminder that there is sorrow even in times of joy."

The music began again, drums, flutes, lutes, and sistra. People stood uncertainly, looking at each another. "It is done, he has made his choice. She is his bride," Mary said softly. "Nothing can change what must now follow."

Sitting at Mary's side, I saw Jesus turn his gaze to her. A long look passed between them. How close son and mother were, even in their differences. At last Mary nodded silently.

She rose, unexpectedly taking my hand and pulling me forward toward the canopy, gesturing for others to follow. One by one, group by group, they did so. Everywhere guests and servants were clasping each other's hands, dancing now, encircling the wedding couple, singing a lively, vigorous song that I knew not but hummed happily. Everyone, even Mary—*especially* Mary—seemed to possess a sense of love and hope, a joyous knowing that we were as one in this moment. Round and round we danced, everything a glorious haze, rich and sparkling like the miraculous wedding wine. Lovely Miriam, gown spiraling about her, Jesus at her side, strong and handsome. Rachel and Joanna, eyes bright and eager, disciples singing lustily, jealous tittering women smiling now, faces soft and kind.

I whirled and whirled until all was a blur. At its center only the face of Jesus, eyes dark and wonderful, his lips smiling, smiling, smiling. *No!* In that instant, Jesus' face changed, everything changed. I closed my eyes, struggled to hold the picture of a happy young man wearing a crown of flowers, but now the crown had turned to thorns.

CHAPTER

35

Choices

Pilate returned from his hunting trip in a festive mood. He'd slain a large bear, soon to be a rug for me. Poor creature. More significantly, he'd stopped at Herod's palace on the way back and found Barabbas languishing in the dungeon. Once again he'd been captured. Pilate was delighted. The fiercest kind of Zealot, a *Sicarii,* Barabbas had killed not only Roman soldiers but Jews he regarded as Roman sympathizers, people who in his opinion had strayed too far from the traditional ways. He was a wild man, hero to some, terrorist to others. I was reminded of the bear.

That evening as I prepared for bed, my husband came up behind me, wrapping his arms about my waist. "Did you miss me?" he asked.

"Of course," I murmured, praying this wasn't a lead-in to questions about my activities in his absence.

Fortunately, he had something else on his mind. "I heard a strange story at Herod's today," he said, slipping off his sandals.

"Don't tell me someone else has been beheaded?"

"More bizarre than that," he said, pulling me down on the couch beside him. "Chuza—the steward—has lost his wife. She's run off to follow one of those messiahs. Joanna's her name—do you remember her? An attractive blond woman, a little on the plump side." Pilate paused, head to one side, smiling wryly. "A few months of living off the land should take care of that."

I remembered Joanna as I'd seen her last, joyously dancing in the courtyard. Perhaps I was staring into space, for Pilate took my chin in his hand, raised it slightly to look into my eyes.

"What kind of woman leaves her husband?"

I shrugged, trying to back away from his gaze. "An unhappy woman, perhaps a searching woman."

Pilate shook his head impatiently. "Joanna had a good life. Her husband is well favored by Herod. What could possibly have been missing from her life?"

"Someone should have asked her."

Reaching for the flagon beside the couch, Pilate splashed wine into my glass. He didn't cut it with water in the usual way. "Claudia, *you* are not searching?" His blue eyes fastened on mine. "There is nothing . . . missing in your life?"

I thought of Joanna's courage as I smiled up at him. "I have a good life. What could possibly be missing?"

To my surprise Pilate urged me to accompany him on an outing to Sepphoris. A series of minor uprisings had delayed Barabbas's trial, but finally Pilate had scheduled it. Though I was not to attend the trial, he wanted me to make the trip with him. We would see a play or two at the city's famed amphitheater and explore the countryside on horseback. Fearing that someone might recognize me from my previous visit, I busied myself fabricating possible explanations. Fortunately, the one person who did recognize me was not likely to tell my husband.

While Pilate's court was in session, Rachel and I, accompanied by an honor guard, wandered through the busy streets. Crowds pushed and shoved in all directions as they examined oranges and dates, amphorae of wine and olive oil, stacks of carpets, and shelves of carvings. What stopped me was a cry: "Mud! Mud! Dead Sea mud! It's the best in the world!"

Tucked in between a spice shop and a storyteller was a booth with bright orange awnings fringed with gold. Its shelves were filled with pottery vessels containing thick, black mud. Why would anyone buy that? I wondered, looking from one elegantly painted container to another.

"You don't need it—*yet*, but Herodias swears by it." A familiar voice spoke up behind me. "She has a mud facial every day and swears it keeps her young. Such foolishness!"

To my amazement I turned to find Joanna standing beside me. Pilate was right; she did look more svelte.

"With your husband officiating at the trial, I thought I might see you here," she said, taking my hand.

I laughed. "You were the last person I expected to see; I thought you'd be far away." Eagerly I added, "Is Miriam here?"

"No, she and Jesus are visiting friends in Bethany. He has asked some of us to go out on our own for a time. We are to serve as examples while spreading his word."

"Surely you aren't traveling alone?"

"No, my companion is Simon, one of the disciples." She nodded to a man in black who stood at a distance watching intently, his sharp, narrow face angrily contorted. He seemed to be glaring at me.

"What a fierce-looking fellow. What example is he supposed to be setting?"

"He is a little different from the rest," Joanna admitted. "They call him Simon the Zealot. Today his heart is heavy for his friend Barabbas."

"You're traveling with a *Sicarius*! Aren't you frightened?"

"He isn't one anymore. Not every Zealot is a *Sicarius,* but of course they are all jealous for Yahweh—that's what makes them Zealots. They desire freedom above all else. No more Roman gods, no more Roman taxes."

"Perhaps . . . in that kingdom of heaven you people talk about, but it won't happen in *this* world." I looked anxiously around, relieved that my guardsmen were temporarily distracted by a street fight. Pilate would have Simon imprisoned in a heartbeat, Joanna too. I turned back to Joanna. "Are you happy?" I asked her. "Do you ever miss Chuza or your old life?"

"Never," she assured me. "Every day I see miracles. The master has made the blind see and the crippled walk. One day he fed five thousand people with only three loaves and two fishes."

Hmmmm. Faith in Isis sometimes healed people, but as for that other miracle . . . I'd have to see it for myself to believe. "How is Miriam?" I asked, changing the subject.

"Radiantly happy. She hopes to have a baby, but the midwives think it unlikely given her history."

I thought of the young woman I'd first met years before at

the Asklepion, so sure of what she did and didn't want. "What about Jesus? Does he mind?"

"Not at all. He tells her that all children are their children and all the children that will follow. The master favors Miriam above all others. He confides in her, tells her things that he tells no one else." Joanna paused in thought. "Sometimes that makes her sad."

"Sad!" I exclaimed, my own longings making me impatient. "She is with the man she loves. How can she be sad?"

Simon still watched me angrily. He looked ready to pull a *sicarius* from his sleeve at any moment and hold me for ransom. For once, I was grateful for my guards, who had begun to eye him suspiciously. Previously instructed by me to maintain a distance, I saw them edging closer. Bidding Joanna a hasty farewell, I wished her Isis's blessings and moved on.

By the time we reached the governmental palace, Barabbas's trial was over. It had ended, as everyone knew it would, with a conviction. "What will happen to him?" I asked Pilate. "What always happens?" he shrugged. For a political criminal there was only one punishment. The ugliest and most humiliating. Barabbas would be crucified.

PILATE AND I RETURNED TO A TRANQUIL LIFE IN TIBERIUS. I spent as much time as possible with Marcella, sailing with her on the lake, building sand castles, reading endless stories, basking in her smiles and laughter. Before my eyes, my daughter was changing from a toddler into a spunky little girl.

One day followed the next, weeks, months. I thought often of Miriam, wondering if I would ever see her again.

How will you live? I'd asked her. "Off the land with Jesus," her reply. Child's talk, I thought, and said so. Miriam had merely laughed. "We'll be rich in all that matters," she assured me. I felt a sharp sting of envy. To be with one's love for however short a time . . .

And then early one evening, I slipped away. Leaving Marcella with Rachel, I went to the room that had become my shrine. It was twilight, the shadows lengthening. Tossing a few grains of incense onto the brazier, I knelt before a golden statue of the goddess. Looking up at Isis's face, strong yet so full of compassion, I imagined her searching the world for the fragments of her beloved Osiris. I felt her anguish and rapture as she sought his hands and his heart, his thighs, his belly, his beloved face. Isis had found them, gathered them to her until he was warm once more, roused to life, eager to fill her womb.

Mother Isis, I can stand it no longer. I must see Holtan.

THE NEXT MORNING I SAT IN MY WEAVING ROOM looking absently AT the lake's sparkling waters caught in early sunlight.

"Your design goes well," Rachel said from behind me. I hadn't heard her enter. "Marcella will love her new tunica."

I glanced up at the pegged skeins of woolen thread. Reds and purples, oranges and yellows, snared by a sudden shaft of sun, blazed dizzily. I reached for a loop of pale rose spun fine as hair. "What do you want?"

"Only to serve, *Domina*."

I looked around suspiciously. Rachel had brought in a bouquet of flowers, was arranging them on the table beside me, her face hidden. "Out with it!" I said, grabbed her arm, pulled her toward me. "Tell me now!" The flowers scattered, slipping unheeded to the floor.

Rachel sighed. "A beggar approached me in the marketplace. He had a message . . ."

I dropped the shuttle. "Holtan!" I exclaimed, turning to face her. "I know it's from Holtan." Thank you, Mother Isis. Thank you.

Rachel hesitated. "Oh, *Domina* . . . your husband loves you. Marcella—"

"Tell me!"

"There's to be an exhibition combat, in Cyprus . . ."

"Cyprus, so near . . . when?"

"The Ides of April."

"That's perfect! A holiday's coming up. Passover, isn't it? Thousands of pilgrims will be pouring into Jerusalem from everywhere. Pilate's few hundred men will be hard pressed to maintain order. He'll be too busy to notice where I am."

Rachel dropped to her knees. "*Domina, Domina,* where is your sight now?"

I pulled away impatiently. "Never mind the sight! I don't care about the future, I only want to be with Holtan now. Was there more to his message?"

"He'll come to Caesarea from Cyprus. He wants you to meet him there. He even wants you to bring Marcella. He says he has a plan—oh, *Domina,* don't do it," Rachel begged, tears filling her eyes. "You have a fine life. Don't go, and please don't take our Marcella."

CHAPTER

36

A Triumph

Rain came late to Judaea that year. Once it arrived, it seemed to last forever. Feeling imprisoned in my villa, I listened to the wind roar down the mountains, roiling the waters of the lake. Then, miraculously, the sky cleared. Orchards and gardens blazed with color. The craggy hills, usually gray and bare, were carpeted with wildflowers. The lake's rim glowed with golden poppies, purple lupine, and red anemones. All I could think of was Holtan's message. Was he already waiting in Caesarea?

"It is time for Marcella and me to take a little trip to the seacoast," I told Pilate at breakfast.

He looked at me, a brow raised slightly. I recognized the expression and braced myself. "Have you forgotten? We're returning to Jerusalem the day after tomorrow."

I pouted, struggling to keep my tone light. "You know I hate that city."

"And you know I must be there."

Pilate's cool determination threw me into a panic that I

fought to conceal. "I will be so much happier, so much e asier to be with . . . once I have had a holiday," I wheedled. "We could go as far as Scythopolis together. From there Marcella and I can travel to the coast for a few days, then join you later in Jerusalem. You cannot expect me to spend the whole spring in that wretched town without the tiniest taste of sea air. Please, darling." My mouth stretched in an effort to smile.

"Claudia, the answer is no."

THE DAY OF OUR DEPARTURE FOR JERUSALEM DAWNED brightly. Frantic with anxiety, I watched Marcella carefully lifted into a litter beside Rachel. Sun gleamed on the golden eagles surmounting the standards at its corners. "I want a horse too, Mama," Marcella pleaded. "Let me ride with you and *Tata*."

Pilate smiled at his daughter's pleading eyes. "The litter is all very well for you now, but next year our little princess will be five. Then you will have your own pony and can ride between us." Smiling broadly, he saluted Marcella, then turned and galloped to the head of the column.

His words sent a chill through me. Next year? Where would we be next year? Blowing a quick kiss to Marcella, I galloped off after him. The honor guard stood at attention. Camels snorted, donkeys brayed, horses pranced nervously. Everyone, it seemed, shared my husband's eagerness to be off. Once I was beside him, Pilate turned and raised his arm, signaling to the assembled caravan. We moved forward.

After a few hours of riding, the village of Scythopolis came

into view. My stomach knotted as we approached the fork in the road, south to Jerusalem, west to the sea. Striving to sound casual, I turned to Pilate. "I still want to go to Caesarea."

"Enough of that. You're coming with me. It's too much trouble to rearrange everything."

"Not at all. Whatever Marcella needs for the journey is in the litter with her. It is not as though she does not have a whole palace full of toys and clothes in Caesarea." *Why was Pilate making this so difficult?* "I will only be gone for a few days," I persisted.

"No! I want you and Marcella with me." He signaled abruptly and the caravan stopped. "We'll eat our noon meal up there." He gestured toward a grassy knoll some distance above the road. Men hurried about covering the ground with rich rugs. Soon the savory smell of roasting meat filled the air. I reclined on brightly woven pillows, between Pilate and Marcella. The hills around us were covered with flowers, purple hyacinths and iris, bright daffodils, and everywhere star-shaped blooms of the purest white. I plucked at a dark green thistle. The tiny blossom at the center was red as blood. I flung it away.

Marcella sat up, shielding her eyes from the sun. "Who are those people, *Tata*?"

I followed her pointing finger and saw a small procession of pilgrims on the road below us. Villagers from Scythopolis, many carrying palm branches, ran to greet them. "Hosanna!" some cried out to the wayfarers.

Pilate smiled condescendingly. "One would hardly call it a triumph."

"Not the kind we are used to in Rome, but perhaps it is to

them," I said. "At least the pilgrims are riding. No one is ragged, and their donkeys look well fed."

Marcella leaned forward. "What are they saying?"

I strained to hear. "It sounds like 'Blessed be he who comes in the name of the Lord.' "

Pilate frowned. "What 'Lord'? Who are they talking about?"

I shrugged, my thoughts returning to Holtan; what was I to do? "Surely no one of any importance," I responded vaguely. "No one we know." My eyes drifted absently, following the train of pilgrims below us. Suddenly I spotted a familiar face. *Miriam! Miriam and Jesus. What now? Where are they going?*

Pilate looked at me curiously. "You know one of those people?"

"The woman with red hair—the pretty one—riding beside the man in white."

Pilate looked again. "Pretty, indeed! I know her too, she's one of the most successful courtesans in Rome."

"Not anymore," I informed him.

"How do you know that?" he demanded. "How do you know her at all?"

I caught myself, realizing that I had already said too much. "Livia introduced us, then I chanced to meet her again—in the market. Love appears to have changed her." I watched as Miriam leaned over and whispered something in Jesus' ear. He turned, head thrown back, as he laughed. *The laugh I remembered from the wedding . . . then the vision that followed. What did it mean? What terrible thing lay ahead for them?*

"What is it?" Pilate wanted to know. "What's the matter? You look frightened. Who is that man?"

Surely it was a figment of my imagination. Had I not problems enough without imagining more? There was nothing I could do to help them. I forced a shrug. "Miriam believes him to be the messiah."

Pilate frowned. "Not another messiah."

"This one preaches only peace," I quickly assured him. I remembered Joanna's words, my own experience with the wine. "He preaches peace and is said to perform miracles. Miriam thinks he is wonderful." I paused a moment, studying the man on the road below. "Perhaps she is right."

I felt Pilate's eyes. "Really?" He watched me intently. "So tell me, Claudia, what constitutes a miracle for you? What would it take for you to think *I* am wonderful, for you to look at me as Miriam looks at that man?"

"Something quite simple." I tilted my head back to look up at him. "Something like allowing me a day or two in Caesarea."

"It would take nearly a day just to get there."

"So? A day here, a day there—is that so important? For me to get my way just once, would that not be a miracle?"

Pilate's dark brows knit in thought. "Very well," he responded. "Enjoy your few days by the sea, but Marcella will remain with me."

"Oh no!" I gasped. "She needs to be with me."

"She'll have Rachel and a nurse."

"I cannot go without her."

"Of course you can. As you said, 'a day or two.' Go now if you like. I'll send an honor guard with you. And soon—very soon, I think—we'll all be together. You and I and Marcella in Jerusalem. You won't tarry long without her."

It was a long trip to Caesarea, yet when I finally reached the palace that night thoughts of Holtan kept me awake until dawn. The governor's palace was a landmark. He would find it, learn quickly that I was there. Remembering all the clever ruses Holtan had devised for our secret meetings in Rome, I was certain that he would find a way to reach me. But he did not. Two days passed without a word from him. Where was he? What was wrong? Searching for him was risky, but how much longer could I wait? Finally, I could stand the suspense no longer. I would begin my quest at the wharf. Surely, I reasoned, anyone there would have news of the gladiatorial combat in Cyprus, possibly even know Holtan's whereabouts.

Pilate's litter waited my use by the palace entrance. It was an imposing affair, canopied in satin and crusted in gold leaf. Pilate's personal flag, borne by a burly soldier, whipped in the breeze. I squared my shoulders and stepped in.

There was nothing I could do about the honor guard—six soldiers. Pilate had ordered them to accompany me everywhere. They would obey those orders no matter what I said. Holtan would find a way to deal with them. I knew he would. In the meantime, there was nothing unusual about my wish to visit the wharf. Ships docked daily bringing messages and papers of state to Pilate. I had taken Marcella there often to watch the cargo unloaded. Frequently we lingered to buy green figs or pink slices of melon from one of the many vendors crowding the wharf. Always we had stood in awe watching the snake charmer sitting cross-legged on his mat, playing a pipe with one black serpent draped about his shoulders while another rose groggily from the basket. Already I missed Marcella and thought longingly of her. Holtan will get her for me, I reassured myself, Holtan can do anything.

The slaves gleamed with sweat when at last they helped me to alight before a large merchant ship. Protected by a half-moon-shaped quay of massive stones, the lone vessel rested against the wharf. A wharf that was curiously deserted. Where was the snake charmer? Even the beggars were gone. Passengers, hurrying to disembark, jockeyed for position on the crowded gangplank with sailors struggling to unload cargo. Some of them seemed almost frantic, the others . . . what was wrong with them?

The soldiers escorting my litter muttered uneasily among themselves. Signaling them to remain behind, I lifted my *chiton* slightly and pushed my way up the swarming gangplank. The deck was a mass of confusion, people shoving one another this way and that. In the midst of it a young officer struggled to maintain order. With difficulty, I made my way toward him. "Looks like a very crowded ship," I said, smiling sympathetically.

"Yes, *Domina.* Many from Cyprus fought to get on. They were eager to pay anything. Now I fear it was our captain who paid too high a price."

My heart contracted. "Why? What's wrong? Some of these people look—"

As I spoke, a familiar face appeared on deck—Julian, Holtan's body slave. He and another man carried a large trunk.

"Where's Holtan?" I cried, pushing toward him.

"He is below. No! *Domina,* wait—" Julian cried as I rushed past him toward the stairs. The officer grabbed me, holding me roughly by the shoulders. "Get off this cursed ship, get off while you can." I shoved with all my might, taking him by surprise. In that instant I slipped loose and ran for the stairs.

Below, the narrow passage was clogged with people laden with possessions, jostling one another as they shoved their way forward. What did caution matter now? "Holtan, the gladiator, where is he?" I cried out. No one appeared to hear or even take note of me. Passengers and crew pushed and fought as though panic stricken. There was a smell too, an awful smell, vomit, and something more. Holding a scarf over my nose, I struggled forward, calling as I went for Holtan.

Finally I heard his voice. "Here, Claudia, behind you."

Turning, I saw him at the end of the narrow passageway shoving his way toward me. I fought my way back through the crowd, at last flinging my arms about him.

"What in Hades are you doing here?" he growled, pushing me back.

I looked up in surprise. Didn't Holtan realize what I had gone through, the risk I was taking? Then, as my eyes swept over him, I saw that his face was pale and lined with fatigue. I wanted to take him in my arms and kiss away the weariness.

"I came to be with you, dear one. Are you not glad? Is this not what you wanted, what *we* wanted? Your message—I came as soon as I could. I thought there would be some word from you. I could wait no longer."

"You should not have come. Go back, go now," he said, shoving me away.

"Go back! Your messenger told Rachel that you had a plan. Whatever it is, I will do it—do anything, go anywhere as long as we are together."

"I did have—I *do* have a plan." Holtan spoke slowly, haltingly.

"But now . . . now I want you to take Marcella and get out of Caesarea as fast as possible."

My lips trembled, my voice caught. "I had to leave Marcella with Pilate. We must get her. You will think of a way, won't you?" I looked up at him expectantly.

Relief flickered in Holtan's bloodshot eyes. "Marcella is in Jerusalem? You can thank your goddess for that. Go back to her. Trust me, go now." His hands still held me at arm's length.

"I won't," I protested, trying to free myself. "I am not going anywhere without you. Do you think I have risked everything to leave you now?"

Holtan braced himself against a door frame. "Then wait for me at your palace." He released me; one hand caressed my hair. "I will send for you later. Just leave now." He pushed me away again, reeling as though drunk.

An engulfing fear swept over me; I struggled for control. Moving once again to face Holtan, I placed a hand on his moist cheek. "There is a plague on this ship and you have got it, haven't you?"

He swayed unsteadily. "Fortuna . . . has played a bad joke on us."

I braced him with my arms. "Since when did you give up so easily?"

"I have seen so many die, Claudia."

"You are not going to die! I won't let you." I looked up at the face I loved so well and saw death waiting. *You will not take him! I will wrestle you to the very bowels of Hades. You will not take Holtan from me!*

CHAPTER

37

Holtan's Request

I sat looking out at the sea. The day had grown increasingly hot; I was grateful for the breeze. Oh, where was that physician? Why did he not come? I had exhausted my memory, wracking my brain for all that I had learned years ago at the Iseneum. The knowledge of herbs that had served me well with Marcella's childhood fevers proved useless. Holtan vomited the potion of passiflora and matricaria. The calming valerian had no effect. If anything, the poultice of mustard seed raised his temperature. Nothing was working. *Mother Isis, save him. Do not let him die! Do not take him from me now!*

Holtan stirred restlessly on the couch beside me. "Where am I?" he asked, waking slowly. His thick, rasping voice slurred the words. Scowling as his eyes found me, he shouted, "I told you to get out of here."

"You are in a safe place. Trust me, dearest, I am going to make you well. I promise that I will."

"Claudia—please! Save yourself while you still can. Get out! Go now, leave me." When I did not respond, Holtan lowered his voice, speaking clearly and rationally. "I will be dead by tomorrow. If you stay, you will die, too." He struggled to sit up, almost falling off the couch.

With a sudden shove, I forced him back onto the cushions. At least now I was stronger than he. I could keep him from harming himself further.

"Where am I?" he asked again. "Is this your palace? Surely you did not take me there!"

I had never before seen fear in Holtan's eyes. I knew it was for me. "No, dearest," I reassured him. "We're in a small inn. My honor guard brought you here. It is a quiet place on the outskirts of town. We have everything necessary." I placed a fresh compress on his brow. "All you need do is rest. You will be well again very soon."

Holtan sighed. "Claudia, my dear, dear Claudia, if the plague does not get you, Pilate will. What did you tell his soldiers about me?"

"That you are an army friend of my father's. You can thank Isis that they were with me. When your slaves and I tried to get you off the ship, city guards blocked the gangplank. No one was allowed to leave. Without my men and their weapons, we would be trapped there with the others. After the soldiers brought us here, I sent them back to the palace."

"They will talk—"

I shrugged. "What else could I do? Hopefully, Pilate's too busy keeping the peace to think of me. All those thousands of pilgrims pouring into Jerusalem for their festival should keep him occupied."

Holtan smiled weakly. "I feel old enough to be your father's friend, but were they not suspicious . . . I can't remember . . ."

"You were unconscious." I soothed him as I would Marcella. "I told them you had had too much to drink, the innkeeper too—a gold coin took care of him."

"Julian? Where is Julian?" Holtan's voice had dropped to a whisper.

I could see the effort of talking had exhausted him. "Julian is downstairs getting food and water. Your other man, Ajax, is outside guarding us."

Holtan took my hand, grasped it tight. "You did . . . well . . . everything right . . . I . . . love . . . you. If you . . . love me . . . go now. Give me that, Claudia. Go . . . while . . ." His grip loosened. Holtan's words slurred and he lay still.

I could not tell if he was conscious or not. His eyes were half open, but he no longer seemed aware of me. Then, suddenly, without warning, he sat up and vomited onto the floor, retching with such violence I thought he would tear out his stomach. Fear and revulsion swept over me. What should I do, what could I do?

Hearing a sound behind me, I turned to find Julian standing in the doorway, his dark eyes wide. I reached into the small leather bag at my waist. Gold coins glittered as I held out my hand. "Take half of these now. You will have the rest when you find that physician and return with him. And—and look at this." Quickly I picked up the ruby amulet that Holtan had been wearing about his neck. "You know the value. It is yours if you remain with us until *Dominus* has recovered."

Julian shook his head, his expression adamant. A large, long-legged man, he crossed the room in an instant and stood at my side. "Keep it. *Dominus* saved my life more than once. I will never leave him. The king of Cyprus awarded him that ruby but three days ago. He wanted it for you."

"Isis bless you," I murmured, tears of gratitude stinging my eyes. I took the tray from him and placed it on the table. "Go now, go quickly. Find that doctor and bring him here." Turning back to Holtan, I dropped my scarf in a bowl of water on the table beside us, wrung it out, and sponged the vomit from his gaunt face.

Hours passed, an eternity, as the sun slipped lower on the horizon. I supported Holtan, holding the vessel, watching with horror and pity and mounting rage while my lover retched again and again. His lips were cracked, his face receding to bone. He retained not even a drop of water and, despite the heat of the day, shivered as though freezing.

It was nearly evening when I looked up to see a tall black Ethiopian standing in the doorway. He slowly advanced into the room, reed-slim in his long blue tunic. Stopping short of the couch, the physician held a cloth to his nose. "Was he on the boat from Cyprus?"

"Yes." I nodded. "What is it? What's wrong with him?"

"A foreign plague that has already killed hundreds. Victims die quickly—perhaps a blessing."

Fear knotted my belly. "I will pay anything," I said, reaching for my pouch.

"Money means nothing. Masters are as helpless as we who are their slaves."

My heart dropped. I had waited so long for this man, hoping that he might work some kind of magic. "You are only a slave?"

"Yes, my *dominus* rents me out."

"But you do know something of medicine?"

He raised his chin proudly. "I was a doctor before my capture. The fee for a consultation is fifty sesterces."

I pulled the coins from my pouch and handed them to him. "Heal him, damn you! Every second we waited for you, he has grown weaker. Will he live?"

The slave-physician shrugged. "*Domina* asks the impossible. A few will live, most will die. The gods decide."

"There must be something you can do."

"What have you given him to eat?"

"I fed him broth, but he vomited it up. He has been terribly thirsty but can keep nothing down."

"Give him cabbage; or if he cannot swallow that, the urine of someone who has eaten cabbage." When I looked up at him incredulously, he shrugged. "Some claim great success from that treatment."

"There must be something else?"

"Try this," he said, pulling a small packet from his bag. "It is dried horehound. Mix it with his wine. Force it down him. Keep him warm. That is all I can tell you except that you must guard your own strength. Everyone who came in on that boat has it. Most are already dead and now it has spread into the city."

"What causes it?" I asked, following him to the door.

"Who knows?" The slave doctor shrugged again. "My Jewish *dominus* says it's Yahweh's punishment for our sins."

"What kind of a god is that! What sins? All Holtan, all any of us, have ever done is merely struggle to stay alive."

I ran back to Holtan, who was vomiting again. When I turned, the slave-physician was gone. "Close the drapes, build a fire," I instructed Julian, who knelt beside the couch. "Then go downstairs, tell them to boil cabbage and make a broth of it. Bring wine. The doctor said some survive. Holtan is a fighter, he has got to be one of the lucky ones."

Soon sweat poured off Holtan's face. The sheet beneath him was soaked. I covered him with a heavy blanket. Julian returned with the cabbage broth and wine. I sent him back to the main hall to get food for himself. Pulling the damp hair from my neck, I skewered it on top of my head, then poured a cup of broth from the pitcher and resumed dribbling drops onto Holtan's parched lips.

Hours passed. I looked outside for a brief moment and saw that the sky was pitch-black. When I turned, Holtan lay flat on his back, his eyes open, but unseeing. Frantically, I flung myself across him. My fingers clutched at his shoulders, still broad and powerful. "Holtan, Holtan, I won't let you go," I sobbed. Clinging to him, crying hysterically, I screamed curses and endearments.

"Claudia!" Holtan's eyes opened. He shoved his hands into my hair, pulling my head back.

Sick with fear and shame I wiped away my tears. What awful things had I been saying—shouting?

"It is over," he whispered. "I had . . . to see you, Claudia. Another time . . . somewhere . . . we will be together." Wearily, he closed his eyes.

Holtan's breathing grew so shallow, I could scarcely hear it. I pressed my ear against his chest and held him tightly. "Oh, darling, do not leave me," I sobbed. My vision returned to me with sickening clarity. Why had I not heeded it? It was my fault that he had come to Caesarea, my fault that he was dying.

"Please don't leave me," I begged, but his eyes remained closed. After a time, I slipped to the floor and sat with my head resting on the couch, one hand in Holtan's.

"DOMINA?"

I jumped. Had I dozed off? Oh no! I stumbled stiffly to my feet, leaning over the couch. It was Julian who had spoken. He was beside me, a gently supportive arm about my shoulders. "*Dominus* is gone."

"Noooooooooo!" I screamed. "He cannot die!"

I ran my fingers through Holtan's sandy hair, down over his face. I kissed his lips, seeking his spirit, longing to draw it into me. Did anything of him remain? His lips were cold, so cold. "He died when I was asleep," I sobbed. "I let him die alone. How could I have slept when he was so sick, when he needed me most?"

"You were with him, *Domina.* He knew that. If you had been with us on the ship, you would have seen many die, the strong as quickly as the weak. You stayed with him. There is nothing else that anyone could have done. Now you must leave—as he wanted you to do."

"Leave?" I repeated blankly.

"Ajax will go with you to the palace. I will see to everything here. You must go. The sooner you get to back to Jerusalem, the better. That is what *Dominus* wanted."

"Perhaps . . . yes." I tucked the ruby into my coin bag and handed the pouch to him. "He would also want you and Ajax to have your freedom, to start new lives. This will make it easier."

"Are you forgetting?" Julian asked. When I looked at him dumbly, he handed me a coin. "For Charon."

I nodded gratefully and placed the coin under Holtan's tongue. Of course, he must have his toll ready. Without it the ferryman would never row him across the Styx. If only I could go with him to the Underworld. My fingers moved once more over my lover's face. Then turning, I left through the door that Julian had opened for me. Kitchen noises and the sound of a child's laughter floated in the air. Released from the thick, heavy smell of the room, I breathed in the fresh morning breeze, knowing that nothing for me would ever be the same.

As my curtained litter moved down the streets, the tread of the bearers' feet echoed eerily on the stone road, an unaccustomed sound in the normally teeming city. A chill passed through my body. When I cautiously parted the curtain, I saw that plague had changed Caesarea overnight. Vendors had vanished. Even the beggars were gone. Shops were closed, streets deserted but for a few darting figures who averted their eyes from one another.

With so little traffic, we reached the palace quickly, but found its gates closed and bolted. I had never seen it so. Even in Pilate's absence the courtyard was always jammed with impatient, jostling supplicants eager to speak with any underling willing to hear their pleas or propositions.

Ajax and the bearers hammered with their fists, shouting loudly for admittance until the massive cedar door opened a crack. A guard peered out.

"Is this any way to greet your *domina*?" Ajax demanded.

Slowly the door swung open and a familiar figure appeared, all leather straps, clinking steel, and blood-red wool. I nodded to Gavius, captain of the palace guard. His greeting was deferential, his bow militarily correct, but the soldier's eyes lingered a fraction too long on my face.

Do I look as bad as I feel? "Pay these men," I instructed him.

Gavius accidentally dropped the coins as he approached the bearers, then backed away as they scrambled for them on the ground.

"Thank you, Ajax." I took the slave's callused hand in mine, looked into his eyes. "Go now, go quickly."

"You as well, *Domina*. Leave this accursed city."

I squeezed his hand, then turned and entered the palace. My legs felt leaden as I ascended the stairs to my apartment. So many stairs.

Leah, a young slave, appeared in the doorway. "Is *Domina* ill?"

I saw the fear in her eyes. "No! Not ill, just exhausted," I hastily explained. "A banquet, much too much wine. Help me off with my things. I want to rest."

I stood woodenly as Leah removed my clothing. Outside, I heard the surf crashing against the cliffs. Waves of fatigue swept over me. I had the sense of standing in a whirlpool, the mosaic floor tipped toward me, the blues and greens of the frescoed room blending with the sea sounds swimming in my head. "Go now," I instructed her. "I will call if I need anything."

Once she left I flung myself on the couch. Bitter tears wracked my body. How could Fortuna have been so cruel? What sort of joke was it to match Holtan in a battle where his strength, courage, and skill meant nothing? "Why, Holtan, why?" I moaned softly over and over until at last I slipped into a deep, exhausted sleep.

When I opened my eyes, Holtan stood beside me, not the wan, helpless creature I had last seen, but the vigorous, confident man I loved so well. "Dearest! You have come for me," I exclaimed, joyously holding out my arms.

Holtan shook his head, just beyond my grasp.

"Please don't leave me again," I begged, tears streaming down my face. I struggled to reach him, crying out as his form slowly faded. "Take me with you!"

An instant later Leah was at my side.

I stared at her in bewilderment. "The man who was here, where did he go?"

"*Domina* must have dreamed."

"It was so real."

"Nightmares often seem real," Leah said, blotting the tears from my face. "Would *Domina* like me to stay with her?"

"Thank you, no. I have nothing to fear from that dream. Go, please, I want to sleep again."

I closed my eyes, longing for death. Holtan waiting so near that I could almost touch him. Others, too, reaching out. Dear Germanicus, tall and handsome, armor gleaming. My joyous, laughing sister. Equals now in love, we have much to share. Mother, with her wise words and gentle warmth, is with me, and beside her *Tata* smiles proudly. How long since I felt the security of his embrace? Oh, *Tata,* I have missed you so! All the dear ones that I have lost. So close now. Holtan, dearest, I am coming . . . Somewhere far off the sound of sobbing. It is so good here, soft twilight, loved ones waiting to take me home. Why should anyone cry? Sobbing, still the sobbing. Who can it be?

And then I know.

A voice, strong and clear, echoes throughout the chamber. *No, Claudia, death is not for you, not now. Your days on this earth will be many. Go back to Jerusalem. Go now.*

The words of Isis. I know that, just as I know that it is she who has sent a vision of Marcella, the child of my body, still so small and dear, sobbing as though her heart would break.

It is dark when I open my eyes again to find Leah leaning over me. "You look much better, *Domina.* The banquet must be wearing off."

I looked at her, puzzled, then remembered. "Oh yes—all that wine. I am better, much better. Please bring me fruit and water."

"Anything else, *Domina*?"

"Yes, tell Gavius to ready a small guard and the fastest horses. At dawn I leave for Jerusalem."

CHAPTER 38

My Vision

The moon had been up for hours. Tired to the bone, I prayed silently as the palace gates swung open. *Isis, goddess of my faith, grant me the strength to do my soul's work.* Taking a deep breath, I urged my horse forward.

The courtyard was ablaze with torches as slaves ran to assist me. There was Rachel, waiting, wrapped in her night garb, a tremulous smile on her lips. "I have been watching for you from the parapet," she said, her voice choked. "I prayed you would return." Stiffly, I slid from the horse, all but falling. I clung to Rachel's sturdy arms, struggling to hold back the tears I had fought throughout the long ride. "Holtan is gone—dead."

"Domina!" She held me closer, whispering. "Did *Dominus* find out? Did he . . . ?"

I shook my head. "Holtan died of plague."

"Plague . . . so even he was not invincible. Are *you* all right?"

Fear flickered briefly in her eyes; I pulled away. "I am

well—as well as I will ever be without Holtan. I want to see Marcella."

"*Domina,* is that safe? The plague . . ."

In my weariness, I snapped at her. "Do you think I would have returned if I there was a chance that I carried it?" Seeing Rachel's face, I softened. "For whatever reason, Isis chose to spare me. It was she who sent me home to Marcella."

We left the courtyard and entered the palace, eerily quiet in the predawn. "It broke my heart the way Marcella kept crying for you," Rachel said as we approached the nursery. "*Dominus* told her that you would be back soon. I was not so certain."

I watched my sleeping daughter from the doorway. Marcella's face was flushed and plump with health. She stirred and slowly opened her eyes. "Mama!" she murmured in a voice husky with sleep. I longed to rush forward, to sweep her into my arms, but held back. Tomorrow . . . "Yes, Mama's home," I said softly. "Sleep, my darling one." Her outstretched arms dropped slowly as she drowsed.

Once out in the hallway, I asked Rachel about Pilate.

"Herod Antipas has come to Jerusalem to celebrate Passover. *Dominus* has gone to his palace to confer."

I wondered briefly what new crisis kept the two men up so late. They were not friends. Only a thin veil of civility covered their suspicious aversion to each other. Pilate held Herod in contempt while fearing his popularity in Rome. The Jewish tetrarch wanted nothing more than to get my husband out of Judaea so that he might rule the country without a Roman presence, as his father had done.

"I hope Pilate's conference is serious enough to detain him all night," I said as we reached the door to my chambers. "How can I answer his questions? I have lost all but Marcella. What if he knows about Holtan, what if he banishes me?" I sank wearily to a couch. "I am not ready to see Pilate; I am exhausted. The roads are clogged with pilgrims, thousands of them. You cannot imagine the dust, the noise. It was a nightmare. I must rest first."

Rachel frowned as she undid the fastenings of my sandals. "Everyone is troubled this Passover season. So much has happened . . ."

"Please, not now. The rumors can wait. I want only to sleep."

"It is more than rumor. The news reached us yesterday from Rome. The *Dominus* Sejanus has been executed. Everyone is talking about it, speculating about the future. What, who will be next?"

"I do not believe it!" I exclaimed, startled out of my fatigue. "The second-most important man in Rome—in the world! Tiberius dotes on Sejanus."

"No longer," Rachel insisted, her voice lowered. "Jealous courtiers managed to come between them. Whether their stories of betrayal were truth or fiction, I know not, but the emperor believed them. He ordered *Dominus* Sejanus's whole family killed."

I gasped as though I had been struck. "What! All of them? Even little Priscilla?" Priscilla with her merry smile and bobbing curls was hardly more than a child. "It is against the law to execute virgins," I reminded Rachel.

"She was not a virgin when the guards finished with her."

I slumped down on the couch. Sejanus had been a kind man, to me at least. How well I remembered good-natured

Apicata with her quips and tittle-tattle . . . Warm friends lost to me forever. "How much more can I bear?" I murmured, shaking my head wearily.

"Better to worry about your husband—and yourself," Rachel advised. "The emperor is surely aware that *Dominus* was Sejanus's man."

A chill ran through me. Poor Pilate, as though he did not have enough to worry about already. Oh, Isis! What if it had been our child taken, our precious girl. No! I would not think about that, not tonight.

Rachel signaled to another waiting slave to prepare my bathwater. "The *Dominus* Sejanus's overthrow is not all that has happened in your absence."

"No more, please."

Rachel looked up, a worried expression on her face. "This concerns the *Domina* Miriam."

I caught my breath. "Very well, tell me."

"She has come to the palace three times this very night begging to see you. The last time the *domina* was sobbing openly."

"Strange." I turned away, unwilling to think what this new development might mean. I struggled to ignore the mounting fear. "What could Miriam want of me?" I wondered aloud. "I saw her riding with Jesus on the Jerusalem road less than a week ago. She looked like the happiest woman alive."

"Then you would not recognize her," Rachel murmured sadly. "Jesus has been arrested. It was Caiaphas's doing," she explained, slipping off my shift. "He and the other high priests are determined to get rid of Jesus."

Sighing, I slipped into the bath. The warm, scented water

seemed to sink into every tired pore. "That does not make sense," I reasoned. "Why would those powerful priests bother with Jesus? He is merely an itinerant rabbi who possesses nothing and wants nothing."

"I do not know," Rachel said, shaking her head. "It is difficult to understand Jesus. He angers people because he confuses them. He had hardly entered Jerusalem before a crowd of Pharisees and Herodians accosted him. 'Is it right to pay taxes to Caesar?' their leader asked him."

"Oh, Isis! There is no right answer to that one."

"No," Rachel agreed. "They wanted to trap Jesus."

"I see. If he says yes, he loses Zealots like Simon and Judas who believe he was born to fight their cause. If he says no, Pilate can easily have him arrested. I suppose that is what happened, why he is in jail."

"No, Jesus was clever. He asked for a coin and they gave him a denarius. Holding up the side with Tiberius's picture on it, he said, 'Render unto Caesar that which is Caesar's.' Then, turning the coin over, Jesus told them to 'Render unto the Lord that which is the Lord's.' "

I sat up in the tub feeling a little better. "That's wonderful!" I exclaimed, "so like him. Pay the taxes. They mean nothing. His kingdom, the kingdom of love and equality, is not of this world."

"It's wonderful unless you happen to be a Zealot," Rachel reminded me. "Jesus has done everything they expected of him, fulfilled each of the ancient prophecies, even to entering Jerusalem like the true messiah they believed he was. Then, just when his Zealot champions expected him to lead them into battle, Jesus vilified their cause before half the city."

Oh, Isis! If Jesus is not to be their messiah, would the Zealots then use him as their martyr?

Before I could voice my fears, Rachel continued. "It is as though Jesus wants to incite *everyone*. Two days ago, he caused a disturbance in the Temple. It's the talk of the city."

I tipped my head back and closed my eyes as she rubbed soapy water into my scalp. "In the Temple? How extraordinary! Were you there?"

"Yes, I was just passing by and heard a commotion in the courtyard. At first I thought it was just the usual—people swarming all over each other to buy offerings. Doves that sell for a few pennies going for twenty times that. Suddenly there was Jesus ranting and raving, overturning cages. Lambs were running in all directions, doves flying in circles. Then he went after the money changers."

"Really!" I exclaimed. Money changers were the lifeblood of the Temple, of Jerusalem itself. Everyone, including Pilate, left them strictly alone. Not so much as a beggar got space in the Temple without paying something to the Sanhedrin. The last thing Caiaphas would want was some upstart threatening his money changers.

Rachel shook her head in bewilderment. "Jesus kept shouting that the money changers had to get out of his father's house. Imagine calling the Temple his father's house."

I remembered talking with Jesus at the wedding, the reference to his *abba*. "That is what he believes," I told her.

"Caiaphas was furious."

"I can well imagine. What about my husband? Where does Pilate stand on all this?"

"The head guard told me that *Dominus* was far more

concerned about another criminal, the one he sent from Sepphoris to be crucified."

"Barabbas?"

Rachel nodded. "He is the man."

"Miriam must have come here because she wants me to intercede for Jesus."

Rachel gave me a frightened glance. "If *Dominus* thinks that you have anything to do with Jesus or Miriam—"

Waves of anxiety and exhaustion swept over me. "I am so very tired, I cannot face Pilate tonight. How can I possibly pretend that nothing has happened to me . . . that I have not lost . . . everything!"

"Do not try, wait till you have rested," Rachel said as she helped me from the bath. She began to towel-dry my hair. "*Dominus* will want to see you, but I will tell him that you are tired from your journey and need to rest."

I waved the towel away. "Please leave me now. I need to be alone."

By myself at last, I sat quietly thinking about all that Rachel had told me. In retrospect, Jesus' fate did not seem so dire. Rome's worst complaint against the Jews was their reluctance to pay taxes. Now here was a popular leader—many believed the legitimate heir—actually advising people to pay their tax. Pilate was certainly not going to side with the Zealots against him. As for Caiaphas and the Sanhedrin, why would the governor try, let alone condemn, an idealistic young man who actually spoke in support of Roman policy? A night in prison was not the end of the world. Jesus would be released in the morning. Pilate would need no urging from me to decide that question. Miriam would soon have her husband back.

As for me, I would never have the man I loved.

Reclining on my couch, I turned and tossed, unable to sleep. Finally, I rose and knelt before my statue of Isis. I would pray for another dream of Holtan. Please come to me, my darling. *Please.* Tears denied for long hours flowed freely as my mind filled with memories. Holtan, the victorious gladiator, Holtan on his deathbed. I returned to my couch but sleep eluded me. Where was he?

When it came at last, sleep delivered a dream more terrifying than anything I could have imagined. Isis sent not my love, but Miriam's. As the nightmare unfolded, my grief merged with hers until I became one with Miriam. Helpless, I watched Roman soldiers nail my beloved to a cross. I longed to rush to him as he begged for water. The hot sun beat mercilessly on his head, uncovered but for a crown of thorns.

Trapped in a spinning reality that would not stop, I saw Jesus at the front of a parade of tragic victims, their pitiful dramas followed by ever greater bloodbaths. Men with crosses emblazoned on their robes rode angrily into battle after battle. I saw women tied to stakes and burned alive, the stench of roasting flesh everywhere as their tortured shrieks mingled with chanting . . . I heard my husband's name repeated endlessly. *Suffered under Pontius Pilate. Suffered under Pontius Pilate. Suffered under Pontius Pilate . . .* My screams mingled with theirs as something held me. Struggling desperately to free myself from the dream, I watched Jesus' face fade until it disappeared. All that remained was the cross, superimposed over endless fields of flame-engulfed corpses. I sat up, the ghastly sight receding as I recognized the familiar confines of my room. The cross, of course, the cross that had haunted me for so long. Pilate was going to crucify Jesus.

"*Domina!* What is it? What is wrong?" Rachel stood beside me, her eyes wide with concern.

I looked about. Sunlight was streaming into the room. "That noise? The shouting! Where is it coming from? What's going on?"

"The priests have brought Jesus to the palace for trial. They will not go into the courtroom because of the statues of Augustus and the other gods. *Dominus* is going to try Jesus' case in the courtyard. It is filled now, mostly by members of the Sanhedrin. No one else can get in."

"Pilate is trying Jesus!" The words from my dream echoed in my head as I scrambled from the couch. "Hurry!" I cried, pulling at my sleeping tunic. "Help me to dress. I have got to stop him."

"They will not allow it." Rachel pulled the gown from my hands. "You cannot go down there!"

"I will find a way. I have got to find a way. I must see Pilate," I said, lowering a tunic over my head and shoulders.

Sandals slapping against the marble stairs, I descended, Rachel at my heels. Pausing once at a parapet, I looked down at the angry mob packing the courtyard. There was Pilate in his crimson magistrate's robes sitting above them on a dais. A path had been cleared before him. Dark-robed priests approached. I ran on down the stairs.

When I reached the anteroom, guards barred the arched entryway, hulking brutes who stood immobile, holding their spears upright. Beyond, I heard loud angry voices and heavy staffs thumping furiously against the paving stones.

Recognizing the captain, a large, florid-faced man, I gave an imperious nod. "I must see my husband immediately."

"That's impossible," he said, blocking me with his broad body. "Jewish law forbids women to be here."

"My husband is the governor. This is *my* courtyard."

"The rule is clear, *Domina.* I have orders from your husband. No disturbances of any kind."

"But I have urgent business with him." The guard stood firm. "Out of my way!" I demanded, pushing him with all my strength. I might as well have tried to move a stone wall.

"Be reasonable," he urged, his sunburned skin taking on a deeper flush. "The crowd is angry. You would not want to inflame them further."

Peering around his broad shoulder, I glimpsed Jesus. He stood, wrists bound, encircled by accusers. Someone had wrapped a scarlet cloak about his shoulders. Across his brow was a crown of thorns.

I gasped. *My dream was already coming true!*

The High Priest Caiaphas confronted Pilate. "This man is accused of corrupting our people. He calls himself a king."

My husband looked up from a scroll and regarded Jesus quizzically. I knew that calm, noncommittal expression. "Well—are you a king, the king of the Jews?"

I strained to hear the reply.

"If you say that I am," Jesus said softly, as noncommittal as Pilate.

My husband leaned forward, his gaze curious as he studied the prisoner. "You have heard their accusations. Have you nothing to say?"

"Do you want to know this for yourself, or because others have spoken against me?" Jesus asked.

I held my breath. Jesus' manner seemed strangely calm, without defenses, almost provocative.

Pilate looked at him sharply. "Am I a Jew? Is it not your people, your chief priests, who brought you here? What have you done to provoke them?"

Jesus continued to regard him almost tranquilly. "They persecute me for reasons of their own."

My husband's gaze shifted briefly to Caiaphas and his father-in-law, Annas, who stood scowling, arms folded across their chests. Turning back to the prisoner, Pilate asked, "And why would they do that?"

"Because I speak of the kingdom of heaven, and they talk only of this earth. I came into this world to bear witness to the truth."

"The truth." Pilate smiled. "What is truth?" he asked, raising an ironic brow.

As Jesus remained silent, I felt an unexpected wave of sympathy for my husband.

"I find nothing criminal about this man," Pilate said, turning to Caiaphas. "Take him and judge him according to your Law."

"You Romans do not allow us to put a man to death," Caiaphas reminded him.

"Death?" Pilate looked startled. "This harmless dreamer does not deserve death."

Caiaphas struggled visibly to keep his voice calm. "This 'harmless dreamer' travels throughout the whole of Judaea and Galilee inciting people with his blasphemy."

"You must go, *Domina*," the guard whispered hoarsely, gesturing toward a group of priests who had noticed me and were muttering among themselves. One priest was pointing at me. "Do you want to set off a rebellion?"

"I must speak with my husband," I insisted, looking about frantically. Clearly Pilate was the one reasoning mind against a rabid mob. A thought occurred to me. "Bring me a tablet and stylus. I will write to him."

The guard towered over me. Chin up, I glared back at him. Finally, he looked away. "Withdraw then," he conceded. "Move back now or I'll have you carried out."

I stepped back from the archway to the anteroom where Rachel watched.

"The guard is right. It is dangerous to be here," she said, her eyes wide and frightened.

"Oh, Rachel, you do not understand. You cannot. You have not seen the things I have seen or heard the words, those awful words. Executing Jesus would be a travesty. He is a good man who wants only peace. My dreams tell me that his death will be the beginning of endless war and misunderstanding. A great darkness will come over the world. No one will remember what Jesus really said and the name Pontius Pilate will live on in some dreadful way. I must stop it."

A servant came with a tablet and stylus. I snatched them from him, my heart pounding wildly as I struggled for words. How could I possibly describe what I had seen in my dream? I could not, and time was running out.

Hurriedly, I scrawled: "Pilate—I warn you, have nothing to do with that innocent man. I have had painful dreams because of him." I handed the scroll to the captain. "Deliver this directly into my husband's hands. Do it now."

At the guard's insistence, Rachel and I remained in the anteroom. The angry voices in the courtyard grew louder, I felt the tension mounting. Finally, I could stand the suspense no longer and began to inch my way back toward the archway. The guard watched my advance, his mouth set in a grim line. I placed a finger across my lips, whispering, "Please. I will stay back out of sight."

Pilate banged the flat of his sword against the table to quiet the impatient crowd. I saw my tablet open on the table before him.

"You brought this man, Jesus, to me, but I find nothing criminal about him." He paused, looking at the angry crowd assembled before him. "Perhaps he does not perfectly appreciate the authority of Rome. For that I will teach him a lesson that he will not forget, but then I will set him free. Jesus has done nothing to merit death."

"No!" Caiaphas growled. His angry cry was picked up by possibly a hundred men who pressed closer to Pilate.

My heart raced. What was he to do? Roman law was inherently equitable. If Jesus had been a citizen of Rome, he could have taken his case to Caesar himself. Even as a mere Judaean subject, he was entitled to justice from the governor. Pilate's duty was clear, yet I knew that fulfilling it might jeopardize Rome's sovereignty and cost my husband dearly.

"It is the custom to set one prisoner free each year at Passover time," Pilate reminded the court. "As a gesture of my good will, I will release Jesus, 'king of the Jews.' "

My blood tingled with relief and pride. It was a master

stroke. Pilate had not only freed an innocent man, but he had reminded the unruly mob of Rome's strength and power. What had the ruler of the world to fear from a simple rabbi? How clever! In that moment I was as proud of him as the day we were married.

But even as these thoughts raced through my mind, the crowd grew even uglier. "Free Barabbas!" someone called out. "Give us Barabbas!" The ringleaders picked up the cry. Soon the whole crowd was shouting: "Barabbas! Barabbas!" as though acclaiming a hero.

"Barabbas! That murderous scum!" the captain of the guard, standing in front of me, muttered.

My heart sank as I saw Pilate's shoulders sag. "It is over," I whispered. "Nothing can save Jesus now."

"Then what am I to do with your king?" I heard Pilate ask.

"Crucify him!" the people shouted almost as one.

"But what crime has he committed?"

"Crucify him!" they cried again.

Pilate looked about the crowded court. Not one man came forward to speak for Jesus.

As my husband hesitated, Caiaphas moved closer, a warning implicit in his voice. "If you set this man free, you are no friend to Caesar. Anyone who calls himself a king is against Rome. Tiberius is our ruler, and no one else."

"Very well," Pilate said at last. "His blood is on your hands, not mine." He signaled to an attendant. "Water. Bring it now in a bowl." The noisy courtyard quieted. I stood perfectly still, watching, waiting. Every eye was on Pilate as he plunged his hands into the basin. "I wash my hands of the innocent blood of this man."

Rachel tugged at my arm. "Come, *Domina,* we should leave."

Tears blinded me as I allowed myself to be led away. Even as I had striven to avert fate, I had been no more than a fly on the wall. I thought of Miriam and Mary. Oh, my Isis, how could they bear it! Excited conversation rippled through the courtyard. I turned back, pushed my way through the archway. What difference did it make now if I was seen? People stood in silent groups, waiting. Standing on tiptoe, I saw Pilate pick up my tablet. He was erasing the wax with the blunt end of the stylus. An impatient muttering spread though the courtyard as he began to write a new message. The palace guards raised their swords threateningly at the protesters. When Pilate had finished, he held up the stylus.

The mob's angry grumbling began in earnest as spectators surged closer to the bench, struggling to see.

"What did he write?" I asked the guard.

The burly man pressed forward. "By Jupiter." He nodded approvingly. "The governor knows how to put them in their place."

"What did he write?" I repeated.

"Jesus of Nazareth, king of the Jews."

"Carve this on his cross," Pilate ordered Caiaphas. "Carve it in Aramaic, Greek, and Latin."

The high priest's face went livid. "You cannot write that! Say instead 'He *said* he was king of the Jews'."

Pilate regarded him coolly. "I have written what I have written."

CHAPTER

39

My Decision

The stairs echoed under my feet. The palace felt deserted. Was everyone down in the courtyard watching that horrid spectacle? I shuddered at the memory of the guards closing in around Jesus. He had been beaten. I saw him stagger. I must not think . . . I hurried faster as though a sanctuary awaited me in my chambers.

It did not.

"Try to rest, *Domina,*" Rachel urged when we reached the anteroom of my apartments. "You slept so little last night."

Rest. Would I ever rest again?

I wanted only to be alone, but when the door at last closed, I knew there would be no such thing as solitude. From every direction memories besieged me. They could not be eluded. All that I had loved, all that I had lost. My beloved family, Holtan, and now this new . . . What meaning was there in any of it? How was I to go on? I rose and walked to the shrine I had created for Isis. Kneeling before her image, I prayed silently. What is your plan for me? Tell me, show me, and give me the strength to do thy will . . .

How long I knelt there I do not know, but slowly I became aware that someone was pounding at the door. In the distance I heard a woman screaming. Now what? I wondered, rising. Moving reluctantly, I hesitated before throwing back the bolt. There in the passageway was Miriam, struggling frantically as two guards dragged her from the door. Others stood watching with swords drawn.

"Release her immediately!" I ordered.

The men fell back but kept their weapons firmly fixed on Miriam.

"Please, Claudia, help me!" she cried. "I must speak with you alone."

I put my arm around Miriam, pulling her into my chamber. Before the guards could say or do anything more, I slammed and bolted the door.

"My dear," I said, settling Miriam on a couch, placing a pillow behind her, "I tried, I truly tried, but what was Pilate to do? You may think him all-powerful, but that is not true. There are hundreds of thousands of pilgrims packed into this city right now. My husband has only a few hundred men in the whole country. It would be days before reinforcements arrived from Syria."

"Jesus can still be saved."

A chill of apprehension swept over me. "What do you want of me?"

"You know about herbs and potions—secret things." Her face was white and strained, her eyes wild. "You can give Jesus something."

Give him something! What madness was this? "Miriam, Miriam, do you not think that I tried everything I knew to save Holtan? In the end it was useless."

"Please," she begged, her arms outstretched. "I know no one in Jerusalem. You are his only chance."

I turned away, unable to face her desperate eyes.

"I have a plan," she insisted, her manner frantic. "When the Sabbath comes the guards will be forced to cut Jesus down. They will think him dead, but with your help he will only *seem* dead. I will claim his body and watch over it until the *therapeuta* from the Essene monastery comes. His healing skills can save Jesus, I know it. The Essenes will hide him. No one will know. It will work, I know it will. Claudia," she pleaded, down on her knees now, "you have got to help me!"

I RAISED MIRIAM TO HER FEET, COMFORTED HER IN MY arms. My dream had revealed Jesus' death so clearly. Mary had known his fate as well. I recalled her deep melancholy at the wedding. How could any mother live with such a burden?

But suppose my dream was false . . . Suppose I could change the outcome of what I had seen . . . Could that be possible? . . . Was it in my power to save Jesus? . . . Passiflora and arnica would calm him while soothing the pain . . . Stavesacres might make him appear dead. "How would you get it to him?" I asked.

"I can do it! Please, Claudia, just make the potion. It is the only way." Her eyes lit with hope as she grasped my hands.

So little hope, yet if I did not try . . .

I WAS ALONE IN MY APARTMENTS WHEN IT HAPPENED. Struggling to escape the ugly pictures that beset me, Jesus' agony, nails . . . nails driven into his flesh and Miriam kneeling before his cross, suffering with him, praying for a miracle. Had she been able to administer the potion? Was it working? *Could* it work?

I must not have noticed the darkening sky. Suddenly a crash of thunder shook the palace. Hurrying out onto the parapet, I saw that the sun had vanished. A great wind came up, breaking awnings and bending trees. The sky turned black. The Temple, revealed in a brilliant flash of lightning, rocked before my eyes.

Rushing back inside I saw the lamp stand sway and crash. The marble floor shifted beneath my feet. "Marcella!" I cried aloud. Feeling my way like a blind person down the darkened hallway, I finally reached her door. My baby was screaming while the nurse beside her struggled to rekindle a fallen lamp.

Taking Marcella in my arms, I stroked her hair, murmuring reassurance. The temblor was over as quickly as it had begun, but the sky remained dark. I cradled my little girl, soothing her, repeating words that I hoped were comforting. How long I rocked Marcella, singing lullabies and chattering foolish stories, I do not know. An eternity. Finally, I heard the sound of heavy footsteps approaching. Someone was shouting orders. Light flooded the room. Pilate stood in the doorway flanked by two torch-bearing slaves. "*Tata!*" Marcella cried, reaching toward him.

Pilate crossed the room in an instant, his arms encircling me as I held Marcella, holding us both tightly.

"What awful thing is this!" the nurse cried hysterically.

"What evil have we done to cause the gods to punish us in this way?"

Pilate glared at her. "It was an earthquake and an eclipse, nothing more. Intelligent people—the only kind fit to care for children—know that." Turning back to Marcella, he gently stroked her hair. "It's just the moon passing between the sun and earth—a natural thing that happens from time to time."

As he spoke, Marcella's sobs ceased. Soon she wriggled free from both our arms and settled herself on the floor. "Let's make an eclipse," she said, assembling her clay blocks. "The blue one will be the moon . . ."

Pilate and I knelt beside her. He was moving the clay blocks as she instructed him. "I love you, *Tata,*" Marcella said unexpectedly. "We missed you, Mama. Don't you love *Tata,* too?"

To my great relief, someone knocked at the door. Pilate scowled in annoyance, but I leaped to open it. There stood Rachel, white-faced, eyes wide with fright. I slipped outside to speak with her.

"Terrible things are happening, *Domina,*" she gasped breathlessly. "Rock tombs have shattered—the bones, the bones, they are spilling out. I was in the anteroom when people began to pour in with awful stories. The great hanging curtain in the Temple—it's been rent from top to bottom."

"See to the slaves," I instructed her. "Calm them." I would have gone back inside Marcella's room, but Rachel stopped me.

"There is something else," she added reluctantly. "Miriam has sent a man here to plead with *Dominus*. He begs a favor."

I looked about the hallway, now bright with lamps. "Where is this person?"

Rachel's expression was apprehensive. "He waits by your apartments."

"Pilate will not want to be disturbed. I will talk with the one you have brought."

Rachel blocked my path. "The Sanhedrin is always spying—Herod, too—looking for ways to discredit *Dominus* with the emperor. You can do nothing but get yourself into more trouble with him." She paused. "Jesus is dead."

Dead... so soon? Had Miriam given him the potion? Could it be working? "Who says this?" I asked, my heart pounding. "How do they know?"

"They say that a soldier thrust his sword into Jesus' side."

Poor Miriam, her frantic scheme for naught. Forcing back the quick tears that stung my eyes, I pushed Rachel gently away. The man stood outside my chambers, slight, barely into his twenties. His white robes were well cut, but wrinkled and badly stained. Was it blood? I wondered. He turned toward me, large eyes entreating.

"Who are you?" I asked. "Why have you come?"

"My name is Joseph of Arimathea. I am a disciple of Jesus."

"How dare you come here?" It was Pilate who spoke. "A disciple, you say?" he asked, striding forward. "Haven't I seen you before? In the Temple, perhaps?" He studied Joseph suspiciously.

"Yes, *Dominus*." Joseph's voice was scarcely above a whisper. "I came to Jerusalem to become a priest."

"But instead you have followed Jesus?" I asked, looking into dark eyes, level with my own.

"Keep out of this, Claudia!" Pilate warned, his voice rising. "Go inside and close the door."

I didn't move.

Joseph's pale face flushed. "I have been a secret disciple—too afraid to speak out."

"And now?" Pilate asked, his impatience mounting. "Why are you here? What do you want?"

"Your soldiers have taken Jesus' body. They bartered for his clothing among themselves. The body will be thrown into a ditch—a pauper's grave. If—if only I might have it. I have a tomb ready. Please . . ." He looked from Pilate to me. Those large eyes again, imploring. What could I do?

Pilate shook his head. "What happened may have been unnecessary, even unfortunate, but Jesus was still a criminal. The sooner this matter is over the better. There are rules to follow."

I moved forward, looking directly into Pilate's eyes. "But they were not followed, were they? The trial was a travesty. Perhaps this time . . . this rule . . . could be broken . . ."

We stared at each other. Slowly his expression softened. He gestured impatiently at Joseph. "Very well, take the body! Do with it as you will. Tell the guards you have my permission. I want to hear no more of this."

Joseph flashed me a grateful look. He bowed several times and backed away down the corridor.

Turning quickly, hoping to escape Pilate and his inevitable questions about my trip to Caesarea, I entered my chambers. Before I could close the door behind me, he was inside. Pilate seated himself on a couch and reached for a carafe of wine. His hand shook as he poured.

"That man—Jesus—I would have set him free, but there were too many dissenters. Caiaphas had the court packed. They were out for blood." Pilate lifted the wineglass to his lips, his face flushed.

"I know, I saw."

"You were there?" Pilate looked at me in surprise. "Claudia, you know the danger."

I shrugged. *What is truth*? Pilate had asked Jesus. Indeed, what did truth matter now? "The dream I warned you of meant nothing," I assured my husband. "I scarcely remember it. What difference will any of this make in a week?" Forcing a smile, I added, "If the day ever comes that as many pray to Jesus for healings as they do to Asklepios, perhaps you will have reason to regret your decision."

He laughed too heartily. "You do have a way with you, Claudia. You can always make me laugh."

It would be two days before I saw my husband again. Jerusalem was in turmoil.

Numerous riots erupted, Pilate hard put to suppress them. To my knowledge he slept not at all during that time. Troops were pulled in from surrounding areas to maintain order in the angry, troubled city. Many who had heard Jesus preach believed that his execution was in some way linked to the earthquake and eclipse. Had he not railed against the Temple? At the insistence of Caiaphas, Pilate posted guards around Jesus' tomb. A boulder was rolled against the entrance and the seal of Rome affixed. All this I heard from Rachel, who, despite my admonitions, went out into the fearful city to gather information.

Where was Miriam? I wondered again and again. Then late Saturday evening she appeared at the door to my chambers looking haggard beyond belief. Her face was blotched, her eyes so red and swollen that I wondered how she could see.

"I thought I was so clever," she told me, her voice tight and hoarse. "I tricked a soldier into giving Jesus the potion. The wretched man thought it was vinegar—Jesus was crying for water. Neither of them had any idea what he was drinking. I thought I had won. The Sabbath was approaching when Jesus lapsed into a coma. He looked dead, but I knew better. Only a little longer, I thought, but then another soldier came. He took his sword and— It is over."

She swayed and might have fallen had I not reached out to steady her. Carefully I led her to a couch while Rachel mixed water with a little wine. "Stay here," I said, pushing the tangled hair back from Miriam's face. "Stay here and rest."

"No, no, I cannot," she said, tossing her head fitfully. "I only came to tell you what happened, to thank you for trying . . . I must go. Mary and Joanna are waiting. They were with me at the cross. We and Joseph were the only ones . . . tomorrow early we will go to rub spices into his dear body and wrap it in linen."

"But the tomb has been sealed, the boulder is far too big for you to move."

"Tomorrow I will find a way."

It was useless to argue. I placed a *palla* about Miriam. "Tomorrow, yes, but tonight try to sleep."

To my surprise, even as she protested, Miriam drifted into a troubled slumber. I sat by her couch long into the night, but eventually slept as well. When I awakened she was gone. Bright sunlight poured in from the balcony. Sunday morning. What would the day bring?

I determined to spend as much time as possible with Marcella. We practiced writing her name together on a new tablet and played with her three kittens. "Tell me about Ariadne," she asked. It was her favorite story as it had once been mine. We lounged on the sun-drenched balcony far above the city. Marcella, perched on my lap, looked up. "Would Ariadne weave a thread for me, Mama? Would she show me the way?"

"Perhaps, if you believe in her . . . and if you remember to reach for the thread."

We were not alone, I felt it and turned. Pilate watched from the doorway. How long had he been there? He looked furious, but his voice was soft as he addressed Marcella. "You'll excuse your mother, won't you, sweet one?" He nodded for me to follow him. Once outside, he grabbed my shoulder, pulling me down the corridor to my apartments. "I don't understand," I gasped.

"Keep quiet! Do you want the slaves to hear?"

At last we reached the massive door, inset with ivory and lapis lazuli. Pilate thrust it open and shoved me inside. Slamming it behind him, he turned to face me.

"What's going on here, Claudia?"

My heart thumped wildly. I needed more than Ariadne's thread. "I don't know what you're talking about," I said, backing away.

"Jesus' body is gone—stolen out of his tomb. Now the guard tells me that his woman has been to the palace twice, that she spent part of last night here in this very room. You were so anxious for me to release his body. Why? What is your part in all this?"

"Miriam is my friend. I told you that in Galilee. She came to me hoping that I might persuade you to pardon her husband. Of course, that was impossible. I knew that. She knew it too, but was desperate. Can you not understand simple feelings?"

Pilate shrugged off the question. As though thinking aloud, his voice lowered. "She was one of the women who went to the tomb this morning. How they expected to roll back the stone, I can't imagine. As it turned out they had no need. Someone had already removed it. All that remained inside was Jesus' burial shroud, lying on the ground as though he had just stepped out of it. Now I ask you"—he leveled his eyes suspiciously on me—"how can this be?"

"How should I know? Ask your guards."

"They claim to know nothing."

"You mean they went to sleep! Those disciplined fighting men?" I looked at him, incredulous.

"We shall soon find out," Pilate answered grimly. "They are being questioned now."

We sat in silence for a time. My mind reeled, trying to imagine Miriam's shock at finding an empty tomb. What did it mean? What lay ahead for her? I felt the weight of Pilate's eyes, watching. What lay ahead for me? Finally, not knowing what else to say, I thanked him for giving Jesus' body to Joseph. "You were kind." How absurd that sounded in view of this inexplicable new development.

But Pilate took me seriously. "I believed it was your wish. I *do* want to please you, Claudia."

I smiled at the irony of his words. "Indeed? It was not always so."

"It is now. Surely you have noticed changes . . . since we came to Judaea?"

"Some changes, perhaps," I allowed, not meeting his eyes.

"Yet you went to Caesarea."

"Yes, I went to Caesarea." I stood still, braced for whatever might follow. When he said nothing, I looked up. "I suppose you know . . ."

"I know about the plague," Pilate answered.

I took a deep breath, searching his eyes. He knows all of it and has chosen to forgive me.

But it was too late. Unspoken forgiveness was no longer enough, nor was fear sufficient to keep me quiet. A sense of power surged through me as I faced him. "As I know all about you."

"Very well then." Pilate's eyes blazed. "Let's talk about Holtan. Because of him I have endured grievous humiliation. Thanks to Livia, your conduct is the talk of Rome. Anyone would advise me to exile you, Claudia. Had the man lived, he'd have taken you from me. I know as well that the two of you would not have rested until you found a way to steal Marcella."

"I cannot deny that any more than you can deny the countless women you have had throughout our marriage—Titania, for instance. Did you imagine I did not know about her—did not know about the other child born to you on the very same day as our Marcella? Yes, I know about your son, the son who died."

Pilate looked down. "I have hurt you badly. I regret it deeply."

"As I have hurt you, which I do *not* regret." As from a distance I heard myself speaking in a tone I scarcely recognized, saying words that sounded not at all like me.

"I see . . . but is forgiveness possible?"

"Do you care after all that has happened?"

He hesitated before continuing. "We've both lost much, must we also lose each other?"

I smiled wryly, remembering my sixteenth year and the young centurion with blue eyes and a heartbreaking smile who had come to my father's villa. I recalled the incantation and the spell, could almost smell the perfume rising from the bath. What a frantic, foolish girl I had been. I remembered the soul-searing waves of jealousy that had all but destroyed those early years.

Pilate touched my cheek lightly. "You loved me once, perhaps too much. Can't you . . . is it not possible for you to love me again?" His hand moved to the sistrum I wore about my throat. "What would your Isis say?"

"That you are a most unlikely Osiris!"

"And your mystagogue . . . would he not say that *every* marriage is a union of Isis and Osiris? Would he not also say that I am the Osiris the goddess has sent to *you*?"

I laughed. What a politician! Pilate was incredible, yet could it be that he was right? Did Isis mean for me to gather and cherish the remaining pieces of *this* union? Memories crowded in, my life's best and worst . . . I felt again the horror and humiliation of my sister's funeral. Pilate, the ambitious one, the man who would do anything, sacrifice anyone, had remained loyal, riding in the funeral procession beside me. It was in those troubled times that our Marcella had been conceived.

"Marcella loves you," I answered at last.

"Is there nothing more for us than that?" His eyes, once so cool, searched mine. "So much has happened to us both—we are wiser now. You are safe, you are well, you are here. Say that you will always be here."

He knew everything and yet he had forgiven me. Holtan was dead and I had been left behind. I must go on for Marcella. I had loved Pilate once . . . It would take time, but perhaps . . . I did not know.

"Yes," I said, finally meeting his eyes. "I will always be here."

Epilogue

After the trial nothing seemed to go right. Nothing that Pilate did met with the emperor's approval. Eventually we were recalled to Rome. There would be no further appointments. I did not need the sight to tell me that it was time for us to begin a new life somewhere else.

When a pleasant dream placed me again at my childhood home, I took it as a sign from Isis. Why not return to Monokos? Pilate, increasingly despondent, did not care where we went.

When we reached the town, we found it changed, no longer the small garrison where I had grown up. Too many people, too many chariots crowding the steep, narrow streets that hugged the hills. What could I have expected after so many years? The best of Monokos remains. The sea mist cool on my skin, the smell of salt and seaweed, the surf sounds at night. Sweet sensations that awaken ghosts of my loved ones, *Tata* and Mother, my beautiful sister with her laughing eyes, regal Agrippina, restless shades never far away.

What I could never have anticipated was finding Miriam here. I had heard rumors that she had been stoned to death in the streets of Jerusalem. Over the years I often prayed to Isis for her soul as I do for the many others lost to me. What a joy to discover my old friend alive and well.

Miriam has changed, her glorious hair flows white now. Many are drawn to the one they have come to call the Magdalene. She meets with them in the crumbling temple of some forgotten goddess and speaks of Jesus. Even Pilate sometimes attends her gatherings. Ironic as it may seem, he draws solace from their meetings. More surprising, he is accepted and forgiven by the faithful.

Discovering Miriam in Gaul has brought unexpected joy to these past years. Despite her great loss, she remains a lively companion. Miriam tells endless tales, most often about Jesus' resurrection. It seems that she returned again to the open tomb of Jesus, this time alone. A strange man awaited her there. He was a gardener, or perhaps an angel. Miriam is unsure about that as well. Sometimes she believes that it was Jesus himself, but instead of rushing to hold her, he insisted that she remain at a distance. It is hard for me to understand that, much less to believe it. But then, "What is truth?" as Pilate is so fond of asking. She is certain that he lives, that he awaits her in the kingdom of heaven. Where that is, I do not know; and Miriam, though certain of its existence, is vague about the location.

Strange to think of Pilate, Miriam, and me bound together in this far-off land, living out our final years in exile. Pilate is frail now, our fortunes greatly reduced. We will never return to Rome. Why would we? The political turmoil has only grown worse. True, Livia and Tiberius are dead. My old enemy, Caligula, reigned for a time as Caesar, just as my sight once told me he would. But he, too, is dead. Now Agrippina's grandson Nero, a worse tyrant if that is possible, has taken his place.

Nero has begun to persecute the followers of Jesus—Christians, they call themselves. I scarcely know what to make of this new cult. A father who sacrifices his own son? A king who dies a criminal's death? Followers of Peter. Followers of Paul. They fight noisily among themselves, arguing about obscure tenets. The one belief they can agree on is that the world is fast coming to an end. Very soon now Jesus will return to reward the faithful and punish the unbelievers with eternal damnation. That last part doesn't sound at all like the Jesus I remember; yet in anticipation of heaven, his followers give away their belongings. Working hard, pressing forward in the Roman way, has scant appeal to them. Their promised treasures are not of this world. No glory for *Pax Romana* in that!

It is easy to see how Nero is able make scapegoats of them. But his cruelties . . . Christians are crucified and burned alive, others fed to lions! I fear for Rachel, who has become one of them and lives now in Rome with Marcella and her family, but wonder why she and the others don't avoid those dreadful deaths by paying lip service to Nero while keeping secret their creed. Still, my sight tells me that the world will not forget the Christians' stubborn bravery. I see in them a true marriage of Yahweh and Isis—courage and conviction but also compassion and charity—and pray this sacred union will not be forgotten in later years.

The presence of my oldest granddaughter here in Monokos gives me great pleasure, a beautiful young woman so like her dear namesake, my mother. Selene and I share a special bond;

I suspect she too has the sight. The inheritance I dreaded to find in Marcella may have passed instead to her daughter. I pray that it serves her better than it has me.

Selene has been especially kind this summer. I feel her glance often and look up to see her lovely eyes clouded with concern. Who knows, perhaps she sees my death. So be it! My life has been long and I have seen and done much. In these last years I have been a good wife to Pilate. I have no regrets, and if my days are numbered they only bring me that much closer to the one who has waited so long.

—Claudia, wife of Pontius Pilate

MONOKOS, IN THE FIFTH
YEAR OF THE REIGN OF
NERO (65 C.E.)

Acknowledgments

Fortuna was kind, blessing me with the inspiration and support of many. In the Stanford classrooms of Patrick Hunt and David Cherry the spark of a half-remembered sermon caught fire and took form.

Writer friends Kevin Arnold, Marlo Faulkner, Lucy Sanna, Nancy and Harold Farmer, Jim Spencer, Phyllis Butler, and Helen Bonner—most particularly Helen Bonner—read and reread draft after draft. Without their patience and creativity, *Claudia* would not have been.

Literary agent Irene Webb guided and encouraged me with wisdom and humor. My editors, first Renee Sedliar and then Claire Wachtel, were latter-day Ariadnes leading me through the labyrinth, their perceptive suggestions crucial.

WHAT WAS LIFE LIKE FOR ROMAN WOMEN?

- Both women and men dyed their hair, and blond was a fashionable colour.
- Wigs were popular, particularly those made from the blond hair of Germans captured in battle.
- Although Roman women were citizens, they were not entitled to vote or stand for political office.
- Pale skin was fashionable and white lead and chalk were used to lighten the complexion.
- Charcoal and saffron were used as makeup.
- Legally, women could marry when they were twelve years old.
- Women's clothing was simple and they wore their hair in elaborate styles to vary their appearance.

- Women's hair accessories included hairnets made from delicately woven gold wires and bone hairpins.

- Purple shellfish was used to dye fabric a range of colours.

- During childbirth women sat upright in a special chair.

- Children were the property of their father, and when couples got divorced children remained in their father's house.

- Men had the legal right to kill their wives if they committed adultery.

HISTORICAL BACKGROUND TO CHARACTERS

Claudia Procula

Claudia is a mysterious figure – very little is known about her life with any certainty. Her name suggests she may have been a member of the Claudian dynasty, which ruled Rome; she is said to be the granddaughter of Emperor Augustus and illegitimate daughter of Tiberius' third wife, Claudia. She was married to Pontius Pilate, the governor of Judea at the time of Jesus' crucifixion. According to the New Testament she warned her husband not to condemn Jesus on account of a dream, which led her to be recognised as a saint in the Eastern Orthodox Church. Claudia is also known by several other names including Procla, Prokla and Perpetua. Letters apparently written by Claudia chronicling her time in Judea were found in a monastery in Belgium and placed in the Vatican archives.

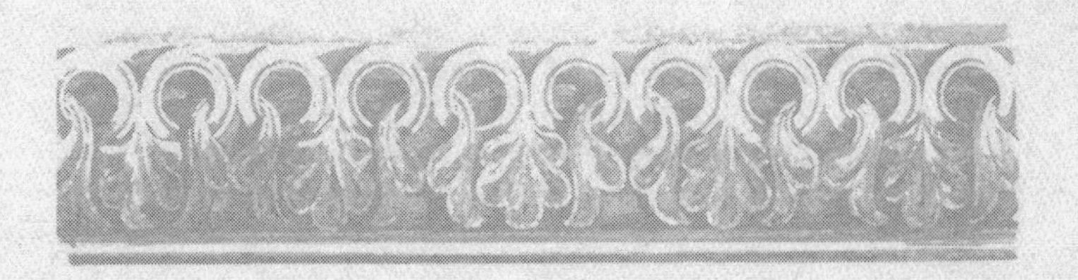

Germanicus

Germanicus was born in 15BC. His father was the Emperor Tiberius' brother, Drusus. In AD4 he was adopted by Tiberius at Augustus' request, becoming second in the line of succession. He was married to Agrippina the Elder, who bore him nine children, six of whom survived into adulthood. A formidable force in Roman politics, he was a general in the army and campaigned in Germania in AD14–16. Germanicus was very popular among the citizens of Rome, which caused tension with Tiberius. He died in suspicious circumstances – showing signs of poisoning – and there was widespread mourning in Rome following his death.

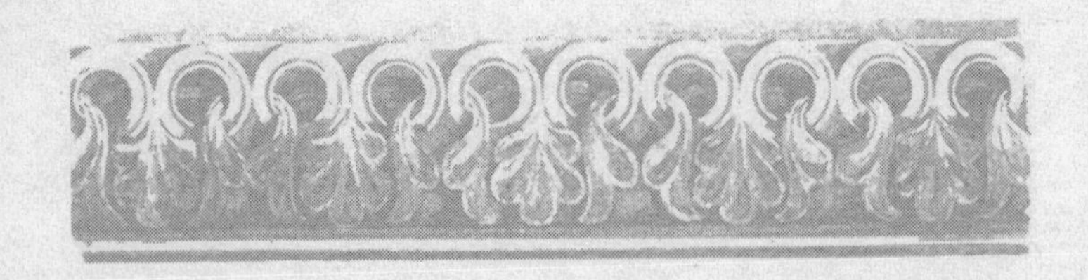

Agrippina the Elder

Agrippina – one of the most prominent female figures in the Roman Empire – was the child of Augustus' only daughter, Julia, and his close ally Agrippa. She was married to Germanicus and together they had nine children, including the future Emperor Caligula and Agrippina the Younger, mother of the Emperor Nero. She accompanied Germanicus on his military campaigns, which was unusual for a Roman wife and earned her a reputation as a model for heroic womanhood. After her husband died in suspicious circumstances, Agrippina boldly accused Piso (the Governor of Syria), Emperor Tiberius and Livia of being behind his death. She was arrested on Tiberius' orders, tried and exiled to Pandateria, where she was subjected to considerable brutality by her guards and eventually starved herself to death.

Pontius Pilate

Very little is known about Pilate before he was appointed Governor of Judea. Not even his birthplace is agreed upon; legends say he was a Spaniard or German but he was most likely a natural-born Roman citizen. He is best known as the man who presided over the trial of Jesus and ordered his crucifixion. Pilate was under orders from Rome to respect Jewish culture and would have ruled in conjunction with the Jewish authorities. However, during his time as governor Pilate appropriated Jewish revenues to build an aqueduct and is said to have ordered the massacre of resistance fighters who opposed the project. He appears to have been extremely unpopular among the Judean people. After his spell as governor he was recalled to Rome.

Caligula

Born Gaius in AD12 at Antium, his parents were Germanicus and Agrippina. As a boy he accompanied his father on military campaigns in Germania and became the army's mascot. He was dressed in a miniature soldier's uniform and nicknamed Caligula – 'little boots'. He became emperor in AD37. Following a good start to his reign, Caligula became seriously ill and his sanity may have been affected. His rule was marred by famine, financial crisis and scandal, and he struggled to maintain his position against several plots to overthrow him. In AD41, less than four years after his accession, Caligula was assassinated by his own guards in a conspiracy involving the Roman Senate.

Livia

Livia was born in 58 BC to aristocratic parents. Her first marriage produced the future Emperor Tiberius and she divorced her husband while pregnant with their second child in order to marry Octavian. They remained together for 51 years but had no children. An ambitious and formidable character, Livia was a trusted consort of Octavian and she enjoyed the status of privileged counsellor, petitioning him on behalf of others and influencing his policies when he became emperor. She remained politically active until her death in AD 29, aged 86.

TIMELINE

Claudia: Daughter of Rome

DATE	EVENT
31BC	Antony and Cleopatra are defeated by Octavian at the battle of Actium
30BC	Antony and Cleopatra flee to Egypt and commit suicide
27BC	Octavian assumes the name Augustus
21BC	Agrippa and Julia (Agrippina's parents) marry
18BC	Julian Laws passed regulating adultery and marriage
15BC	Germanicus is born
14BC	Agrippina (the Elder) is born
12BC	Agrippa dies
11BC	Augustus forces Tiberius to divorce his wife and marry Julia (Augustus' daughter)

DATE	EVENT
4BC	Herod the Great dies
2BC	Julia is exiled by Tiberius for adultery
AD4	On Augustus' orders Germanicus is adopted by Tiberius
AD4–6	Tiberius' campaigns in Germania
AD6	Judea becomes a Roman province
AD12	Caligula is born at Antium
AD14	Augustus dies of natural causes; accession of Tiberius; legions in Rhine and Danube mutiny
AD14	Julia (wife of Agrippa and Tiberius and mother of Agrippina) dies
AD14–16	Germanicus' campaigns in Germania

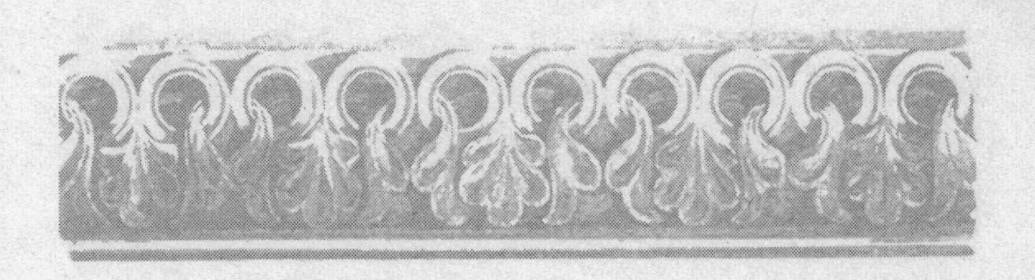

DATE	EVENT
AD15	Agrippina the Younger (daughter of Germanicus and Agrippina, and mother of the future Emperor Nero) is born
AD17	Germanicus is sent to the East and some time later dies in Antioch under suspicious circumstances; widespread mourning of his death in Rome
AD26	Tiberius retires to Capri
AD29	Agrippina the Elder is exiled to Pandateria
AD 29	Livia dies aged 86
c.AD30–31	Sejanus is accused of plotting to overthrow Tiberius and is executed; Jesus is crucified on order of Pontius Pilate, Governor of Judea

DATE	EVENT
AD33	Agrippina the Elder starves herself to death on the Island of Pandateria
AD37	Tiberius dies; accession of Caligula (Gaius); Nero is born
AD41	Caligula is assassinated at the Palatine games at Rome; accession of Claudius
AD43	Invasion of Britain by Roman forces
AD54	Claudius dies; accession of Nero
AD59	Nero has his mother, Agrippina the Younger, assassinated
AD60	Boudicca leads a rebellion in Britain
AD61	Boudicca's rebellion is suppressed

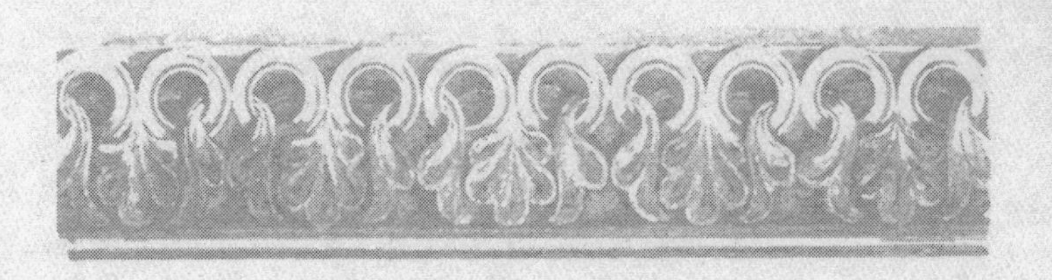

Bibliography

Adkins, L. and Adkins, R. *Handbook to Life in Ancient Rome* (1998: Oxford University Press, Oxford).

Balsdon, J. *Roman Women: Their History and Habits* (1962: The History Book Club, London).

Cherry, D. *The Roman World: A Sourcebook* (2001: Blackwell, Oxford).

Dupont, F. *Daily Life in Ancient Rome* (1989: Blackwell, Oxford).

Ford Russel, B. 'Wine, Women and the Polis: Gender and the formation of the city-state in archaic Rome', *Greece and Rome* (2003) 50 (1), pp. 77–84.

Lefkowitz, M. and Fant, M. *Women's Life in Greece and Rome* (1982: Gerald Duckworth & Co).

Le Glay, M. et al. *A History of Rome* (1996: Blackwell, Oxford).

Paoli, U, *Rome: Its people, life and customs* (1964: London, Longman).